CORK CITY LIBRARY
Leabharlann Cathrach Chorcaí

www.corkcitylibrary.ie

Tel./Guthán (021) 4924900

This book is due for return on the last date stamped below.
Overdue fines: 10c per week plus postage.

D0231422

Catch A Falling Star

Also by Ken McCoy

Hope Street
Cobblestone Heroes
Annie's Legacy
Two Rings For Rosie

Catch A Falling Star

Ken McCoy

 **Visit the Piatkus website!**

Piatkus publishes a wide range of best-selling fiction and non-fiction, including books on health, mind, body & spirit, sex, self-help, cookery, biography and the paranormal.

If you want to:
- read descriptions of our popular titles
- buy our books over the internet
- take advantage of our special offers
- enter our monthly competition
- learn more about your favourite Piatkus authors

VISIT OUR WEBSITE AT: **www.piatkus.co.uk**

All the characters in this book are fictitious and any resemblance to real persons, living or dead, is entirely coincidental.

First published in Great Britain in 2002 by
Judy Piatkus (Publishers) Ltd of
5 Windmill Street, London W1T 2JA
email: info@piatkus.co.uk

The moral right of the author has been asserted

A catalogue record for this book is available from the British Library

ISBN 0 7499 0618 9

Set in Times by
Phoenix Photosetting, Chatham, Kent
Printed and bound in Great Britain by
Biddles Ltd, Guildford

To my grandchildren

To Laura and Grace and Sophie and Luke,
And William and Wunon, who's small.
Old-fashioned names for new-fashioned folk,
Unspoiled by this world, bless 'em all.
I know what you're thinking, has this man been drinking?
'What sort of a name's Wunon?' you say.
Well, it's due to arrive on New Year's Eve,
And is known as the Wunon the Way.

Go, and catch a falling star,
Get with child a mandrake root,
Tell me, where all past years are,
Or who cleft the devil's foot,
Teach me to hear mermaid's singing,
Or to keep off envy's stinging,
And find
What wind
Serves to advance an honest mind.

'Song' by John Donne

Part One

Chapter 1

Yorkshire, March 1954

A dry-stone waller took off his cap and wiped the sweat off his brow with his forearm as he squinted at the walkers on the hill above him – two small figures silhouetted against leaden clouds, leaning forward and pushing determinedly against the slope and wind. The man shaded his eyes with his hand, and when he identified them for what they were he spat on the ground and muttered to himself, 'Gippo brats.'

The girl was thirteen and her brother was nearly ten. They were too far away for the watching man to see their distress. Had the children spotted him they might have tried to enlist his help, and under the circumstances he would have given it; his bigotry wouldn't have stopped him helping kids in this sort of trouble. But as far as the children knew, the nearest adult was in the village, which was ten miles away by road but only six as the crow flies and, as Dove had an unerring sense of direction, that was the route she'd chosen. Earlier, they'd tried to flag down several passing vehicles, but their personal appearance did them no favours. No one in their right mind would stop for a couple of gippo kids.

The boy instinctively paused to examine a half-buried piece of German bomber which had crashed into the hillside more than a decade ago, at the height of the war. His sister turned and grabbed at him, dragging him away from his find. He obeyed without protest, which was unusual for him.

The journey took them two hours, by which time it was almost noon. The exhausted pair sat down on a rock and surveyed the village in the valley below them. An escaping ray of sunshine slanted across the sulking sky and brought a cluster of pantiled roofs briefly to life, like an usherette shining a torch to identify a cinema seat. It drew the children's eyes to a blue lamp above the police station door and they headed straight for it without hesitation or discussion. They presented themselves at the desk where the girl banged her flattened palm hard on a loud, brass bell, which caused an aging constable to hurriedly stuff his *News of the World* into a drawer. The lines in his forehead creased into canyons when he saw the likes of what had disturbed his quiet Sunday morning. Both faces were grimy grey with dried rivulets of clean skin on their cheeks, telling of recent crying. This softened the way he spoke to them.

'How can I help you?'

Dove's hair was long, dark and dishevelled. Beneath the grime she was unusually pretty, with faint freckles and an intelligent shine in her bright-blue eyes.

'We've come to report a death, Mister.'

Her accent was a hybrid of Yorkshire, Irish and Welsh. It was what the policeman would have expected from such a person, a gippo. He stared at them for a moment then heaved a heavy ledger onto the desk.

'Can I have your name please, Miss?'

'Dovina Mary McKenna.'

'Henry Malachy McKenna.'

Their names were laboriously entered in the ledger, then the policeman looked up.

'Of . . .?' he asked.

The girl shook her head, not understanding. She checked with her brother. He didn't understand either. The policeman enlightened them.

'Where are you from? Where do you live?'

'Miles away,' Henry said. 'In a waggon.'

The policeman looked puzzled.

'A caravan,' clarified Dove.

'A proper one,' said Henry. 'Not a tin one.'

The pencil rattled against the constable's false teeth as he tried to recall the location of a recently spotted proper caravan. 'Is it in a field off the Riccall Road?'

The name of the road seemed to ring a bell with Dove. She nodded.

'It's a very pretty caravan,' said the policeman. 'Quite big if my memory serves.'

4

'That's because it's a showman's waggon,' Dove said. 'It was our granddad's.'

'Right. You say you've come to report a death?'

He regarded the children with an air of mistrust. Gippo kids were not to be trusted. If it turned out to be a pet dog or cat, or even a horse, he'd send them on their way with a rebuke for wasting police time. On the other hand they were obviously upset, so there was no need to add to their sorrow. He liked kids and these were probably no worse than most; probably better, given half a chance.

'So, who – or what, is dead?' he asked.

'Our mam,' said Dove.

Both sets of eyes stared up at him. Wide and sad. He coughed, excused himself, went through a door and came back with a sergeant.

'This is Dovina Mary McKenna, and her brother, Henry, Sarge. They've come to tell us that their mother has passed away.'

Henry corrected him, 'No she hasn't, she's dead.'

Dove glanced down at her brother with reproach in her expression, then back at the two policemen. 'She died at twenty-two minutes past nine this morning,' she said. 'I checked the time on her watch.'

'It's gold-plated,' added Henry, as though gold-plated was a guarantee of its accuracy. 'She were all right yesterday. Then she got a right bad headache.'

'She told us she'd be all right with a good night's sleep,' said Dove. 'She said she had a stiff neck and she was really hot and then she got this rash and she asked me to wrap a towel round her face to keep the brightness out.' A tear trembled in the corner of her eye. 'I said if she wasn't better by this mornin' I'd fetch a doctor myself, even if Dad hadn't come home.'

The two policemen looked at each other and the sergeant asked, 'You say your father didn't come home last night? Do you know where he is?'

The children shrugged, then Dove said, 'He went off with a bloke in a lorry. He never tells Mam where he's going and this usually sets her off crying and we usually take no notice, but this was different, wasn't it, Henry?' She waited for Henry to nod that it was different before she continued, 'We sat up with her all night, an' she got worse. So when it got light we tried to stop a car or a lorry ... but nobody'd stop for us.'

5

'It's 'cos they think we're gipsies,' explained Henry. 'But we're not really.'

'We're entertainers,' said Dove. 'Gipsies sell pegs an' stuff an' tell fortunes. We're show-people. Well, I am – our Henry's still learning.'

'I can juggle,' the boy said, his grief momentarily forgotten.

'Only with three balls,' said Dove.

Henry's face fell and he muttered, 'I'm good at drawing.'

His sister put an arm around him. 'Yes, he is,' she confirmed. 'He's very good at drawing.'

'Tell me about your mother,' said the sergeant, who wasn't interested in the boy being good at drawing.

'Well,' said Dove. 'We kept going back in, and after a bit my mam said not to leave her again because every bone in her body was aching. She said she'd be all right so long as we didn't leave her on her own … she were crying and screaming a lot and we didn't know how to help, did we, Henry?'

'No, we didn't.'

'Then after a bit she sort of went to sleep.'

'Then she died,' said Henry.

The sergeant frowned and cleared his throat. 'Get on to this, Arthur,' he said, gruffly. 'Better send an ambulance … you never know.'

'What about …?' The constable gestured sideways with his head. 'It's got to be *him*.'

The sergeant nodded, then returned his attention to the children. 'Could you, er …' he cleared his throat again. 'Could you tell me your father's name?'

'Malachy Joseph McKenna,' said Dove. 'He's from Ireland.'

'You can tell by the way he talks,' added Henry.

The sergeant let out a long sigh as the constable spoke into the telephone, directing an ambulance to the caravan. 'I think we may have your father here,' he said.

The puzzled look on the children's faces forced him to explain further. 'He was arrested for … never mind.'

'Drunk, prob'ly,' guessed Henry.

His sister nodded her agreement. 'Was he drunk?' she asked.

The look on the sergeant's face gave Dove her answer. 'I'd better tell him about your mother,' he said.

'No,' insisted the girl. 'That's my job.'

6

The constable came off the phone. 'There's a car and an ambulance on the way, Sarge. I've told them to ring in as soon as they get there, so we can confirm ...' his voice tailed off under Dove's stare.

'She's definitely dead,' she assured him. 'I checked with a mirror and everything.'

The sergeant forced a smile. 'I'm sure you did.' He unlocked a door at the side of the desk and showed them into a room with just a table and four chairs. 'If you wait in here we'll bring your father through.'

Malachy McKenna's beery breath preceded him through the door. When he saw his children his shallow brow furrowed and his eyebrows knitted together into a caterpillar of wiry, black hair. A fleeting look of embarrassment flashed across his hard face and his lips tightened. The sergeant indicated a chair for him to sit on. The two men sat down and faced the children.

Dove studied her father with acute distaste. 'We didn't know what to do, with you not being there,' she said. 'Mam said she'd be all right, but if you'd have been there, you could've done something.'

'What are ye talkin' about?' Malachy's voice was still hoarse from last night's drink. He looked to the sergeant for an explanation but the policeman was looking at Dove, whose own eyes were fixed on her father's face. Her voice went quiet.

'Mam were taken very poorly last night and she died this morning because we didn't know what to do.'

'We're only kids,' said Henry.

Malachy stared at them both. What blood was left in his face drained from it. 'Holy Mary, Mother o' God ... what're ye tellin' me?'

'Mam's dead,' said Dove. 'And we think you should have helped her, but you were too busy drinking pints.' She got to her feet and took Henry's hand. 'I'll see you back at home ... if they let you go.'

It was obvious from her tone that she didn't care if they kept him there for ever.

7

Chapter 2

The children's grief at the loss of their mother would have been greater had she not been an emotionally incontinent woman who would shed a tear at the breaking of a cheap cup or a blow from her husband; and there were many of each. Dilys McKenna was from Wales and had a piercing soprano voice which could crack a wine glass at twenty yards. She would juggle three wooden balls and sing "Oh, Oh, Antonio", accompanied by Dove playing the banjo and Malachy singing along in his tremulous, Irish tenor as he struggled, mainly unsuccessfully, to keep three wooden clubs aloft, at the same time thumping a bass drum strapped to his back with a foot pedal. They scraped a living and troubled neither the dole office nor the taxman.

As parents they were unimpressive. The mother wept and moaned her way through life. Even as she sang, she wept. And people often put money in the hat simply because they felt sorry for a woman with such a piercing but tuneless voice. In the end she had something to moan about – a dose of meningitis.

When sober, Malachy's demeanour was one of hearty belligerence, with a menacing hint of danger simmering below the surface. When in drink he would lose control and speak with fist and boot. Alcohol would turn him into a violent and cruel bully, even to his children, who tried to keep out of his way in such circumstances. After his wife's death, he wrongly figured the act had lost its backbone and vowed to give up travelling from fair to fair and settle down in one place; at least for a while, so his children could get the education they'd been missing. This was the thinking of the sober Malachy. He augmented their earnings by working with a travelling tarmac gang, which aroused interest from the police.

In his spare time he would teach the children to juggle and ride the unicycle and eat fire and walk on stilts and one day they'd all join Billy Smart's circus and won't that be grand? Better than entertaining a load of drunken gipsies at the Appleby Horse Fair.

But Friday and Saturday nights were reserved for drinking; and when he came home in a drunken rage the children would cower in their bunks and face the wall and pretend to be sound asleep – even then they regularly felt his fist in their backs, as he roared around the confines of their wooden home before dropping into a stupor. Then he'd wake up the following day with no memory and ask Henry where he got such bruises and his son would answer, 'You did it, Dad.'

Dove would confirm this and say she'd show him her own bruises if she wasn't a young woman now. She'd tell him that living with him was like living with Doctor Jekyll and Mr Hyde and that she'd leave home and take Henry with her as soon as she could before he killed one of them. Malachy would wring his hands, denying all memory of it and promise never to touch the drink again and may God strike him down if he did. Then the following Friday he'd be at it again.

The waggon had belonged to Malachy's father-in-law, from whom his wife inherited it. The back was partitioned off into a bedroom for the parents, and the children slept in ornately carved bunk beds just beyond the living area. The original wooden wheels had been replaced with pneumatic tyres which made the waggon much smoother and easier for Boris, the massive Clydesdale, to pull. The exterior was painted in a dark plum with ornate gold and green scrollwork, and a blue and white checked canopy over the stable-type door at the front.

The living area was small but functional with upholstered bench seats and a foldaway dining table. A ten-gallon water tank was bolted to the ceiling and boxed in with rosewood. Water was heated and food was cooked on a calor gas stove. For convenience the original wood-burning fireplace had been converted to paraffin, but the old mantelpiece still remained with its burnished steel bars and uprights topped with brass finials, and above these was a beautifully engraved mirror. There was a bow-fronted chest of drawers with shining brass handles, and almost every wooden surface inside the waggon was decorated with intricate carving and gold-leaf scrollwork.

Up until Malachy's wife's death all their clothes had been washed once a week in a peggy tub which took a while to heat with pans of water transferred from the stove. It was the only domestic chore Mrs McKenna was ever any good at. But now the weekly wash was taken to the handiest laundry. The peggy tub, and its associate, the mangle, had been discarded because they took up too much space. There was just one easy chair – Malachy's. His wife's chair had been also discarded as surplus to requirements, upon her death.

A prefabricated wooden 'thunderbox' was carried in a large storage box beneath the bed of the waggon, and would be erected around a chemical toilet on each camp site.

Six months after his wife's funeral Malachy set up camp on a small piece of common land on the southern outskirts of Leeds. The council only moved illegal travellers on when the public moaned about the mess and health risk, but a picturesque caravan and a friendly horse elicited not a single complaint. Besides, Boris saved the council having to cut the grass and provided keen gardeners with a source of fresh manure.

The day they arrived, Henry finished helping his dad erect the 'thunderbox', then he went off to investigate his new surroundings. In the distance he could see the motionless winding wheels of a nearby worked-out drift mine and allowed his imagination to turn the adjacent pit-hills into the Rocky Mountains, as seen at the pictures. He was drawn towards them and found himself walking across a field of dusty chickweed when his feet kicked against something wooden. The boy knelt down and tugged at the overgrown vegetation, revealing a short row of railway sleepers, each one about eight feet long. He inserted his slender hands between two of them and pulled with all his might but couldn't make them budge. However, his curiosity had been aroused. Beneath these sleepers was a mystery which he could not allow to remain unsolved, so he searched around until he found a rusting bicycle frame. Dragging it back to the sleepers, he jammed the front forks between the end two and levered them apart, congratulating himself on his ingenuity. Beneath the gap was an empty blackness. Henry dropped the bicycle frame into the hole and began counting. He'd tell his dad how many seconds it took to hit the bottom and his dad would tell him how deep it was. There was a diminishing clatter as the metal frame bounced off the walls of the shaft, but no final crash.

'Wow!' Henry was impressed by such things.

Ten minutes later, both Malachy and Dove were trying the same experiment, only this time with stones. A couple of stones sent back a faint, echoing 'ching' as they hit something metallic, but others sent back no sound at all.

'It must be bottomless,' concluded Dove.

Her father gestured towards the distant colliery and accurately guessed, 'It'll be an old ventilation shaft for that pit.' Then he rubbed his dark, unshaven chin. Railway sleepers were worth money, but the hole they were covering could be a useful dump for all their rubbish; rubbish was the cause of most travellers being moved on. He pushed the disturbed timber back into place.

'How deep d'you think it is, Dad?' asked Henry.

'Deep enough fer you two ter stay clear. It'll prob'ly be flooded down there by now. Fallin' down there would be loike droppin' off the edge of the world. Jasus! – ye'd nivver be found agin.'

Malachy stood on the sleepers and slowly looked around, surveying the landscape and giving approving nods to what he saw, like a farmer viewing a lush valley he might wish to buy. The steaming cooling towers of Skelton Grange power station dominated the skyline. To his left were acres of low, wooden sheds growing forced rhubarb and behind him were the winding wheels of several distant pits. A pall of smog hung over the urban perimeter of Leeds city centre, produced by the factory chimneys which stabbed the sky like a hundred dirty fingers. The old Yorkshire saying 'Where there's muck, there's brass' brought a grin to his face.

'We'll be all right here fer a good long while,' he decided. 'Just as long as none o' them didicoys don't come spoilin' tings fer us in them rusty ole tin cans they live in. I might have a word wid yer man Tordoff; he'll see we're not bothered.'

Len Tordoff was the proprietor of Murphy and Sons, Tarmac Contractors. The name of his firm was written on the side of a Thames Trader truck and nowhere else; least of all any pieces of incriminating paper. Estimates were given verbally and hands would be spat on to seal the contracts. Bad debts were avoided by payment in advance. Guarantees were lavish, limitless, freely given – and worthless.

'They're a bunch o' rascals all right,' said Malachy to his children. 'But anyone stupid enough ter employ us deserves ter be robbed.'

'What about old people who haven't got much money?' asked Dove.

'What about them?'

The anger in his eye warned Dove to take a step back – her father was not a man to appreciate reasoned argument. In any case he had bought her and Henry respectable clothes and arranged for them to go to St Joseph's School in Hunslet.

Dove was put into Senior Two and Henry into Standard Four; Henry would sit his state scholarship in February. Both could read and write which meant they could hold their own in everything but the arithmetic lessons, for which they were both sent to the transition classes four times a week until they caught up. Dove was too old to sit her scholarship but, as she had no academic ambitions, this didn't worry her. Although they had both been baptised Catholics, neither had been confirmed so they were ordered to receive instruction twice a week on Thursday evening and Sunday afternoon.

'Yer should get loads o' points on the Mass register,' said Alice Webster, who wore a caliper on her leg and with whom Dove shared a double desk. She'd already heard Alice referred to as 't' lame lass', and had determined never to call her that herself.

'What's the Mass register?'

'Miss Molloy takes it every Monday mornin,' explained Alice. 'Yer've got ter tell 'er what Mass yer went ter and whether yer went ter Confession, or Communion, or Benediction, or if yer've done any novenas and stuff like that.'

'What's Miss Molloy like?'

Alice wrinkled her nose. 'She's all right with me because of me leg, but she's a miserable old trout really.'

'That's what I thought.'

'They had me in the transition class because of me sums. I can do English and stuff, and I love poetry. I know loads of poems – but I'm no good at sums.'

'Nor me,' said Dove.

'What're you good at?'

Dove had to think. 'Music,' she said, eventually. 'Our Henry's good at drawing and I'm good at music.'

'We do music once week on a Friday. Singing mainly ... our Tom says I've got a voice like a rusty violin. Can you sing?'

'A bit ... how does this Mass register thing work?'

Dove's Mass attendance had been restricted to weddings and funerals and the occasional time her father's conscience pricked him and he dragged them off to the nearest church – which wasn't very often.

'Well,' explained Alice. 'For everythin' yer do yer get points. Yer get more points fer eight o'clock Mass than for eleven o'clock – 'cos the late masses are for old people.'

'Then what?'

'Then at Easter, Father O'Dea brings a load o' presents into school. One for each kid and the ones with the most points gets first pick.'

'What did you get last year?'

'Some plasticine.'

Plasticine didn't seem much of a reward for all that hard work, then Alice explained, 'I were off poorly wi' me leg an' I went in nearly last. I'm gonna try an' go in first this year. There's allus a big present if ycr go in first. It were a bike last year.'

'Can you ride a bike?' Dove asked. 'You know ... with your leg?'

Alice shook her head. 'No. If I got a bike I'd most prob'ly give it to our Tom. When he were in the Juniors he once won and he picked out a doll's house and gave it to me. He could have had a bike but he picked out a doll's house.'

'Blimey!' commented Dove. 'I think a lot about our Henry but I'm not sure I'd go that far.'

'That's 'cos your Henry's not a cripple. He's allus looked out for me has our Tom. He's a gormless lump, but he allus sticks up for me. I wouldn't mind if you won it though.'

'Wouldn't you?'

'No ... I quite like church as well. I might be a nun when I grow up.'

To Dove, coming top of the Mass register seemed a reasonable goal. It might also secure her place in heaven if she unselfishly set her sights on a present for Henry, who would be eleven on Easter Sunday, as he pointed out after examining the class calendar.

A bike would be the best birthday present he'd ever had. By far.

'Yer can come wi' me,' said Alice. She had never had a best pal, which was something she had in common with Dove – albeit for different reasons.

'Right,' said Dove. 'I will.'

Alice gave her a lazy wink and a broad smile. To the other children they soon became 'the gippo and the crippo' which drew them together and Dove found Alice to be amusing and bright. Had she not been off poorly with her leg she would have passed her scholarship – if she'd been better at sums.

Boris provided Dove and Henry with pocket money from what they charged the local children for a short walk round the field on his broad back. He could carry three at a time and, at twopence a go, they soon made enough to go to the local pictures to see the Saturday matinee.

Dove and Henry would arrive at school early to take advantage of the hot water in the washroom. Once a week their respective classes went to Hunslet swimming baths, where the two of them luxuriated under the hot showers; and the unwashed musk which usually accompanied them became a thing of the past. Despite the cruel taunts, life wasn't too bad.

'Take no notice,' their father would advise. 'Mostly they're jealous. Show them how ye can juggle – an' take yer banjo one day. That'll show them what class o' people ye are.'

But Dove and Henry wanted to blend into the background and become normal kids, not jugglers and banjo players. 'He'll be tellin' us to go to school on stilts next,' muttered Henry.

'I hate living in this waggon,' Dove said. 'We've got no proper lavvie and no telly. Nearly every kid in our class has got a telly.'

'I wouldn't mind a gramophone,' Henry said.

'I wouldn't mind a bedroom of my own,' said Dove. 'I'm entitled to a bedroom of my own at my age.'

'Have you heard of Frankie Laine?'

His sister nodded. 'Never heard any of his records, though. Alice says I can go to her house to listen to her records. She's got her own bedroom.'

Every Sunday, throughout the whole of the autumn and winter Dove went to eight o'clock Mass with Alice and a reluctant Henry, who didn't share his sister's ambition to be the one to claim the much envied Big Present. It was enough that he had to waste three valuable hours a week being prepared for their Confirmation in March. Drawing was his hobby – that and making model aeroplanes. The day after his mother died, he'd gone missing and had been found by Dove examining the wreck of the German bomber they'd passed the previous day. He rarely went with her to Confession, Communion or Benediction and he didn't do one single novena; not even for the repose of the soul of his dead mother. All this religion ate too much into his drawing and modelmaking time. He was currently constructing a Hawker Hurricane from balsa wood and glue. It would go the way of all his other models, fly for a while until it became damaged beyond repair. 'Tested to destruction' he called it.

'D'yer want ter come back to our house? I've got a new Rosemary Clooney record.'

'Will it be okay with your mam?'

Dove and Alice were on their way home from Benediction one Sunday afternoon. It was the first time Dove had been invited into a friend's home – most of them were put off by her gipsy associations.

'Why should she mind? I'm allowed to bring friends home.'

'Okay.'

Alice lived in a three-bedroomed council house on the Blackmoor Estate with a neat garden and a motorbike and sidecar parked outside.

'It's me dad's' said Alice, with a hint of pride. 'He takes us out in it sometimes.'

Her dad was a small, cheery man who gave Dove the same lazy wink his daughter had perfected.

'Dad, this is Dove,' said Alice, as they walked through the door.

'How do, love. By heck! you're a bonny un.'

'Don't be so embarrassing, Dad.'

There was a radiance about Dove that made heads turn, not least Alice's older brother's, who appeared at the lounge door. Tom had never seen Dove before, having already won his scholarship to grammar school.

'And that big long streak o'trouble's our Tom,' said Alice.

Dove gave him a smile, which Tom returned, awkwardly. He thought girls like Dove only existed on cinema screens. Alice's

15

mother came down the stairs, her hair hidden within a turban. She wiped her hand on her pinny and held it out to Dove.

'I'm Alice's mam, pleased to meet you, love. She's told me a lot about you.'

'Can we play some records?' asked Alice. 'That's why she's come round.'

'Go through, love,' said Mrs Webster, nodding the girls towards the living room, 'and I'll make us a bit o' summat to eat. D'yer think yer dad'd mind if yer stayed fer a bit of tea?'

For all Malachy cared, Dove could have stayed all night. 'No, he wouldn't mind at all, and I'd like that, Mrs Webster, thank you.'

In the corner of the room was a walnut-veneered radiogram and a chrome rack full of 78 rpm records. Alice selected one, slid it carefully out of its sleeve, placed it on the turntable and gently lowered the pick-up arm into the outside groove.

Rosemary Clooney's "This Ole House" had the two of them dancing round the room, as did Guy Mitchell's "She Wears Red Feathers". Mr Webster came into the room with a guitar.

'Oh Dad! Yer not gonna play that, are yer?' Alice turned to Dove. 'He used to play in a band during the war. Yer know, all this oneski, twoski, threeski stuff.'

'I play the banjo a bit,' said Dove, not knowing why she'd said it. Maybe she just wanted to be part of this happy, normal family.

'What kind?' asked Alice's dad. 'Four string, five string?'

'Well, mine's only got four.'

Alice protested. 'Dad, we're supposed to be listening to records.' But her father had gone.

Mrs Webster popped her head round the door; there was flour on her nose. Dove had always wanted a mam who had flour on her nose now and again. A proper mam.

'He's the biggest kid in the house,' said Alice's mother, before disappearing.

Dove smiled. She liked this family and wished she belonged to one like it. Mr Webster appeared with a banjo, far superior to the one she played.

'Here, it might need tuning a bit.'

Dove took it and gave it a strum. 'Can you give me a C, Mr Webster?'

He obliged and within a minute Dove had it in tune and was

playing and singing "How Much Is That Doggie in the Window".

Alice's dad beamed broadly with admiration. 'By heck, lass – yer play it like a pro. Where'd yer learn ter play like that?'

'I've been playing since I was six. We used to be entertainers, then my mam died.'

There was an uncomfortable silence, broken by Mrs Webster's entrance. 'Was that you I heard? I must say, I've never heard it played as well as that before.'

'She's been playin' since she were six,' said Alice, proud of her friend. 'She's brilliant, isn't she?'

Tom appeared with a large saucepan and two wooden spoons and Alice took a harmonica from a drawer. 'I'm not very good,' she said. 'But I can just about play "Put Another Nickel In".'

With Tom on percussion, the four of them formed an impromptu skiffle group. They played for an hour until Mrs Webster came in with a tray loaded with toasted pikelets, buttered scones and a huge, steaming teapot.

'There's rhubarb crumble later,' she said.

'Aw, Mam! It's allus flippin' rhubarb.' Alice turned to Dove. 'Me dad works at t' rhubarb sheds. It's a wonder we haven't got rhubarb growin' out of us ears.'

'Hey!' said Mr Webster. 'It's good for yer is rhubarb.'

'Rhubarb keeps yer regular,' chorused Alice and Tom, obviously beating their dad to his favourite rhubarb maxim.

'Well, it does,' he grumbled, good-naturedly. 'Yer could set t' Town Hall Clock by the Webster family bowels.'

'Dad!'

After they'd eaten they played again until the neighbours complained. It was the best time Dove could remember.

On 4 November, Malachy had left for his Friday night drinking session. The children were apprehensive as usual, but it was something they'd learned to live with.

'He could get into bother for leavin' us on us own,' said Henry. 'If somebody found out, they'd make him stop in, then he wouldn't come back all bad tempered an' throwin' his weight about.'

'If he found out we'd told, it'd be worse,' Dove pointed out.

'No, as soon as we're big enough we'll run away. We don't need him with us to join a circus.'

'When shall we do that?'

'You've got to be at least eleven. They won't take you if you're under eleven.'

Dove was guessing, but it instilled hope in Henry and gave her time to think and organise things without him nagging her all the time. There was a tentative knock on the door. Dove opened the top section and saw Tom standing way below, looking breathless.

'Who is it?' asked Henry.

'Tom,' said Dove, 'Alice's brother.' Then to Tom, 'What're you doin' round here?'

'I thought I'd best come an' tell yer.'

'Tell us? What about?'

'It's Mischievous Night.'

A surprised grin lit Dove's face. 'What? Are you goin' mischievin'? Hey, Henry, Tom wants us to go mischievin' with him.'

'Hey, yeah, I'll come.'

'No,' said Tom. 'I didn't mean that. I've come to tell yer ter watch out. There's some kids from our estate talkin' about comin' and settin' fire ter yer caravan.'

Dove looked in the direction of the council estate, part of which was still under construction.

'They know yer dad goes out on a Friday,' said Tom. 'They're gonna light a fire underneath, then fire rockets at yer when yer run out.'

'Who told you?'

'I heard 'em talkin' about it last night. They wanted me ter go with 'em. They don't know yer a mate o' mine.'

Dove smiled. She didn't know she was a mate of his either, but she liked the idea.

'How many of them are there?'

'Six of 'em. They're all meetin' up at 'alf past seven. Maybe if yer not in,' he suggested, 'they'll not bother.'

Henry said, 'I've got a great idea.'

Dove said, 'Oh, heck!'

It was a pitch-black, moonless night; ideal for those bent on mischief. Windows and doors would be mysteriously knocked on; gates would be removed and taken to adjacent streets and jumping crackers put in dustbins. But six boys from the Blackmoor Estate had a more ambitious project in mind – to burn out the gippoes.

There was a light inside the waggon as the attackers ran silently across the field towards it, two carrying dry wood, one carrying a can of paraffin and three carrying fireworks. The boys had planned their operation in meticulous detail, even down to their alibis. If questioned, they were all watching television at the home of the eldest – in the company of his parents, who fully condoned their actions. But only with it being gippoes.

The three firework carriers stayed back while their cronies advanced, faces blackened with Cherry Blossom shoe polish and keeping low and stealthy in the manner of Green Beret Commandoes. They issued owl hoots and low, mysterious whistles to each other, which none of them understood, except that it added to the adventure of the occasion.

From round the back of the waggon appeared an eight-foot tall man. His white face was illuminated by a flaming torch he was carrying and he was dressed from head to foot in black. He directed his torch at the enemy and shot balls of fire at them as an amplified, ghostly voice screeched, 'Kill the little buggers, kill the little buggers!'

All six youths backed away, uncertainly, as the giant strode, inexorably, towards them. A rocket caught fire in one boy's hand, setting off others. He screamed in pain and flung his remaining fireworks away. Then out of nowhere came the sound of thudding hooves and a whinnying horse thundered towards them, its rider shooting balls of fire at them, just like the giant; and all the time the ghostly voice kept up its tirade.

'Kill the little buggers!'

It was all too much for the boys. The one with the paraffin flung the can away and turned on his heels, followed by the others. Another one was crying in pain as he held his burned hand. Within a couple of minutes it was all over. The attackers had gone.

Tom came out from the back of the waggon, holding a loudhailer in his hand; the one used by Malachy at the fairgrounds. Henry the stilt-walker emerged from the darkness, his giggles arriving before he did. Tom wore a broad grin as he opened the waggon door to let out light for Henry to see by. The boy took off his coat, unhitched his long trousers and jumped expertly to the ground. Malachy had taught him well.

Boris came trotting towards them with Dove on board, her legs stretched out across his back like a wishbone about to snap. The horse wore a bridle but no saddle. She slid off the great beast and patted its neck.

'Well done, Boris.' She turned to Tom and explained. 'He used to work in a circus, that's why bangs don't bother him.'

Tom joined her in the patting. 'Best laugh I've 'ad in ages. It'll be all round the estate tomorrer. Them kids'll be a right laughin' stock.'

Dove giggled. 'I thought you had a real scary voice.' She imitated him. 'Kill the little buggers ... '

Henry said, 'Them Roman Candles were great. I got ten shots from minc.'

'I thought one of 'em were gonna go up in smoke,' said Tom, who had supplied the fireworks. 'We'd have been in dead trouble then.' He didn't look too worried.

'*We'd* have gone up in smoke if you hadn't have come round,' Dove reminded him. 'If they got hurt, they've only themselves to blame.'

Tom shrugged. 'I think it were Melvyn Jubb what got burned. Their lass goes ter your school.'

'Mary Jubb?'

'Yeah.'

'She's in my class,' said Dove. 'She's a bighead ... and she's got a right gob on her.'

As Henry had disappeared into the waggon to get changed, Tom stuffed his hands deep into his trouser pockets and kicked at a stone, in the manner of someone who had something to say but didn't know how to express himself. Dove watched it fly off into the darkness and sensed his awkwardness.

'Penny for 'em,' she said.

He scratched his ear, then screwed up his face and looked away from her.

'I er ... I wondered if yer might want ter ... yer know ... go out with me.'

She didn't know what to say. No boy had asked her this before. They were either wary of her background or intimidated by her beauty.

'What? You mean, go to the pictures and stuff?'

'Yeah.'

'Be your girlfriend, you mean?'

He nodded. 'It's all right if yer don't want ter. I just thought I'd ask, that's all.'

'Well ...' She tried to think of a reason why not without offending him.

'Well what?'

'Well ... I don't know much about you.'

'Yer know I've got regular bowels.'

Dove couldn't help but laugh. 'When?' she asked.

'When what? ... When do I go to t' lavvie?'

'When are you taking me to the pictures?'

'Does this mean you'll go out with me?'

'Only to the pictures,' Dove said. 'I think we should see how we go on. I read in *Woman's World* that regular bowel movements might not be a basis for a relationship.'

'It's something to build on,' said Tom. He reached into his pocket and brought out a brown paper bag. 'Me mam made some parkin,' he said. 'I thought yer might like a piece.'

'Thanks,' she said. 'I like parkin.'

She took a piece and they munched contentedly for a while. Tom finished first and waited for Dove to finish hers before he asked, 'Shall we ... kiss each other or summat?'

'If you like.'

She held him around his waist as he pressed his lips onto hers. They held the kiss for a few seconds before parting. Neither of them was overly impressed. But they would both remember it with fondness.

'That was nice,' she said.

'Yes,' said Tom, 'very nice – do you want some more parkin?'

That night Malachy came home drunk, unaware that his children had saved his home from being burned to the ground. He swore and slapped them both, then took to his bed. They told him about the incident the following day and he laughed long and loud and said how proud he was. Neither mentioned him hitting them. It did no good.

'I don't think you're right in yer head,' said Alice. There was something in her voice which brought a suspicious smile to Dove's face.

'Why's that?'

'Goin' out with our kid ... he's a right gormless lump.'

'He's all right is Tom ... and he's very nice looking.'

'Doesn't stop him bein' a right gormless lump.'

'He passed his scholarship,' pointed out Dove. 'So he can't be all that gormless.'

'I didn't say he wasn't clever,' said Alice. 'He came top of his class last term – I said he were gormless.'

They were walking around the school playground. The two of them were inseparable.

'Hey up! It's the gippo and the crippo,' called out a girl, who then proceeded to imitate Alice's limp, to the amusement of her friends.

'Take no notice,' said Dove. 'She's as thick as two short planks is Jubby.' She turned and pulled a face at the sniggering Mary Jubb, tapping her forefinger against her temple to indicate imbecility. 'Me dad told me never to talk to idiots,' she called out. 'And you're the biggest idiot in the school, Jubby.'

'Your dad's a gippo,' sniggered the girl.

'He's not, actually,' said Dove, evenly. 'Anyway – at least I know who my dad is.'

Doubting other children's parentage was the latest popular insult.

'Your dad could be anybody,' said Alice. 'I've heard you look a bit like the Co-op milkman.'

'Actually,' said Dove to Alice, 'I think she looks more like the Co-op horse.'

'More like the Co-op horse's arse,' returned Alice, warming to the subject.

Mary Jubb reddened and glared at them both. Repartee was not her forte. She was the big sports star of Senior Two: captain of the netball and hockey teams and the school's fastest runner – including the boys. She had also set her heart on being first among the prizewinners on Easter Sunday. For this she had two close rivals, Dove and Alice; Alice's brother had been responsible for the belittling of her own brother on Mischievous Night. The nasty injury to his hand wasn't reported to the police as it might have invited too many awkward questions. It was her parents who would have provided the alibi. She changed her tactics from insults to a sporting challenge; a contest she knew she could win.

'Hey, crippo. Racc yer to t' gate ... give yer twenty yards start for a bob.'

Alice said nothing. Mary smirked. 'Sorry, forgot yer can't count. Twenty's the number what comes after nineteen.'

Alice blushed at this assault on both her weaknesses.

'Hey, Jubby!' Dove called out. 'There are two types of people. People who can't count ... and people like you, who don't count.'

It was a line she'd got out of *Woman's World* and stored for the right occasion. She took Alice's arm and they went on their way, chatting animatedly and sending the message to Jubby that her jibes weren't worth further argument.

It was during a games period that things came to a head. Sister Siobhan had taken a bag of old tennis balls into the school playground and instructed the girls from Senior Two to form themselves into groups and throw the balls to each other, thereby honing their throwing and catching skills. Meanwhile Sister Siobhan, who had no interest in, or aptitude for, any kind of sport, took herself off to the staff room to roll herself a cigarette – her one vice. She was standing in for Miss Johnstone who had rung in sick. As soon as she was out of sight the girls stopped their throwing and catching and stood around in groups, chatting and laughing with the odd suspicion of cigarette smoke drifting into the air. Sister Siobhan watched the girls through the window and planned on leaving it for half an hour before going out to supervise a final ten minutes of throwing and catching. She frowned when she saw a volley of balls being hurled at Alice by Mary Jubb and her friends, some bouncing painfully off Alice's body. Then Jubb thrust out a pointing arm, obviously instructing the lame girl to go and collect the missiles, no doubt to rearm her tormentors for a second assault. The nun watched in some fascination to see how the girl dealt with the situation. It was a cruel world and she'd be doing Alice no favours by stepping in to help; or so it had been decreed by Sister Clare the head teacher. Nevertheless, if it got out of hand, Sister Siohan would step in.

She took a deep drag of the thin cigarette and sensed a feeling of disappointment as Alice almost slunk off to collect the balls. Then, instead of handing the balls back to Mary Jubb she threw four of them, one by one, to Dove McKenna. The nun's fascination mounted as Dove began to juggle with them. Word went round and the rest of the girls in the playground wandered over to watch, in noisy admiration. Mary Jubb's hands went to her hips in annoyance. The spectators clapped and cheered when Dove began to show off, spinning around as she juggled; tossing the balls in the air from behind her back. Then, with a broad grin, she shouted, 'Here, Jubby – catch 'em,' and hurled them, one by one at Mary Jubb, each ball bouncing off the girl's head with a painful ferocity. The nun laughed out loud at this and looked up at the sky as if thanking the Boss for His divine retribution.

Maybe it would knock some of the conceit out of young Jubb and make her a better person. She knew about the Mass register rivalry and deplored the whole idea. Tempting children into attending devotion simply for material gain couldn't be right.

'I'll get yer back, gippo.'

Sister Siobhan didn't hear Mary Jubb's threat, which Dove pretended not to hear. The nun would have been mortified had she realised this simple incident had ignited a flame of revenge in Mary Jubb which would very soon explode in Dove's face and change the course of her life.

stamped on the brake but his foot met with no resistance. For a critical two seconds he gawped down at his useless footbrake; time which would have been better spent steering the car away from Alice. By the time he looked up, he'd hit her.

There was no screech of brakes to alert Dove to her friend's accident. The car had no brakes to screech. It was the sight of people pointing and running which made her walk to the corner out of curiosity. If nothing else, she'd be able to see if Alice was coming; if not she'd go to school on her own.

An angry crowd was gathering round the car, which had eventually stopped fifty yards past where it had struck Alice. She was still underneath it. Some women were berating the driver, who had stayed inside his vehicle for safety.

'The poor lass is a cripple! She'd no chance o' gerrin' outa yer road. Why dint yer bloody stop?'

'I hope they lock yer up an' throw the bloody key away!'

The hapless man shivered with shock and locked his doors as the crowd increased and word got round. Dove pushed her way through and her heart shuddered with shock as she saw a callipered leg sticking out from beneath the car. She knelt on the ground beside a man who was talking to Alice, jammed between the exhaust and the ground. A pool of dark blood was edging out into the road; the man was holding Alice's hand.

'Yer'll be all right, love,' he was saying, with more encouragement than hope in his voice.

'Alice,' said Dove. 'Are you okay?'

It seemed such a stupid question, but Alice smiled at the sound of her friend's voice. The shock had numbed the pain.

'Is that you, Dove?' she asked.

'Yes ... what happened?' Another daft question.

'I don't know,' Alice said. Her voice was little more than a whisper. 'I think I'll be off school for a bit, though.'

'Yer'll be as right as a bobbin afore yer know it,' the man assured her.

The skin had all been scraped off one side of her face by the rough road surface. Blood saturated her coat and her limbs were sticking out at frightening angles. Dove began to cry. Alice turned her head and gave her best friend one of her lazy winks.

'I don't suppose I'll beat Jubby now,' she said. 'Make sure yer beat her, won't yer?'

28

Chapter 3

Henry passed his scholarship and couldn't wait for his dad to come home so he could tell him. He took the letter from his pocket and handed it to Malachy.

'What's this?'

The boy couldn't keep the smile of pride from his face. 'It's from school, to say I've passed me scholarship.'

'Is it now? Well so long as ye don't go round thinkin' ye better than the rest of us.'

Malachy read the letter with an increasing scowl on his face. 'What's this? School uniform? How the hell am I supposed ter pay fer a school uniform?'

'They said if we can't afford it we can get a grant.'

'So, that's what ye told 'em is it? That we're so poor we need their charity.' He cuffed Henry round the side of his head.

'Ow! I didn't say anything of the sort, Dad,' complained the boy, 'I'm only telling you what they told us ... and I'm sick o' you hittin' us for nothing.'

'Are ye now?' roared Malachy.

Henry stood his ground and cringed, waiting for a blow that didn't come.

Malachy had his hand raised, then lowered it. 'Well you go back an' tell them we don't need their charity – and you don't need no uniform neither!'

'Can I go out, then?'

'Ye can go ter hell for all I care – an' don't bother comin' back.'

Henry went out to stroke Boris then decided to head for Alice's house. He wasn't on house-visiting terms with any of his own school friends, although they all found his own home an

25

interesting place to visit. Mrs Webster opened the door and gave him a big smile.

'Is our Dove here?'

'Yes, she is, and I believe congratulations are in order, young man.'

She stepped back from the door to allow him through. Pans steamed on the cooker and there was flour on her pinny. A proper mam. He and Dove had never had one of those.

'I expect yer dad's pleased. I know we were when our Tom passed his scholarship.'

'Oh, yeah. Me dad's dead chuffed,' lied Henry.

Dove had heard his voice and shouted down the stairs. 'Is that our Henry, Mrs Webster?'

'It is love, shall I send him up?'

'If you must.'

Henry grimaced at his sister's mock antipathy and trudged up the stairs to Alice's bedroom where she and Dove were playing Lonnie Donegan records.

'Me dad won't buy me a uniform,' he said, matter of factly.

'The miserable pig!' said Dove. 'Do you want me to have a word with him?'

'Not much point,' said Henry.

'Course there's a point,' argued Dove. 'If you go to St Michael's you can get your O Levels and get a good job.'

'We won't stop round long enough though, will we?'

He had a point. 'If you want a uniform, we can go busking,' Dove said. 'It'll not take us long.'

'I'm not bothered about a uniform. I just wanted him to be pleased wi' me.'

'Well I'm pleased with you,' Dove said.

'So am I,' said Alice.

A knock came on the door and Tom popped his head round. 'Hey! I gather there's someone in the house who's nearly as clever as me.'

Alice hurled a pillow at him. 'There's no one in the house who's as *daft* as you,' she shouted. Then to Henry, 'Promise you won't turn out as daft as him.'

Henry grinned. He liked being here, among a normal family.

The following day, Dove took some money from her dad's box and bought her brother a fountain pen as a reward. Malachy

always assumed any money she took would be for 'w
things' and Dove took full advantage of this. If Malachy w
surprised at how much 'women's things' cost, he never qu

'Don't let Misery Guts see it,' advised Dove when she g
the pen. Secretly she agreed with Henry's prediction th
wouldn't stay around long enough for her brother to take
tage of a grammar school education.

Tom and Dove's courtship was a chaste and innocent affai
a friendship of kindred spirits. She was as much a friend to
she was to Alice. Once a week they went out together, the
the time they spent as a threesome, or a foursome if Henry
along. It wasn't until after Alice's accident that Tom made
too far. A move which both surprised and excited Dove. M
was precipitated by the pain he was feeling. His sister's a
had shocked them both; it happened a few weeks before E

Alice had been late that morning; it wasn't easy to make
with her handicap. Dove would be waiting round the
outside the paper shop, but she wouldn't wait for eve
McKenna was the best friend a girl could have, even if
show signs of mental weakness by going out with Tom.

A pre-war Austin Ten was struggling up Buttergill Lan
smoke belching from its exhaust, the driver cursing his
being unable to afford to have it properly repaired.
week's overtime should do it. In the meantime the ol
would have to soldier on. If it packed in he'd have to
everyone else did – go to work by bus.

The hill levelled out to give the old car some respi
making the long descent towards the centre of Leeds. T
stayed in second gear to prevent the car running out of c
the brakes were fairly useless, certainly no good in an en

Alice stood at the kerb and tried to gauge the spe
approaching Austin. It wasn't going very fast, and a long
vehicles followed in its wake. Waiting for it to pass woul
another couple of minutes. Dove might have gone by th

She stepped off the kerb, swung her crippled lim
forward and caught her foot on a slightly upraised manh
sending a painful vibration up her leg. The approachin
forgotten as she hopped around, crying with pain. 1

'Don't worry,' said Dove, through her tears. 'Hey! I can just see Jubby's face when I come first.'

Alice was smiling at this thought when she died.

Two weeks after the funeral Dove called round to see Tom. Mrs Webster came to the door. Her face was still gaunt with grief, her eyes empty and sad. She forced a smile for Dove's benefit.

'Is Tom in, Mrs Webster?'

'Come in, love. I'm sure he'll be pleased ter see yer.' She took a coat off a hook. 'Look, I'm goin' round ter a neighbour's for a bit. Mr Webster's at work, so yer can have the house ter yerselves.'

Tom looked up and said hello to Dove as she walked into the lounge.

'Your mam says she's gone to a neighbour's so we can have the house to ourselves.'

He nodded. Dove sat down beside him on the settee. She hadn't seen him since the funeral. That day his face had been fixed into a stony, tearless gaze. Whatever he felt inside, he refused to let it come out. The following week had been spent in tears. His eyes were dry again now, but tears weren't far below the surface. She put an arm around him and rested her head on his chest. They sat in silence for while; then Tom said, 'I haven't told anybody, but it was my fault.'

'What was your fault?'

'Our Alice getting run over.'

'Don't be silly, Tom, you weren't even there.' She sat up and looked at him. There was guilt in his eyes.

'It was my fault she was late,' he said. 'If she hadn't been late she wouldn't have got knocked down.'

'How do you mean, Tom?'

'I couldn't find me pencil case and I was in a hurry so I took our Alice's. That's why she was late, she was looking for it. Me mam told me. I daren't tell her it was my fault.'

'It wasn't your fault, Tom. It was circumstances. We all contribute to circumstances – that's what my dad says. Mind you, I think he's an expert at contributing to circumstances.'

'I didn't ask if I could take it because I knew she'd kick up a fuss, and I had an exam.'

She took his hand. 'Stop blaming yourself, Tom. It's doing no good.'

29

'If I hadn't taken her pencil box she'd be alive today ... and why didn't I just shout up and tell her I was taking it? She'd have gone mad with me, but she'd be alive.'

'If "ifs" and "ands" were pots and pans, there'd be no need for tinkers,' recited Dove.

'Does your dad say that as well?'

'No,' she smiled. 'That was one of me mam's.'

Tom went quiet again and Dove allowed him his silence.

'Me dad's been offered a job in New Zealand,' he said, at length.

Dove allowed the news to sink in before replying, 'What doing?'

'Showin' 'em how ter grow rhubarb. He applied for it before Alice ...'

He stopped. He wasn't ready to talk about Alice's death in normal conversation. Dove helped him out.

'I don't suppose he'll be taking it now.'

'Well yer suppose wrong. If he stays here, he'll mope himself ter death, me mam as well. He wrote to accept it this mornin'.'

'Oh,' said Dove, suddenly sad. 'I shall miss you.'

'I'm not going.'

Dove squeezed his hand, surprised at this. 'Why not?' she asked. She secretly hoped it might have something to do with her, but she knew she was being silly.

'I want ter stay on at school,' Tom explained, 'then go straight into the RAF.'

'RAF? You never mentioned it to me before.'

'I've been doing a lot of thinking these last few weeks. I want ter be a pilot. Yer need qualifications ter be a pilot.'

'That's what our Henry wants to be ... mind you, he changes his mind every week.'

'So,' said Tom. 'I'll be staying with me auntie and uncle in Bardsey.'

'What? That stuck-up Auntie Margaret?'

'She's not so bad when you get to know her ... and Uncle Frank's all right. He's very much like me dad.'

'What about your cousin, what's his name?'

'Our Michael? He's a bit of a prat, thick as two short planks, but I can always ignore him.'

'Bardsey eh? It'll be twopence to talk to you once you move to Bardsey.'

Tom grinned, his first since he'd been called out of class to be told his sister had been killed. 'It'll only cost *you* a penny.'

'So, we can still see each other, then?'

'Course we can,' Tom said. He turned to look at her. His eyes were kind and guileless and she felt comfortable in his company. 'Dove, what're you going to do when yer leave school?'

She shrugged. 'Never thought about it much ... I suppose I always assumed I'd stay on the road with my family.'

'Is that what you want?'

'Dunno, I quite fancy being a proper musician.'

'What – a banjo player?'

She laughed. 'I can play the guitar as well, only dad sold it just after mam died. I think he was a bit skint.'

'I've got one you can borrow. Me dad bought me one, but I never learned to play. Neither did Alice.' He thought for a while, then said, 'Yer can have it if yer like. It's no use ter me.'

'You can't go giving presents away, what would your dad say?'

'He'd say it'd gone to a good home. My dad thinks the sun shines out of yer ... backside.'

'You can say arse if you want, I'm not a prude.'

'In that case, we all think the sun shines out of yer arse,' he said. 'Our Alice did, especially.'

'She was my first best friend.'

'Our lass thought the world of yer,' said Tom. 'With her bein' crippled, she didn't seem to have any friends. Not real friends. Yer used ter stick up fer her, didn't yer?'

'She didn't need much sticking up for.' Dove laughed at a memory. 'She once told Jubby she had a face like the Co-op horse's arse.'

Tom laughed as well. 'I'm glad she got to know you. She deserved someone like you.'

'That's a sort of a compliment, isn't it?'

'Sort of.'

He kissed her, gently at first, then with a passion which unnerved her slightly, but she allowed him his way because it wasn't at all unpleasant; on top of which, she was imagining the anger this would arouse in her dad if he could see her now. Maybe this lowered her inhibitions as she didn't resist when he undid the buttons on her cardigan and ran his hands across her budding breasts; pressing his lips into her mouth and making her gasp for breath. She was becoming aroused when he gave a sudden moan and slumped back, closing his eyes and allowing his breathing to subside. Then his face went crimson with embarrassment and his eyes filled with tears.

'Sorry,' he said. 'I shouldn't have done that.'

'Maybe I shouldn't have let you,' she said, buttoning up her cardigan.

'No, it were my fault. I shouldn't have done it.'

'Why did you stop?' Dove had a good idea why, but she wanted his confirmation.

'Something happened that ... that shouldn't have happened.'

'Oh,' she said. Her eyes were drawn to the tell-tale stain on his trousers. 'I see.'

'I bet yer think I'm rotten.'

She shrugged. 'It's human nature. You can't stop how you feel.'

'It's not right though,' he said. 'Not at a time like this.'

She didn't argue, but she did feel slightly cheated. Then she wondered how she could word this when she went to Confession. She'd committed a sin of impurity with a boy. *A sin of impurity with a boy?* That could mean anything. The priest might think she'd actually *done it*. What sort of a penance would she get for that?

'I'll fetch yer that guitar,' he said, turning away so the stain wasn't on view. When he came down he'd changed his trousers and Dove pretended not to notice. He handed her a handsome-looking acoustic guitar. Dove ran a finger over the strings to check it was in tune. It was.

'Tom, it's a really good one.'

'I know. Me dad never buys rubbish when it comes to instruments.'

'Well look, I'll borrow it and –'

'Dove, I don't want it back. Our Alice once mentioned that I should give it to you.' He was tearful again and annoyed at himself for showing such weakness in front of Dove. She took the guitar from him.

'One day, I'll make Alice proud of me,' she promised.

'She always was proud of yer.'

'I mean really proud.'

*

32

Dove had sneaked a look in Miss Molloy's Mass register and noted with some satisfaction that she was in first place in front of Mary Jubb. The word was that no one in the school was anywhere near her and Jubb; this would have pleased Alice. The additional church attendances leading up to her recent confirmation had given Dove enough points to overtake everyone. All she needed was Confession, Communion and eight o'clock Mass and she was home and dry. Rumour had it that the top present was definitely a bike again.

On the night before Palm Sunday, Dove confessed her sin with Tom.

'Father, I was kissing a boy and he got, er ... overexcited.'

'Did you commit a sin of impurity with him, my child?'

'Well, we weren't being *very* impure, Father. In fact I was quite surprised when it happened.'

'I see. You will find that some young men have very little self-control where the flesh is concerned. You must be wary of that at all times.'

'I will, Father.'

'For your penance say three Hail Marys, now make a good Act of Contrition.'

'Thank you, Father.'

That night, Malachy had gone out as usual and arrived back in the early hours. Both children heard him come in and waited for the inevitable rage. When Malachy was in drink all the injustices the world had inflicted on him magnified in his mind. His dead wife was the object of his self-pity as he staggered home. He was weeping when he kicked the door open.

'Bastards!' he shouted from outside.

His children heard him staggering up the wooden steps, tripping and falling back with a loud curse. Eventually his shadow, formed by the moon shining through the open door, fell across them. They braced themselves.

'So it was my fault, was it? My fault she died? I know what ye tink o' me ... ye little shits!'

Dove was in the top bunk and out of range of his boots, so he kicked at Henry. The boy screamed in fear and pain. She turned over and flung herself at her drunken father.

'Leave him, Dad!' she shrieked. 'You're going to kill him!'

'It wasn't my fault she died!' he wept.

'I know it wasn't, Dad.'

'Know? What the hell d'ye know!' His eyes blazed with irrational anger and he hit her with his open palm; it landed on her ear with a blistering smack, knocking her on top of her brother. Then Malachy collapsed on the floor and wept himself to sleep. He was getting worse. Dove knew they'd have to run away before much longer.

Blood was running from her ear. She lit a paraffin lamp and held it over her frightened brother. His face was pale with shock and blood drizzled from either nostril. He was sobbing.

'I think he broke me arm, Dove. Are you okay?'

She nodded and took his arm, gently. 'Try and hold it up.'

He winced with pain and lifted it up, slowly. 'It hurts like mad,' he said.

'It's not broke,' she diagnosed. 'You wouldn't be able to lift it if it was broke.'

'It still hurts.'

'See what it's like in the morning. You might have to go to hospital.'

Henry nodded and looked at her. 'What we gonna do, Dove?' he asked. 'I'm really scared of him.'

They both looked down at their snoring father, lying on the floor with his arms crossed over his gently heaving chest and saliva drooling from the corner of his mouth. He was harmless now – until the next time.

'He'll be fartin' soon,' forecast Henry, bleakly. 'That'll be nice.'

Dove and her brother left the caravan at dawn. Loose change had spilled from Malachy's pockets onto the floor; enough to pay the bus fare to Leeds Infirmary.

Henry was diagnosed as bruised but unbroken. 'You must have lost, because I haven't seen the other feller in here,' smiled the doctor when Henry told him he'd been in a fight. The man looked at Dove's ear and asked: 'Did you get mixed up in it as well?'

Her ear was still ringing, but it was seven-thirty and she needed to be at Mass by eight o'clock.

'I got caught on my ear, it's nothing.'

'I'd like ENT to take a look at you.'

34

'Honest, Doctor it's nothing ... '

'Let me be the judge of that.'

It was turned eleven when they emerged from the hospital, Dove with a bandaged head and Henry with his arm in a sling. Mary Jubb would now be in the lead – that was the most depressing thing about the whole affair.

Malachy showed genuine concern when they got back. 'What the hell happened ter you two? You haven't been fightin' in church, have yer?'

They stared at him with blank faces.

'It was a joke,' he said.

'We've been to hospital,' said Dove. 'Henry thought you'd broken his arm, but it's only badly bruised. He's got bruised ribs as well where you kicked him.'

'Holy Mother o' God! What have I done?'

'The doctor said you nearly burst my eardrum.'

Anger flared. 'So ... ye told them it was me what did it?'

'No Dad,' said Dove. 'But we will next time.'

The two of them walked past him and stepped up into the confines of the waggon, where Dove lit the stove and fried a panful of sausages for her and Henry. They sat inside for the rest of that Palm Sunday morning, wondering what the future held for them. If there was to be a future.

In the afternoon she found herself heading for Tom's house. Malachy had gone to see a man about something or other and Henry had gone off with a pal from school; Dove realised that with Alice now gone she had no friends. Apart from Tom.

He saw her from the window and came to the door, concern on his face.

'What happened to you?'

She saw no reason to cover up her dad's transgressions. 'Dad came home drunk last night. Henry's worse than me. Fancy a walk?'

Tom's face coloured with frustrated anger. Had this been some boy, he'd have known what to do – go round and take it out on his nose; but dads were a different matter.

'Maybe you should tell the police,' he said, as he took her hand.

'What, and get taken into care? I'd rather take my chances with my dad. He's okay when he's sober. The worst part is I missed Mass this morning because of it. I took Henry to the Infirmary and

35

the flipping doctor insisted on treating me. By the time we got out it was too late.'

'I don't suppose God'll mind.'

'It's not God I'm worried about. It's the Mass register.'

'Oh, *that*.'

Dove detected a strong element of disapproval in his voice. 'I thought you came first once,' she said.

'Sort of.'

They strolled down the street in the afternoon sunshine. Everything seemed so much more normal here than in Dove's life. Two women, chatting at a gate, said 'good morning' to Tom; their sympathy for his bereavement was unspoken, but obvious. A man was mowing his front lawn and a gang of children were playing a noisy game of rounders. They all had homes, every one of them. Solid, permanent havens of brick and timber which stayed put and were there every night when they came home from school and would be there the following morning.

'I won't win, now,' Dove said. 'I promised Alice I'd beat Jubby. It was the last thing I said to her. If I'd managed to get to Mass this morning, I'd have won.'

Tom shrugged, 'So – why don't you lie?'

'I can't do that,' Dove said. 'Anyway, I'd have to say which Mass I went to and someone's bound to know I wasn't there.'

'Say you went somewhere else because you'd been to the Infirmary. Say you went to Saint Anne's.'

He made it sound so simple.

'I couldn't do that. You can't tell lies about the Mass register. It's like telling a lie to God.'

Tom smiled, 'Scared of a bolt of lightning, eh? I think God's got better things to worry about.' He inclined his head towards Dove's bandaged ear. 'Vicious dads for one thing.'

Dove thought about it and shook her head. 'No,' she said, making up her mind. 'No one ever lies at Mass register.'

They strolled in silence, then Tom said:

'I did.'

'Did what?'

'I lied at Mass register. Quite a few times, actually.'

'You mean ... when you won that doll's house for Alice?'

'Yeah,' he admitted.

'Oh Tom! Alice thought you were a hero – a selfless hero.'

'Maybe I was ... I could have chosen the bike.'

'Maybe she'd have thought differently if she'd known you'd cheated.'

'What she didn't know didn't hurt her,' he said, philosophically. He kicked at a stone and they both watched it tumbling down the street. 'I didn't start off by lying.' He kicked it again. 'One Sunday I didn't go to church at all. It was David Cohen's fault.'

'David Cohen?'

'Yeah, he's a Jew – he lives next door but one. I talked him into playing football one Saturday morning instead of going to syna-gogue, so he said it was only fair that I should go fishing with him instead of going to church the next day.'

'Tom,' said Dove. 'What's that got to do with the Mass register?'

'I'm just comin' to it if you give me a chance. Anyway, yer know how these teachers go on if yer miss Mass? I daren't lie and say I'd been to Saint Joe's, just in case someone said they hadn't seen me. So when Miss Booth called out the Mass register, I said I'd been ter The Holy Name for a change because Saint Joseph's got very full at nine o'clock Mass. She said it didn't really matter – and after that I just got carried away.'

'Didn't you feel guilty?'

'I did, actually ... but it was all a bit too tempting for me. I think maybe I'm a bit weak. I kept convincing myself that giving prizes for going to Mass isn't right; next thing you know they'll be paying kids to go to church. David Cohen reckons if that happens, us Catholics won't be able to get into church for all the Jewish kids.'

'He's a bit of a comic, is he ... your mate David.'

'He's okay. I must say, mam and dad were a bit surprised when I came home with this big doll's house an' told them how I'd won it. It were massive – Vernon Ferguson helped me to carry it home.'

'I know, I've seen it. Why didn't you choose the bike?' asked Dove.

He went quiet and squeezed her hand. 'I don't know – I didn't feel all that good about what I'd done,' he said. 'And maybe I thought if I didn't choose a present for meself it wouldn't be so much of a sin.'

'Did you ever tell the priest in confession?'

'Oh yeah ... that wasn't a problem. I just told him I'd been telling lies, which was true. They never ask for details.'

She remembered her recent confession and wondered if she should tell Tom. Or would it just embarrass him?

'Did you confess what *we* did?' she asked.

'What *we* did? We didn't actually do anything ... did we?' He looked keenly at her. 'What about you?'

She lowered her eyes and Tom's face took on a look of realisation. 'You did, didn't you? You thought we'd been all wicked and sinful.'

She reddened and nodded her head, slightly. 'I wasn't sure,' she said.

'What did you say to the priest?'

'I told him I was kissing a boy and he got overexcited.'

'Overexcited?'

'I didn't know what else to call it.'

'What did the priest say?'

'He told me that some young men have very little self-control where the flesh is concerned and that I must be wary of them at all times.'

Tom burst out laughing and Dove was forced to smile as well. He contorted his face, pretended to grab at her with clawlike hands and said, in a ghostly voice, 'You must be wary of me at all times, my dear.'

Dove laughed and ran away from him, up a narrow footpath that led into an overgrown recreation ground. Tom caught her and pulled her to the ground; then became immediately concerned that he might have hurt her.

'Sorry, Dove, are you okay?'

'Course I'm okay, I'm not made of china you know.'

'I know.' He put his arm around her and asked, 'What penance did we get?'

'Three Hail Marys.'

'Can't have been much of a sin,' he said. 'I got more than that for nicking apples off old man Benson's apple tree.'

They sat together in the afternoon sun, comfortable in each other's company. Dove unwound her bandage and Tom examined her ear.

'Nothing much to see,' he said. 'It's a bit red, that's all ... and there's a bruise on the side of your face. He's not much of a man, isn't your dad, doing this to his own children.'

38

A long silence followed, and then Dove said, 'The more I think about it, the more I think it was a really nice thing to do.'

'What was?'

'Choosing a doll's house for Alice.'

'Oh, that.' He'd rather hoped her mind was on more carnal things.

'And I don't suppose God will blame you,' she added.

'There's a bit more to it,' said Tom, grinning at a sudden memory. 'Yer should have heard everyone when I walked up to this doll's house. All the lads started hooting, calling me a lady boy ... I were as red as a beetroot.'

'Did you tell them who it was for?'

'I didn't think it were any o' their business. Do you still have Monday Assembly?'

'You mean when Sister Clare reads out the good deeds of the week?'

'Yeah,' grinned Tom. 'Well, first assembly after Easter, she read out that I'd won the Mass register prize and told the whole school I'd chosen a doll's house. She'd no need to tell them, but she did – I think she had her suspicions about me. Oh, you should have heard 'em, Dove. I thought they'd never stop laughing. Then in class, Miss Booth started takin' the mickey out o' me. She once asked me if I wanted to sit wi' the girls. Everyone started titterin' like monkeys.'

'You should have told her you'd picked it for Alice. They must have known about her.'

He shook his head. 'Our Alice wasn't at Saint Joe's then. She was mostly in and out of hospital and when she wasn't she was at a special school in Crossgates. Anyway, Miss Booth never liked me and I knew a way of getting my own back.'

'Own back ... how do you mean?'

'Well, I let them all have their fun for a couple o' weeks because I knew me mam and dad would be going to see Sister Clare to ask if Alice could start the following September. And I knew they'd mention the doll's house to her and how proud they were of me for giving it to my sister when I could have chosen a bike.'

'You crafty monkey.'

'Me dad allus said yer should never tell people how wonderful you are – it's much better if they discover it for themselves. He

39

reckons me mam hasn't discovered how wonderful he is yet but she will, given time.'

'So,' said Dove, 'what happened?'

Tom grinned and lay back in the grass with his hands cupped around the back of his head. 'Oh, it were brilliant, Dove,' he said. 'After me mam and dad had gone, Sister Clare called me into her office and asked me why I didn't tell everyone I'd picked the doll's house to give to my poor, lame sister.'

'Was she embarrassed?'

'Oh, yeah – I told her me dad said if you're going to do something for somebody, just do it, and don't show off about it. If yer show off about it, it means you're doin' it as much for yourself as for them.'

'What did Sister Clare say?'

'She said something like, "Well, Thomas, there's a lesson to be learned here," and said I could go. Then at Monday Assembly she got up and told everyone what I'd done and how wrong they'd all been to make fun of me when they didn't know the true facts, and they should all bow their heads and pray for forgiveness – all except me of course, because I was the only one who hadn't done anything wrong.'

Dove was laughing at the irony of it all. 'Go on,' she said, 'what happened then?'

'Well, everyone bowed their heads and started sayin' prayers. I stood on a chair and was looking round to check that there were no slackers, and I noticed Miss Booth looking daggers at me. I stared back at her until she looked down and I saw her lips moving. Honestly, Dove, it were brilliant.'

Dove laughed and lay down beside him, 'I still can't lie about going to Mass,' she said.

'That's because you're a better person than me,' Tom said. 'I've always been a gormless lump ... according to Alice, anyway.' He cupped her head in his hands and kissed her on her lips. 'I don't suppose you fancy another three Hail Marys worth, do you?'

'Watch it, Webster. I've been told to be wary of young men like you at all times.'

Miss Molloy eased herself onto the seat behind her high desk, from where she had an elevated view of the girls of Senior Two. She wore her hair in a bun to add gravitas to a face which, otherwise, would have been difficult to take seriously, mainly because of her nose. It was inordinately long, with a bridge which was threatening to break through the flimsy film of skin, and a permanently red tip which she camouflaged with face powder. This rarely lasted long, due to her habit of constantly rubbing it. She was aware of her physical imperfection and thus had treated Alice with understanding and compassion. Laid across her desk, behind the inkwell, was a bamboo cane which she kept on display as a deterrent.

Mixed-sex classes were restricted to the junior school. For boys and girls to associate during the dangerous years of puberty was tempting providence. None of these girls had passed their scholarship and in some eyes were classed as intellectual failures, destined for factory work and general drudgery. There were forty-four girls in her class, many of whom had slipped through the net and would have done well in grammar school.

'Quiet!'

There was enough authority in the teacher's voice to subdue the whispering. They knew if she had to tell them twice it meant someone would be in trouble. She lifted the lid of her desk, removed two ledgers, then closed it before peering at the girls over the top of her glasses, checking for absentees rather than going through the attendance register.

'Anyone absent?'

There was only one empty desk, Alice Webster's. The girls glanced round and several voices called out,

'No, Miss.'

'Right, I'll get straight on to the Mass register. This is the final day and I'm pleased to say that two of the girls in this class are ahead of anyone else in the school. It might well have been three girls, but for poor Alice Webster.'

She then looked down and studied the register, and the girls thought she was bowing her head in remembrance of their late classmate, so they did the same. Miss Molloy was puzzled when she looked up, then she realised what was happening and took advantage of the situation by leading the children in prayer:

'Eternal rest grant unto Alice, Oh Lord, and let perpetual light shine upon her. May she rest in peace ... Amen.'

Then she put the cane away as it seemed an inappropriate thing to have on display at such a time. She rarely used it, other than to point at the blackboard or to rap on her desk to restore silence. When she looked up again, Mary Jubb was grinning from ear to ear.

'Would you like to share the joke with the rest of us, Jubb?'

Some of the children sniggered and the grin went from the face of Mary Jubb, who had heard about Dove not making it to church. The teacher began to call out the Mass register and the girl's grin returned when it got to the aitches.

'Harrison?'

'Ten o'clock Mass, Miss.'

'Hopkins?'

'Confession, Communion and eight o'clock Mass, Miss.'

'Well done, Hopkins. Jubb?'

'Confession, Communion and nine o'clock Mass, Miss.'

'Slept in did you, Jubb? Never mind, I believe this puts you in the lead.'

Mary Jubb folded her arms and sat back with a triumphant smirk. Miss Molloy glared at her, then allowed her eyes to drift over to Dove, the other main contender. McKenna was the lesser of two evils. She then returned her attention to the register and arrived at the Irish contingent.

'McGinty?'

'Communion and nine o'clock Mass, Miss.'

'McGee?'

'Eleven o'clock Mass, Miss.'

McGee withered under the teacher's disapproving glare.

'McKenna?'

'Confession,' Dove paused and looked at Mary Jubb's smirking face. Then she remembered Alice's last words before she died. *'Make sure yer beat her, won't yer?'*

'. . . Communion and eight o'clock Mass, Miss.'

Mary Jubb's smirk turned to disbelief, then to anger. She held up a hand to lodge a protest. Dove half raised her own hand and added, 'I went to Saint Anne's near the Infirmary, Miss . . . with me having to go to hospital with my ear . . . is that all right?'

'I don't see why not.' The teacher gave her a smile. 'Well, McKenna, barring miracles, you seem to have come first.'

Dove blushed as Miss Molloy went through the rest of the register. She could hardly believe what she'd done. Tom had put the idea into her head, but even so, lying at Mass register had to be a mortal sin ... and dying with a mortal sin on your soul meant going straight to Hell and no appeal for clemency. Still, all she had to do was stay alive for a week or so and she was home and dry. On Sunday she'd choose the bike and the following week she'd confess her sin. She'd go to the same priest who only gave her three Hail Marys for getting Tom overexcited. Missing Mass because you've had to go to hospital isn't a sin, so all she had to say in confession was that she'd told a lie. As Tom said, priests never ask for details. It all seemed so easy. Anyway, she hadn't lied nearly as much as Tom had. In view of recent events she didn't feel as guilty as she otherwise might. God owed her a favour.

It was the following Wednesday that the bombshell arrived. No one in the school really knew what the big present was, but a bike was definitely the hot favourite. It was the only big present anyone ever wanted. Dove was hoping they'd swap a girl's bike for a boy's bike as she didn't want Henry to be made fun of for riding round on a bike without a crossbar; he had enough to put up with. Miss Molloy had just taken the class register when Mary Jubb's arm stabbed the air. The teacher looked up.

'What is it, Jubb?'

'Please Miss, me dad says they haven't had an eight o'clock Mass at Saint Anne's for two weeks due to one of the priests havin' flu. Me dad says the first Mass is nine o'clock Mass, Miss.'

The teacher didn't immediately see the significance. 'What's this got to do with anything?'

'Dove McKenna said at Mass register that she went to eight o'clock Mass at Saint Anne's, Miss.'

Miss Molloy's eyes swivelled on to Dove. 'McKenna, did you go to eight o'clock Mass on Sunday or not?'

Dove was in trouble. 'I 'er ... I don't remember, Miss.' The colour of her cheeks told of her guilt.

The teacher stared at her in disbelief. Her face went pale with anger. 'You don't remember? Of course you remember. Did you go to eight o'clock Mass or didn't you? Yes or no?'

Dove bowed her head miserably and mumbled, 'No, Miss.'

There were was a rumble of disapproval from the class.

'It's not fair on us if she's been tellin' lies, Miss,' called out one girl.

'She's a gippo, Miss,' said Mary Jubb, smugly. 'Mc dad says yer daft if yer believe owt a gippo says.'

'I don't need your father's unchristian opinions, thank you, Jubb.'

'It was only that once, Miss,' said Dove. 'And that was because the hospital wouldn't let me out in time.'

The class was giving this mitigating circumstance due consideration when Mary Jubb called out, 'If yer lie once, yer lie all the time.' She followed it with, 'Liar, liar, pants on fire.' The chant was taken up by the rest of the class.

'QUIET!' roared Miss Molloy. 'You're supposed to be young ladies, not children.' She glared at Dove. 'Do you have anything further to say for yourself, McKenna?'

'I promised Alice I'd beat Jubby!' blurted Dove without thinking. 'It was the last thing she asked me to do before she died.'

There was a silence as the class digested this latest turn of events. Dove was already regretting involving Alice in her crime. Miss Molloy's expression turned to disgust. The girl had now shown her true colours.

'Blaming a dead girl for your own lies is a most heinous sin, McKenna. Come out here.'

Dove hesitated.

'NOW!'

With bowed head, Dove moved down the short aisle between the desks. Feet lashed out at her as she walked, kicking at her ankles, hurting her; but she didn't react.

'Hold out your hand.'

The teacher gripped Dove's fingertips to ensure her hand was fully stretched. The cane lashed down into her palm; Dove blinked but showed no pain and drew her hand away, thinking her punishment was over.

'I haven't finished, yet, McKenna. Keep your hand there until I say different.'

Another five strokes lashed into her hand with increasing ferocity as Dove's face remained impassive. Six was the maximum ever imposed. Tears of pain and humiliation were bubbling just below the surface. She bit into her lip, producing a trickle of blood which went unnoticed by the teacher, who was determined to dislodge what she took to be defiance off this girl's face. After the sixth stroke Dove had lost count and her hand still remained outstretched. Miss Molloy took this to be further impertinence and gave her a final lash, delivered with all her strength. The cane snapped to a chorus of 'oohs' from the class. Dove's stoicism finally crumbled as the last blow broke through her pain threshold. She bent double, clutching her hands under her armpits, crying profusely.

'That was very cruel, Miss.'

'What?'

'She said you were very cruel, Miss,' called out Mary Jubb. 'I think she deserved it.'

'We're not interested in what you think, Jubb,' snapped the teacher, unhappy now at having made Dove cry with pain. If the girl had howled at the first stroke she'd only have given her a couple.

'Dovina McKenna, stand out in the corridor,' she said, uncertainly. 'We'll see what Sister Clare has to say about all this.'

As Dove closed the door behind her, Mary Jubb's hand stabbed the air once again.

'Please, Miss, may I go to the lavatory?'

'You may,' muttered the teacher.

Mary Jubb's smirk accompanied her to the door. In the corridor she stopped and stood face to face with Dove.

'Just so yer know. I made it up about there bein' no eight o'clock Mass at Saint Anne's. Yer see, I knew you were lyin' – gippoes allus lie.'

The sneer on Mary's face was too much to bear. Dove's fist curled into a ball which she slammed into the girl's nose producing a howl of pain and a spurt of blood. She followed it up with a flurry of punches that sent Jubb to the floor, where she curled into a ball as Dove kicked her in the ribs. The classroom door opened and Miss Molloy stood there, horrified; but Dove had taken off and didn't stop running until she got back to the waggon.

When Henry came home at lunchtime, his sister was sitting on a step, staring into the distance, wondering what was to become of her. Life with her father had become intolerable. Had their mother still been alive it might have been different. Now that Alice was dead, she missed her mother, as inadequate as she had been. Fortunately she had been still alive when Dove had her first period. Although she hadn't had the sense to forewarn her daughter, she was there to quell the tears and reassure Dove that the 'curse' was nothing to worry about and that it happened to all girls. They'd had a talk about boys and all the pitfalls of sex and Dove had been amazed at her mother's forthrightness. But with her and Alice both gone, she missed having someone to confide in. A father such as Malachy was the last person she could turn to for help and advice. He was cruel and dangerous and impossible to live with. Running away seemed the only option. She became aware of Henry's presence, and said, without looking at him, 'I'm running away.'

'Fair enough, I'm coming with you.'

'You can't, you've just passed your scholarship.'

'What difference does that make?'

'None, probably,' conceded Dove.

'Well then.'

'If we take the waggon,' she mused, stroking a non-existent beard, 'Dad'll come after us. If we just disappear, he'll probably shout and carry on, but he won't bother looking for us. He'll just wait for us to come back; then give us both a good hiding.'

'So ... we don't come back then.'

'No.' Her answer was firm and unequivocal.

'What're we gonna do?'

'Make plans,' said Dove. 'We've got all the Easter holidays to make plans.'

Henry's eyes danced with excitement. 'I'm eleven on Sunday. We could join a circus.'

'Maybe,' said Dove, as if that was just one of many options she was considering.

The following day they simply stayed at home. Their dad never asked questions about school so there was no need to lie to him. The day after that was Good Friday, the first day of the Easter holidays. Time for Dove to make plans.

Chapter 4

For the benefit of the school Malachy had assigned himself an address. Sheraton Drive was the nearest road to their waggon and it had no number 13 of its own so Malachy had adopted the number and collared the postman to inform him. It was Easter Saturday before the first (and last) letter was delivered. The postman just caught Malachy as he was leaving for work. He stuffed it into his pocket and climbed into Len Tordoff's truck.

That evening an old man bought a newspaper from a village shop just north of Leeds and was reading with interest about Yorkshire's first match of the season, against Middlesex. He'd played a bit in his youth and had often gone to Headingley to watch the Yorkshire greats, such as Len Hutton and Herbert Sutcliffe.

Montgomery Catchpole was three miles out of the village now and heading north. Beneath his battered trilby the hair on the top of his head was a distant memory; just a shiny dome encircled by a wild hedgerow of snowy white locks, left very much to their own devices and extending into a spectacular beard.

To the casually watching world he was just another tramp, but within his own mind he was a traveller – an adventurer, ending his days in freedom. Those who took the time to pause and say 'hello' saw a great pride in his eyes which belied his appearance. He would bestow upon them his most benevolent beam and send them on their way feeling somehow better for having encountered him. A large raindrop splashed onto the newspaper, the first of many.

'Oh dear,' hc said, and stuffed the paper into one of the pockets of his army greatcoat. 'Oh dear, oh damn damn dear!'

He reached over his shoulder into his rucksack, grabbed the protruding handle of an umbrella, unsheathed it like an ancient swordsman and tried to push it open in one continuous movement – but was hampered by broken spokes. He then spent a rain-soaked minute trying to straighten them out before giving up and settling for what cover it could afford him.

The rain came down heavily as he pressed on. His advancing years had taken their toll of his legs and he knew he couldn't keep up this arduous life for ever. It was a depressing thought.

How he wished his wife could be with him. As he walked, he remembered that final moment, his last words to her before he killed her.

'Thank you for a lovely life, Elisabeth.'

He'd kissed her on her cracked lips; then stifled the last breath back inside her body with a pillow. He didn't press too hard as he didn't want to cause any more pain; as if her having cancer wasn't enough, dementia was irreversible, undignified. Especially in a woman such as Elisabeth who had always been bright and articu-late and . . . dignified.

Tears had smudged his vision as that final injection of morphine sent her to sleep. The doctor had quietly left, with a sympathetic promise to return tomorrow to give her another shot; but her pain would have returned long before then and her agony would have been unbearable for both of them. Unfortunately the doctor was much too busy to come more than once a day. 'Can't you give her enough to last her until you come back?' the old man had asked. The doctor had shaken his head and explained how he was wary of giving her an overdose.

This was Montgomery's last act of love for the woman he'd known and loved since they were both fourteen years old. It had been a gentle love. No fierce passion or fights or infidelities. He had smothered the last remnants of painful existence from Elisabeth's fragile body; then he'd left. He didn't want to face the questions, the rigmarole of a funeral and the church service. And most of all he didn't want to see her being lowered into a dark hole in the ground. He wanted to remember her in the sunshine and full of life.

He'd done all his mourning for her during the weeks he'd watched her life slowly ebb away. It had been the saddest of times. He'd watched over her as the colour and vibrancy drained from her face. He held her hand until it no longer gripped his; and he'd looked into her eyes until the brown turned to grey and no light was left within. He'd watched over her until the only thing she had left to remind the world of her mortal existence were her moans of pain. And then he'd said his goodbye to her. There were others who could do the rest.

When he brought the pillow away, he saw she'd left this world with a smile on her face. Where it had come from he didn't know, except that it was her final gift to him; a smile which would allay any suspicion. Montgomery's tears dripped onto her lips as he kissed her for the last time.

The old man had been on the road a year now; an idea that had taken his fancy more than once. If Elisabeth had been well enough to come they'd have tramped the roads together. And wouldn't that have been a fine way for them to say their good-byes to the world? As things turned out, it wasn't to be, but she'd left him with his memories of her. And no one could take those away.

It was dusk. The unremitting rain had soaked into his ponderous coat and he was on the lookout for somewhere to pitch his tent and fill his water bottle. As he rounded a bend, he saw the solution to both his problems in front of him. Out of the mouth of a boy, carved in stone and set in the wall, was a stream of spring water, collecting in a stone trough. According to a weathered inscription it had been put there many years ago in memory of Alderman Cusworth, to slake the thirsts of passing animals and travellers. And at the far side of the wall was a field. The grass was perhaps a bit too long to be called an ideal campsite, but it looked inviting, nevertheless. The old man looked skywards and smiled. 'Thanks, Elisabeth,' he said. 'You never let me down.'

He cupped his hands into the stone trough and took a deep drink. It was cool and sweet and as flavoursome as many a wine he'd drunk. How she would have enjoyed this.

Malachy was already at the bar when a didicoy called Pikey Scullion came in, soaked to the skin from a sudden flurry of rain. The Fountain Head was full of Saturday night drinkers, mainly Irish construction workers. Wages and back-handers would be paid; men hired, but never fired – rule of the house to avoid bloodshed. Instructions would be given, deals struck and pints consumed. A few hours into the evening the tone would grow livelier and more animated. Malachy would normally be persuaded into song, accompanied by a fiddler and an accordionist. There would be fights; minor scuffles as points of view were forced home – but they would be over quickly.

Scullion caught Malachy's eye, nodded and moved to join him. They weren't exactly friends. They weren't the types to foster friends. Just two men who simply shared a mutual dislike of the human race, especially after a few drinks.

'Where've been hidin' yersen, Malachy, lad? We've not seen yer round t' fairs for a bit.'

'The wife died on me,' said Malachy. 'I been workin' fer Lennie Tordoff. You still thievin'?'

Pikey shrugged, as if there was no insult implied in the question, which there wasn't. 'As and when,' he said. 'We had a nice little pick-up last week in Derby. Stuff's a bit too warm ter shift straight away though.'

'Ye mean Beulah won't let ye?' cackled Malachy.

'She got her head screwed on, has me ma,' grunted Pikey. 'She's an ugly old cow but she sees us right.'

'An' how's your Sid?'

'Our kid?' said Pikey. 'Still as thick as pig shit – Ma treats him like a baby.'

The evening wore on and Malachy was called upon to sing.

'I've nothin' ter sing about,' he said.

'What's up wi' yer ... yer miserable bugger?' taunted Pikey. 'Yer like a broken pisspot — all on edge.'

'And wouldn't you be on edge if ye had ter put up with the likes of my family?'

'Family, yer mean them kids o' yours?'

'I do. They're the only family I've got — apart from a gobshite of a brother who's away in America with his arse pocket stuffed with dough and nivver a penny ter spare for me, nor a mind ter come ter me wife's funeral.'

He took a letter from his pocket and pushed it across the table to Pikey. It was from school. The didicoy read it with a smile slowly contorting his harsh face.

'Lyin' and fightin' eh?' he smirked. 'I wonder where she gets it from.'

Malachy's eyes blazed with rage, his fist tightened on the

50

handle of his pint glass. 'Mind yer mouth!' he snarled. 'Or I'll mind it for yer.'

'Okay, okay, calm down. I were just takin' t' piss, that's all. No need ter take it personally.'

Pikey gulped his drink as Malachy allowed his temper to cool. Then his mouth creased into a cruel grin once more.

'Hey,' he whispered, loud enough for all around to hear. 'I bet lyin' and fighting's not all she's been up ter. She's not a bad lookin' tart isn't your daughter. I bet she puts it about a bit. Yer could make a few quid out of her if yer played yer cards right.'

Malachy sprang to his feet, kicked away his chair and squared up to the sniggering didicoy. 'I'll bloody kill ye, ye dirty-mouthed bastard!' he screamed.

Pikey Scullion rounded the table and, with a beckoning hand, invited Malachy forward. 'Kill me, eh? I'll tell yer summat, yer thick paddy. If anyone's gonna get killed ternight it's not gonna be me.'

Scullion had spent years as a bare-knuckle fighter and knew he could take the Irishman. As Malachy was trying to focus his beer-glazed vision, Pikey floored him with a single heavy blow. When he came to, the didicoy's grinning face was staring down at him and the momentarily distracted drinkers returned to what they had been doing. There'd be other bouts as the night wore on. Scullion held out a hand and pulled Malachy to his feet.

'No harm done, hey lad? Just takin' t' piss, that's all.'

Malachy wiped the blood from his lip and snarled. 'I owe ye one fer that.'

They drank in silence for a while as Malachy mulled over his problems. 'What will I do with her?' he asked, after a while. 'Aw, Jasus, man. I can't be chasin' round all over the place findin' schools for her ter be kicked out of.'

'Yer could try teaching 'er a proper lesson,' suggested Pikey, trying to keep his face straight so that he might be taken seriously. 'A lesson she'll never forget. She needs teaching a lesson till she screams for bloody mercy and promises she'll never be a bad girl again.' His drink-sodden eyes glazed for a moment as he drew vicarious pleasure from the thought of what Malachy might do to his beautiful daughter. 'Give her a good beltin' on her bare arse. I'll do it for yer if yer haven't got the stomach.'

'Stomach?' roared Malachy. 'Who says I haven't got the

stomach? I'll attend ter me own problems with no help from you!'

'Well make sure yer do.' Pikey Scullion concealed a smirk behind a huge hand. 'I'll come wi' yer an' make sure yer do it right.'

'I need no help nor advice from you. I've me own way o' doin' things.'

'Well, what're yer asking me for then?'

Malachy sank his pint and wiped a sleeve across his mouth. 'Ah, go to bollocks,' he grunted.

Pikey was dangerously drunk as he drove Malachy home. It was a night that would change many lives. And end one.

Henry was putting the finishing touches to a detailed drawing he'd done of Boris earlier in the day. Dove was peering through the window into the darkness, wishing the rain would stop. Running away in bad weather hadn't been part of her plan. She glanced down at his drawing.

'Not bad,' she commented. 'In fact it's quite good.'

'I'd paint it,' he said. 'If I had anything to paint it with.'

'I'll get you some paints,' she promised. Her father's money box would finance the purchase.

Malachy burst in and flung the letter on the table. 'What's all this about?' he roared.

Dove took a tentative step forward and picked it up. It was from school:

Dear Mr McKenna,
It is my unpleasant duty to inform you that your daughter, Dovina Mary McKenna, has been telling quite serious lies about her Mass attendance record in order to dishonestly obtain an expensive Easter Day prize. On being found out in this lie she assaulted the pupil who, quite rightly, brought this dishonesty to our notice. In view of this I regret to say that your daughter is forthwith expelled from this school. A copy of this letter will be sent to the Local Education Authority. It is unlikely that she will be allowed to finish her education in a Catholic school.
Yours faithfully,

Sister Maureen Clare

Dove looked up at her father and said, defiantly, 'I only lied about one Mass, last Sunday – and that was your fault.'

'My fault? he roared. 'Everyting's my bloody fault!' His hand came arcing round, knocking her to the floor.

'I only did it once, Dad. I promise,' Dove sobbed.

'That's right, Dad,' said Henry. 'She only did it once ...'

His father turned on him. 'An' you're just as bad, you an' ye stupid pictures,' he raged, snatching Henry's drawing and tearing it into shreds.

The boy opened his mouth to protest and was silenced by a punch in his stomach, which knocked the wind out of him. Malachy returned his anger to his daughter.

'An' who am I supposed ter believe? You or a holy bloody nun?'

He aimed a kick at her ribs. She winced with pain and shuffled away from him; then she got to her feet and pushed Henry out of the door. 'Run, Henry!' she yelled. 'Before the mad bugger kills us both.'

Her insult brought a roar of rage from Malachy, prompting Henry to jump to the ground and run clear. He turned to see how his sister was faring. Tears of helplessness rolled down the boy's cheeks as he listened to the sound of his sister being cruelly beaten by their father. Malachy was dragging her from the waggon now and shaking her by the scruff of her neck.

Above the wind and the rain Henry couldn't hear any sound coming from Dove; she sagged in her father's grip and the boy feared the worst. He followed at a distance as his dad dragged her across a field in the direction of the mine shaft; her feet scuffed twin tracks into the sodden ground. After a few yards, Malachy let her drop in a heap, then he turned and strode back the way he'd come. Henry made a few tentative steps towards his sister and stopped as his father re-appeared, carrying a length of rope. Scarcely breaking stride, he stooped to grab Dove's collar, then continued to pull her, roughly, across the field; vicious profanities dripped from his mouth with every step he took.

When he reached the shaft he dropped her to the ground and began to heave at the railway sleepers. There were seven in all. He moved six and left the middle one in place. Then he took the rope and roughly lashed it around Dove's ankles. To Henry's immense relief she let out a cry of pain. At least she was alive. She was talking now, her words broken by sobs of fear.

'Dad ... what ... what are you doing to me? ... I haven't ... I haven't done anything.'

Malachy slapped her face again. 'Haven't done anything?' he rasped. 'Ye bring shame on the whole bollockin' family and ye say ye haven't done anything? Jasus girl! Ye need teachin' a lesson an' I'm the feller ter do it.'

He tied the other end of the rope around the remaining sleeper and pushed Dove, shrieking with terror, into the hole. The jerk almost broke her ankles as she dangled upside down, six feet into the shaft. Her screams echoed down into the black depths and she wet herself. It soaked into her clothes and ran towards her head and mingled with the blood from her nose, her tears and the rain. It ran across her forehead and into her hair, before dripping down into the dreadful blackness beneath her.

The pain in her ankles was unbearable and she knew this was it. She was going to die; murdered by her own father – a*nd with a mortal sin on her soul!* She crossed herself and tried to remember the Act of Contrition, forcing out the words as they came into her head:

'Oh my God I am sorry ... and beg pardon for all my sins, I ... I detest them above all things, because they ... because they ... they offend Thy infinite goodness, because they deserve Thy dreadful punishment ...' She paused as her voice echoed back up to her. She thought it might be her dad; her only hope of life. But there was nothing. She couldn't remember any more of her prayer and she hoped she'd done enough. It was the contrition that counted, not the words.

'Sorry,' she said, 'Amen.'

It would have to do. Where was Henry? She hoped he hadn't stopped running. He'd be able to tell someone what had happened. Tell them where her body was. Please God, get me out of here. I'm truly sorry for telling such a bad lie.

Everything was misty now. The blood had gathered in her head and was taking away her pain, her fear – and her life.

Malachy was sitting on the edge of the hole, looking down at his daughter as he sipped on a bottle of whisky. He was soaked to the skin, his brain completely befuddled by the drink – convinced his cause was just.

'Ye can dangle there till ye see the error of ye ways. D'ye hear me, girl?'

His own voice came back to up him but no sound came from Dove. He took her silence to be dumb defiance; which inflamed him even more.

'I said, did ye hear me, girl?'

The boy stood watching as his father killed his sister. Murdered Dove. Henry's quaking terror had frozen to a petrified numbness. His eyes had widened like those of a rabbit caught in a car's headlights, resigned to the inevitable. Then he came out of it. Suddenly he didn't care what happened to him. Adrenalin began surging wildly through his veins and a growl formed deep within his skinny body. Whatever was happening was beyond his control. The sound coming from his mouth was that of some vicious, cornered animal which was prepared to fight to the death.

He set off running, with tears streaming down his face. His father caught a glimpse of him from the corner of his eye just as he was raising the bottle to his lips. The boy hurtled into him with a force equivalent to many times his weight. Malachy dropped the bottle down the hole and slowly teetered after it, like a felled tree, unconcerned – as if unaware of what was in store. Henry stood there and watched his father fall from sight. Then he heard a sharp cry that could only be his sister. The boy ventured to the edge of the hole and saw his father hanging on to Dove, his right hand gripping her left wrist.

They were now lit by the moon, coming out from behind a departing raincloud. The shock of her father grabbing at her had jerked Dove back into consciousness. She looked down and there he was, trying to drag her into the awful depths where he alone belonged. There was anger and confusion in his eyes; he was unable to understand how and why he was here. His hand began to slide, slowly and relentlessly from hers. Dove, more through instinct than any feeling for this man, tried to hold on to him with her free hand, but she had no strength; he had taken all that away from her, and now he was paying the price.

His eyes were on hers as he slipped from her grasp and fell down into the bottomless blackness. The sound he made was more of exasperation than fear. One second he was gripping on to her hand, adding to the agony in her ankles, then he was gone, and now there was only the sound of pattering rain. She felt the mist returning and managed to tell herself, *at least Henry will be safe now.*

Pikey Scullion lay slumped against a tree. He was dead to the world now, but the drunken didicoy had seen enough of what had happened to know that Malachy's death hadn't been an accident – but was his mind too clouded by drink for him to remember? And if he did somehow remember, would he think his mind was playing tricks on him? He had stopped by the tree to relieve himself; then his legs had collapsed under him.

'Dove, are you okay?' called out Henry.

His voice injected her with new hope. Determination. 'I'm okay, Henry.' She could scarcely summon up a whisper.

'Dove, hold on, I've got an idea to get you out,' he called down.

'I was hoping you might.'

She was glad he had an idea. He was quite good at ideas. But there was no way Henry could pull her out using just his own strength.

Her brother untied Boris and ran with him over to the hole. He tied the horse's tether around the sleeper and knotted it to the rope from which Dove was hanging, then he led the horse slowly back, pulling the sleeper away from the hole and Dove with it. In the remains of her consciousness she protected her head as she was dragged clear. Gravity was already draining the blood from her head and back into her body as her brother untied her bonds.

As if to signal the end of the torment, the rain had stopped and the moon illuminated the scene with its monochrome glow, instilling optimism. Henry brought a tarpaulin from the waggon, laid it on the wet grass and eased Dove on to it. Then he brought blankets to cover her with.

They lay side by side, looking up at the stars as they allowed the terror to subside.

'I'm glad you're not dead, Dove,' Henry said, after a while.

Dove was oddly calm after her ordeal, as though it had all happened to someone else. 'Oh, yes,' she said. 'Why's that?'

'You know.'

'Is it because you love me?'

'What if I do?' he said. 'You're my sister, aren't you?'

'I love you as well, Henry,' she said. Then she fell into a deep sleep, induced by shock and exhaustion, and woke up nestling against her brother, with the moon pale and low in the western sky and dawn not far away. Henry was staring upwards. He sensed Dove was now awake. A shooting star appeared and fell down towards the horizon. He nudged his sister.

'Dove, look – a shooting star.'

They watched it fall from sight and Henry said, 'It's lucky when you see one of them. We're going to have good luck today.'

'We could do with some,' Dove commented. One of Alice's poems came into her head and she began to recite it:

> 'Go and catch a falling star,
> Get with child a mandrake root,
> Tell me where all past years are,
> Or who cleft the Devil's foot ...'

She stopped because she couldn't remember any more. There was a long silence before Henry asked. 'Where'd d'you learn that – school?'

'No, it was one of Alice's favourite poems ... I really miss Alice. I wish she were here now, she'd have loved to have seen that.'

'There might be another one,' said her brother.

For a while they both scanned the skies in hopeful silence but soon their thoughts were on other things.

'I pushed him in,' Henry said. There was no guilt – he was just telling her.

Dove didn't respond. Her mind was suddenly racing with awful images of what had gone on last night. She began to shiver.

'I pushed him in,' Henry repeated, as if he hadn't heard her. 'Will I have to go to Confession?'

'Only if it was a sin,' Dove said. 'And if you savin' my life's a sin, I'm not bothered about bein' a Catholic.' There was a rising anger in her voice.

'Neither am I,' said Henry.

'Henry.'

'What?'

'I don't think I can walk. And I need to get out of these wet things or I'll catch my death.'

'If you don't mind me saying so, Dove, you niff a bit as well.'

It was as though he'd just sliced through the slender thread from which her sanity was suspended. She burst into tears. 'Well if you must know, I peed myself. And it's not very nice hanging upside down by your ankles when you're peeing yourself.'

'Sorry, Dove,' Henry said. 'I think I'd have done more than pee meself. I think I might have –'

'All right!' she sobbed. 'I know what you might have done. The thing is, what am I going to do?'

He thought for a while, then suggested, 'I could hitch Boris up and bring the waggon over here.'

Dove didn't hear him. She was back down the hole with death only a few heartbeats away. Henry got to his feet and went to hitch Boris to the waggon, with one eye on his shivering, sobbing sister; he'd never seen her as unhinged as this, and he was at a loss to know what to do. After a few minutes he brought the waggon to within a few feet of her.

'Okay, Dove?'

She looked up and, without a word, got to her knees and crawled painfully up the six shallow steps, across the carpeted floor and onto the bottom bunk.

'I'll warm you some water up,' he said. 'Then you can have a bit of a wash.'

Without waiting for a reply, which wasn't forthcoming anyway, he filled a panful of water and placed it on the stove. Dove still said nothing as Henry hunted round for a clean towel and flannels. Once the water was bearably hot he poured it into a bowl which he placed on a small table beside his sister's bed. Then he pulled out the screen which Malachy had bought to preserve his daughter's modesty within the cramped confines of the waggon.

'You can have Dad's room when we get properly organised,' Henry said. Then he went outside and was unhitching Boris again when Dove's curiosity got the better of her misery.

'What're you doing?' she asked, dully.

'I'm off to put the sleepers back,' he said. 'Then no one'll know.'

Dove nodded; he was right. No one need ever know what had happened to their dad. All they had to say was that he hadn't come home. When her brother came back, half an hour later, she was washed and beneath the covers in her bunk, staring blankly into space. Her eyes were damp and her arms were wrapped around her body. Protecting herself from any further harm.

'Done it,' Henry said. She made no response and Henry didn't know how to deal with it. 'Right,' he said. 'We'll have another couple of hours kip and make a start. I'll drive.'

He closed the door and climbed onto the bunk above her. Despite her obvious distress he felt safer now than he ever had in his life. She'd get over it in her own way – he hoped. Dove was the only family he needed.

A finger of dawn light crept across the roof of the waggon, bringing a smile to Henry's face. He began to sing:

> 'Happy birthday to me,
> Happy birthday to me,
> Happy birthday dear Henry,
> Happy birthday to me.'

In the darkness beneath him, Dove's face relaxed into a faint smile. Her brother's innocent and friendly voice cut through her fears and horror and somehow swung the balance of life back in her favour. With Malachy gone it now seemed that the good outweighed the bad.

'Henry,' she said.

'What?'

'Sorry for being so soft, but I was very frightened.'

'I know,' said Henry. 'It must have been a right bugger down that hole.'

'It was that all right.'

'He can't hurt us now,' he said. 'So there's no need to worry, really.'

'I suppose not ... Henry.'

'What?'

'Happy birthday.'

Pikey Scullion woke up at dawn with his head banging with a fearsome hangover. He stumbled to his truck. The sleeping children didn't hear the engine cough into life and the spinning wheels spew up a spray of mud as he pulled off the sodden grass onto the road.

He headed for his family's caravan five miles away, formulating the excuse he would give to his cow of a mother for staying out all night. One of these days he'd shut her foul mouth for good. He might have done it some time ago had she not been so useful. Beulah Scullion was the brains of the family, Pikey was the brawn and, at twenty-three, Sid was the baby – chronologically and mentally. Their father – or fathers – were never mentioned. Every time Pikey had expressed any curiosity in this direction he had been rewarded with a blow to the head. He was twelve years old before he realised his real name was Bernard. The name Pikey better matched his swarthy, gipsy appearance; inherited, so he'd been secretly told by those in the know, from an itinerant Spaniard who had once spent a night with Beulah. Sid was almost as large as his brother, but where Pikey was dark haired and rock hard, Sid was mousy haired and jelly soft.

Pikey drew the vehicle to as quiet a halt as he could manage, hoping to sneak in as they slept. The Scullions' caravan was what Malachy would have described as a tin can: cream and rust, six berth, with a portable outside toilet.

As Pikey stepped out of the truck, the door to the privy was kicked open, revealing his mother sitting there with her skirt around her ankles and her face puce with anger.

'What bleedin' time d'yer call this?' Her voice was hard and deeper than either of her sons'. 'Been out wi' one o' yer slags, have yer? Well don't expect us ter wait till yer've had yer bleedin' beauty sleep. We're off ter Netherton Fair, an' I want ter be there good an' bleedin' early.'

Pikey lowered his eyes, strode across to the wooden toilet and kicked the door shut. The turmoil in his stomach, exacerbated by *that* sight of his mother, caused him to double up and vomit on his boots. He wiped his mouth on his sleeve, went into the caravan and pulled his younger brother out of bed.

'What's to do, Siddy boy? The sun's up, Ma's festerin' in the crapper and you're snorin' like a pig.'

Sid rolled onto the floor, protesting that it wasn't time to get up yet. He curled into a ball as Pikey prodded him with the toe of one of his vomit-sprayed boots, then, realising the opportunity, he wiped them clean on Sid's pyjamas.

Beulah was outside, washing her hands and face in a water barrel. 'Sid! ... Get that pan on. We'll have a fry-up, then we're off. Pikey, get this van hooked up. I want a good pitch at Netherton. I don't want ter be stuck behind the bleedin' waltzers like we was at York.'

Pikey appeared at the door. 'I thought we were barred from Netherton, Ma?'

'That were bleedin' years ago. It'll all be forgot now.'

'I bet that geezer whose nose yer broke hasn't forgot,' sniggered Pikey. 'Are we selling them sparklers at Netherton, Ma?'

Beulah threw a dirty towel at him. 'Yer haven't got the brains yer were born with ... an' I thought our Sid were the barmy bugger in the family.'

'I just thought, that's all.'

'Well, yer know what thought did. Them jewels is worth proper money. Them punters at Netherton won't have two coppers ter scratch their arses with. On top o' which, the stuff's still a bit too warm ter be movin' on. I know a bloke in Manchester ... he'll give us a fair price.'

'How much d'yer think?'

'Well, t' papers reckon they were worth fifteen grand ... which'll be over t' top. They allus say it were more for t' insurance. Where did yer get ter last night, any road?'

'I were out wi' Malachy McKenna.' A sudden image of Malachy being pushed down some hole flashed into his mind, then went as quickly as it came.

'Malachy?' grunted Beulah. 'Haven't seen hide nor hair of him for God knows how long.'

'So? How much d'yer reckon, Ma?'

'I'm gonna ask him fer five grand. With a bit o' luck we'll get three.'

Pikey gave a crooked grin. The thought of his share of three thousand pounds drove away the vestiges of his hangover.

'Pull up at that spring, Ma.' They'd been on the road for an hour; Pikey's mouth was dry and his system dehydrated. 'We can pick up some water. My mouth's as furry as a buzzard's crutch.'

Beulah cackled at her son's remark as she pulled up by the spring; a regular stopping point for them and many other travellers. Had Montgomery Catchpole known this he might have thought twice about the safety of his campsite. The brothers got out and Pikey held his mouth under the stream of water, gargling and spitting noisily into the trough. Sid was looking over the wall.

'Hey up,' he said. 'There's a tent over yon.'

Within seconds Pikey was over the wall, with Sid on his heels. The old man woke up and was blinded by the sudden sunlight as Pikey yanked the tent away from its pegs. 'Who's this?' he roared. 'Christ! It's bleedin' Santa Claus.'

'Hey up! There's Santa's sack here, Pikey,' sniggered Sid, picking up the old man's rucksack.

Pikey thumped his brother on the arm. 'Go on,' he snarled. 'Tell everyone what they call me. I'm gonna have ter top the owd bugger now.'

'Aw, Pikey ... Ma said we hadn't ter top no one.'

'Leave me alone!' protested Montgomery, unable to make out his tormentors because of the dazzling morning sun.

A kick to his head, followed by a flurry of blows knocked him into oblivion. Their victim's life was saved by Beulah sounding the horn.

Pikey and Sid piled back into the truck with all the old man's belongings, including his tent. Their mother drove away just as a farmer clopped around the corner at the reins of a horse and cart. She watched, keenly, through the rear-view mirror and whistled a sigh of relief as the horse and cart didn't stop at the spring.

'What the bloody hell were all that about?' she snarled, savagely at them.

'Some owd dosser,' said Pikey, rummaging through the rucksack. 'He looked like Father bleedin' Christmas.'

'Jesus! What's the point in robbin' an old dosser? How is he ... yer didn't ...?'

'Nah, I should have. Our Siddy told him what me name was.'

'So, yer'd risk bein' hung just for a few owd rags, would yer? Have yer got no bloody brains inside that thick skull o' yours? An' there'll be nowt in that bag what's worth owt,' she said. 'I don't know why yer botherin'.'

'Yer never know, Ma,' grinned Pikey, holding out two rings and a locket in his grubby palm. 'I've got me a nice present from Santa. These should be worth a nice few bob.'

There was a noticeable new jauntiness about Boris as he picked up his great feet. Perhaps it was the absence of Malachy's sixteen stones, or perhaps the lightness of Henry's touch on the reins. The horse had never really responded to the heavy-handed way Malachy used to drive. When she was alive, their mother had mostly taken the reins and Henry had her touch. The sheer horror of the previous night's events was tightly wrapped in their minds and would slowly unfold over the next few weeks. Memories and fears and guilt would all be dealt with one by one. One step at a time. Right now that awful memory was tempered by a new dawn in their lives. A new freedom.

'Boris seems happy,' said Dove, as she eased herself down beside her brother. 'Ouch!' Her ankles were grazed and badly swollen. In her mind she'd been composing a letter to Tom. He had a way of seeing through a lie, so she must be very careful what she wrote. Her boyfriend was entitled to a letter, if not the truth. They'd been to the pictures together nearly every week since Mischievous Night. Malachy thought she'd been going with a girl; the less he knew the better. Their kissing had grown adventurous. It would have been nice to kiss Tom one last time. Maybe one day.

A church steeple appeared in the distance, probably a Prodidog church, Henry thought, as opposed to a Catlike, but it reminded him.

'Dove, shouldn't we go to Mass, with it being Easter Sunday?'

'I can't walk.'

'Do you think *I* should go?'

'Since when were you so keen on going to Mass?'

'I'm not but ... it's the day Jesus rose from the dead.'

'I think I know how he felt.'

Her brother was slightly shocked at this hint of blasphemy, then he took to thinking that maybe she was right. Maybe this was the start of a new life for both of them.

'They'll be giving out the presents this morning,' she said. 'Jubby'll be riding round on her new bike with that big daft grin on her face. I wish I was there so I could wipe it off.'

'You've already wiped it off once,' Henry pointed out.

Dove smiled to herself and gained some satisfaction from the memory. Then she remembered her promise to Alice and the smile faded. And suddenly the spectre of her father's face returned, as it disappeared into the blackness. She looked at her brother and asked, 'Did you see dad's face when he ... when he let go of me?'

Henry didn't return her gaze, he just nodded. 'I don't think he knew what was happening to him,' he said.

'Probably didn't realise what he was doing to me. As long as I live I'll never touch alcohol.'

'Nor me neither,' said Henry. 'He'd have woken up this morning not remembering a thing, asking where you were.'

'And you'd have said she's hanging upside down in the hole, Dad, dead as a nit.'

'I wonder what he'd have said to that? Probably blamed me.'

'Do you think you'll miss dad?' asked Dove.

63

The boy considered his reply carefully, 'When he wasn't drunk, he was okay. What about you?'

'Well, personally, I thought he tended to get over-critical ... especially when he'd had a few.'

Henry, who was miles away and didn't seem to spot the sarcasm in her remark, said, 'I wish it hadn't been me who killed him.' Then he added, quietly. 'You tried to save him, didn't you?'

Dove shrugged. 'That was just instinct, I think ... He probably wasn't worth saving.'

They didn't speak for a while as they watched the countryside go by; the solid clip-clopping of Boris's hooves soothing their troubles. They'd been sticking to the back roads and keeping the early sun to their right, heading vaguely north. It was a fine morning. Low mist carpeted the ground as the sun drew out the moisture. For the first hour it had been like riding along the top of a cloud. The trees were just bursting into bud and the hedges were decorated with wild flowers. Tractors began buzzing busily across fields and a horse rested its head on a fence to watch its distant cousin pass by. Dove threw it the remains of an apple she'd been eating and Boris tossed his head as if to say, 'What about me?'

'It was the drink that killed him, not you,' Dove said. 'If he'd killed me they'd have only hanged him, so what's the difference? As far as I'm concerned he killed himself.'

It seemed a wise and appropriate point of view and Henry felt a little better. Being a murderer was no life for a boy. He turned his thoughts to more practical matters.

'Dove ... do you think we'll get found out?'

Dove had been thinking about this for the three hours they'd been on the road. 'I honestly can't see how. Remember what dad said?' She did an accurate impersonation of Malachy's Dublin accent. *'Fallin' down dere would be loike droppin' off the edge of the world. Jasus! – ye'd nivver be seen agin.'*

'What shall we say if anyone asks about him?' asked Henry.

'Who's going to ask?'

'Len Tordoff?'

'We'll probably never see him again,' said Dove. 'He'll think dad's gone off with us.'

'What about people at the fairs?'

'We'll say as little as possible. Just that he cleared off and left us. They'll believe that of him.'

64

'They will an' all,' agreed her brother.

'I found twenty-one pounds in his box, so we're okay for money for a bit.'

'We can do our act around the fairs,' suggested Henry. 'With us bein' kids we can prob'ly make more money.'

'Prob'ly can,' said Dove. 'Give me the reins, you go find dad's map. We might as well find out where we are. There's usually a fair in Netherton on Easter Monday.'

No sooner had she taken the reins when she spotted the flash of water coming from a carved stone head in the roadside wall just ahead.

'Whoa, Boris.' She pulled on the reins and guided the horse up to a stone trough into which the spring was pouring.

'What's up?' Henry sounded slightly worried. 'Why have we stopped?'

'Water.'

Her brother gave a relieved 'Oh' and went back to looking for the map.

She watched Boris busily slurping away then called out, 'Grab a bucket an' top up the tank.'

Henry was about to say, 'What did your last slave die of?' when he remembered Dove's ankle. He pushed the map into her hand, unhooked a bucket and jumped out. The water looked cool and clear. He nudged the horse to one side, cupped his hands and helped himself to a drink.

'Tastes like champagne,' he called out. 'Boris'll be drunk if we let him have any more.'

Dove laughed. 'What would you know about champagne?'

There was a moan from the far side of the wall. Henry froze and held up a finger for Dove to be quiet.

'What?' she asked.

'Did you hear that?'

'Hear what?'

The moan came again. Boris pricked up his ears and Dove heard it this time. Henry took a couple of frightened steps towards his sister and whispered, 'It's coming from over the wall.'

'Well, go have a look then.'

'Not on me own, I'm not.'

'Well, I can't come with you.'

Henry frowned, defeated. He turned and put a foot on the ledge of the trough, then another on the carved head. The moan came again, sending his heart racing. He took a determined breath and leaned over the top of the wall.

A voluminous-trousered knee was protruding above the long grass, like a small, torn wigwam. There was a movement and he made out a bloodied face.

'What is it?' called out Dove.

'It's a bloke. I think he's hurt.'

Henry warily climbed into the field beyond the wall and stood a safe distance from the moaning figure.

'Are you all right, Mister?' he called out.

The old man tried to prop himself up on one elbow and answered in a cultured voice which seemed comically incongruous, considering his current predicament.

'I've had better days.'

Understatement always impressed Henry. He took a step forward and knelt beside the injured man, who pressed his arm on the boy's shoulder and sat up. There was a nasty gash above his right eye and blood had congealed in his beard. His other eye was almost closed and heavily bruised.

'You look as if you've just done ten rounds with Rocky Marciano,' said Henry, who was a big fan of the world champion.

'I could have done with Mr Marciano's help,' groaned Montgomery, holding his head.

'Henry,' shouted Dove. 'What's happening?'

The boy got to his feet and went to the wall. 'There's an old bloke here. He's hurt his head. I think we'd better help him.'

'I can't,' pointed out his sister.

Henry grimaced and turned to look at the man. 'Can you get up, Mister?' he asked, hopefully.

'Perhaps – with your help. I doubt if I can climb over the wall though.' He looked at the waggon looming at the far side of the wall. 'Is that your vehicle?'

'Yeah,' said Henry. 'Me an' me sister's. She's hurt her ankles, so she can't help.'

'Oh dear – I am sorry.' His sympathy sounded genuine, despite him not having met Dove yet.

'There's a stile down there.' Henry pointed to a spot about twenty yards away. 'Can you manage that?'

The old man levered himself to his feet and leaned heavily on

66

the boy. 'With you beside me, young man. I can conquer the world.' There was a smile in his voice now, despite his obvious discomfort.

Henry grinned. 'Just like Rocky Marciano, eh, Mister?'

'Just like the undefeated Rocky.'

Dove watched with mounting curiosity as the two figures stumbled over the stile and approached the waggon. The old man was of medium height and, going by his gaunt face, probably quite scrawny under that coat, which was possibly the heaviest thing about him. He gave her a smile, which she returned.

'I hear you've hurt your ankles,' he said. 'I do hope I'm not going to add to your troubles.'

Henry slid the steps out from under the waggon and fixed them in position.

'Can you manage?' asked Dove. 'We have a bed you can rest on if you like. I'm Dove, by the way.'

The old man stretched out a long, bony hand and shook hers, graciously. Then he proffered it to Henry.

'And that's my brother, Henry.'

'I cannot tell you how pleased I am to meet you, Dove and Henry. You have well and truly saved my bacon.' He licked his lips. 'I don't suppose you have any, have you?'

Dove moved back and allowed him to gingerly mount the shallow steps. He reached the doorway and leaned against the frame as he examined the interior. 'Good heavens! A veritable palace. Are there any ... any *larger* people I should meet?'

'No,' said Dove, 'just us.'

She waited for him to enquire what a couple of children were doing on the road on their own. Instead he smiled and said, 'I should mind my own business, shouldn't I?'

Dove felt unqualified to comment. 'We have some eggs and sausages if you're hungry. But first we have to find somewhere to park up.'

Henry appeared with a bucket of water. He stood on a stool and poured it into the tank as the old man limped to Malachy's bed. Brother and sister looked at one another and shrugged. Neither knew what they'd let themselves in for.

'Would you mind if I took off my coat and hung it out to dry? It's still wet from last night's rain.'

'Course you can,' Dove said.

'Ah, thank you, young lady.'

He took off his coat and handed it to Henry, who hung it on a hook just outside the door.

'My name is Montgomery,' said the old man, easing himself painfully onto the bed. 'Montgomery Catchpole, and I won't be troubling you for long, so don't worry. I'm just grateful that there are Good Samaritans in this wicked world; restores one's faith in human nature. And my faith needs restoring, especially after what happened to me. Eggs and sausages did you say?'

Henry went out for a second bucket of water and Dove handed the man an apple. 'Have this to be going on with.' Montgomery bit into it, hungrily, as the girl said, 'You can stay with us till you feel better.' She sensed a decency in him that was rare in the adults she'd come across.

Montgomery slept for an hour until he was awakened by the smell of frying sausages. He gingerly bathed his face then ate his meal with an elegance they were unused to. Malachy had been a noisy eater and their mother had always held her knife like a fountain pen and sniffed a lot, as though the smell of her food wasn't to her liking. But Montgomery ate silently and efficiently, slicing his sausages into manageable portions instead of stabbing at them with his fork and chewing them bit by bit. The children watched and copied; they knew his way was right and their parents wrong. Malachy and Dilys had been wrong about most things.

'Mr Catchpole, what happened to you?' asked Henry, after Montgomery had laid his knife and fork to rest, side by side, neatly on his empty plate.

'To the best of my recollection I was attacked and robbed,' said Montgomery. He patted his pockets and his eyes lit up when he found a packet of cigarettes. 'It seems they didn't take everything.' Further investigation of his pockets produced a box of Swan Vestas. He looked at the children, questioningly, and held out the cigarette packet. 'Do either of you smoke?'

It seemed such a grown-up thing to ask; they appreciated this.

'No thank you, Mr Catchpole,' said Dove. 'We don't.'

'Very wise. Dreadfully expensive habit – got hooked when I was your age.' He was looking at Dove. 'Shouldn't be encouraging you really, but at my age it's one of the few pleasures left. You can call me Montgomery by the way.'

'How many robbers were there?' Henry asked.

'Two, I think ... I couldn't see them properly because of the sur in my eyes.'

'What did they steal?' asked Dove.

'Oh, just my rucksack. There was nothing in it of any great intrinsic value, but to me it contained items of inestimable worth.' His eyes misted over and his brow furrowed into a sad frown. 'There was a small tent, a few items of clothing, several books ... and some mementoes of my marriage.'

'That makes you sad, doesn't it,' Dove said.

'Yes it does, Dove. I didn't have much to remember my wife by – just a few photographs, her rings and a locket. I could sit and look at them on an evening ... and remember her.'

Dove assumed his wife must be dead but she didn't think it proper to ask. Henry had no such inhibitions.

'Is she dead?'

Montgomery nodded. 'Sadly, yes. She died a year ago. We'd been married fifty-one years. It was a good marriage ... I loved the old girl dearly.'

'I bet she was a nice lady,' said Henry.

'Bless you, Henry, she was. I never expected her to go before me. I felt cheated in a way – you see it's not the sort of thing you prepare yourself for. Husbands should always die first. Wives are so much better at surviving alone. I suppose that's why I ran away.'

Dove's eyes widened with a mixture of surprise and amusement. 'You ran away? Who from?'

'Not who,' smiled Montgomery. 'More *what*. Death is such an *occasion* for some people and I didn't want to be surrounded by fussing people – relatives and friends. All with good intentions – but they were simply a reminder of what I'd just lost. They'd have been telling me I wouldn't have to face my loss alone; but you see I *wanted* to be alone. Out here on the road she's with me all the time; sharing my discoveries, guiding me when I'm lost. I'm afraid I'm one of those people who talk to themselves – only in my case I'm talking to Elisabeth – that's Elisabeth with an S by the way. She was always particular about the S. Never knew why, but it seemed impolite to ask. It's very important to let people enjoy their idiosyncrasies without trying to apply logic to them.'

Henry hadn't a clue what he was talking about, but it sounded very interesting. Dove could see the romance in his story.

'Is she with you now?' she asked.

Montgomery closed his eyes. The children watched him intently; then the old man nodded and smiled.

'Yes, she's here. I can bring her back. It's easier with the photographs, but I still have her up here.' He tapped the side of his head.

'We should report it to the police,' decided Henry, then he winced as Dove kicked at him, under cover of the table.

'I doubt if the police will do much good,' said Montgomery, who had spotted the kick. 'And I don't suppose you want them asking any awkward questions.'

Henry paled and Dove's eyes narrowed. 'What sort of awkward questions?'

Montgomery shrugged. 'Questions that are none of my business but the police might think are theirs. Such as what are a couple of children doing living on their own?'

'Our parents aren't around any more,' said Dove, flatly. 'And we don't want people fussing.'

Montgomery smiled and said, 'Touché.'

Neither of them knew what touché meant, but it seemed to signal an end to his curiosity, which was okay by them. His hunger satisfied, Montomery retired into Malachy's partitioned-off bedroom, from where he emerged mid-afternoon. The swelling and bruising to his face looked worse, but he seemed brighter. He walked through to the front of the waggon where Dove and Henry sat side by side.

'I think one of them was called Pikey,' remembered the old man. 'He seemed annoyed that the other one had mentioned his name.'

'Sounds like Pikey Scullion,' said Dove. 'He's a thug. He's got a brother called Sid. They do the fairs. What did they look like?'

'I didn't see their faces.'

'Did they have a Guinness label instead of a tax thing on their truck?' asked Henry.

'I didn't get to see their truck either. In fact I didn't see much at all.'

'Bet it was the Scullions,' said Henry.

Dove nodded, 'I wouldn't put it past them,' she said. 'Them Scullions are didicoys. They'd slit their own grannie's throat for half a crown.' Then she asked, '*Are* you going to report them to the police?'

'Would it do me any good?'

Dove shrugged. 'Don't know – you might get your stuff back, if they haven't sold it by then.'

'Which they probably will have, eh?'

'Probably,' said Dove.

He ran his hand through his beard as if giving the matter full consideration. 'Tell me – what are didicoys?' he asked at length.

'Like gipsies, only they're not,' said Henry.

'It's what Romanies call them,' said Dove.

'A derogatory term by the sound of it . . . and what are you? Are you true Romanies?'

Dove laughed. 'We're neither Romanies nor didicoys. This is a show waggon. We're travelling entertainers.'

Montgomery's face lit up. 'Entertainers *and* Samaritans? A worthy combination. Tell me about this entertaining.' He seemed to have forgotten about reporting the Scullions to the police, which suited the children.

'We juggle,' boasted Henry, 'and play the banjo and sing and walk on stilts.'

'*Some* of us can do all the lot,' said Dove. '*And* ride a unicycle.'

'I can ride a unicycle,' protested Henry.

'I'm afraid I have no talents to match yours,' admitted Montgomery. 'Unless of course you count my being a virtuoso on the spoons.'

The countryside went peacefully by, and for the first time since his wife had died, the old man craved company. But not just any company. He was taken with these children in a way he'd never taken to anyone. His marriage had never been blessed with progeny. How his wife would have loved a pair of children such as these.

Monty smiled once again at the memory of Elisabeth, then he looked at Dove and Henry. With these children he could see a way to becoming a full partner in their lives, if he played his cards carefully. 'It seems I have much to learn about life on the road,' he said.

Henry grinned at him. '*We've* got a lot to learn about every-thing. We left school a couple o'days ago an' we're not going back.'

71

'Oh dear, I don't like the sound of that.'

'We're better educated than most gipsy kids,' said Dove. 'We can read an' write an' do sums an' stuff.'

'How long have you been on your own?'

The children looked at each other. It had been only a few hours but it had seemed an age.

'Just today,' said Dove. 'Our mam died a few months ago and our dad went off and left us.'

'He won't be coming back,' Henry assured him. 'He tried to kill Dove.' His sister glared at him. He was giving away too much information.

'Bit of a brute was he?'

'When he was drunk,' said Dove. 'And we'd rather not talk about him any more.'

'We want to forget him and get on with our lives,' added Henry. 'It's my birthday today, I'm eleven.'

'I'm fourteen,' Dove said.

The old man smiled. 'Happy birthday, Henry.'

'Thanks.'

'Will he be coming after you?' asked Montgomery.

'Who?'

'Your father.'

'No,' said Dove, firmly. 'No one will be coming after us.'

'Ah,' breathed Montgomery, relieved. 'Such freedom. And all your lives spread out in front of you. How jealous I am. How will you earn your living?'

'We're entertainers,' Dove reminded him.

Montgomery could see no approach other than a direct one. He cleared his throat and said, 'You know, I'd love to come along for the ride.'

There was a silence as the children considered this. The old man thought he might have asked for too much too soon, so he added, 'Only for a while, until you can walk properly again.'

Henry favoured the idea but kept his opinion to himself. Montgomery threw in a sweetener. 'I could help with your education.' He tapped the side of his head. 'I have a wealth of knowledge locked up inside here. Geography; history. I could tell you about our great authors and teach you mathematics.'

'Were you a teacher?' asked Dove.

'Not exactly ... I was a librarian. You see, I have always had a love of books and a thirst for knowledge. Elisabeth used to say I was a walking encyclopaedia. All my life I've had a bursting ambition to travel and see all the places I've read so much about.'

'Is that why you ran away?' Henry asked.

'I suppose it is,' mused the old man, stroking his beard. 'Trouble is I'm somewhat restricted by lack of funds. My pension doesn't allow for foreign travel.'

'So you do have a bit of money, then?' asked Dove. There was a practical motive to her question.

'Enough for me to live on.'

A long, contemplative silence followed as Boris clip-clopped on. Dove turned over the pros and cons in her mind. On balance, having an adult with them might prevent a few eyebrows being raised.

'I'd want dad's old room for myself,' she said. 'You'd have to have one of the bunk beds.'

'The bottom one,' said Henry, who had always wanted the top bunk.

'The bottom bunk would suit me fine.'

'And you'd have to say you're our uncle.'

Montgomery beamed with pleasure. 'I think *great* uncle might be more believable,' he said. 'And more remote – in case anyone became inquisitive. Any other conditions?'

'I can't think of any, but if I do ...' said Dove

Henry gave a laugh.'Welcome on board, Uncle Monty,'

'Uncle Monty?' the old man tossed the name over in his mind. 'Why not? ... Uncle Monty it is.'

'Told you,' Henry said to his sister.

'Told me what?'

'Told you we'd have some good luck.' He turned to Monty. 'We saw a shooting star last night. They bring you good luck, don't they?'

'Well, I must say, I'm flattered if you consider me a form of good luck,' Monty said. 'I do hope I can live up to it.'

As the trio watched the world pass by for a while, a contented smile lit Monty's face. 'What a wonderful place to call your home.'

'How d'you mean?' asked Henry.

'Well, look around you, this is your home. The sky, the fields,

73

the birds. Your world isn't fenced in. You're not confined by walls and conventions.'

Dove said, 'I wouldn't mind a proper bathroom.'

'With a warm lavvie,' said Henry. 'I'd love a warm lavvie.'

'And a telly,' added Dove. 'And a gramophone – we don't even have electricity.'

'Oh, believe me,' Monty said, 'you'd be stifled in a house. You're a pair of nature's Bohemians. Freewheelers. Exempt, unregulated, unshackled, self-sufficient, self-governing.'

'Are we really?' asked Henry, impressed by his newly discovered status.

'All that and much more.'

Dove smiled at their new companion then hobbled into the waggon and picked up her banjo. To their left was a river, sparkling in the afternoon sun. A young man in a boat was rowing a young woman, who smiled and waved to the picturesque trio in the gipsy caravan. Dove began playing and singing, "Cruisin' Down the River". Her two companions joined in with gusto. Henry dropped the reins for a few seconds and found Monty a pair of spoons, which the old man began playing with remarkable skill. The pair in the boat joined in with the singing and for a memorable few minutes the river was alive with music and laughter. It was the best any of them had felt in years, including the couple in the boat, who were trying to sort out a difficult time in their courtship. They waved goodbye as the waggon slowly pulled away from them. Dove was sure she heard the young woman shout 'Thank you', but she didn't know why.

Chapter 5

As the sun dropped down towards the hills in the west, Dove instructed her brother to turn off the road on to a cart track, which, according to a weathered wooden sign, led to Caldthwaite Pond. The rutted track took them through a dark tunnel of overhanging trees before swinging almost at a right-angle down to the edge of a large, unruffled lake. The wooded tops of the hills in the distance were dramatically lit by the setting sun which cast a rim of radiant light among the distant trees and fields; and all of this was mirrored in the dark, calm water. The trio were stunned into silence by the abrupt beauty of it all. Boris stopped without being asked, as though sensing the magic of the moment.

A man emerged from the trees, carrying a small sack. He walked quickly to the lakeside and hurled it into the water, then retraced his steps without seeing the watching trio. Three pairs of eyes focused on the expanding rings left by the splash. The sack bobbed up to the surface, then disappeared again. Boris twitched his ears. Dove listened and said, 'Did you hear it as well, Boris?'

'*I* heard it,' said Henry, jumping down and running to the water's edge.

'What is it?' asked Monty. 'I didn't hear anything.'

'There's something in the sack,' Dove said. 'I heard a sort of whimpering.'

Henry had his shoes and socks off and was already up to his knees. Monty said, 'Oh dear,' but Dove reassured him.

'He can swim like a fish.'

Henry was up to his waist now; he plunged forward and swam a couple of strokes.

'About there,' Dove shouted.

Henry's head disappeared and his thin legs kicked momentarily in the air as he performed a neat, surface dive. A minute later the ripples he left in his wake had cleared and there was no sign of him.

'Oh dear,' said Monty. 'I don't like the look of this. I don't like it at all.' He looked at Dove and infected her with his panic.

'I'd better go in after him,' she said, not knowing how.

'Oh, damn damn dear!' moaned Monty. 'I'd go in myself but I'm not much of a swimmer.'

Henry's head suddenly broke the surface. A broad grin of triumph was on his face. He held the sack out of the water and kicked on his back towards the bank. Monty stumbled towards him and helped him out. The children watched impatiently as Monty fumbled with the rope which tied up the sack.

'What is it?' called Dove as he finally undid the knot.

The boy reached inside and pulled out a small dog. He laid it on the ground. 'It's a puppy,' he shouted. His voice was heavy with disappointment, 'I think he's dead.'

Henry looked at his sister; his eyes were wide with sadness and Dove felt for him. Monty did too. The old man knelt down, laid the dog on its side and gently squeezed its stomach. After a few moments water began to spurt from the animal's mouth. Monty picked it up and stood it on all fours as it vomited.

'He's alive!' cheered Henry, dancing around. He ran towards his sister, as Monty tended to the dog. 'Can we keep it, Dove? I've always wanted a dog.'

'I don't know; can I see him?'

Monty carried the distressed animal to her and laid it on the floor of the waggon. The puppy struggled unsteadily to its feet and began to carry out an investigation of its new surroundings, its busy nose sniffing for food. Dove grinned broadly at her brother. 'I've been wondering what to get you for your birthday.'

Henry gave a loud whoop. 'Does this mean he's mine?'

'I suppose so.'

Henry cuddled the dog in his arms and let it lick his face. He looked at his sister. 'This is a lot better than any old bike.'

'It'll have to be – it's all I can afford.'

'I think I'll call him Jesus,' decided Henry. 'Because they both came back from the dead on Easter Sunday.'

'I think calling a dog Jesus might be considered blasphemy by overly devout Christians,' said Monty. 'Besides, I believe *he* is a *she.*'

'Fair enough,' Henry conceded. 'I'll call her Prince.'

The sun was just about to make a reappearance as they turned in to the field housing Netherton Easter Fair. A man in a greasy trilby hat stepped out in front of them.

'Are yer wanting a pitch, love?' he asked. 'Most o' the good uns were taken last night.'

'We don't need to set up or anything,' said Dove. 'We're entertainers.'

'Yer'll need a class three trader's ticket,' said the man.

'How much?'

'Seven an' a tanner.'

Dove handed the man a ten-shilling note, took a ticket and her half crown change from him then clicked Boris into action. Around the perimeter of the twenty-acre field was a scattering of caravans, lorries and vans; behind them was a rumbling of traction engines. Then, in a colourful encampment of their own, stood a variety of wooden caravans. Gipsy vardoes; bow-topped waggons; spindle-sided four-wheeled and two-wheeled carts; ledge waggons; brush waggons; and straight-sided waggons – which were also known as showman's waggons.

Dove headed for these. Questions might be asked about her dad but she had to handle this some time. A quiet word in one ear should spread the word and satisfy the general curiosity.

A red, green and gold gipsy vardo caught her eye, the most ornate waggon in the encampment. Dark smoke trailed from a small, tin chimney projecting from the roof. Outside, a fire was burning with something cooking on a spit. Dove sniffed the air.

'Hedgehog,' she said.

Monty pulled a disbelieving face.

'It's hedgehog all right,' confirmed Henry.

A leather-faced, toothless gipsy woman came to the door and peered out, shielding her eyes against the dawn light.

'Morning, Mrs Lee,' called out Dove. 'The hedgehog smells good.'

'Doesn't mean yer'll get any. Malachy still sleepin' it off, is he?' she cackled.

'Me dad went off and left us,' called back Dove, pulling Boris to a temporary halt.

'Did he now?'

'Me mam died last year.'

'I heard.' The woman offered no condolence. 'And I'd expect no better from Malachy McKenna. Nor any man I know, for that matter.'

'We're better off without him, that's for sure,' said Dove.

The woman nodded. 'On yer own then, are yer?'

Henry appeared and called out, 'Morning, Mrs Lee.' He earned another nod.

Monty peered around the door. 'Good morning, Mrs Lee,' he shouted, smiling broadly.

'This is our great uncle Monty,' explained Dove. 'He's looking after us now.'

The woman stared at Monty's black and blue face and muttered, 'Looks like he's the one what needs lookin' after.' Then she stared long and disconcertingly at Dove, causing the girl to lower her gaze. As the old woman disappeared into the dark of her home, Dove flicked the reins, setting Boris into motion.

'We shouldn't have to do any more explaining,' she said. 'Old Betsy Lee'll do all that for us.'

'You looked worried,' Monty observed.

Henry supplied an explanation, in the absence of one from his sister. 'She's a proper Romany,' he said. 'She's supposed to be able to see inside people's minds and see into the future an' all that stuff. They say she's a true woman.'

'True woman?'

'Everything she says is supposed to come true,' said Dove.

'She's supposed to be really good,' Henry added. 'I didn't like the way she was looking at me.'

'Why? What have you got to hide?' asked the old man.

Dove scowled. 'We haven't got anything to hide.'

'Sorry – I wasn't being nosey,' said Monty, mentally kicking himself. He went back into the waggon lest he put his foot in it again. There was something these children weren't telling him and if that's how they wanted it, so be it.

A thought struck Henry as he guided Boris into a vacant space. 'I hope the Scullions aren't here. There might be trouble if Monty sees 'em.'

'I've never seen 'em at Netherton Fair yet,' said Dove, trying to remember if she had or not.

'Best keep outa their way if we do see 'em,' said her brother.

At the end of the line of caravans was a long, dark-blue waggon with the words 'Madame Tossard's Travelling Waxworks' painted in large gold letters on the side, and underneath: 'You'll think they're alive!' The children had never seen the attraction before and laughed at the name. Dove turned in beside it and pulled Boris to a halt.

'People queuing for the waxworks will need entertaining,' she grinned to Henry.

Henry passed the grin on to Monty. 'Always park near where there's likely to be a queue.' Then, as an afterthought, he added, 'That's what me dad used to say, anyway.'

Dove looked sharply at him and her brother dropped his eyes. They'd promised not to talk about their father. According to her, if they didn't talk about him, they wouldn't have to think about him. He'd be gone from their lives quicker that way. But the manner of Malachy's passing would be hard to forget. Monty caught the look passing between them and knew there was something they hadn't told him; and he thought to himself, Maybe their secret's as dark as mine.

While Henry unhitched the waggon and got Boris organised, Monty fashioned a dog collar from one of Malachy's old belts and attached a rope to it to keep Prince in check. Dove watched them as she leaned against the open half of the door.

'You two go for a walk if you like,' she said. 'I'll just organise a bit of a repertoire. I haven't done any busking for a while.'

So, with the puppy darting excitedly around their heels, Monty and Henry strolled round to watch the showpeople setting up their attractions. Henry's nose led him to a hot-dog stand. The man had set up early to attract custom from the stallholders. He tossed a handful of frankfurters into a pan and awaited Henry's order.

'One scabby donkey between two bread vans,' said the boy, determined to enjoy his birthday.

'With or without onions, sir?' asked the hot-dog man.

'It's me birthday today, I'm eleven.'

'In that case I'll only charge yer twopence.'

'That's what you normally charge,' Henry pointed out, looking at the price list.

'Tell yer what,' decided the man. 'Yer can 'ave three for a tanner – I can't say fairer than that.'

79

'If I tell you a good joke can I have one for nothing?' asked Henry.

'Only if it makes me laugh.'

Monty's face broke into a broad smile.

'Right,' said the boy. 'A man goes into the doctor's and he says, "Doctor – I can't say me effs, me tees or me aitches ..." and the doctor says, "Well, you can't say fairer than that!"'

Henry laughed uproariously at his own joke and Monty joined in. The hot-dog man's face twitched, then he allowed a laugh to come through, but it was the boy he was laughing at, not the joke. He handed Henry a hot-dog and said, 'Happy birthday, now bugger off.'

'You couldn't stick a few candles in it, could you?' asked Henry.

The man looked at Monty and pleaded, 'Will you take him away, please?'

As next-door neighbours and class three ticket holders, the two of them were invited for a free viewing of Madame Tossard's Travelling Waxworks, which consisted mainly of the Royal Family, George Bernard Shaw, Charlie Chaplin and George Formby. Recognition of the latter trio was greatly helped by a shaggy beard; baggy trousers, bowler hat and walking stick; and a ukulele. The Royal Family looked only vaguely familiar and were identified mainly by their crowns and regalia.

'I have ter make do an' mend when people pop off,' admitted Madame Tossard, aka Clarice Unsworth. 'When the king died I swapped his crown for a ukulele. I always thought his late Majesty had a strong look of George Formby.'

The gates opened at nine o'clock and by mid-morning a queue had formed to see if Madame Tossard's waxworks really did look alive. People at fairs expect not to be impressed and they weren't disappointed. They emerged into the daylight and encouraged others to pay a visit, not wanting to be the only ones who were wasting their money. ·

Henry strolled along the length of the queue, high on his stilts, dressed in a top hat, tail coat and long, striped trousers, his normal height of four feet five now almost doubled to an impressive eight feet. Dove sat on the top step of the waggon, played her banjo and sang a variety of comic songs which had spectators laughing as Monty, with the puppy at his heels, collected the money with a sweeping bow and a theatrical 'Thank you.'

80

After a while he handed the hat to Henry and accompanied Dove with his spoons. By lunchtime they had taken over three pounds.

'We never made this sort of money with mam and dad,' said Dove, as the three of them sat eating fish and chips inside the waggon. 'A third of it's yours, Monty.'

'I wouldn't hear of it. Board, lodging and your excellent company is all I need for wages.'

Dove shrugged and didn't argue because it was probably fair. She looked at Henry and said, 'I don't know about you, but I could do with a bit of a break.' She looked at her mother's gold-plated watch. 'We'll leave it till half past one and start again. With a bit of luck we should make another three quid this afternoon.'

'There'll be different people here by then,' Henry explained to Monty. 'So we can do the same routine again.'

'I learn something every second I'm with you,' said the old man.

Dove went for a lie down as Monty and Henry rode on the steam-driven, nineteenth-century carousel, clinging to the necks of the polished wooden horses as they whirled around and leaped over imaginary jumps. Monty swore it was the same one he'd ridden on as a boy. They marvelled at the automatons dancing and marching to the mechanical music of the fairground organs and laughed at the failure of a diminutive man to ring the bell with the hammer only minutes after his hefty wife had managed it with ease.

A wedge of children watched Punch hit Judy with his stick and laughed when the crocodile stole the sausages. The Filey Brass Band began to play and Henry hit three coconuts with three balls, failing to dislodge a single one and insisting they'd been stuck on with glue.

'Yer'll need yer bleedin' head stickin' back on after I've done wi' yer,' scowled the yellow-toothed old crone running the shy, between puffs of her clay pipe. 'I reckon I can fart stronger than you can throw.'

'Pooh!' said Henry. 'So that's what it is.'

Dove sat in the easy chair with her feet up on the table, watching the fair through the window and running the events of the past few days through her mind. The shock of what her father had subjected her to had somehow been balanced by his punishment. The architect of her terror had paid the ultimate penalty and there was no more to fear. She tried to gauge her sense of loss, but felt nothing. Her mother's death had made her cry, because despite her being a miserable, self-centred woman, she hadn't been cruel. Neglectful perhaps; incapable of giving her children the love they so craved – but not cruel. Not like Malachy McKenna, whom God had chosen to punish. Which reminded her: there was still the little matter of the mortal sin of lying at Mass register to confess – or had she already been forgiven? Certainly her contrition as she hung upside down, waiting for the end, had been sincere. She'd never been so contrite. And the Act of Contrition was what it was all about. So, that was it, she was forgiven. No need to bother a hard-working priest with an unnecessary confession.

Mrs Lee stood at the entrance to her fortune-telling booth, a cheroot in her mouth and a red and white spotted, silk bandana on her head, looking the part. On the wall of her booth was a glass frame containing faded photographs of her reading the palms of the likes of Frankie Vaughan, Freddie Mills, Bessie Braddock and Stanley Matthews; and above the door was a sign proclaiming 'Gipsy Lee – Fortune Teller to the Stars.'

As if sensing Dove was watching her, she suddenly turned and headed in the girl's direction – much to Dove's consternation. A minute later, the top half of the door swung open.

'Gone off an' left yer, has he?'

'What? Oh, you mean my dad?' said Dove, averting her eyes from the gipsy's searching stare. 'Yes, he left us on Saturday.'

Mrs Lee came in, uninvited, and sat down opposite her. 'Give me yer hands,' she said, her eyes firmly fixed on Dove's. 'No, don't look away from me. Look *at* me.'

Dove nervously forced her gaze to meet the gipsy's blackcurrant eyes, glistening from deep within her wizened face. The girl held out her hands, palm upwards. The old woman held on to the tips of her fingers, but she didn't shift her gaze from Dove's face. She suddenly shuddered and said, 'He's gone into the dark, hasn't he?'

Dove was startled and the gipsy knew she'd hit a nerve. She could still see her father's disappearing face; and the look of surprise on it. Drink had spared him the terror of that moment – as if he deserved such mercy.

82

'He's gone for good, hasn't he, girl?' Her eyes flickered over Dove's face, eagerly searching for an answer.

Dove figured the old woman was fishing for information, so she composed herself and said, non-committally, 'Well, he didn't say when he'd be back.'

The gipsy gave an ear-splitting cackle and slapped her knee. 'No ... I don't suppose the bugger did!'

She looked down at Dove's hands then back at her face. 'Men will cause you trouble. I see four men – three good men ... and two bad men.'

'That's five men.'

She was sceptical of Mrs Lee's gifts but nevertheless felt very uncomfortable at having her soul searched in such a manner.

'I see death in your life,' said the gipsy. 'Many deaths.'

Dove thought of her mother and father and Alice. People died all the time. It would be amazing if the gipsy couldn't see death in her life.

'Do you see anything to cheer me up?' she asked.

Mrs Lee shook her head, then she nodded. 'There will be – music will be your life.'

A guitar hung on the wall behind her, and a banjo stood in the corner. It didn't take much working out.

'Anything else?'

The gipsy didn't get a chance to answer for she was distracted by a commotion in the fairground.

'I think there's a fight going on,' Dove said, nodding towards the window.

The gipsy followed her gaze, then looked back.

'Cross my palm,' she said, quickly.

Dove took a shilling from her pocket, then changed her mind and swapped it for half a crown, which she dropped in Mrs Lee's outstretched hand. The gipsy's withered fingers closed over it as she stood up. 'Remember my words,' she said, as she went out. 'Watch out for the bad men.'

Henry was having a good birthday and loved fairgrounds despite the ever-present undercurrent of danger and dishonesty that somehow accompanies fairground folk – especially old crones on coconut shies. Playing them at their own game was the only way to win.

Determined not to be cheated, Henry returned to the coconut shy and bought three more balls, then, when the old woman wasn't looking, hurled a half brick he'd previously secreted by his feet. The brick glanced off one of the coconuts before clattering into the board at the back. The coconut toppled to the ground and the old crone looked around in amazement. Henry threw two more balls to complete his turn, the third he stuffed into his pocket to avert suspicion. Both balls hit coconuts but failed to dislodge them.

'Can I have a coconut please?' he asked, innocently.

'If yer bloody must.' The old woman spoke without removing the pipe from her mouth. 'Not one o' them big uns, they're for grown ups.'

Henry chose a medium-sized coconut which he hit against a rock and split it in four pieces. He handed one to Monty, who ate it with relish as he congratulated Henry on his marksmanship and guile.

'I've only ever had coconuts at fairs,' said the boy. 'Coconut shies an' coconut macaroons. That's the only time I ever have coconuts.'

'That's all they're designed for,' said Monty. 'That and coconut milk.'

'And coconut matting,' added Henry.

'Milk, macaroons and matting,' laughed Monty, who felt at ease having a nonsensical conversation with this amusing boy. Elisabeth would have doted on him.

'I wonder if there's a stall selling paint boxes an' stuff.' Henry said.

'Is that a hobby of yours?' enquired Monty.

'Sort of,' said the boy. 'I like messing about with paints. I'm good at drawing ... but all they ever did in our family was sing daft songs and juggle an' stuff.'

'So, you don't want to be an entertainer?'

'I don't mind. It's just that I'm nowhere near as good as Dove ... neither were me mam and dad.'

'She does seem an exceptional young lady.'

Henry shrugged. 'She's all right.'

Their conversation was curtailed when a stallholder in the distance caught Henry's eye. For a second he contemplated manoeuvring Monty in the opposite direction, but his sense of justice prevailed.

84

'That's Mrs Scullion over there,' he said to Monty. 'Your stuff might be on her stall.

'Might it indeed?

Monty pushed through the crowd without hesitation, with a very wary Henry in his wake. The Scullion brothers were in the beer tent, having left the running of the bric-à-brac stall to their mother. Beulah Scullion was a large-faced, mean-eyed woman in late middle age. Her skin bore a legacy of volcanic adolescent acne and her grey hair was straggly and abundant. Had Beulah been a kind and decent woman she could have sued her face for defamation of character and won substantial damages.

When he came within sight of her, Monty's resolve wavered. 'Oh dear, oh dear,' he said. 'I'm surprised she has any surviving sons. She looks like something that would eat its young.'

Elisabeth's rings were the first things to catch his eyes. He took the gold wedding ring from a ring tree and examined it carefully. Then he handed it to Henry for his young eyes to read the worn inscription. The boy deciphered it before reading it out loud.

'To Elisabeth from Montgomery ... oh heck!'

He stood transfixed as Monty picked up his late wife's engagement ring and laid the two rings side by side in the palm of his hand. He held them out to Beulah Scullion, who scratched her wispy chin.

'Twenny quid for the pair,' she said; her voice was as coarse as her complexion. 'And yer've got a bargain, Mister.'

Monty's bony fist closed over the rings and squeezed until the knuckles pressed white through the flesh. 'Where are the rest of my things?' There was ice in his voice that made Henry shudder.

'Here, put them rings back or I'll call a copper.'

'Madam, I'd be obliged if you would.'

Henry felt apprehensive. He didn't want to become involved with the law; nor did Monty as it happened, but the boy didn't know that. However, the old man felt confident in calling the woman's bluff. His voice became loud and theatrical.

'These rings were stolen from me by a pair of cowardly thugs who left me to die.'

A crowd of curious onlookers had begun to gather round. They saw the guilt written in large letters across Beulah's face.

'Here!' she protested. 'I never had nowt ter do wi' nowt like that. My lads bought 'em from a feller in a pub, fair and square.'

Henry spotted a rucksack behind her. 'Is that your rucksack, Monty?'

Monty's eyes followed Henry's pointing finger and recognised the bag. He glared at the woman.

'Madam, you're a liar and your sons are thieves and thugs. Hand over my bag before I call the police.'

There was a steely authority in his voice that neither of the children had noticed before. The woman hesitated, then she saw the face of one of her sons at the back of the crowd.

'Sid! ... Come and sort this barmy owd bugger out, will yer.'

But Sid had seen and heard enough, and was gone before she finished. In the meantime Henry sneaked round the back of the stall and rescued the rucksack, which he handed to Monty. The old man placed the bag on top of the bric-à-brac and began to open it with a flourish. He waved a theatrical arm and announced to anyone within earshot who was interested – which was everyone:

'Inside this bag, ladies and gentlemen, there should be various books, some photographs, and other items. I know this because this very bag was stolen from me two days ago, as were these rings which belonged to my late wife.' He held up the rings for all to see.

'Here, yer can't have that bag!' screamed Beulah Scullion. 'Sid! ... Get back here, yer useless pillock!'

Her eyes glazed over with guilt as Monty took out a handful of books and a box, inside which was a bundle of photographs.

'Voilà!' he exclaimed. 'My books, my photographs and my bag. You are a thief, madam ... and your cowardly sons attacked me and left me for dead!'

The onlookers began to mutter their disapproval and moved angrily towards Beulah. Henry grabbed Monty's arm and was dragging him away as the stall turned over and Mrs Scullion emerged, screaming and cursing at the crowd which had now turned into a horde of happy looters. Other stallholders, who didn't know what had happened, rushed to the rescue of their beleaguered colleague; then word carried to the beer tent that the gippoes were attacking the locals. The Filey Brass Band, as if well drilled for such an eventuality, laid their instruments on the ground and formed a defensive ring around them, vigorously fighting off all intruders. Within minutes a wholesale battle had broken out.

'Oh dear, what have I done?'

Monty's authoritarian demeanour seemed to collapse as he hurried with Henry away from the scene of mayhem. Once clear of the fighting they stopped and looked back.

The crowd from the beer tent were in the process of heaving at the helter-skelter, the owner of which was stranded at the top, where he'd gone to rescue a pair of terrified children. He had pushed them, screaming, down the shute into the safety of their mother's arms, but he himself hadn't the courage to follow because the ride had begun to topple, to the delight of the cheering crowd. He clung, doggedly, to the top platform like the captain going down with his sinking ship; all that was missing was his final brave salute to the world. Six feet from the ground he abandoned ship and jumped clear, happy to escape with a broken ankle.

Mrs Lee was scarcely out of the door before Henry and Monty approached at speed. Dove called out to them through the open window.

'What's happening?'

'We found the Scullions,' shouted Henry. 'Monty got his stuff back. I think they might be after us.'

'Oh dear,' gasped Monty as Henry bundled him up the steps. 'Did we really start all this?'

'They don't need much of an excuse to start fighting,' said Dove.

'So, it happens a lot then?'

'Now and again,' said Dove. 'Henry, do you think they recognised you?'

'It were only Beulah Scullion,' Henry told her. 'She hardly knows me.'

Henry hurriedly put the harness on Boris, then coaxed him back into the shafts as an excited Prince played between Boris's hairy feet, yelping as the horse flipped her over with an irritated flick of its hoof. Henry picked the dog up and threw it, unceremoniously, into the waggon. They needed to get away before the Scullions found them or the police turned up. Monty was sitting inside, with sweat pouring down his bruised face as Henry clicked Boris into motion.

'Are you okay, Monty?' asked Dove.

'Oh, it's nothing. Just an adrenalin surge. I always used to get this whenever I'd given a particularly tricky performance on stage.'

'Stage?' she queried. 'Were you an actor or something? I thought you worked in a library.'

'That's what I did when I was, er, resting. That is ... between theatrical jobs,' he explained. 'Then I ended up doing it full time. But I was thirty years on the stage – well, on and off the stage – mostly off.'

'Does that mean,' called out Henry, 'that all that stuff with Mrs Scullion was acting?'

'Every word,' he admitted. He looked up at him as he wiped his brow with a handkerchief. 'What did you think?'

'Well, you had me fooled,' grinned the boy. 'Maybe you should check your stuff – make sure it's all there.'

Monty tipped the rucksack upside down and emptied the contents on the floor. He frowned as a large, coloured handkerchief dropped out last; tied up into a small sack. The contents rattled.

'I don't know what this is,' he said, 'but it's not mine.'

Dove had the knot undone in a flash. Jewellery spilled all over the floor, flashing in the light. Rings, gold bracelets, brooches and pearls.

'Blimey!' she said, her shout stifled into an amazed gasp. 'It's jewels.'

Henry dropped the reins and bounded in, kneeling beside his sister, delicately picking up a long string of pearls. He looked up at Monty, hopefully.

'Are we rich?'

Monty smiled. 'Not unless we're as dishonest as the men who robbed me and left me for dead.'

'Aw ... right,' said Henry, disappointed.

'Besides,' Monty added. 'Keeping this could get us into more trouble with the thieves.'

Dove said, 'Well, we can't just give it back to them. We ought to ...' A distant police car siren cut off her train of thought.

'I've got an idea,' said Henry.

'Oh heck!' said Dove.

Dove and Monty nodded their agreement as he outlined his plan. Henry took the reins and clicked Boris into action, pulling him to a halt as they passed close to the Scullions' caravan. A sliding side window was partially open. Monty handed Henry the knotted handkerchief full of jewels. Without moving from his seat, the boy threw the miniature sack expertly through the gap and noted with some satisfaction that it had landed on a table, in full view.

As they approached the gate, a police car pulled to one side to let them pass.

'What going on?' called out an officer through the window.

'Everybody's fighting,' said Henry. 'We're going before they wreck our waggon.'

Dove popped her head round the door and pointed. 'Hey, Mister! There's a lorry over there with a Guinness label instead of a tax thing.'

The policeman eyed the battle in the distance with a marked lack of enthusiasm and nodded to a suggestion by his partner; then he looked up at Dove.

'Guinness label, eh? Well, we can't have that. We'd best deal with that first.'

'It's towin' an old caravan,' said Henry. 'I should have a look inside if I were you.'

'Would you now? And why's that?'

Henry injected an element of surprise into his voice, as if policemen shouldn't need telling such a thing. 'That's where they keep all the stuff they nick.'

'It's like Aladdin's cave in there,' added Dove.

'They nicked some stuff off us,' said Henry. 'But we got it back.'

'They nick stuff and sell it,' said Dove. 'Everybody knows about them. I should have a look while you're waiting for the fight to calm down.'

'It'll need ter calm down a lot before we get involved,' the constable muttered, driving off in the direction of the parked lorries. It was something to do while they waited for reinforcements from Pickering.

As Boris pulled the waggon out into the road, Monty congratulated the children.

'Quick thinking. That should teach our thieving friends a lesson.'

'Slow 'em down a bit as well,' Dove said. 'I reckon the police'll have a few tricky questions to ask about the jewels.'

'My guess is that we could have slowed them down for a year or two,' said Monty.

'Dove,' said Henry, cuddling Prince on his lap.

'What?'

'I've had a right smashing birhday.'

Beulah Scullion emerged from the fracas with a suitcase full of bric-à-brac in either hand, her eyes angrily searching the crowd for her sons. Pikey, her eldest, was in the process of kicking a man who was lying prostrate on the ground; Sid appeared beside him and joined in. The man on the ground curled himself into a foetal ball and howled in agony as heavy boots hammered at his ribs. Beulah swung a suitcase at Pikey's head, sending him spinning to the floor. He sprang to his feet with fists clenched and eyes blazing, but the fire went from them as he recognised his mother.

'Come wi' me, yer barmy bleeders!' she snarled. 'Some buggers's run off wi' that rucksack.'

The brothers looked at each other then followed their mother, neither offering to relieve her of a suitcase. Several minutes later they stopped by Gipsy Lee's fortune-telling booth.

A sweat-soaked, breathless Beulah Scullion asked, 'Did yer see an old bloke wi' a white beard an' a black eye? He had this lad with him. They were carryin' a rucksack what they'd nicked off us.'

There was heavy menace in her voice, but Mrs Lee was unimpressed.

'If yer want a readin' it'll cost yer.'

Pikey Scullion had her by her throat, choking her. 'Me mam asked yer a question.'

Mrs Lee could see the pschycotic gleam in his eye and knew better than to goad him further. 'I saw someone like that runnin' over there.'

The gipsy pointed to where the Netherton Leek Contest was being held, the opposite direction to Dove's waggon. She had no great feelings of loyalty towards Dove and her family, but she hated the Scullions and their bullying ways.

'Why did they go over there?' asked Beulah.

'How should I know. I'm not a bleedin' mind reader.'

Pikey pointed to a sign above Mrs Lee's head. 'Accordin' ter that, you are!'

Mrs Lee's cracked lips formed a thin grin. 'Yer don't acshally believe all that crap, do yer?'

Beulah put down the cases and shoved the gipsy into her booth, where she fell against her crystal ball, injuring her back. She turned to her sons.

'What the hell am I doin' carryin' these bloody cases? Here, take 'em, yer lazy, idle sods. Dump 'em in t' van then we'll have a good look round.'

The police had wisely parked their car out of sight. They were looking through the caravan window at the approaching men. The one called George observed, 'They're big buggers.'

His partner agreed. They took out their handcuffs and stood out of sight as the brothers entered with the cases. With expert slickness the two constables slipped the cuffs on the Scullions before the brothers could even register surprise.

'What ... ?' began Pikey.

'Just a precaution, sir. We'll apologise profusely if we're wrong.' George kept his manner civil. Even with handcuffs on these two looked as though they could cause damage. He pointed to the jewels laid out on the table. 'If you could just explain where you got these jewels from.'

'What the bloody hell are they doin' here?' gasped Pikey.

'Oh, so you're saying they're not yours,' said George. 'In that case we'll have to check our lists of stolen property. In the meantime I wonder if you could explain why you're displaying a Guinness label where your road tax ought to be.'

George's partner glanced outside at the battle being fought in the distance. A group of youths were making off with various brass band instruments, one small boy struggling beneath the weight of the big drum. A wailing siren signalled the arrival of the Pickering police. 'I think the cavalry's arrived, George. They can deal with the disturbance. We've got bigger fish to fry.'

The man whom Pikey had been kicking hobbled towards the caravan. His face was a mask of blood and he was supported by a sharp-faced young woman who was obviously goading him into making a complaint. They stopped a safe distance away. At her insistence he pointed at Pikey.

'He did this ter me,' he shouted, spitting out a broken tooth. 'That big bugger. Got me when I weren't lookin', or I'd 'ave ... '

He jumped back in fright as Pikey lurched towards him, only to be restrained by George.

'Don't make things worse than they already are, sir,' the policeman advised.

'They're animals,' shouted the young woman. 'They want damn' well lockin' up.'

'Right, madam. I'd better sharpen me pencil,' said George, taking out his notebook. He called out to the injured man, 'I'll take your details in a minute, sir.'

Not wishing any such involvement, the pair walked quickly away. The brothers stood there, dumbstruck at this devastating turn of events. Beulah arrived and peered through the door as her sons were being read their rights.

'Aw, bloody hell fire,' she said as she spotted the jewels laid out on the table.

'And who's this – another of your victims?' enquired George.

The brothers' reply was cut short by a fierce frown from Beulah.

'Just bein' neighbourly,' she said. 'What's the problem?

'I'm afraid your neighbours will have to come down to the station to help with our enquiries,' said George. 'And you are . . .?'

'Mary Smith . . . fortune teller.'

'If you could wait outside, Mary, perhaps we could take a statement from you.'

Beulah turned, as if to go, then reached behind the door and picked up a fire axe, which she wielded in George's face with great ferocity.

'On the floor, coppers!' She spat the words out.

The two policemen almost beat her spit to the floor. 'You should think about what you're doing, Miss Smith,' said George.

'Shut yer cake'ole, else I'll chop yer bleedin' head off!'

The blade of the axe was touching George's neck and the threat in her voice seemed real.

'Gimme the keys ter them bleedin' handcuffs!'

The blade was scratching his skin, drawing blood.

'All right, all right,' said George, who reached in his pocket and brought out the keys. Compliance with her every request seemed the best route to survival. His colleague made no sound at all.

'And yer car keys.'

There was a clicking of locks and George felt a violent kick in his ribs.

'Stop that, Pikey!' commanded Beulah. 'Just handcuff the buggers to a cupboard handle. What we need is time. Gag 'em as well.'

Five minutes later the Scullion family were in the lorry, driving back the way they'd come.

'What do we do do now, Ma?' asked Sid.

'Shurrup an' let me think.' She lit a small cigar and leaned a fat elbow out of the window as she drove. 'We'll head down south for a bit,' she decided. 'Use another name.'

'Yer mean like Smith?' said Sid.

Beulah took her hand off the wheel and slapped him around his head. 'I mean like something original.'

'The scuffers'll be lookin' for three of us,' Pikey said. 'A woman an' two fellers. Mebbe we should split up fer a bit. I don't fancy goin' back ter Strangeways.'

'Yer prob'ly right, lad. We'll dump this truck at Jimmy Duggan's an' get him ter fence the stuff ... then we'll split up. Sid can come wi me an' you go off on yer own.'

'Suits me,' said Pikey. 'I wish I could get me hands on that old bastard. He must've dumped them sparklers in our van, then shopped us to t' scuffers.'

'Oh, we'll catch up with him,' vowed Beulah. 'No fear o' that ... but we'll deal wi' it in our own good time.'

'He'll wish he'd never been born,' snarled Pikey. 'Should've finished him when we had the chance.'

'Yer've already finished one too many,' grumbled his mother. 'Think yersen lucky yer were never caught fer that.'

'He started it,' said Pikey.

'Fellers do tend ter start things when yer havin' it off wi' their women.'

'He came at me with a brick.'

'Aye, an' you finished him off with a knife. It's a good job his woman knows how ter keep her mouth shut.'

'She knows what'll happen if she doesn't,' sneered Pikey. 'I made that very clear.'

They pulled out to overtake a slow-moving waggon. 'Isn't that your mate Malachy's waggon?' said Beulah, then she cackled to herself. 'Here, I'll give the thick paddy a fright.'

Pikey turned and looked at the show waggon being pulled by a large, black horse. Dove was at the reins. He suddenly had a weird mental image of her running across a field and pushing Malachy down a hole. No, that wasn't it. Malachy had been dragging her across this field, then he tied her up and dropped her down the hole. Well, somebody went down the hole ... and it couldn't be the girl because she was there, in front of his eyes. Jesus! What sort of a state must he have been in to dream up something so strange, and so clear? It crossed his mind to stop the waggon and check that Malachy was still alive; then he thought better of it. Pikey shook the image out of his head and vowed not to drink so much in future if this is what it did to your brain.

Dove recognised the Scullions' lorry and for a heart-stopping moment her eyes met Pikey's. It seemed as though Beulah was trying to force them off the road. She sawed on Boris's reins as the side of the vehicle almost clipped the horse's ears.

Monty called out. 'What was that?'

Dove waited until she was sure the lorry wasn't stopping. 'It's the Scullions,' she shouted. 'Looks like they got away.'

George almost broke his wrist in freeing himself. His colleague had been kicking at the door as George yanked at the handle. Finally it came away.

'She threw the keys in the corner,' said his partner. 'Under the table.'

George had them both unlocked within a few seconds. He opened the caravan door and felt a steadying hand on his shoulder.

'Let's think about this, George,' said his colleague. 'We had them arrested, then an old woman overpowered us and left us fastened up with our own handcuffs. How's it going to look?'

'Not good,' George conceded.

'They'll be miles away by now. Odds on they won't come back round here for fear of being arrested.'

George nodded his head. 'Probably ... best thing all round if they don't come back.'

'Save everybody a lot of trouble.'

'And us a lot of embarrassment,' said George. 'I think we should give the Pickering lads a hand. The fight seems to have calmed down.'

Part Two

Chapter 6

November 1957

Dove was laughing at the antics of Alfie Bass in the new ITV comedy series, *The Army Game*. Bootsie always got one over on Snudge, played by Bill Fraser. The 12″ Baird TV was perched on a shelf, purpose made by Monty, who had introduced electricity into the waggon by means of a diesel generator.

'If the Russians can send a Sputnik into space,' he'd said, 'I'm sure we can have electricity in this caravan.'

'Waggon,' Dove had corrected him.

'A home by any other name,' Monty had smiled.

Having power into their home had marginally eased her antipathy towards it; or maybe the softening of her attitude towards the quaint but crammed dwelling wasn't caused by the arrival of electricity but by the departure of her father. She tried not to think about him, but he was always there, at the bottom of that hole. Henry never mentioned him nowadays and Dove often wondered if his silence was caused by guilt. Many a time she had been about to broach the subject, to reassure him that pushing Malachy down the hole was the price they'd both had to pay for Henry saving her life, but each time her brother seemed to sense what was coming and had forestalled her. But she knew the guilt was always there. Maybe it would be different if their father had had a proper burial, instead of just lying there, alone and unloved – missed by no one.

After the first year they'd stopped going to fairgrounds, thus avoiding awkward questions about Malachy's whereabouts from his old associates. He didn't seem to have had many friends, only enemies and creditors. Dove had got fed up pointing out that her father's debts were nothing to do with her and anyway she was skint – and no, she wasn't going to sell the waggon to settle up. It was this last demand that had made up her mind to stay clear of her father's old haunts. Blackpool had been lucrative, as had the east coast resorts: Scarborough, Bridlington, Filey and Whitby. The police didn't bother to move them on quite as much, especially when they set up on the beach. They'd even done a couple of weeks at Butlins.

Dove was the driving force behind the trio. Henry and Monty pretty much went along with her ideas – until today.

It had been on the news that the Russians had now sent a dog into space, which Dove thought was cruel. Prince had gone off with Monty and Henry, who was now thirteen and rapidly outgrowing his sister. She looked at her watch, the one she'd inherited from her mother. Eight-thirty. Where were they at this time of night? You'd have thought they'd stay in with her, today of all days: her seventeenth birthday.

The top half of the door swung open and the pair of them stood there with matching schoolboy grins despite the sixty-year age gap.

'Happy Birthday to you,' sang Monty. Henry joined in and Dove hated the embarrassment of it all. She was a young woman, not a child to be sung at. Monty slid open the bolt on the bottom half of the door and walked in, still singing. Prince scampered in between their legs, and Dove's eyes scanned the two of them for the birthday present she assumed they'd bought for her. But nothing was apparent.

'Where've you been?'

Monty's grin broadened. 'To a brewery.'

She sniffed for evidence but the air was clean. 'A brewery?'

'A brewery,' repeated Monty.

'Where you get beer from,' enlightened Henry.

'You don't say.'

Monty and Henry looked at each other, wondering who should go first.

'We've got you a birthday present,' said the old man.

'Sort of,' said Henry.

'Thank you very much,' said Dove. 'You shouldn't have.' There was a silence, broken eventually by Dove. 'What sort of present?'

Monty looked down at her. 'Well, it's not so much a present as a –'

'As a what?'

'As a contract for you to sign.'

'A contract?'

The old man took an envelope from his pocket and handed it to her. 'You see, Melbourne Brewery owns hundreds of pubs in the north of England and they want you to do a tour.'

'A tour? You mean like a pub crawl?'

Henry laughed, 'A singing tour, dope,' he said. 'Two gigs a week for a year. They're paying fifteen quid a week.'

'Plus five pounds a week expenses,' added Monty. 'For train fares, bed and breakfast, stuff like that. One of their directors heard you at the Horse and Groom last Saturday. He came over and had a word with me – I told him I was your manager.'

'Manager?'

'Well, I am ... in a way.'

'He struck a good deal,' said Henry. 'They only wanted to pay twelve pounds and three quid expenses.'

'Do they know I'm only seventeen?'

Monty said, 'Doesn't make any difference, so long as you don't drink alcohol.'

'Well, there no danger of that.'

She looked at Henry, who held her gaze for a second before lowering his eyes. He was reminded of the vow she'd made the day after their dad died. Monty caught that same exchange of glances, which he'd seen on and off since he'd first met them. But it was none of his business.

Fifteen pounds was a lot more than the average collective weekly money they'd made from busking. And now that winter was upon them, her working in pubs and folk clubs was their only source of income. The previous two winters had been difficult. Dove had done various jobs from cleaning to waitressing, just to keep food on the table. Monty's contribution was cook, handyman, comic songwriter and teacher.

'When spring comes we can do the busking as well,' pointed out Henry.

'I thought you didn't like busking.'

'That's because I'm not very good at it. Have you heard from Tom?'

'No,' she said, brusquely. 'Why do you keep going on about Tom?' Her heart skipped a beat every time she heard his name – just like in the song.

'So, what do you think?' asked Monty, slightly irritated by the conversation's sudden change in direction.

'I think twenty quid a week will come in handy,' said Dove. 'I'll want you both to come with me, though.'

'There's at least three days between gigs,' pointed out Henry. 'We can drive the waggon to most places in three days.'

Dove got to her feet and planted a kiss on Monty's cheek. 'Thanks, Monty,' she said. 'It's a great present.'

Monty looked guilty. 'I suppose in a way it benefits us all,' he said. 'Makes me a bit of an Indian-giver. I've got you a present of work, from which I will no doubt benefit.'

'Work I enjoy,' she pointed out.

'And work you're very good at, Dove,' added Henry. 'Best comic singer he'd ever heard. That's what that bloke from the brewery said.'

'Comic singer? How d'you mean, comic singer? I thought I was a folk singer.'

'Not when you sing them songs Monty wrote. You should have seen that bloke laughing. He said he thought his legs'd never dry.'

'Henry McKenna, don't be so flipping smutty!'

'I'm only saying what he said.'

'He's right, I'm afraid,' said Monty. 'Folk singers are a penny a dozen, but comic singers, they're the ones who draw the crowds.'

'But they're not even my songs – you wrote them.'

'Most of them,' conceded Monty. 'Some had already been written by various people, all called Anon. What you add is comedy timing ... plus you've got a very nice voice.'

'Nice – is that all it is, nice?'

Monty considered this and nodded. 'You make a very agreeable sound and you're in tune. What more could one ask in a singer?'

'One could ask for a voice like Maria Callas – or at least Kay Starr.'

'Neither of whom have your comic timing.'

Dove scratched her ear, pensively. She'd had ambitions to become a great folk singer, any kind of singer, but deep down she knew her limitations. Comic singer it was then – with a few folk songs thrown in; a reversal of her act up until now.

'I'll need to write you some more material,' Monty said. 'You'll need a full hour. That's er ... that's what we've promised them.'

'We?'

100

'Two half-hour sets. Do the serious stuff in the first set. I'm writing a parody on the Everly Brothers latest, "Wake Up, Little Susie".'

She raised an amused eyebrow, 'Now called?'

Monty always changed the titles. '"Woke up, a little boozy",' he said. 'Thought it might go down well in a public house.'

Alone in her room at the end of the waggon, Dove took out the letter from Tom's aunt, a curt four lines telling her it was better she didn't write again as Tom was trying to forget that sad part of his life and everything connected with it. She felt like writing back and asking if Tom was trying to forget his parents as well, or was his attempted amnesia only directed at old friends. The fact that the letter hadn't come from Tom himself spoke volumes as to its veracity. No doubt Auntie Margaret in her posh house in Bardsey knew of Dove's background and thought her unsuitable for her nephew. Dove had figured this out when she'd tried to telephone him, only to be given short shrift from the aunt at the other end.

'Who wishes to speak to him?' The woman sounded a bit like the Queen would if she had flat, Leeds vowels.

'Dove McKenna.'

'I'm afraid he's unavailable, Miss McKenna.'

Then the phone had gone dead and Dove had spoken a few choice words into the unhearing mouthpiece before slamming it down.

Having to communicate via a Post Office box number made life difficult, but judging from the letters she *had* received from him, Tom should now be in the RAF and Dove had no way of knowing where he was stationed. It had been two and a half years since she'd last seen him and she often wondered if the longing she felt for him wasn't simply caused by that absence which is supposed to make the heart grow fonder. Her lifestyle deprived her of male friends. Tom was the only boy she'd ever kissed – until her first gig for the brewery.

Chapter 7

The Gimcrack Arms was at the Leeds side of York, so they parked the waggon on the Knavesmire racecourse and spent the day wandering around the old city before making their way to the venue. They walked, with awe, around the great Minster; and the hallowed ambience reminded Dove of the Mass register which had got her into so much trouble, and how God hadn't been there for her when she needed Him. Or had He? Maybe it was God who made Henry knock her dad down the hole, then save her. That's the sort of thing any God worth his salt would do.

'How come prodidogs have all the best churches?' asked Henry.

Dove nudged him and whispered, 'Monty's a prodidog.'

Her whisper was amplified by the echoing atmosphere and Monty smiled. 'I believe it's got something to do with your name-sake,' he said. 'Henry the Eighth.'

'And don't you dare start singing it in here!' muttered Dove. 'Just because it's not a Catholic church.' She turned to Monty. 'He knows a very rude song about Henry the Eighth.'

'I suppose the nuns taught it to you,' said Monty.

Henry and Dove grinned. The thought of nuns teaching rude songs about Henry the Eighth somehow stripped the vast cathedral of its dignity.

Dove was topping a bill of three: two local acts – a skiffle group with a tea-chest base and washboard; and a young man who was to make a valiant stab at Paul Anka's "Diana", which had just been knocked off the top off the charts by Buddy Holly's "That'll be The Day".

The three of them were sitting at a reserved table near a small stage on which the skiffle group were setting up. The piano lounge and the snug had recently been knocked through into one room in order to provide live entertainment. The old lounge had been suffering in recent years from customers' reluctance to sing. The landlord blamed it on this rock 'n' roll rubbish and promised the brewery that as soon as the fad had worn off things would be back to normal and people would be singing "Put Another Nickel In" like good uns. But Elvis Presley was now on the scene and he didn't look like going away in a hurry, so the brewery had decided to move with the times and provide music shows of their own.

One of the group caught Dove's eye. He was a tall, fair-haired young man, with fading acne, a cheap guitar and a nice smile, which she returned; then she blushed when the rest of the group began to tease him about her.

They began with "Cumberland Gap" which, earlier in the year, had been Lonnie Donegan's first number one hit. Dove felt her foot tapping despite the slightly discordant sound the boys were making. She looked round as the room filled up and wondered, nervously, if she could keep this lot entertained for a full hour. Up until now she'd only been required to do one half-hour set; tonight she would have to virtually carry the whole evening. The other two acts were just local amateurs, playing for beer money. She felt an attack of nerves coming on.

After he had introduced their third number, "Gamblin' Man", the fair-haired young man waved her up onto the stage.

'I do believe he's inviting you to join them,' said Monty.

'I'm not sure of the words.'

'You know *my* words.'

'Give over, Monty, I can't sing your words, we'll get kicked ou ...'

Henry had her guitar out of its case in a flash and thrust it into her hands. 'Show 'em how it's done, Dove,' he called out, to the amusement of the audience.

'Yeah, Dove, show 'em how it's done,' echoed the drummer, who had been working hard to keep the group together.

The two other guitarists fell silent as Dove began playing. The fair-haired youth took out a mouth organ and waited for an opportunity to come in. Dove had acquired all Lonnie's records after Monty had bought them a Dansette record player, but she'd never felt confident about playing the numbers in public, until now. She had often amused Henry and Monty with her impression of

Lonnie Donegan's reedy voice and now it was the audience's turn to be amused. On top of which, Monty had altered the words of "Gamblin' Man" so that it now included many cheeky double entendres, which the audience picked up on without difficulty.

It soon became obvious to the rest of the group that it was unwise to interfere with the work of an accomplished musician and performer such as Dove so, at the end of the number, they took centre stage to receive the tumultuous applause accorded her, then made their exit, leaving her alone and unannounced, as the unsuspecting MC was apparently in the Gents. Monty made his way onto the stage.

'Ladies and gentlemen,' he said. His theatrical training sent his voice booming to the back of the room, without the aid of a microphone. 'The Master of Ceremonies is er ... indisposed.'

'Yer mean he's pointin' Percy at the porcelain,' called out a coarse-voiced woman.

'Madam, I wouldn't have put it so indelicately myself,' said Monty.

'Hey, there's nowt delicate about our lass,' shouted a man, presumably the woman's husband.

Someone shouted, 'Shurrup an' lerrim gerron with it!' This had most of the room laughing as Monty held up a hand for quiet.

'Ladies and gentlemen. For your delight, nay, delectation – that shimmering star of stage and silver screen – Miss Dove McKenna.'

Laughter gave way to enthusiastic applause as most of the audience hadn't realised they'd already been watching the top of the bill.

'What d'you mean, silver screen?' enquired Henry when Monty returned to his seat. 'Our Dove's never been on the telly.'

'It's what you call alliterative licence, m'boy. Got carried away, I suppose. But you never know what lies ahead.'

Her impromptu entrance had extinguished her nervousness; and the audience's reaction to Monty's remark about the MC made her realise that the folk songs might not go down too well. Quick thinking was called for.

'I was going to sing an old country and western song entitled, "Git Down Off the Gas Stove, Granny, Yer Too Old To Ride The Range",' she announced with a broad smile. This drew more laughter. 'Instead, I should like to continue with my version of, "Puttin' On The Style".'

For the whole of her first set she worked her way through every Lonnie Donegan song she knew. To the delight of the audience.

Behind the stage was a small office-cum-dressing room to which she retired to retune her guitar. The fair-haired youth was waiting for her, sipping a glass of beer.

'You're good,' he said.

She sat down on the only chair and ran a thumb across her guitar strings. 'Thanks. I need to tune this back in.'

'Not just good – special,' he said.

'Thanks again. Can you give me an E on your mouth organ?'

The youth obliged and Dove held her ear to the guitar as she teased a couple of strings back into tune.

'Nice guitar,' he said.

'Yes – my boyfriend gave it to me.'

'Your boyfriend?'

'Yes, his name's Tom.'

She looked at him to check for a reaction and noticed, with some satisfaction, a flicker of disappointment in his eyes.

'I wish I had a girlfriend who gave me expensive presents,' he said. 'Or any kind of girlfriend for that matter.'

'I can't believe a good-looking boy like you hasn't got a girl-friend.'

He shook his head. 'I'm not very good with girls. They all seem to run rings around me. Strange creatures.'

'Is that how you see me? A strange creature.'

'I see you as untouchable. It's just as well you've got a boyfriend because I wouldn't dare ask you out.'

'So, you would if I hadn't?'

'Hadn't what?'

'A boyfriend – you'd ask me out if I hadn't got a boyfriend?'

'I wouldn't dare.'

'That explains it then.'

'Explains what?'

'Why no one ever asks me out.'

'You've lost me now. I said women were strange creatures. What about your boyfriend? Doesn't he ever ask you out?'

'He's in the Air Force.'

She was hedging; keeping her boyfriend but allowing the youth a window of opportunity. He opened a satchel and took out a piece of sheet music.

'Present for you,' he said, handing it to her. 'It's not a guitar, but then again, I'm not your boyfriend.'

'Thank you.' She read the title and gave a shudder. "Catch a Falling Star". It brought back memories of *that* night. 'I've never heard of it.'

'Perry Como,' he said. 'It's his latest. I bought it for us to try – thought we might skiffle it up a bit. But it's a ballad – you can't really skiffle ballads. It's got guitar chords; give it a go in your next set.'

'I can't learn a new song in half an hour.'

'It's dead simple. Even I can play the chords and there's more chorus than verse.'

'I suppose I could give it a try.'

'Tell you what – learn the chords and stick the words on your guitar. Here, I'll write them out for you as you're practising.'

Her comic songs went down well. She had the audience in the palm of her hand as she came to the end of the set.

'I'd like to finish with a song that my friend from the skiffle group ... ' she stopped as she realised she didn't know his name.

'Norman,' he shouted.

'A song that Norman tells me will be number one next week.'

She picked out the opening chords and launched gently into Perry Como's ballad that held good and bad memories for her, mainly good memories of Alice.

After the audience finally let her go, she went back to the table. 'My word, Dove, you're full of surprises,' said Monty, as he finished off a pint. 'When did you learn that song?'

'In the interval. Norman gave me the sheet music. It's actually quite easy to learn.'

'It was the best thing you did. The audience were quite impressed, as was I.' He leaned towards her, conspiratorially 'Y'know, sometimes one's first interpretation of a song is the best version. I haven't heard Mr Como's record, but he would be hard pressed to better what I heard tonight.'

Norman was hovering behind her; Monty looked up at him, then back at Dove. 'I believe someone wants to see you,' he said. 'Sit down, young man. I assume you're Norman.'

'Yes, sir, and I just wondered if I could buy you all a drink.'

'A wealthy suitor!' exclaimed Monty. 'Just what we've been

106

waiting for. I hope you'll be able able to keep our Dove in the manner to which we hope to become accustomed,' he winked at Henry. 'Eh, Henry?'

'Monty! I do hope you're not drunk,' scolded Dove.

'Drunk with life and music and beautiful friends.' He suddenly became morose and his eyes misted over. 'If only my Elisabeth were here.'

'Oh, Monty, you *are* drunk,' groaned Dove. 'We'd better get you back.'

'Can't you just stay for one?' pleaded Norman.

'Well, I don't drink, I'm only seventeen.'

'So am I. You don't have to drink alcohol.'

'I'll take him home, Dove,' volunteered Henry. 'Will you be okay?' He looked up at Norman with a challenge in his eyes that said, *look after my sister or else.*

'I'll be okay, Henry,' she assured him. 'Just get Monty back.'

With his arm around Henry's shoulder Monty moved, unsteadily, towards the door.

'Who is he?' asked Norman.

'My great uncle. He doesn't usually drink.'

Someone at the bar called out 'Last Orders'. 'What about you?' said Norman. 'I could get you a Babycham.'

Dove had never heard of it, but it sounded innocent enough. 'Okay,' she said. 'Then I'll have to go.'

She'd had two before they finally walked out into the cold November night; enough to loosen her inhibitions. Norman took her guitar from her.

'I can carry my own guitar,' she said.

'I'm being what's called gallant.'

'So, if I come to a puddle will you throw your cloak over it so I won't get my feet wet like Walter Raleigh did for Queen Elizabeth?'

'If I had a cloak, I might, but I've only got me donkey jacket.'

'Doesn't have the same ring to it, does it?' she giggled. 'The gallant Sir Walter throwing his donkey jacket over the puddle.'

'Didn't she have his head chopped off?'

'No idea. I only know the bit about the cloak and the puddle.'

'I think she had his head chopped off. Fancy chopping someone's head off after thcy'vc laid their cloak over a puddle for you. See what I mean about women being strange creatures?'

107

'All right, if I come to a puddle I'll walk round it.'

Dove was enjoying herself. A flirtatious, nonsensical conversation with an amusing boy her own age. They came to a small, public garden. She walked through the gate and sat down on a bench concealed from the road by bushes. Norman sat beside her and laid his arm across her shoulders as she pulled her coat around her.

'It's a bit nippy,' she said.

He eased himself close and hugged her to him. 'Is that any better?'

'Yes, thanks,' she said. 'Much better.'

They sat for a while, enjoying the moment – Dove's first adult liaison.

'Whereabouts do you live?' he asked after a while. 'Here I am, walking you home and for all I know you might live twenty miles away.'

'Not far,' she said, suddenly uncomfortable about telling him she lived in a waggon. 'Just up the road.'

'Right ... I live in Acombe. I can walk you home and catch the late bus.'

'You can go now if you like. I can make my own way home. I'm a big girl, you know.'

'Sir Walter wouldn't let you go home on your own. Why should I?'

Their lips touched as she turned to face him, frozen for a hesitant moment before they kissed. A gentle, featherlike, ground-testing kiss. Neither spoke as they came apart momentarily, then kissed again. Deeper this time. The cold of the night thawed away as they clung to each other, kissing, holding, cuddling, stroking. After a time his hand ventured inside her coat and paused to check for resistance, then inside her blouse. Another pause. Dove felt she should have stopped him. But she didn't.

'Norman, I've never done anything like this before.'

'Like what? We're only kissing. Do you want to ... you know, go further?'

'I don't know ...' then she added, cheekily, 'How far would the gallant Sir Walter have gone?'

Norman smiled in the darkness. 'He was apparently a bit of a lad, was Sir Walter.' He unhooked her brassiere, then slid a tentative hand over her breast, holding it gently, waiting for her reaction.

'I can see why Walter got his head chopped off,' she said.

Her hand went, instinctively, down to his groin where she felt his hardness. She wanted to touch him, but daren't because she was scared where it all might lead.

'Go on,' he encouraged, breathlessly.

She was tugging at his zip when heavy footsteps approached, causing them to move apart and Dove to adjust her clothes back to respectability. A torch shone in their eyes.

'We shut the gates at eleven,' said the silhouetted figure behind the glare. 'It's two minutes to, now.'

'Right,' said Norman. 'We'll, er ... we'll be off then.'

'Sorry if I spoiled yer night. Yer'll just have ter get started earlier next time.' There was a snigger in the man's voice and Dove felt like kicking him.

She and Norman walked in silence, each regaining composure. 'I'd like to see you again,' he said. 'Do you have a phone number or anything?'

'Not at the moment. What about you?'

'Don't ring me, I'll ring you, eh?'

'No, it's not like that. We're not on the phone.'

'Really? Must be hard to get gigs then.'

'Monty organises all that; anyway, I've got a year's contract with the brewery so I don't have to chase gigs for a while.'

He stopped and took a card out of his wallet. On it was printed:

Norm Ogilvie
The Rebels Skiffle Group: York 48721

'That's my number,' he said. 'My old man works at a printer's.'

'Oh, and what do you do when you're not skiffling, Norm?'

'Still at school,' he said. 'Doing my A Levels – and no one actually calls me Norm. I just thought it sounded a bit more, you know, showbiz.'

The heat of the moment in the garden had cooled as she realised they were nearing the Knavesmire and the moment of truth.

Dove stopped at the end of a street. 'I live down here,' she announced; then, taking her guitar from him, she added, 'You'd better go for your bus or you might miss it.'

'I've got half an hour yet. I'll walk you to your door.'

'It's okay, honest –'

'I insist.'

109

He took the guitar from her and walked beside her. 'My mum said if I take a girl out, I should have the common courtesy to see her safely to her door.'

'Your mum sounds nice.' Dove eyes were frantically scanning the houses to see which one she could claim as her own. One that looked deserted, preferably. She could say Henry and Monty must have gone to bed.

'Which one?' he asked.

'This one.'

She stopped beside a large detached house with no lights on.

'Blimey, your folks must be well off. I'll see you to your door.'

Dove placed a deliberate edge on her voice. It was the only way out of this. 'Norman, you're being pushy. I don't like that in a boy.'

'Sorry, I was just ... '

She pecked him on the lips and snatched the guitar back from him. 'I'll ring you,' she said, unlatching the gate and walking up the drive. She paused and said, over her shoulder, 'Oh ... and thanks for the music.'

As she reached the front door, she turned and saw him looking at her, slightly bemused at this abrupt end to the evening. She snapped her fingers in mock annoyance. 'No front door key,' she called out, then made her way around the back.

A light came on and the back door opened just as she reached it. A stooped old woman poked her head out and looked directly at Dove. 'Do I know you?' she asked, sharply. 'What do you want? ... I'll call the police.'

Dove looked back down the drive to where Norman was still watching her. She walked around the back of the house, out of his line of vision and past the woman, then ran at the garden fence, throwing herself and her guitar over it. The woman was now shouting angrily but Dove wasn't listening. She was busy running across gardens and jumping over fences. All she wanted to do was get out of this stupid, unnecessary situation. Norman could think what he liked, she'd probably never see him again. Unless he came to one of her gigs! The thought stopped her in her tracks. Oh my God! He probably would, as well. She wouldn't be hard to track down. The brewery were advertising her in all the local papers. Jesus, what would she tell him?

She made her way back to the main road and checked that

Norman wasn't around before she continued on her way. The excitement of the evening had been spoiled by the stark realisation of how abnormal and limiting her lifestyle was. Why couldn't she live in a normal house like other girls and have boyfriends and a bathroom and people round to tea instead of being ashamed of where she lived? Because that was the truth of it. She was ashamed.

It was a dishevelled Dove who came home that night. Monty was snoring and Henry was jamming the sound out with a blanket stuffed in his ears. Dove's entrance woke him up.

'Blimey, Dove! You look as if you've been dragged through a hedge backwards. What's happened?'

'I'll tell you what's happened. Living in a stupid place like this is what's happened. How am I supposed to have a proper life living in a stupid place like this?'

'I thought you were beginning to like it.'

Dove flung her guitar case into a corner. 'Well, you know what thought did! I hate living here. The sooner we get out of here and live somewhere decent, the better.'

Monty snored on, as though her distress wasn't worth waking up for; which didn't improve her temper. She stormed into her tiny, claustrophobic room, slammed the door behind her and flung herself onto the bed, sobbing.

Chapter 8

Leading Aircraftsman Webster lay on his bed, browsing through the *Doncaster Star.* Outside, on the parade ground, a flight sergeant was putting the squadron drill team through its paces. Tom had been excused drill due to a swollen toe he'd incurred at football. His flight sergeant had insisted it was self-inflicted and had cancelled Tom's 48-hour pass as punishment. But the MO, acting as mediator, had persuaded the irate NCO that Tom's football skills were as valuable to morale as was an efficient drill team.

'We're hardly likely to win the Wing drill competition, sir, with him in charge,' Tom had commented, confidentially, to the medical officer. 'He marches like Groucho Marx. The lads can't do it for laughing. And if I don't rest me toe, I'll not be fit for the semi-final. A couple of days rest at home'll be just the ticket, sir.'

The MO, who was also the trainer of the squadron team, had agreed, and had restored his invaluable right winger's cancelled weekend pass.

Tom's eye scanned the entertainments column. He'd no intention of spending precious leave with his Auntie Margaret in Bardsey. He and a friend, Johnnie, had planned a boozy couple of nights in Doncaster and district, not far from their RAF camp at Finningley. An advert in the paper caught his eye.

For One Night Only. Thursday, 12th December 1957
The Fabulous Dove McKenna. Amusing songstress and
recording artiste.

She was appearing at a Leeds pub and Thursday was the second day of his pass. Tom knew there could only be one Dove

112

McKenna who sang amusing songs, so he planned to be there. She had never been far from his thoughts and it was because of her that he'd joined the RAF as a National Serviceman rather than sign on for eight years. It had been her suggestion in one of her letters. Those two years, she'd said, should tell him if he wanted to make a career of it or not. Why she hadn't written to him since he'd been called up had baffled and hurt him. He'd left strict instructions with Auntie Margaret to send all letters on. It had never occurred to him that his auntie had her own ideas on the subject of the itinerant Dove McKenna.

Pikey Scullion lurched unsteadily along Vicar Lane in Leeds. He was heading in the general direction of the Robin Hood Hotel for the family meeting, and he was drunk. It would be the first time he'd seen his mother and brother in two and a half years.

After they went their separate ways with the proceeds of the jewellery theft, Pikey had ended up in the West Country. He'd spent all of his share on a three-month bout of high living with women of low morals before reverting to the family business of thieving and working the fairs – until he'd got a message from his mother saying it was time for a family meeting.

Winter drizzle fell unheeded on his long, greasy hair; his hands were stuffed deep into the pockets of his ragged overcoat and the soles of his shoes flapped at every step. The last two years had treated him badly. He carried a pronounced limp – a legacy of a burglary gone wrong – and a disfiguring scar running from his right eye to the corner of his mouth, giving him a permanent leer. The limp plus the drink had him falling against walls for support. Anyone unwise enough to stare at him was treated to a mouthful of abuse, which sent them hurrying on their way. A passing policeman looked hard at him before resuming his beat; arresting Pikey for being drunk and disorderly would be more trouble than it was worth. He was a big man with an obvious capacity for violence. People were giving him a wide berth as he meandered from kerb to wall.

He staggered inside the door of the pub and fell, heavily, against a table, sending drink and glasses crashing to the floor, knocking himself unconscious. When he opened his eyes he coughed and spluttered at the drink his mother was pouring over his face.

113

'Nice ter see yer again, yer big drunken pillock,' she said. 'Have yer been keepin' well?' She looked at Sid. 'Best get him back ter t' van. No point pourin' more drink down him. It'd prob'ly kill him.'

Beulah Scullion's two thirds of the proceeds of the jewel theft had mostly been spent on a new caravan. It was a long, chrome affair, polished regularly by Sid and well appointed within. All in all it was a vast improvement on the one they'd had to abandon at Netherton Fair. She'd given Sid enough money to buy himself some new clothes and drink himself senseless a few times, and the other third share had gone to Pikey. The rain spattered on the caravan roof as she regarded her sons over a table laden with bottles of beer. Pikey had sobered up sufficiently to start drinking again.

'The law's not lookin' for us,' she said. 'Nor have they ever been. We've bin runnin' away from 'em like blue-arsed flies for two an' half years and all fer nowt.'

Pikey had a bottle opener hanging around his neck like a medallion. He flicked the top off a bottle of Double Diamond. 'Yer mean we've bin runnin' away from nowt?' He held the bottle to his mouth and took a deep swig, undecided as to his reaction just yet.

'But we weren't ter know,' said Beulah. 'Them two coppers must've kept it ter theirsens. Can't say as I blame 'em – the dozy sods.'

Pikey was turning belligerent. He slammed the bottle down on the table. 'How come yer've only just found out?'

'Hey! There were nowt ter stop you findin' out fer yerself,' snapped his mother. Then she gave the nearest she could muster to a smile. 'I got pulled in fer tradin' without a licence last week. I gave 'em a dodgy name, but one o' the buggers recognised me. Then a sergeant told this bobby to go check t' records and see if there's owt outstandin' on Mrs Scullion. He must've been gone over half an hour.'

'Tell him how worried yer were,' sniggered Sid, who already knew the story.

'Worried?' she said. 'I'll tell yer how worried I was. By t' time that bobby got back I'd have struggled ter get a tram ticket between t' cheeks of me arse!'

Sid grinned, it was the second time he'd heard this. Pikey

pulled a revolted face as a gross image of his mother presented itself. 'Don't be so bleedin' coarse!' he grunted.

Beulah ignored him and continued: 'He had this smarmy look on his face when he came through t' door an' I thought, "That's it, Beulah, lass — that's you bein' looked after by Her Majesty fer a few years".'

'So, what happened?' demanded Pikey, impatiently.

'Nowt happened,' said Beulah. 'That's what I'm tryin' ter tell yer. No record o' that business wi' them coppers. No mention of us nickin' them jewels.'

'Yer mean I've been lookin' over me shoulder fer nowt for all this bloody time?' exploded Pikey, thumping a fist down on the table and making a half-full bottle fall over and tip its contents onto Sid's lap. 'Some bastard's gonna pay fer this!'

'Look what yer done, yer barmy pillock!' howled Sid.

Beulah sneered at Pikey. 'Oh aye? ... an' which bastard would that be, exactly? Here I am, thinkin' I've got some good news fer yer, an' all yer do is bleedin' moan.'

'I'll tell yer what bastard,' said Pikey, savagely. 'That old bastard what stuffed us. Him what found our sparklers in his bag an' planted 'em in our van, then shopped us ter t' bleedin' scuffers.'

'What d'yer expect after what yer did to him?' growled Beulah. 'He were entitled ter be a bit bleedin' vexed.' She drummed her fingers on the table. 'If yer hadn't robbed him in that field, none o' this would have happened.'

Pikey glared at her. 'How d'yer mean, if I hadn't robbed him? That's what we do, innit? That's how yer brought us up. That's all we bleedin' know.'

'Okay, okay ... it's done now. All over an' done with.' Beulah's finger drumming continued. She knew something about the old man but she was reluctant to tell Pikey lest he do something stupid. But she was angry at the old man as well. Her anger won the day.

'I found summat out about that owd feller,' she said. 'Remember he were with a young lad at Netherton Fair?'

'Oh aye? What about it?' growled Pikey.

'Well, it were Malachy's lad. I thought I knew him at the time, but I couldn't place him. Anyroad, I've bccn askin' round an' both o' Malachy's kids have bin seen wi' this same owd gimmer a few times. No sign o' Malachy. Nobody seems ter know what happened to him.'

'Is that right?' said Pikey, rubbing his unshaven chin.

'Aye,' said Beulah. 'His girl's a bit of a singer now. Clubs an' stuff. It's ter be hoped she sings better than her dad. He sounded like me granny when she caught her tit in t' mangle.'

Sid burst out laughing at this but Pikey continued to rub his chin.

'Well that's very interestin' is that,' he said. 'Very bloody interestin' indeed.'

'What yer sayin', lad?' asked Beulah.

'Am sayin' nowt, Ma. Not till I've had a good look at summat. I'll need ter take yer truck for a couple of hours.'

This time Dove had no supporting acts. She was on her own. Monty had arranged for her to record "Catch A Falling Star" to catch the Christmas market, with him and Henry selling them at each gig. They'd had a thousand made and had already sold over two hundred. The B side to Perry Como's version of the song was "Magic Moments", Dove's B side was a Monty Catchpole song about a man with a nose like an onion. Both songs popular in their own way.

'The Albion Music Shop in Leeds has just taken two hundred on sale or return,' announced Monty. They'd stopped off at a telephone box on their way to the gig. Conducting business without a telephone had become increasingly difficult, so Monty had arranged with an old bookseller friend in Leeds to take all their calls, which he picked up twice a day.

'We'll need to sell them before Christmas,' said Dove. 'No one buys Christmas songs in January. That leaves four gigs between now and Christmas to sell six hundred records.'

'There are always other Christmases, Dove,' said Monty. 'In January we'll record a couple of your comic songs, then we're not restricted to deadlines.'

'Have you found out where we can park the waggon?'

Monty nodded. 'Apparently there's a field about a quarter of a mile away; the brewery have arranged for us to use it.'

'Good of them. I hope they don't knock it off my expenses.'

'They won't,' Monty assured her. 'You're their star turn, you know that, don't you? Oh, and before I forget, they've got a twin bedroom going spare in the pub.'

116

Most pubs had the odd room to spare and were always willing to offer Dove a bed for the night.

'Twin?' enquired Henry. 'That means two beds.'

'I'm not sharing with you,' said Dove. 'If that's what you think.'

'Ugh!' said her brother. 'I just thought me and Monty could share for a change.'

'Don't be so unchivalrous, Henry,' scolded Monty. 'Young ladies need their own room from time to time.'

Pikey Scullion spotted the advert as well; this one was in the *Yorkshire Evening Post*, underneath a glowing review of Dove's last appearance in Huddersfield. He'd been back to the field where he'd last seen Malachy and searched around for half an hour before his feet had kicked against the sleepers. Then he prised them apart and, just like Henry had three years previously, he dropped stones down the hole and listened for a thud; only he didn't hear a thud, not a proper one – a faint metallic chink as the stone bounced off something, but no thud. He sat and drank beer by the side of the shaft, planning his strategy and hurling empty bottles, one by one, down into the darkness. Drunk now, he lay flat on his stomach and shouted down the hole.

'If there's any thick paddies hidin' down there, yer can come out now.' He listened for a reply but only his own voice echoed back up to him. Then an idea struck him. 'Hey, Malachy, I reckon yer must be a bit thirsty by now.' He got to his feet, stood perilously near the edge and urinated down the hole, laughing maniacally. 'Here's a drop o' used beer fer yer, Malachy lad.'

The unusually pretty girl whom Tom had first met three years earlier had developed into a heart-melting beauty. He was standing at the back of a crowded room with his RAF pal when she walked out on stage. This time there was a microphone and full sound system to cope with the large room. Over 200 people had each paid two and six entrance money to come and see Dove, such was her burgeoning reputation. The brewery was getting good value for its twenty pounds a week.

'Good grief! Is that her?' said his friend. 'You forgot to tell me she was a goddess.'

117

Tom said nothing; he was hoping the goddess hadn't taken up with one of the gods. His friend was right, she was bewitching. Her beauty should have been at odds with her comical act, but somehow the two went together. She finished the first set with a Doris Day ballad, "The Black Hills of Dakota" and the audience were spellbound. Tom knew if the gods hadn't already got her, it was only a matter of time.

'I'd have thought she was a bit out of your league, old boy,' remarked Johnnie.

'Don't be so stuck up, Johnnie. She's one of us, not one of your lot.'

'My lot?'

'Yes, your lot. She lives in a caravan, I lived in a council house; you lived in a house with a drawing room and a study, and you talk like the bloke on the nine o'clock news.'

'You're an inverted snob, Webster. Watch out, the goddess approaches.'

Dove hadn't seen Tom. She was heading for Monty, who was propping up the other end of the bar. Tom called out her name.

'Hiya, Dove.'

She'd heard this greeting a hundred times in the past, and was smiling even as she turned to him.

'Tom!' She hurled herself at him.

He hugged her and felt a warmth for which he'd been longing ever since she'd left. Monty looked over and smiled. He'd heard about Tom. She needed to meet friends her own age. Johnnie looked on with ill-disguised envy.

'I demand to be introduced to this person,' he said. 'Before I disintegrate with lust.'

'Mind your manners, Johnnie,' warned Tom. 'Dove, this is Johnnie.'

'Pleased to meet you,' beamed Dove, sparing the bedazzled Johnnie just a glance before returning her gaze to Tom.

'Oh Tom, I've missed you. I thought I'd never see you again. I thought you'd gone off me.'

'Gone off you? I thought you'd gone off me, what with you not writing any more.'

'Not wri . . . ah.'

'Ah what?'

'Your Auntie Margaret said you didn't want me to write to you

118

any more. I tried phoning but she cut me dead. I think she thought I wasn't good enough for you.'

Johnnie gave a shrill laugh that turned many nearby heads. 'Who is this Auntie Margaret?' he said. 'Is she mentally limp? Does she carry a white stick? How can a vision like you not be good enough for anyone – especially an oik like Webster?'

'Johnnie's doing National Service with me,' Tom explained. 'Hence the meeting of opposites.' He turned to Johnnie. 'Would you mind if I had Dove to myself for a few minutes?'

'I'd understand if you wanted her to yourself for a lifetime, dear boy. Don't mind me. I shall just languish here and pine.'

'I'll bring him back in ten minutes,' laughed Dove. 'I've got another set to do.'

She led Tom through to another, quieter room, inhabited by just a few local drinkers and the landlord's dog. They sat at a table for two and intertwined fingers across the table, staring at each other; not speaking at first.

'Can I get you anything, Dove?' called out a barman.

'Just an orange juice and ...?' She looked, questioningly at Tom, who was still otherwise engrossed. 'Tom, what do you want to drink?'

'Oh ... a pint of bitter, please.' He got to his feet. 'Here, I'll get them.'

'No need, they're on the house,' said the barman.

A murmur of amazement came from the locals who had never heard of such a thing. Not in this pub, anyway.

In the privacy of their corner, Dove gave Tom a look of appraisal. He wore his hair in the compulsory short back and sides manner, which pretty much identified him as being in the armed services. Most young men favoured the Tony Curtis or James Dean look. Some went as far the DA, with their hair swept together at the back like the rear end of a duck, hence the acronym. Tom fingered his hair, self-consciously.

'The RAF hasn't caught up with modern hair styling. Every time I let it grow my flight sergeant marches me to the barber. He doesn't like me, doesn't my flight sergeant.'

'Never mind, you can always show him who's boss when you get to be an officer.'

Tom shrugged. 'Maybe.'

119

She gave him a questioning look. 'Are you still going to make the RAF a career?'

'Still making up my mind,' he said. 'I applied for the OTU – the officer training unit – but they said I'd need to sign on for at least three years. So I thought I'd see my National Service out before I made my mind up.' He looked at her and smiled. 'As per a certain person's advice. Besides, officer cadets doing National Service tend to get the mickey taken out of them something cruel.'

'I'd have thought you could give as good as you got in that department.'

'I wouldn't put money on it,' he grinned. 'I'm being posted to Gib next month ... I'm quite looking forward to that.'

'Gibraltar?' She tried to hide her disappointment. No sooner had she got him back than he was going away again. 'How long for?'

'Until my time's up – about a year. Then I'll decide whether to sign on or not.'

'Oh.' She sounded disappointed but it was more to do with him going away than him not having signed on as a regular.

'Hey! It was your suggestion,' he said. 'Do my National Service, then sign on after that if I liked it.'

'I know ... I'll miss you, though.'

'I'll get leave,' Tom said. 'Should manage to get home a couple of times.'

'That'll be nice. I'd hate to lose touch now that I've found you again.'

'Me too.'

'Do you have a girlfriend?'

'Not at the moment. There was someone, but she wasn't special enough to ask her to wait for me.'

'Would she have, if you'd asked?'

'Possibly. She was very cut up when I broke it off.'

Dove laughed. 'You gave her the brush off, now we're getting to the truth.'

'I'm just nineteen, she was seventeen. It's too young to get serious. My dad says a man isn't ready for marriage until he's in his thirties.'

'I like your dad. How is he ... and your mam?'

'Oh, they're fine. They never mention Alice in their letters.'

'I miss Alice.'

120

Tom's face became suddenly serious. 'I miss her like hell,' he said; then the frown cleared. 'I thought I might go and see mam and dad while I'm in Gib. Apparently it's fairly easy to cadge a lift and swan off down to Australia. Not sure how I'll get over to New Zealand, though.'

The barman set their drinks in front of them and looked at Tom. 'Where yer stationed, pal?' he asked.

'God! Is it that obvious?' groaned Tom, running his hand across his hair. 'I'm at Finningley.'

'Oh aye, Brylcreem Boy, eh? Did my stretch in the Infantry ... mainly Malaya,' he reminisced. 'Although I were stationed in Singapore for six months. Not a bad billet, Singapore. Wouldn't mind going back there once they've sorted themselves out. Malaya was a rough owd place though. Just got back in time. Some o' the lads out there got held over because o' Korea. Two years were enough for me.'

'See any action?' asked Tom, with interest.

The barman stared into the middle distance. 'Oh aye,' he said. 'I saw some o' that all right. Lost a few good mates an' all.' He went back to the bar and Tom's eyes followed him.

'Blokes like him make me feel like a fraud,' he said. 'All I do is push a pen around and play football. I've never heard a shot fired in anger.'

'And do you want to?' asked Dove, her curiosity tempered with concern. She'd read somewhere that, in the forces, people with ambitions to get shot at usually got their wish.

'Wouldn't mind a bit of action, somewhere where the enemy can't shoot straight,' he said grinning. 'No fear of that in Gib – unless they start arming the apes.'

Dove laughed. She was pleased to hear he'd be safe in Gibraltar. He was such a comfortable person to be with. The thought made her smile and shake her head. Comfortable – a poor substitute for love. His face was still boyish and easy on the eye – but it wasn't the face of a fighting man. This thought kept the smile on her face. He didn't really look like a man yet. Tom narrowed his eyes, suspiciously.

'Dove McKenna, what are you smiling at?'

'You make me smile, you always have.'

'You used to do that. It used to make me really mad. Those little smiles of yours – little private jokes at my expense.'

121

'Not at your expense, Tom,' she protested. 'Never at your expense. I'd never laugh at you, honest. I always ... you know.'

'Know what?'

'I always ...' she hesitated, then went on, 'I always thought a lot about you.' Maybe she actually loved him, she didn't really know; and until she did it would be wrong to say it.

'Me ... you an' all,' said Tom, awkwardly. 'That's probably why I packed Pauline in.'

'Pauline?'

'Me girlfriend. I always measured girls against you. None of them ever measured up.'

'So, there's been a lot of them has there?'

'A few ... What about you? Have you got anybody?'

Dove remembered the last time she'd been asked that question. That time she'd said Tom was her boyfriend; maybe he always had been. 'The sort of life I lead I haven't time for boyfriends,' she said.

'I believe you, thousands wouldn't.'

She shrugged. 'It's sad but true.'

Tom took a sip of his drink and asked, 'Did you ever catch up with your dad again?'

'No ... never clapped eyes on him since the day me and Henry ran away.'

'You never told me why you ran away.'

'I had a problem at school ... '

'I heard about that.'

'And a problem with dad's drinking.'

'The bastard hit you again, didn't he?'

Dove nodded. 'He went a bit too far. So we parted company.'

'Good for you.' Tom squeezed her hand. 'Where do you think he went – back to Ireland?'

Dove knew this line of conversation would force her into lying and she didn't want this. 'I don't want to talk about him,' she replied. 'I want to talk about you.'

'Me? Oh, I suspect my life's been dull compared to yours. I don't know whether I'm doing the right thing not signing on for longer and giving this RAF thing a real go. If I'd joined the officer cadet unit I'd be learning to fly now. Being a pilot's all I ever dreamed of.'

'I'll keep my fingers crossed. Everyone should have a dream.'

'What's your dream, Dove?'

Their eyes met and Tom knew he'd never see another face as beautiful as hers as long as he lived.

'I want to live in a house,' she said.

'Still living in the old waggon, eh?'

'Yes. It's in a field just down the road. I'm not sleeping there tonight, though. Monty and Henry are, but I'm not ... I'm having a night of luxury in one of the pub bedrooms.'

Whether she was trying to tempt him or not, she didn't know herself. Having him with her would be nice. She'd never spent a night with a young man. Tom gave an exasperated frown.

'Blast! I have to be back at camp at twelve. Which means the eleven o'clock bus.'

'Oh,' said Dove. 'I see.'

Each tried to hide their disappointment. Tom was weighing up the pros and cons of going back to camp a day late and taking his punishment. He studied her face again. If she wasn't worth it, nothing was.

'Maybe, when you get your house,' he said, 'you'll come out into the garden and wave at me as I fly over.'

'Maybe I will.'

Tom thought, Or maybe I'll be living in your house with you; but he kept this thought to himself. Having too many dreams could lead to disappointment. Their paths weren't destined to cross all that frequently in the coming year. A lot could happen in that time.

'I'm glad to see you're putting dad's guitar to good use. I must mention it the next time I write to him. What's all this about you being a recording artist?'

Dove giggled. 'Oh, that was Monty. We hired a studio and made a record. We sell them at gigs. I'll give you a couple if you like. You can send one to your dad.'

'Who's Monty? I hope he's not a rival for my affections.'

'Oh, Monty's a real charmer. If he was fifty years younger you wouldn't stand a chance. We found him the day after we left dad. He'd been beaten up.'

'Oh dear.'

'I'm glad we found him,' Dove said. 'He's been a great help. He's been giving Henry lessons for one thing.'

'Sounds as though he's been giving you elocution lessons.'

'Does it?' She seemed surprised. 'He is a bit of a stickler for pronunciation. I think it's just rubbed off on us. Monty's like that.'

'He sounds an interesting bloke.'

'He is – I'll introduce you to him later.'

They sipped their drinks and chatted happily until Dove looked at her watch. 'Time to get back to work,' she said. 'Mustn't keep my public waiting. Will you still be here after I've finished?'

'I'll stay as long as you like,' he blurted; then he smiled to cover up his embarrassment. Dove kissed him, lightly, on his lips.

'What would happen if you went back to camp late?' she asked.

'I'd be put on report. Extra duties, roasting from my flight sergeant. I'll stay if you want me to.'

'I want you to.'

Monty came over to join him as they waited for Dove to prepare for her next set. He held out his hand.

'Montgomery Catchpole. Dove may have mentioned me.'

'She mentioned a Monty. I assume that's you.'

'That's what the children call me.'

'Children?'

'Oh, sorry. I always regard them as children. I mean Dove and Henry of course.'

'How is Henry?'

'Oh, he's growing into a fine young man. He's upstairs right now, watching television. Takes good care of me.'

Johnnie was pressing at his elbow, awaiting introduction.

'Montgomery, I'd like you to meet the honourable Johnnie Plumley-Shreeve. One day to be a peer of the realm.'

'Delighted to meet you, Montgomery,' said Johnnie. 'Although it'll be many a long year before I don the ermine. The pater's as fit as a fiddle.'

'Hereditary peer, eh? Never met one of those before.'

'Papa's the peer, Lord Plumley-Shreeve of Tewkesbury. I'm just the plonker – according to Webster here, anyway.'

'You are what you are,' said Tom.

'You do realise,' said Johnnie, 'that in the good old days the likes of you would be sweating beneath my stairs, catering to my every need.'

'Right now,' said Tom, 'I'm a Senior Aircraftsman and you're not, which means I outrank you, so mind your manners and get your betters a drink.'

Johnnie clicked his heels and threw Tom an exaggerated salute before turning to Monty. 'What'll you have, Montgomery?' he enquired. 'You're obviously a man of some quality, a cut above the common herd. It's up to us to keep the lower orders in their place.'

'I'll have a pint of mixed, please.'

'Tell him how your ancestor got his knighthood,' said Tom after Johnnie had ordered a round of drinks. He grinned at Monty. 'You must hear this, it's his party piece. Trouble is, it's apparently true.'

Johnnie took the drinks from the barman and handed one to Monty. He'd told this story many times before, mainly at dinner parties where he'd revelled in the digestive problems of the guests after he'd related it.

'Webster's referring to my noble ancestor, Sir Mortimer Shreeve, who was Groom of the Stool to King Henry the Eighth.'

'Groom of the what?' interrupted Monty. Then he grimaced, 'You mean ...?'

'I most certainly do,' confirmed Johnnie. 'The king had an ornate, bejwelled construction called an easement, upon which he sat to evacuate his royal bowel. According to the family annals, it was apparently during a particularly difficult session upon this easement that he vented his frustration by ordering the decapitation of Anne Boleyn. It was my ancestor's function to attend His Majesty's needs by offering him advice and encouragment, handing him warm, damp cloths with which to wipe his nether regions, and various other associated duties. It was at the end of a particularly triumphant evacuation that, still perched upon his kingly porcelain, His Majesty drew his sword and ordered my ancestor to kneel before him. In mind of what had happened to the Queen, Mortimer was understandably apprehensive. However his apprehensions came to nought when he felt a light tap on his shoulder and heard the words, "Arise Sir Mortimer." Knighthoods have been awarded to far less heroic men.'

With that, Johnnie sank his pint in one go and placed the empty glass on the bar. 'Your round, Webster, you low blister.'

'He also reads P.G. Wodehouse,' said Tom.

'You mean your ancestor was awarded a knighthood for being a lavatory attendant?' said Monty.

Johnnie roared with laughter. 'Precisely, my dear fellow – and when Sir Mortimer retired he was given a baronetcy. It's a matter of great family pride. Would that such a thing could happen today – an injection of lavatory attendants into the Upper Chamber would improve the place no end. Make a change from some of the the decrepit relics they have there now.'

Dove didn't disappoint the audience with her routine of Monty's comic songs and no one applauded louder than Tom, except perhaps Johnnie, who accompanied his clapping with a piercing, unaristocratic whistle. Dove had worked out the value of false tabs and, at the end, went off to shouts of 'More' – and returned to centre stage and a single spotlight. She sang "Catch a Falling Star" to an audience stunned that she could switch from comedy to this with such accomplishment and style.

As the applause turned into further shouts of 'More', she calmed them down with her hands and a smile.

'Before I came here tonight,' she said, 'my aged grandmother asked me if I'd be singing "Catch A Falling Star". I said, "Yes, Grandma, I will," then she asked, "And do you think the nice people there will buy your record, so that you can buy me a new wheel for my wheelchair? Because if not, I won't be able to go outdoors and feel the sunshine or hear the birds ever again." I said,"I can only try, Grandma."'

'I wrote that,' whispered Monty into Johnnie's ear.

'Mongomery, you have a masterly touch with a pen.'

Dove's sad face broke into a broad smile. 'Records are on sale at the back, folks. Please don't disappoint my dear old grandma.'

They laughed at her cheek and roundly applauded her whole act. It had been the best night they'd had in a while.

Even Pikey Scullion clapped.

Chapter 9

'I shall tell our dear flight sergeant you said to get stuffed – with the rough end of a ragman's trumpet.'

'Johnnie!'

'Worry not, old boy. I'll dream up some spiffing excuse to get you off the hook.'

'I'd prefer you didn't say anything,' said Tom. 'I'll make up my own excuse ... I'll tell him I had my wallet stolen and I'd lost touch with you and they wouldn't let me on the bus so I had to walk back – which took a while because I've got a bad toe. They already know about my bad toe.'

'But you limped back as fast as you could, for Queen and country?'

'Yes, something like that.'

'They'll clap you in irons and lash you to within an inch of your life. My excuse would be more original.'

'He's exaggerating,' said Tom to Dove, who seemed worried.

Monty had already gone to bed, suspicious, but not critical of Dove's and Tom's arrangements. Spending the night together in the pub was inviting trouble and gossip so she'd graciously given up her room to Henry and Monty, leaving the waggon free for her and Tom.

As the two of them strolled through the chill night, Dove remembered a similar walk with Norman, when she pretended she lived in someone else's house because she was ashamed of her own home. With Tom she felt no such shame; being with him was right. He smiled when the waggon came into view. 'You know, I always envied you living where you do.'

'I've grown to hate it.'

'Hate it?' Tom sounded surprised.

'Oh, don't get me wrong,' she said. 'I'd be sad to see the back of it. It's been my home all my life and I'd be even sadder to lose Boris. He's been there ever since I can remember.'

'It must be convenient right now, though.'

'Yes, it is. But one day I want a house where you go upstairs to bed; with a garden and neighbours and a proper bathroom, and a dresser with photographs on, and a coal fire to sit round in the winter and do toast.'

'And a husband with pipe and slippers?'

'Him as well.'

'Dove, you're probably the only teenager in England who longs to be conventional.'

'Unconventional's okay until it becomes inconvenient, and living in a mobile box is inconvenient – take my word for it. You never shake off the gippo tag.'

Tom stroked Boris as Dove opened the door. 'He seems to remember me,' he called out.

'How could he forget you? I certainly didn't.'

Cold moonlight played on her face as she looked down at him, darkening her eyes and the red of her lips. His heart began to thump as he realised the certainty of what they were going to do that night.

'You're beautiful, Dove,' he said.

'You're not so bad yourself.'

She pushed open both halves of the door and switched on a light.

'Electric light eh? What are you plugged in to – one of the street lamps?'

He was joking but the expression on her face told him it was a poor joke.

'See what I mean?' she said. 'Everyone thinks we're thieves, just because we don't live conventionally.'

'Dove, I was joking, honest.'

'I know, Tom. It's just that everyone makes the same jokes and it gets a bit wearing sometimes.'

'Dove, I'd never do anything to hurt you.'

She moved towards him and kissed him. 'I know, Tom ... I'm glad you're here.'

She led him through to her tiny room and they sat down on the

128

bcd. 'This is my world,' she said. 'And I've only got this because my dad's not around any more.'

There was just enough room for a bed and a built-in cupboard where she kept all her clothes and belongings. On one wall were pinned two photographs: one of Lonnie Donegan, and one of her mother.

'Who's that?' asked Tom.

'It's my mam when she was about my age.'

'She's not as pretty as you.'

'Don't be cruel.'

'I'm not being cruel, I'm being truthful. You could have had a picture of Marilyn Monroe pinned up and I'd have said the same.'

On the opposite wall hung a banjo and a ukulele; there was a good feel about it, and a sweet smell.

'I could live here,' Tom said. 'It smells of you.'

'I do hope you're not being personal, Tom Webster.'

He put his arm around her. 'I'm being personal, all right, Dove. It's the nicest smell in the world.'

'Thank you.'

'You know, Dove, from what I've seen tonight you could become a big star.'

She smiled. 'Oh, I don't think so, Tom. To be a big star you need a big voice. I'm easy listening and amusing. If music hall wasn't dying on its feet I might have had a future there.'

'Something good will become of you,' he said. 'I'm sure of that. I've always been sure of that.'

They talked for an hour about old friends and ambitions. Memories of Alice had them both close to tears, and memories of Mischievous Night, when they'd foiled the arson attempt, had them laughing.

'Kill the little buggers,' smiled Dove. 'I'll never forget that as long as I live.'

'I could hardly say it for laughing,' grinned Tom. 'What about you, galloping towards 'em on Boris, shooting fireworks at 'em?'

'And our Henry on his stilts!'

They fell back on the bed, laughing and holding on to each other. Then their eyes met and the laughter ebbed away. Tom kissed her, gently, on her lips.

'I've been wanting to do this all night,' he said.

'Me too.'

She returned his kiss, warm and lingering this time. Passions were aroused as they moved into each other, pulling at each other's clothes. Then Dove broke away.

'Tom ... if we're going to do it, I want to do it properly. It's my first time.'

'And mine,' he said, a little too hastily, she thought; but she didn't take him up on it.

'I don't want to be fumbling about, struggling with buttons and things. You go through there and ... ' she hesitated. 'And get undressed and I'll wait for you in here.'

'Okay.'

He got to his feet.

'Bolt the outside door,' she said. 'And don't come in until I tell you.'

'Okay.'

He closed the door on her and undressed quickly, not wanting to keep her waiting when she called to him. The paraffin stove had been left on a low light. He shivered and turned it up, then bolted the outside door and waited.

Dove took her time, wondering if she was doing the right thing. She was about to commit another mortal sin – or didn't she believe in all that stuff any more? A lot of it seemed very far-fetched. What was she worrying about? She hadn't been to church in nearly three years. But it was still there, her Catholic conscience. It was too late to worry now, she was in too deep. Not that she wanted to back out. The prospect of what was to happen was far too exciting to be stifled by religious beliefs. There was a rosary hanging from her bedpost. It had been her dad's and had hung there, unused, for as long as she could remember. Fat lot of good it did him. She unhooked it and put it in her jeans pocket. To do *it* within sight of a rosary would be just a bit too blasphemous.

She eased herself out of her brassiere and opened the wall-cupboard door. Inside was a mirror; and inside the mirror was Dove McKenna; naked, nervous and excited. She looked critically at herself and wondered what Tom would think. Then she turned sideways to examine her profile. No one had ever called her fat, although her stomach was perhaps a bit plump. She pulled it in and pushed out her breasts; but beneath her self-critique she knew she was beautiful. She lay on the bed with one leg coquettishly raised, but modestly leaning inwards; then she spread her hair

130

across the pillow and put a languid arm behind her head, the other across her breasts.

There was a long mirror outside on the wall beside the sink. Tom scowled at his reflection; as naked and fragile as a peeled banana. How could Dove fancy a skinny bugger like him? He expanded his chest and flexed his biceps like Charles Atlas in the 'You Too Can Have A Body Like Mine' advert, and realised that the comical addendum to this advert was more appropriate in his case: 'If You're Not Careful'.

'You can come in now.'

His heart hammered away. He took a deep breath and pushed open her door, one hand modestly covering his groin. Dove was well concealed beneath the bedclothes, having dismissed her alluring pose as too tarty. Her eyes were glued to him as he nervously rounded the bed and climbed in beside her.

At first they just lay in each others arms, enjoying this first moment together. Then Dove felt him hardening into her and rubbed herself against him. They kissed and he ran his hand over her breasts, then around her back and across her bottom as she slid her hand down between his legs and stroked him. This was the most beautiful moment of her life and it would get even better. It was to be the first time for both of them and Tom knew it must be now or it would be too late.

A deafening bang startled them. For a mystified moment they clung together.

'What the hell was that?' said Tom.

The bedroom door burst open and Pikey Scullion stood there, his scarred face beaming with drink and malice. In his hand was the sledge hammer he'd used to let himself in.

Dove and Tom pulled the bedclothes up around their necks. She recognised Pikey immediately and went rigid with fright.

'Who the hell are you?' asked Tom, trying not to show fear in his voice.

'Me,' grinned Scullion. 'I'm her Uncle Pikey. Surely yer remember yer Uncle Pikey, Dove lass. You an' that owd gimmer pal o' yours shopped us ter the scuffers. Tried ter nick us jewels off us.'

'Do you know him?' asked Tom.

Dove nodded, uncertainly. 'He's no uncle of mine,' she said. 'What are you doing here?'

131

'I've come ter pay yer back fer what yer did to us. Tryin' ter get us locked up.' He looked at Tom, as if for sympathy. 'I mean, that's not nice, is it? Trying ter get me an' me baby brother an' me dear old ma locked up.'

'You'll get locked up if you hurt us,' warned Dove, weakly.

'I don't think so, darlin'. Yer see, I know all about yer dad.'

'What about my dad?'

'He were me best pal and I know what yer did to him. That wasn't nice neither.' He looked at Tom for support. 'She's not very nice, this girlfriend o' yours.'

'Look,' said Tom. 'If you want to talk, have the decency to let us get dressed first.'

'And who says I want ter talk ter you, yer little gobshite?' he roared.

Dove and Tom cowered under the blanket. Pikey was a big man, bigger even than Malachy. He put down the hammer and, with both hands, pulled viciously at the bedclothes and threw them to one side; exposing Dove and Tom's nakedness. But his eyes were only on Dove.

Tom went for him in desperation, landing a couple of ineffectual blows. Scullion contemptuously jabbed a heavy fist into his face and knocked him back on top of a terrified Dove. She screamed.

'For God's sake! What do you want?'

'I want to know where your dad is. No, I tell a lie. I know where your dad is. I just want to know what it's worth fer me ter keep quiet about it.'

'I don't know what you're talking about,' protested Dove, shocked at what he knew and wishing this nightmare would go away.

Tom lay across her, semi-conscious, with blood pouring from his nose across her breasts and onto her stomach. The sight seemed to excite Pikey. He grabbed one of Tom's legs and yanked him off the bed so that he could get a proper look at Dove, her body now smeared with Tom's blood.

'I were there that night,' said Scullion. 'That night yer did yer dad in. Pushed him down that shaft. I were there. I saw the lot.'

'He was trying to kill me,' sobbed Dove. 'We had no choice.'

He yelled, triumphantly, 'Ah! So yer admit it, d'yer?' Up until that moment he'd still had his doubts. 'Yer admit shovin' yer old man down that hole. I wonder what the scuffers'd make o' that? It's murder that is ... an' yer know what they do ter murderers.'

She curled herself into a ball to avoid his piercing eyes. 'We didn't murder him.' Her voice was hoarse with shock and fear.

'Leave her alone, you bastard!' Tom had come round enough to make a grab for Scullion's legs and was repaid with several vicious blows, which continued even after Tom had gone quiet.

'Stop it!' screamed Dove. 'You'll kill him.'

Scullion looked back up at her. His face creased into a malevolent beam once again.

'Okay, darlin', I'll leave him alone. It's you I want.'

'You lay one finger on me and I'll scream.'

'Scream all yer like. There's no one round here ter hear yer.'

'I'll tell the police. You'll get locked up for years for this.'

'Tell the police? Yer not listenin' ter me are yer? ... What will yer tell 'em about yer dad? How will yer explain pushin' him down that mine shaft when I tell 'em what I know?'

He gave a coarse, drunken laugh. 'Yer see, lass, I've got a bit of a hold on yer.' He held out his gnarled, grubby hands, expansively. 'But I'm norra mean man. All I want from yer is what yer were going ter give this little gobshite anyway. Only wi' me it'll be worth yer while. It'll save yer goin' ter prison fer life. You and your kid.'

She shivered with horror. He was right. He could get them both locked up. 'Please, isn't there any other way? I've got some money ...'

A greedy glint lit his eyes. 'Money? Where is it?'

'It's in my bag through there. You can have it all.'

'I'll be takin' it all, don't you worry, love.' Then the vicious grin returned. 'And I'll be takin' you as well.'

He had his trousers off now and was holding both of her ankles, pulling her legs part. She fought to keep them together so he leaned over her and slapped her hard across her face. Dove tried to scream but the strength had gone from her voice.

'Malachy should 'ave given yer more o' this,' he snarled. Then he gave a brown-toothed smile. 'Hey, I'll do a deal wi' yer. You keep yer legs open an' I'll keep me mouth shut.'

He laughed, loudly at his own wit and Dove continued to struggle. The humour vanished from his face.

'Listen,' he snarled. 'If I have ter go from here without what I came fer, I'm goin' straight ter t' scuffers.' He hit her again, this time sending her into merciful oblivion.

Scullion stared down at Dove's naked, unconscious body and he knew that no girl as beautiful as this would ever give herself to him willingly. He allowed the vision to imprint itself on his memory, before satisfying his brutal lust.

She awoke to find him pushing himself off her. The searing pain inside her told her that the worst had happened. She folded herself into a ball again and vomited with fear and disgust on the mattress. When she opened her eyes he had gone and she was consumed with loathing, for the world and everything in it.

Tom recovered consciousness, staggered to his feet and sat on the bed. He pulled at Dove's hand until she stared up at him, her brows tugging together above empty eyes.

'What did he ...?'

But her eyes had already answered his question.

'Oh God! ... Oh my bloody God!' He ran, naked, to the outside door and screamed into the night. 'You ... you bastard!' Then he sank to his knees and sobbed like a child. Out of respect he got dressed before he went back to her. His face was a mass of lumps and bruises and streaked with blood and tears.

'I'm so sorry, Dove,' he wept. 'I'm ever so sorry. I shouldn't have let this happen to you.'

He knelt down and gathered her clothes, then held them to her as though making a peace offering. Dove took them, silently. He left her to get dressed, away from his intrusive eyes. She was sitting on the bed when he tapped on the door and pushed it open just enough for him to ascertain that she was decent.

'I'll, er ... I'll go and ring the police. Shall I ask for an ambul –'

'No!' she said, quickly. 'For God's sake, didn't you hear a word he said?'

Tom tried to recall what Scullion had been talking about, but couldn't. 'Love, he's got to be caught,' he said, gently.

Dove's face was now sodden with tears as she looked up at him. All the energy and exhuberance and life had drained out of her. Her voice had dropped to little more than a whisper.

'Tom!' she said. 'He could ...' She took several deep breaths. 'He could put me in jail for life.'

'What? Dove what are you talking about?'

'He saw Henry push dad down a ... down a very deep hole. We could be done for murder.'

'Down a hole?'

'That's why we ran away.'

'Your dad was a vicious bully.'

'Tom, we killed him.'

'Dove ... I don't know what happened, but I do know it wasn't murder.'

'Oh yes, and how do you know?'

'Well, was it?'

'No.'

'That's how I know then.'

She sank her head into her hands as Tom stood by, uselessly.

'I'm going to get Monty and Henry,' he said, eventually.

Dove said nothing.

'Is that okay?' he asked. 'You'd better come with me – I don't want to leave you on your own.'

She nodded and pushed herself to her feet. Then she took his hand and said quietly, her eyes anywhere but on him, 'It wasn't your fault, Tom. You did your best.'

'It wasn't good enough though, was it? I'm not sure how I can live with that.'

'I'm glad you were with me. It would have been worse if I'd been on my own.'

'Yes,' he said. 'I'm glad I was with you as well.'

Monty listened, gravely, as Dove told the story of how Malachy had died. Starting from when he'd beaten them and forced Dove into missing Mass and her subsequent expulsion from school.

The old man nodded in admiration when she came to the part where Henry had come to the rescue. She had already suffered the embarrassment of admitting to what she and Tom had been doing when she told the story of events leading up to the rape. It was the first time she or Henry had spoken about either of their parents. Up until now the subject had been taboo.

'Well done, Henry,' Monty said. 'It was a fine thing you did.'

'I killed my dad,' Henry pointed out.

'You saved your sister's life, that's the only way to look at it.'

Tom felt even more useless knowing that an eleven-year-old

boy had been more use to Dove than he had been. Dove spotted this and took his hand.

'I'm surrounded by people who risk everything to try and save me,' she said.

Tom tried to smile but winced in pain. His face was covered in plasters and iodine. 'You should go to the hospital,' said Monty, for the umpteenth time.

Tom shook his head. 'Dove's the one who needs to go to hospital. She's suffered a hell of a lot more than me. I'm not going anywhere until this thing's sorted out.'

'Tom,' Dove insisted. 'There's nothing to sort out. I don't want to go to jail.'

'Nor me,' said Henry. 'But I don't want him to get away with it, neither.'

'I wholeheartedly agree,' said Monty. 'Scullion must be brought to book for what he did. On top of which you'll never rest easy knowing he has something as damaging as this on you.'

'What do we do, then?' asked Dove, faintly. The shock of her ordeal was seeping through to the surface.

Tom and Henry cast worried glances in her direction. She gave them a smile that said 'I'm okay' but they knew she wasn't.

'We *think*, that's what we do,' said Monty, stroking his beard and staring into the middle distance.

They all went quiet, racking their collective brains for what to do next.

'You know,' decided Monty, at length. 'This is all a question of conscience.'

'How do you mean?' asked Tom.

'I mean, if Dove and Henry don't feel guilty about the death of their father, then nothing else matters.'

'I don't understand,' said Dove.

'Look,' said Monty. 'I know for absolute certain you didn't murder your father. What about you, Tom?'

'I'm as certain as you are.'

'There you are, you see. That's four of us. Who else in the world matters?'

'The police for one thing,' Henry said.

'Ah, you must lie to the police.'

'Lie?' said Dove. 'Monty, we can't lie to the police.'

'I'm afraid you have no option, Dove. If you tell them the truth you'll have to explain why you put the sleepers back; and why you didn't tell anyone; and why you ran away.'

'But they'll find us out,' she protested, weakly. 'I'm no good at lying.'

Henry laid a protective arm around his sister's shoulder. Monty was too wrapped in thought to notice her distress.

'On top of which,' he said, 'this all happened just after you were expelled from school for being violent towards another girl.'

'The girl was a bully,' said Tom. 'Everyone knew that.'

Monty regarded Tom for a moment and said gravely, 'It happened the week after their father put them both in hospital with his drunken violence. They had motive and opportunity and there's a witness.' He turned to the children. 'It all adds up, I'm afraid.'

'So,' summed up Henry. 'We've had it then?'

'You have if you insist on telling the truth.' Monty suddenly smiled and took Dove's limp hand in his. 'Look, Dove. There's nothing wrong with telling a lie if telling the truth will bring about an injustice. Call it Catchpole's Law.'

'He's right,' said Tom. 'It's Scullion's word against yours. The word of a rapist and a thief against yours. Who are the police going to believe?'

'What do we say?' asked Henry, who much preferred Monty's idea to the alternative.

'You tell the truth,' Monty said.

'But ...?' said Dove.

'As far as it goes,' he continued. 'You will express surprise but not much regret at the news that your father may have been murdered. They will ask you about your relationship with your father and you will both tell him the truth about his drunken rages.'

'He was in jail for being drunk the night mam died,' said Henry.

'Tell them everything,' Monty went on. 'About being expelled from school, and why. Keep nothing back ... except of course...'

Three pairs of eyes were glued to him. 'Except you didn't see hide nor hair of him the night he died. He went off to work that morning and he didn't come home that night. Instil that thought into your minds until you believe it yourselves. The following

137

morning, when there was no sign of him, you did what you'd been planning to do for some time. You ran away from him.'

Dove and Henry nodded, slowly. Monty continued, speaking his thoughts and ideas out loud.

'The police will ask you if you ever thought it odd that your father never caught up with you ... and in fact was never heard of again. What will you say to that?'

The two of them thought for a while then Dove said, quietly, 'I'd say we thought he'd gone back to Ireland.'

Henry nodded vigorously. 'That's what we thought. And we said "good riddance to bad rubbish", didn't we, Dove?'

'That's the ticket,' said Monty. 'Wipe that awful night from your memories. It didn't happen. At some point the police will ask both of you outright if you killed your father. It may well be asked in a kindly manner. They might say they wouldn't blame you if you did kill him, they'd have done the same in your shoes. Don't fall for it. Stick to your story.'

Dove and Henry nodded their understanding as Monty racked his brains to figure out all the possible permutations of what Dove might be asked.

'Now, Scullion says he saw you push your father down the hole.'

'It wasn't her, it was me,' said Henry.

'I know, I know,' said Monty, impatiently. 'Just let me think.' After a few moments he was nodding his agreement to his own thoughts. 'Tell the police exactly what Scullion said to you. But make it clear you hadn't a clue what he was talking about.'

'Right,' Dove said.

Monty looked at her. 'Have I covered everything?'

'What if they ask who *you* are?'

The old man went quiet for a moment, then said, 'Good question, Dove; but with respect they'll think I'm just another itinerant traveller with no fixed abode.'

'You've only got to open your mouth for them to know that's not true,' observed Tom.

'Thank you, Tom, I shall take that as a compliment. But I suspect my voice contradicts my appearance. I've met many an articulate knight-of-the-road on my travels. If I'm asked, I shall say I'm a distant relative who responded to a distress call when your father disappeared. I'm your late mother's favourite uncle, related to her by marriage. The police will have too much else to think about without checking my authenticity. They'll pay as little regard to me as they will to the fact that Henry doesn't attend a formal school.'

'That never bothered anyone when I was a kid,' admitted Dove.

Monty placed a hand on her shoulder. 'It's been my experience over the last two years that the authorities leave the travelling fraternity to organise their own affairs.'

'Scullion said he was getting revenge for what we did at Netherton Fair,' said Dove. 'Should I mention that to the police?'

'It would do no harm at all to tell them what he said to you about the jewels,' Monty said. 'Henry and I will say it came to our knowledge that the Scullions had got stolen jewels in their caravan and that you reported it to the police at the time. They should have a record of it, and of their subsequent action.'

He looked round at them all. 'Any other business before I declare this meeting closed?'

They all shook their heads. The old man rose, slowly, from his chair. 'I think now's the time for us to ring the police.' He took a close look at Tom's face. 'And an ambulance.'

'For Dove more than me,' Tom said.

Chapter 10

Pikey Scullion glared at the two detectives at the other side of the table, a sergeant and an Inspector Sykes. Sitting beside Scullion was a solicitor, who looked less than enthusiastic at having to represent him.

'I'm sayin' nowt until yer get Malachy's body outa that mine shaft in Leeds. That lass shoved him in, I saw her wi' me own eyes. She murdered her own dad – her own flesh 'n' blood – then she accuses me o' rape.'

'Mr Scullion,' said the inspector. 'I just want to go over your story of what happened on the night of the twelfth of December?'

'Christ! How many times do I have ter tell yer? I went to the lass's caravan to ask her why she killed her dad.'

'Nothing to do with a grudge you had against her regarding certain stolen jewels?'

'What stolen jewels?' Pikey knew he was on safe ground here. Beulah had already confirmed that the incident hadn't been reported to the police.

'The stolen jewels in your caravan at Netherton Fair,' said the inspector. 'She reported you to the police and you thought you'd take revenge.'

'If she reported me, then yer'll have a record of it,' said Pikey, slily.

'We're checking on it.'

'When yer find she's been lyin' about that, as well as me rapin' her, will yer let me go?'

'There's always the matter of breaking and entering, robbery, and the serious assault on Mr Webster.'

'He bloody started it.'

'And what did Miss McKenna say about her father's death?' asked the inspector.

'She said something about he was trying ter kill her, which wasn't how I saw it,' muttered Pikey, unhappy now that even if he did get away with raping Dove he'd be done for assault on Tom. 'Malachy were sittin' at the side of t' shaft, shoutin' an' carryin' on. Then she ran up an' pushed him in. That's God's honest truth.'

Inspector Sykes regarded him with acute distaste. 'So, you witnessed a murder, but didn't you see fit to report it at the time. Why was this, Mr Scullion?'

Pikey frowned as he searched for a plausible answer. 'Because I didn't,' he muttered, '... and that's that. It doesn't mean ter say it didn't happen though.'

'So, you didn't report it because ... you didn't. Are you getting all this down, Sergeant?'

The sergeant nodded without lifting up his head.

'And you're sure it was Dove McKenna?'

'I saw her wi' me own eyes.'

'But, weren't you drunk?'

'I'd had a few. But I'll tell yer summat. When I went round ter tackle her about it, yer should've seen the look on her face. She did it all right – an' she knew I knew. That's why she tried ter keep me quiet.'

'And how did she do that?'

'I've already told yer. She said she'd let me have a shag if I kept me mouth shut.'

'Really?'

'Well, I could hardly turn an offer like that down ... have yer seen her?'

'And what was her boyfriend –' the inspector looked at his notes '– Mr Webster, doing during all this?'

'Boyfriend?' Scullion spat on the floor. 'Bloody fairy ... He tried ter get funny wi' me, so I had ter give him a slap.'

'You mean you savagely assaulted him.'

'Ah, call it what yer like. I never raped her though.'

The inspector stared at the man for a long time before shaking his head in disgust. He gave the sergeant a peremptory nod.

'Bernard Scullion,' said the sergeant, getting to his feet.

'Me name's Pikey.'

'I'm arresting you for robbery and assault on Mr Webster. There may be more serious charges to follow. You do not have to say anything, but anything you do say may be taken down and used in evidence against you.'

'I would like it placed on record that my client has reported being witness to a murder,' said the solicitor. 'I assume you'll be following this up.'

'We'll inform the Belle Isle Police,' said Inspector Sykes, with almost no enthusiasm. 'I believe this alleged pit shaft falls within their area. And if they see fit to carry out a search and find nothing we'll add wasting police time to his charge sheet. That should really impress the judge.'

'Why has nowt been seen o' Malachy since that day?' shouted Scullion. 'Answer me that!'

'His children seem to believe he went back to Ireland,' murmured the inspector. 'And with Malachy McKenna's record as a parent, that seems entirely feasible.'

A nurse hovered attentively over Dove's bed as Inspector Sykes cleared his throat.

'I'm pleased to see you looking a bit more, should I say, yourself, Miss McKenna. I'd, er, I'd like to ask you a few more questions. Normally we'd do this down at the station but under the circumstances –' he glanced up at the nurse '– we can do it here. Do you mind if my sergeant takes notes?'

'No,' said Dove. 'Have you checked on the jewels the police found in their caravan at Netherton Fair?'

'We can't find any record of it.'

'But I reported it to two policeman in a car. Henry and Monty were there.'

'Your brother and Mr Catchpole have confirmed your story, but the Netherton police have no record of any such incident.'

'That's strange,' said Dove. 'We definitely reported them – and Pikey knew about it. That's why he attacked me. Revenge for us telling on him and his rotten family.'

The inspector cleared his throat. 'Dove ... Scullion has made a serious allegation about your father. You told us yesterday that you haven't seen him since the day you ran away?'

'That's right.'

'And you think he might have gone to Ireland.'

142

Dove gave a non-committal shrug. The inspector looked at his sergeant, then back at the girl.

'Scullion seems to think he's dead.'

'I know.'

Inspector Sykes gave a frown. 'How do you know?'

'He was saying something about how I'd killed him, and if I wouldn't let him . . . have sex with me, he'd tell the police.'

'Let me get this clear. Scullion broke into your caravan. . .'

'Waggon.'

'Then he accused you of killing your father?'

'Well, he went on about the jewels and us shopping them to the police at first. Then he came out with all this stuff about my dad.'

'And he offered to keep his mouth shut if you had sex with him?'

'Yes.'

'Was he drunk?'

'Yes.'

'And what did you say?'

'I said I didn't know what he was talking about and if he wanted money, he could have all I had.'

'And then what did he do?'

'He punched me . . . and when I came round he was on top of me and I knew he'd . . .' She was in tears now.

'He'd had intercourse with you? I'm sorry to be so blunt, Miss McKenna, but I must hear you say it.'

'He'd had intercourse with me.'

'But you were unconscious during the time it happened?'

'Yes . . . but it definitely happened.'

'I believe the medical examination supports that,' said the inspector, softly. He paused for a long time as he looked at his fingernails. Dove knew the big question was coming.

'Just one last thing, Miss McKenna. Did you kill your father?'

She gave him her most incredulous look.

'I'm very sorry,' he said, 'but I have to ask. You've already told us your father mistreated you. You might have been driven to it by fear. It may well have been a perfectly justifiable action.'

Monty had coached her well. She looked steadily at him. 'I didn't kill my father. I swear on my brother's life and my mother's grave that I didn't kill my fathcr or push him down any stupid hole or anything else that awful man says I did.'

143

Suddenly she felt a surging hatred for Pikey Scullion who had robbed her of everything; of her beautiful moment with Tom, which she'd never get back; of her virginity; of her money; and now he was trying to rob her of her freedom.

'Inspector,' she said. 'If my dad's down that hole then someone pushed him down and it wasn't me. And I'd be interested to know how Pikey Scullion knows he's down there.'

Tom sat on the edge of her bed. 'I've been discharged,' he said. 'How are you?'

'I'm just waiting for a doctor to give me the all clear,' said Dove. She looked up at him and read the question on his mind. What her mother had called the 'curse' was now adding to her discomfort. It was the first time in her life she'd considered it a blessing.

'I'm not pregnant, thank God. It happened at the wrong time.'

'Or the right time,' said Tom, relieved for her.

'There isn't a right time for something like that.'

'I'm sorry. I didn't mean ... you know. So, no damage was done?'

'Nothing serious. Not physically, anyway.'

'Good.' There was a long silence before he said, 'The MO came over from camp to see me. Apparently I'm off the hook as far as being late's concerned.'

'Tom,' Dove asked. 'Did they ask you about Scullion raping me?'

'Yes.'

'And what did you tell them?'

He sat for a long time before replying; his face was racked with remorse. 'I told him how Scullion broke into the waggon and threatened us and beat me up.' He looked her in the eye, then lowered his head and shook it.

'Tom, what's up?' she asked.

'Oh, Dove, I'm sorry. They asked me if I'd actually seen him ... committing the rape. I told them I was unconscious ... I'm an idiot, I just wasn't thinking quickly enough. I should have lied and told them I'd seen the whole thing.'

'Its okay, Tom. I wasn't expecting you to lie.'

'No, but it would have helped you if I had.'

'How do you mean?'

144

He lowered his voice as a nurse clattered over the polished ward floor. 'After the police left,' he said, 'Monty came in to see me. Somehow he'd overheard them talking about Scullion's version of what had happened.'

'Scullion's version? What's he been saying?'

Tom reddened. 'Look, Dove, I'm only repeating what Monty heard. I know it's not true.'

'Tom, just tell me.'

'Scullion's saying you offered him sex in exchange for him keeping his mouth shut about you killing your dad.'

'Oh, I see.'

'You wouldn't do a thing like that ... would you?'

Dove detected doubt in his question. 'No, Tom,' she said, firmly. 'I wouldn't.'

'Of course you wouldn't,' he said. 'I know you wouldn't ... why did I ask you? Oh hell! I'm getting all this wrong, aren't I?'

She said nothing.

'Dove,' Tom said. 'I don't feel very good about this. I feel as though I'm ... as though I'm not worthy of you. I've been no help whatsoever ... God knows what you must think of me.'

'Don't be silly, Tom.'

Although, somewhere deep inside her, she knew her feelings for him had changed. In fact, her whole outlook on life seemed to be changing by the minute.

'I've cancelled the next two engagments,' announced Monty as he came through the door the following afternoon. 'The brewery were very understanding.'

'Thanks, Monty.' Dove was sitting on a floor cushion, trying to read a book.

He tapped the side of his head, sat down on a chair and gave her a fatherly smile. 'I have no way of knowing how long such a wound will take to heal,' he said. 'If you need more time, you only have to say. Oh, by the way, Tom left a telephone message to say he's leaving for Gibraltar sooner than expected. He'd like to see you before he gets posted.'

'Right,' she said, non-committally, returning her attention to the book. 'I'll have to see.'

Monty looked at her, but decided not to pursue it. It would be a shame for her to heap further hurt and humiliation on Tom by not seeing him before he left. But that was Dove's decision. She knew what she knew.

But Dove didn't know. Losing her virginity in such a way had created much confusion within her. Such a violation had stripped her of her dignity and her pride. It would be hard to give herself fully to a man, the way she'd been about to with Tom. Heart and soul, mind and body.

'I spoke to Inspector Sykes, as well,' Monty said. 'To ask if any progress had been made with looking for your father.'

'And?'

'The Leeds police are looking for him right now.'

'Doubt if they'll find him. Dad said the bottom of that hole would be flooded. He could be miles away.'

Monty nodded. 'Better if he's not found,' he said. 'Best thing all round.'

'I sometimes wish he'd had a proper burial, though,' Dove said, closing the book. 'Even he deserved a proper funeral.'

Monty thought about Elisabeth and how he'd missed her funeral. 'Funerals are for the benefit of the living,' he mused. 'The dead have already taken their leave.'

'So, when your time comes, you don't want a funeral?'

He smiled and shook his head. 'I'd prefer not to be left around to rot. Just stick me under a pile of stones. Let my memorial be your memory of me ... and when you have children, tell them about me.'

They had parked the waggon in a frosty field just north of Leeds. Henry came hurtling in.

'There's a copper on a bike. I think he's coming here.'

The three of them were sitting, expectantly, when a police helmet bobbed into view over the top of the stable door. Beneath the helmet was a young face, out of breath after an arduous cycle ride. And serious.

'Dovina McKenna?' he called out.

'Yes.'

He introduced himself. 'PC Goodacre. They told me I'd find you here. How are you feeling?'

'I'm okay, thank you. Come inside if you like.'

'Oh, right, thanks very much.'

He mounted the steps, pushed open the bottom door and stepped inside. He saw Dove looking at his feet and followed her

146

gaze. One trouser bottom was folded into a bicycle clip and the other tucked into his sock. 'Lost one of me clips,' he said, to the top of her head.

She looked up and returned his smile with interest. The constable was taken aback by her sudden beauty.

'Right,' he cleared his throat. 'Well, there's been some developments regarding the search for your father.'

'Developments?' said Dove. 'What sort of developments?'

'A body's been found.'

'You mean my father's body?'

'Well, there's no way of identifying it at the moment.'

Monty butted in. 'Surely, Constable, you don't want the girl to identify a three-year-old body?'

'Oh no, sir. Apparently there's not much left of it. We just wondered if you could be of any help. Would anyone have any dental records or anything?'

There was a long pause as Dove and Henry tried to work out the implications of this.

'I think he had a tooth out a few months before he died,' volunteered the boy after a while. 'D'you remember, Dove? He was a right big baby about it.'

'That's right, we had to go with him.'

'So,' said the policeman, relieved at how easy it all had been. 'You can tell us who this dentist is, can you?'

Apparently Malachy's body had come to a halt 200 feet down on a bicycle frame, which, in turn had become wedged in a narrow part of the shaft. An explorative search with a winch and a hook had brought his remains up first time, without the need for anyone having to go down. Dental records confirmed it was him.

'His skull was fractured,' the young policeman told Dove and Henry. 'He probably died as he fell. Knocked his head against the side.'

'So, he didn't suffer?'

'No, not at all ... by the way, we recovered the money Scullion stole from you. You can collect it from the station whenever you like.'

'Thank you,' Dove said. 'It'll pay for dad's funeral.'

There was a frost in the air which decorated the trees and lent the burial a sort of bleak beauty.

147

As the priest blessed the descending coffin, Dove looked around. It was a thinly populated send-off: just her, Henry, Monty and the undertakers' men. PC Goodacre was standing a short distance away, with his bicycle leaning against a miniature memorial.

Dove had dutifully placed a notice in the *Yorkshire Post* on the off chance it might prise out a few of his friends and relatives. None came. Malachy's parents were dead and his only brother, Francis, lived in America. Bad blood existed between them. It could be many years before Francis McKenna knew his brother was dead.

Neither Dove nor Henry knew exactly how old their father was when he died, so the coffin bore a simple brass plate engraved with his name, Malachy Joseph McKenna.

As he sank beneath the ground she tried to summon up a loving recollection of him which might encourage a mournful tear, but the memory of that awful night had obliterated any good times she might otherwise have dredged up. She bowed her head and glanced sideways at Henry, who was picking his nose. Dove nudged him with her elbow as he flicked his pickings into the grave.

'That was very disrespectful.'

'I was just remembering how he tried to kill you,' muttered Henry. 'That was disrespectful as well.'

'Two wrongs don't make a right.'

The priest ended his Latin dirge and frowned at the bickering pair before moving away, followed by the undertaker's men. The young policeman approached, his helmet respectfully tucked under his arm.

'Nice of you to come,' Dove said. Her eyes flickered downwards. He obviously hadn't found the missing cycle clip.

'I had to,' he smiled, guiltily. 'Sergeant's orders.'

'Oh.'

'Scullion's been charged with your father's murder,' he told her. 'He was seen in a pub the night before you ran away, fighting with your dad. They were threatening to kill each other.'

'I'm glad,' said Dove.

'Will he get hung?' asked Henry. His face had gone white.

The policeman nodded. 'I expect so, if he's found guilty – which I reckon he will. Whether he gets it commuted to life imprisonment's another matter.'

148

Monty gripped Henry's shoulder, tightly. 'They have to prove it was intentional,' he said. 'That might be tricky.'

'They didn't find it too tricky with Ruth Ellis,' commented the policeman. 'Bad do, that. If you ask me, Scullion's a lot worse than her. My guess is, he'll swing.'

Henry turned and ran away; twisting in and out of the gravestones. Dove set off after him. The policeman gave Monty an apologetic glance.

'Maybe I should have kept my big mouth shut.'

'Maybe you should, Constable.'

'The Belle Isle Police will need a statement from them two,' he said. 'The murder was committed on their patch.'

'The children can't tell them anything they haven't told you,' Monty pointed out.

'Belle Isle will still need to take their own statement ... and them two will probably need to give evidence in court.' He inclined his head towards where Dove and Henry had gone.

'Oh damn damn dear!' cursed Monty. 'As if they haven't been through enough recently.'

Dove caught her brother up at the gate. He was out of breath, sitting on a low wall, coughing out clouds of frosty breath, like a bronchial smoker. The boy looked up at her, with worried eyes.

'What am I going to do, Dove? It was me who killed dad, not Pikey Scullion.'

'Henry, Scullion's an animal, he deserves to die.'

'But he knows we did it.'

'He thinks *I* did it,' Dove corrected him.

'Will we have to go to court?'

'I imagine so.'

'Dove, we'll have to tell more lies. Only these lies are more terrible than the lies we told before. These lies could get him hanged ... or us.'

Dove sat beside her brother and put her arm around him. 'I don't know what to tell you, Henry. As you say, it's him or us ... and you know what he did to me.'

'But they wouldn't hang him just for what he did to you.'

'How do you mean, *just*? What happened to me was awful.'

'I know, Dove, I'm sorry.'

'In some countries they'd hang him,' she said. 'They would have in this country in the olden days. He's a bad man.'

149

She could have added, 'He destroyed my life', because that's how she felt. Maybe if they hanged him it would satisfy this violent and burgeoning hatred she felt for the man. Maybe she'd begin to feel like a normal person again.

Or maybe not.

'Will we definitely have to go to court, Monty?' Dove asked, later that day.

The paraffin stove had melted the film of frost on the inside of the waggon windows and replaced it with condensation. Monty rubbed one of the panes clear with his hand. Boris was outside, happily enshrouded in a new woollen blanket embossed with his name, his head busy inside a feedbag. The horse was a valued member of this small, but special, family; as was Prince, asleep in the corner. A family which mustn't come to any harm, not if Monty had anything to do with it.

He thought for a while. 'Well ... in view of Scullion's insistence that it was you who killed your father, I imagine the prosecution will want you to give evidence. Their barrister will try and crack you in court, I'm afraid.'

'Crack us?' said Henry. 'Oh heck! I don't like the sound of that, Dove.'

'They'll ask you all sorts of questions to try and break your story,' said Monty. 'You must engrave upon your mind the story you told the police. You must believe it to be true. Convince yourself. Remember, it's not your doing that Scullion got himself into this mess. You didn't point the finger at him. He did that himself out of sheer malice, and now he's due to pay a terrible price.'

'I don't know,' muttered Henry. 'It doesn't feel right to me.'

'It never will feel right, Henry,' Monty said. 'It's the way things must be.'

'I'll feel as if I've killed him *and* my dad.'

'The cause of their deaths,' said Monty, 'will have been their own cruelty and evil. Remember that, Henry. The only way to salve your conscience would be for you to sacrifice yours and Dove's freedom for his.'

'How do you mean?' asked Henry.

'I mean,' explained Monty. 'That if you confess to your father's death, they'll know that both you and Dove have been lying. For your sister to be branded as a liar plays right into their hands.'

'Oh.'

'In a nutshell,' continued the old man, 'he'll doubtless get off the rape charge as well. He'll walk free and both of you will be facing very serious charges.'

'Henry,' said Dove. 'It's up to you. I understand how you must feel, having an innocent man's life in your hands.'

'Not so innocent,' said Monty. 'But it's a quandary, I'll grant you.'

'What would you do, Monty?' she asked.

The old man said, without hesitation, 'Given a choice between you and him, I'd let the vermin hang. Do the job myself if necessary.' He regarded Henry, fondly. 'Young man, a minute of your life is of more value to this world than fifty years of his.'

'What if the choice was *you* or him?' asked Dove.

'Rather than let him get away scot-free, I'd still let him hang. We don't live in a perfect world, Dove. Choices have to be made. Politicians do it all the time. I had a friend in the First World War who was shot for cowardice. The poor chap had just had enough. Got the shakes, went a bit potty, turned tail and ran. He was worth ten of Scullion. No, I wouldn't sacrifice the remnants of my life for the likes of him.'

They both looked at Henry, who appeared to have the worries of the world on his shoulders. He gave his sister a troubled smile.

'I'll not let you get into trouble, Dove,' he said. 'I'll be all right.'

Henry dreamed of Pikey Scullion most nights. The man was a monster, walking along a dark, echoing corridor, with heavy-booted steps; a black mask was covering his face and his hands were tied behind his back. Around the monster's neck was looped a hangman's noose, and through the mask his evil eyes glowed like hot coals. And now his hands were free and around Henry's neck, squeezing the life out of him. A trapdoor beneath their feet slammed open and Dove was down there, with Scullion clinging to her, cursing him and swearing vengeance. Now it wasn't Scullion at all but his father, wild eyes blazing at him as he disappeared down the hole, which was a hundred miles deep and full of blackness and horror. Henry would wake up, crying and sweating. Monty would be there and very soon Dove as well, but for all their best efforts their words of comfort wouldn't chase the nightmare

151

away. What was needed was a plan, and one thing Henry was good at was making plans. Everyone said this.

He would go to the police and tell them it was he who pushed his dad down the hole, not Dove. She wasn't even there. In fact she still didn't know anything about it. He'd say they'd run away because they'd planned it for ages – just as they'd told the police. He hadn't told anyone about pushing his dad down the hole, no one – especially not Dove – because she would want him to do the right thing and own up and he didn't want to get locked up. She was like that was Dove – very honest. He'd done it because his dad was cruel and he couldn't stand it any more. He'd had enough. He'd just gone potty.

This was Henry's master plan. To keep Dove right out of it so it didn't implicate her or make her a liar – so Scullion wouldn't get away with what he'd done to her. He knew he'd get into trouble, a lot of trouble. But it would end his guilt and his nightmares. There was nothing worse than the nightmares.

Inside the police station Inspector Sykes put down the telephone and muttered a curse under his breath. 'Hell and bloody damnation!' He stamped to the door of his office and called for his sergeant.

'I've just heard from Belle Isle, Sergeant. Two more witnesses have turned up in the Scullion case; apparently a man and a woman saw Scullion and McKenna in the pub car park that night, best of friends – which cancels out the violent argument witness.'

'So . . . what's happening, sir?'

'The Department of Public bloody Prosecutions is dropping the murder charge, that's what's bloody happening,' the inspector sighed. 'Insufficient bloody evidence. It was always a bit tenuous.'

'I bet Scullion's chuffed,' commented the sergeant. 'What about the rape charge?'

'We're not proceeding with that either. Scullion's lawyers have already got the girl marked down as a liar with that accusation about the jewels. They've also come up with some evidence that she was kicked out of school for beating another pupil up, which doesn't help her reputation as an innocent young girl. The only witness to the rape was unconscious, as was the girl.'

'What do you think, sir?' enquired the sergeant.

152

'Me? I think Scullion's as guilty as hell ... of the murder and the rape. But my opinion counts for sod all.'

'What's left?' enquired the sergeant.

'GBH, breaking and entering, and robbery,' said the inspector. 'In the meantime I'd like to check on this stolen jewellery business. It seems an odd story for the three of them to just make up like that.'

There was a knock on the door. A constable poked his head round. 'There's a young lad at the desk, sir. Insists on speaking to you.'

'Young lad? Does he have a name, Constable?'

'Henry McKenna, sir.'

'Right,' the inspector said, slowly. 'I wonder what our Henry wants?'

The boy sat opposite him in a shrunken slump. His heart was fluttering and his worried eyes scanned the blank walls. Would he be allowed out of this place once he'd told them his terrible secret? Probably not. Inspector Sykes smiled at him – a warm, genuine smile. A smile Henry would have liked to have seen on his father's face, just once. A man with a nice smile like that was hardly going to lock up a boy for pushing his cruel father down a hole. Henry smiled back, knowing deep down the policeman wouldn't be smiling in a few minutes, once he had confessed to being a murderer. No one smiled at murderers.

'Good morning, Henry. Tell me, how's your sister bearing up?'

'She's okay, sir.'

He'd heard Inspector Sykes's subordinates call him 'sir ' and therefore it was only right and proper that Henry should do the same.

'So, what can I do for you, Henry?'

'I've got something to tell you, sir.'

'Now there's an unfortunate coincidence, Henry, because I've got something to tell you.'

'It's about Pikey Scullion killing my dad, sir.'

'Really.' The inspector leaned his elbows on the table and laced his fingers as though in prayer, deep in thought, his thumbs resting against his mouth. He looked at the boy, and with faraway eyes, said, 'Henry. Please tell me you've brought me evidence that will convict Mr Scullion.'

'No, sir, I ha –'

'In that case, Henry, it's all a bit of a bugger.'

'What is, sir?'

'Life, Henry. Life can be a right bugger at times.'

'Sir, I've come to tell that I –'

'You see, Henry, the murder charges against Scullion are being dropped.'

'What?'

'Dropped. Sorry, lad, what were you saying?'

'I er, I was wondering what you were talking about, sir.'

'Ah! People are often wondering that. I was saying that we're dropping the murder charge,' said the inspector, gloomily. 'I thought I'd tell you before you went rambling on. You see, unless you have conclusive evidence, we haven't enough to convict him … even though he's still the odds-on favourite.'

'Oh,' said Henry. 'I see.'

The crushing burden bearing down on his heart was evaporating by the second, floating away like an escaping balloon and leaving in its wake a vacuous smile on the boy's face. The inspector looked at him through narrowed eyes.

'Henry, lad. What are you smiling at? This is bad news.'

Henry thought quickly. 'I'm smiling because I was worried about giving evidence. Now I don't have to … sorry.'

'So, that's why you came, eh? Well, there's no need to be sorry. Giving evidence isn't my favourite occupation … and it's part of my job.'

His sergeant entered and beckoned the inspector to come outside. Henry sat there, tapping his feet on the floor in time to the tune going on inside his head, "Blue Suede Shoes".

The inspector returned. 'Scullion's signed a confession admitting to the offences of breaking and entering, robbery and assaulting Tom Webster,' he said.

'So they're not doing him for what he did to our Dove?'

'I'm afraid not, Henry. But he'll still be locked away for quite some time. It'll also save your sister a very harrowing experience in court.'

It occurred to Henry that his and Dove's lives could have taken a tricky turn for the worse had he got his confession in first. He gave the policeman a crumpled grin and exhaled a long breath. 'I think our Dove will be pleased,' he said.

Inspector Sykes smiled. 'I'll be sending someone round to tell her officially.'

Henry's face dropped. 'I'd prefer it if no one mentioned that I've been here. She'll think I'm ever so silly being frightened of giving evidence.'

'You have my sympathy, Henry. I've got an older sister myself. They can be a pain in the backside.'

He got to his feet and held out a hand for the boy to shake. 'If our paths cross again, Henry,' he said. 'I hope it's in happier circumstances.'

Henry shook the man's hand and left the police station. He couldn't get out fast enough.

The cycling policeman had been and gone by the time Henry got back. Dove was standing at the door and came out to meet her brother.

'We've just heard a bit of news,' she said. 'That policeman's just been.'

'What sort of news?' Henry suspected what the news was, but he didn't say.

'You'll be happy to know they've dropped the murder charge against Scullion ... so you won't be responsible for an innocent man being hanged ... and guess what?' she added.

'What?' he asked, innocently.

'They've dropped the rape charge as well.'

'Oh heck!'

Henry put his arms around her. She held on to him and sobbed into his shoulder. He felt a fraud not telling her he knew all this already. Eventually she moved away and dried her eyes.

'It's okay, Henry,' she said. 'It's not the end of the world.'

'What about the other charges?' he asked. Once again he knew the answer.

'He's confessed to breaking in and assaulting Tom.'

'That's something. At least you won't have to go to court now.'

'I know,' she said. 'I didn't fancy going to court. According to Monty, Pikey's barrister could say all sorts of rotten things about me and get away with it. He might even have said something about dad.'

'I think you're well of out of all that, Dove.'

She nodded. 'With his record the police reckon he'll get about three years for the other offences. On balance, I think I'm okay about it all.'

Monty appeared over her shoulder. 'We can all get on with our lives now.'

'We can, can't we,' said Henry, climbing up the steps.

Dove took his arm. 'Monty and I have just been talking about how different things would have turned out if you'd gone to the police and confessed. Doesn't bear thinking about, does it?'

'No,' he said. 'It doesn't, does it?'

'Where've you been, by the way?' she asked. 'You've been gone all morning.'

He shrugged. 'Just out ... you know, walking and stuff.'

Chapter 11

A gloomy Christmas came and went and when Tom hadn't heard from Dove he sent her a goodbye letter via Monty's contact in Leeds. She waited until she was alone before she read it as she'd no idea of what her reaction would be on hearing from him again, so unsure was she of her feelings for anybody or anything. Some days it was as though nothing had happened to her and on other days she felt almost suicidal. And the worst thing was that she had no one to confide in – no one who could translate her thoughts and fears into something that made sense. Monty tried his best but he was an old man – a dear old man, but old nevertheless; and Henry – well, he was just Henry.

Dove closed the waggon doors and shut the windows to keep out any outside influence; then she took unnecessary care to open the envelope, not wanting to tear the letter inside:

Dear Dove,
I would really have liked to have heard from you one last
time, but I think I understand. I blame myself for
coming back into your life. Can't tell you how sad and
sorry I am.
Isn't it all a pig?
I hope you have a really nice life.
Lots of love,
Tom

She read it over and over again and felt anger and unease that she couldn't summon up a single tear of sadness at his leaving her; or any guilt for the unspoken blame she'd heaped upon him. What was wrong with her? She knew, deep inside, that the tears were there; frozen by Scullion's violation of her. He'd violated her body, her dignity and her emotions.

She hadn't told Tom of her true feelings because she didn't know how to put them into words. He'd left without being told to leave; because he felt his being near her hurt her too much. He left her because he loved her and couldn't bear the revulsion he seemed to cause when he touched her. It all seemed so irrational. Every time the thought came into her mind she physically shook her head to rid it of such nonsense; but it kept coming back, that same stupid thought. And it was here again as Tom's words stared up at her from the page.

It was all Tom's fault.

No, not his *fault*. Of course it wasn't his *fault*. But he was the cause of it. Take Tom out of the equation and how much different would her life have been?

Alice would still be alive because she wouldn't have been late for school; she wouldn't have lied at Mass register so she wouldn't have been expelled and her dad wouldn't have got angry; and ... Stop it, Dove! ... And if Tom hadn't turned up that night she would have stayed in the pub not in the waggon and Pikey Scullion wouldn't have ... Oh for God's sake!

She was crying now. Not for Tom, for herself. Maybe for her sanity. The whole world didn't make sense any more. She hadn't worked since that night – the very thought of facing an audience made her feel physically sick. Monty had cancelled her gigs indefinitely until she was well enough to go back on stage. How long that would be was anyone's guess. Pull yourself together, Dove McKenna! You're still alive, thanks to your brother; maybe even thanks to Tom. Who knows what would have happened to her if Tom hadn't been with her that night? Would Scullion have been so keen to make his getaway? So, why did she blame Tom? Was it because Pikey Scullion, the real villain, was locked up for attacking Tom and not her? Was that it? Was it because the law was saying that her being raped didn't matter, that it wasn't a crime – but Tom being punched a few times was? Was it the injustice of it all that constantly troubled her? She put the letter back in the envelope, looked out of the window and nodded to herself.

Yes, maybe that was it.

*

'I want to start doing gigs again,' Dove said to Monty. It was March 1958.

'Are you sure?'

'It's been three months. I need to get back to normal. Maybe going on stage will get me out of myself.'

'I understand the feeling,' said Monty, enthusiastically. 'The stage is another dimension. You become a different person. Your talent will transport you to a magic world few of us have known.'

'Good grief, Monty! You do go on,' she said. 'I'm doing gigs in pubs – not starring in a West End show.'

He smiled. 'I know. But I never had your singular talent. I was only ever one of many, part of a company. But I knew the magic of the stage and loved every minute of it.'

'I thought Henry should come in with us as well. He used to hate being left in the waggon, doing his lessons.'

Mony nodded his agreement. 'He has a great capacity for learning has young Henry. However, you're the boss. I'm sure my pupil will have no objection. I will notify the brewery.'

Dove had scarcely spoken about her rape since the day Scullion had been locked up for assaulting Tom. 'You might have to bear with me, Monty,' she said. 'It's a nightmare that won't go away in a hurry.'

'I'd like to say I understand, but how can I?' Monty said. 'I know that time has a habit of chasing away the demons.' He thought of Elisabeth's last moments on earth. 'I know it has with me.'

Part Three

Chapter 12

October 1959

The newly released prisoner looked up and down the road in the futile hope that at least his brother Sid might have come to meet him. The grimy grey fortress of Armley jail cast its threatening shadow over him as he headed down Hall Lane towards the centre of Leeds. He'd done just short of two years and it had been hard time. Although he'd never been convicted of rape the word had somehow got into the prison that he was a rapist who got away with it. Fortunately Pikey was a big man and able to look after himself to a certain extent, but there's always someone bigger, especially inside. And there are always more waiting if you knock one down. Jails are full of thieves and thugs and even murderers who claim the moral high ground over sex offenders. Even his mother had disowned him.

Pikey had let the truth slip to Sid during a prison visit and Sid, despite being sworn to secrecy, had passed it on to Beulah who, deep down, already knew the truth. She had no illusions about Pikey. No way would a girl like Dove McKenna give herself up to the likes of him. Her son disgusted her; and Beulah had low standards. As a way of life she accepted thieving, thuggery, blackmail – even murder under extreme circumstances – but she drew the line at rape. Her absence from the prison visitor's room sent a message to Pikey, a loud and clear message. He was now on his own.

The much-awaited euphoria of walking out of the prison gates was short lived. The driver of a passing car glanced curiously at him. Pikey's circumstances couldn't have been plainer if he'd been carrying a sandwich-board saying 'Just Released'. Scarred

163

face, prison pallor, short haircut and cheap suitcase pretty much identified him for what he was. He glowered and swore at the driver, forcing the man to return his attention to the road.

As Pikey listened to the uneven sound of his limping boots clattering along the stone-flagged footpath he weighed up his options and found they were few. He carried his world in this suitcase; he had no proper home to go to, unless you counted a men's hostel; he had no job, no skills and little money. As far as he could work out, he only had one option: thieving.

Pikey made his way to Leeds Market – busy on a Wednesday morning. In the past he'd relieved shoppers of many a purse and traders of many a wallet. He slowly worked his way through the bustling crowds down Butcher's Row, picking up two handbags in the process, each one momentarily deserted by bargain-hunting housewives, loading their shopping bags with choice cuts of meat. He'd observed this in the past. Some dizzy women paid for their shopping, then laid down their handbags while they filled their shopping bags. It was a bad habit, but one that paid well as far as Pikey was concerned. He then made his way into the Market Tavern, or the 'Madhouse' as it was more commonly known.

The handbags contained a total of seven pounds, three and six, a ruby ring and a pension book. Pikey grinned. He'd just made half a week's wage in five minutes. With his skills he wouldn't need that old bag Beulah, or his idiot brother.

The drink served to fester a lust he'd been harbouring since the day the cell door had clanged shut on him. A savage lust when he thought about that night, and what he'd done to her. And he knew he'd do it again; he couldn't help himself. He would lie in his cell, practising the prisoner's popular form of sexual release and fantasising about what he'd do to her. He'd take what he wanted and finish her off. It would be a new beginning for him and an end to her. That's how it was to be.

164

Chapter 13

Tom had elected to walk to the church. They'd become engaged the day he arrived home after completing his National Service, she having talked him out of signing on for eight years. She preferred her man at home, not gadding around the world where she couldn't keep her eye on him. Tom had become articled to a Leeds solicitor and hated every minute of it.

'There's still time to leg it,' said Johnnie, marching in step beside him. 'I lent my car to the bride's brother. It should be parked outside the church and I have spare keys in my pocket.'

'Why should I not want to get married?'

'Because you're still a child.'

'Oh yeah,' grinned Tom. 'I can see the look on everyone's face. I'd be shot on sight.'

'Who by?'

'Her brother, for a start. He'd take it very personally, would her brother . . . tell yer what, though.' Tom removed his top hat. 'I feel a bit of a prat walking to church in this fancy suit. Flat cap and donkey jacket would have done me.'

'It would certainly have been more appropriate,' commented Johnnie.

They marched on in silence, attracting amused stares, which Johnnie acknowledged with toothy grins and sweeping bows.

'I wish you'd pack it in,' said Tom.

'Oh dear, such a long face and this is supposed to be the happiest day of your life.'

The day was sunny with a scattering of yellow leaves on the path. Tom kicked at them with his patent-leather shoes.

'Perhaps you should have persevered,' murmured Johnnie. 'Not be put off at the first sign of trouble.'

'What're you talking about?'

'You know very well what I'm talking about.'

There was a long silence, broken only by the scuffing of shoes through leaves. Dove's silence after the incident had told him how she felt. He'd sent her his address in Gibraltar via Monty's bookseller friend, but had received no letters. So, when he got back he didn't look her up. No point in embarrassing her after all she'd been through.

'Anyway,' he said. 'It's too late now.'

'So, that's why you're going through with it, is it? Because it's too late not to?'

'I never said that.'

'You don't have to,' Johnnie said. 'She's still single, isn't she?'

'No idea,' said Tom.

'Ah,' grinned Johnnie. 'You didn't even have to ask who I'm talking about. Anyway, you can take it from me, she is.'

'How do you know?'

'As your best man, it's my duty to have your best interests at heart. I made it my business to know. The lovely Dove is as free as I am. Never had a man since . . .' He didn't need to continue.

'She could have done with a man then,' said Tom, 'instead of a shirt button. Which is what she had that night.'

'From what I hear, that gorilla would have given King Kong a run for his money. Blaming yourself is plain daft.'

'You weren't there, Johnnie!' said Tom, sharply. 'You didn't see the look on her face.'

'No,' persisted Johnnie. 'But I can see the look on your face right now. And it's not the look of a man who's relishing the prospect of marriage to the lovely Monica Utterthwaite.'

'You've never liked Monica, have you?'

'Well, she's a bit too forceful for my liking. I'm not struck on forceful women.'

'She does like her own way, I'll grant you that,' conceded Tom. He tapped the top of his hat. 'All this was her idea, you know.'

'Tell me something I don't know.'

'My mam and dad have come all the way from New Zealand; they wouldn't be best pleased if I let everyone down.'

'I had a long chat with your parents yesterday. There must have been a blip in the genes for them to have produced an oik like you.'

Tom had long since learned to ignore Johnnie's insults. 'You'd have liked Alice,' he said.

'I would have fallen in love with Alice had she inherited your share of the Webster genes. What do you think Alice would have said to your giving up on her best friend in favour of Miss Utterthwaite?'

Tom stopped and looked at Johnnie as though he'd dealt him a low, lethal blow. Johnnie smiled, ingenuously. The church was a hundred yards away, and getting out of a wedding limousine were Monica's ample mother and diminutive father. Tom pulled a face.

'My future in-laws,' he informed his friend.

'Perhaps even your future,' said Johnnie. 'In twenty years' time I suspect Monica will look not unlike her mother does now ... and you may well have shrunk to the size of your father-in-law. Forceful women feed off their men.'

'Don't talk silly.'

'You know, I suspect it happens at night,' Johnnie went on, warming to the theme. 'Perhaps during coitus – a few ounces at a time. There are many unsolved mysteries within the marital bed.'

'Pack it in, Johnnie ... Mrs Utterthwaite.'

Tom put on his top hat in order to doff it to Monica's mother. She gave him a double-take and said, 'Oh, it's you. I didn't recognise you. Straighten your cravat, Tom. You look as if you'd never worn one before.'

She reached towards his neck, but Tom backed away. 'It's okay, Mrs Utterthwaite. I can manage.'

'Well?' she said, turning from side to side.

'Well what?' asked Tom. He looked at Johnnie, who shrugged his ignorance.

Mr Utterthwaite was standing behind her, puffing out his cheeks and miming something as she asked, 'I want you to tell me the truth, Tom. Does this dress make me look fat?'

It was more of a challenge than a question. Her husband was shaking his head, vigorously. Tom stared at her for a long time, wondering how on earth he'd arrived at this crossroads in his life. Having to tell a flattering lie to a woman who got up his nose; then walking into a church to marry someone who couldn't hold a candle to the girl he truly loved. He glanced upwards at a

167

criss-cross of vapour trails in the sky, and in that enlightened moment, he saw what he was doing. Allowing events to carry him along without protest.

'Well?' asked Mrs Utterthwaite.

He spotted Johnnie's MG, parked by the side of the road, tempting him. Perhaps it was this avenue of escape which gave him the courage to say, 'The dress is fine, Mrs Utterthwaite ... I think it's all the food you eat that makes you look fat.'

Neither Tom nor Johnnie could believe he'd said it. They backed away as the woman's mouth opened and shut, then turned and ran to the car. Her husband's face lit up with delight, then fell sombre as she turned to him. He and his shocked wife watched in dumb amazement as Tom and Johnnie raced away with a screech of tyres, just as the bridal limousine came in sight.

They'd travelled several miles before Tom said, 'What the hell have I done?'

'I think you just cancelled your wedding, my old son.'

Chapter 14

Dove was staring out of the waggon window, her eyes following a single-decker West Yorkshire bus as it pulled up at a stop to take on more passengers for Otley. The leaves on the trees lining Otley Road were beginning to turn yellow amd gold. Soon the ground would be covered, and the mild autumn would be replaced by November fog, followed by December. She hated December as much as she hated Easter. December was the month of rape and Easter the time of murder.

They had rented a pleasant site on one of the many farms within the northern boundary of Leeds; and short of living in a proper house, her life was almost satisfactory. Monty had taught her to drive. He didn't have a licence himself but he was a good teacher and she passed first time. Now they owned a 1948 Morris Eight, which Boris regarded with suspicion when it was parked too close to him.

She had more good days than bad now. Her relapses into morbid depression were few and far between. Monty and Henry had handled these times by simply leaving her to it. Nothing they could do or say would chase away the demons. Only time could do that. Sympathy, understanding and patience was all they could offer. Her mind was on Tom as PC Goodacre arrived on his motorbike.

With great care, the constable heaved his vehicle up on to its stand, took off his crash helmet and approached the waggon. She opened to door to greet him.

'PC Goodacre. How nice to see you.'

'Nice of you to remember my name, Miss McKenna.'

'It's an easy name to remember.' She looked past him at his motorbike. 'You're obviously coming up in the world.'

169

He followed her gaze and gave an embarrassed smile. 'My mother's sewing machine's got a bigger engine than that; but it's better than a pushbike. My sergeant calls it a fart-box ... begging your pardon, Miss.'

'Is this an official visit?'

'Er, no. In fact it's strictly unofficial. I heard you were here and I thought I'd call round.'

'We've been here a few weeks actually,' Dove said. 'It's a handy base now that I've got a car. Had you any particular reason for calling round?'

She had a vague notion he might have some romantic motive and she was looking at him in a new light. He was a few years older than her, plain looking, a bit on the thin side and his hair didn't look as if it would cling on much past thirty but he had an honest face and she hadn't been out with anyone since ... she had trained herself not to think about that night.

'Er, yes actually,' said the policeman.

If he asked, Dove had decided to risk it. After all he was a policeman. She could hardly come to any harm going out with a policeman.

'It's to do with Pikey Scullion,' he said.

A dark cloud descended over Dove. The smile dropped from her face and any frivolous, romantic notions in her head went right out of it, never to return. The name Scullion was enough to push her over the edge, so fragile was her grip on normality. The constable became concerned at the grief he'd apparently caused. She sat down and asked in a low voice, 'What about him?'

The policeman shuffled his feet, uncomfortably, then cleared his throat. 'He, er ... he was released last Wednesday.'

'Oh.' Dove knew he wouldn't be locked up for ever but the sentence seemed to have passed so quickly.

'Time off for good behaviour and all that,' said PC Goodacre.

'Should I be worried?' Her eyes told him she already was.

He shrugged. 'I doubt it. If he commits any sort of offence they'll just sling him back inside to finish his sentence. He's staying at a men's hostel in Beeston – reporting to Holbeck Police Station once a week.

'Not with his mother?'

'No, it has to be a fixed abode. His mother doesn't like to stay in one place too long – can't imagine why.' He grinned at his little

170

joke, then took a step backwards and replaced his helmet. 'Like I said, it's not an official visit. I just thought you were entitled to know.'

'Thank you, Constable. I appreciate that.'

Two hours later, Monty entered the waggon and flopped down in the easy chair. He opened the *Yorkshire Post*.

'Oh dear!' he remarked, 'how sad.' He looked over the top of the paper at Dove. 'Mario Lanza died last Thursday.'

Dove was genuinely upset to hear of the death of the second of her pin-ups in two days. 'Oh heck! Erroll Flynn Wednesday, Mario Thursday,' she said. The two matinée idols were as near as she'd got to a love affair in nearly two years. 'All the good-looking blokes are popping off like flies.'

'Not all of them,' said Monty. 'I'm as fit as a fiddle.'

Dove flashed him a smile and pushed the spectre of Pikey Scullion away. There were more important men in her life. 'Talking of good-looking men, where's Henry?' she asked.

'I left him in Leeds,' Monty said, 'picking up a batch of records. I believe there's a young lady down there he's got his eyes on. I've told him to take a taxi back.'

'Young lady ... Henry?'

'He's not a little boy anymore, Dove. He'll be sixteen soon.'

'How do you think he's doing with his studying? Will he be ready to take his O Levels?'

The old man shook his head and sank behind his newspaper. 'Ah, we had a chat about that this morning and decided to take a moratorium on his studies — in view of the fact that the authorities won't allow him to sit his examinations until he's been properly assessed. I picked this up this morning.'

His mottled hand came out from behind the paper and handed Dove a letter. She read it and placed it back in his waiting hand.

'That's just jargon,' she said. 'I don't understand half of it. What's it mean?'

'It means he'll have to do an approved course leading up to his exams. Which will be awkward, considering our lifestyle.'

His voice came from behind the newspaper, which always irritated Dove. 'And what does Henry think about it all?' she asked.

'He knows he needs qualifications to get a decent job,' Monty

171

replied. 'But I've told him that time is on his side – and he's accepted that.'

'I suppose he's got a full-time job working for us.'

Monty nodded his agreement. 'Road manager and record sales. It's enough to keep him busy. His time will come.'

'I heard Tom's out of the RAF,' Dove said. 'I thought he'd sign on again, but apparently he got engaged to some woman instead.'

Tom had been temporarily pushed out of Dove's thoughts by Pikey. She'd heard Tom was getting married and the thought disturbed her. Not enough for her to go charging over to Leeds and bursting into the church; but it disturbed her, nevertheless. The deep wound inflicted by Scullion had been slow to heal; and the scar would always be there. And now he was back, skulking in the shadows of her mind.

'PC Goodacre called round earlier,' she said, as casually as she could.

'Goodacre?' Monty ran the name over in his mind.

'The one with the cycle clip missing.'

'Ah, that PC Goodacre. What did he want?'

'He came to tell me Scullion was released last Wednesday.'

'Oh dear.' The old man put down his paper and looked up at her. 'And how do you feel about that?'

'Not good.' It was an understatement.

He nodded. 'I think we should all feel not good, with an animal like him loose on the streets.'

'PC Goodacre reckons I should be okay. If Scullion puts a foot wrong they'll put him back inside to finish his sentence.'

'People like Scullion are unpredictable,' Monty warned. 'He belongs to a violent substratum of society which doesn't observe normal rules. We must be on our guard at all times.' He stared into space for a while, as though digesting his thoughts on the matter; then he returned his attention to his newspaper.

Dove switched her own thoughts to something else and found no comfort. 'Tom should be married by now,' she remarked. 'I hope he's happy.'

No comment came from behind the paper. Impatiently, she lifted it from his hands.

'Did you hear me? I said Tom should be married by now.'

Monty looked at his watch. It was just after midday. 'I imagine

172

so,' he said. 'I expect the ceremony will have been in the morning, most are.'

Fear of Scullion and the loss of Tom combined to reduce Dove to tears.

'Oh dear!' Monty got to his feet. 'Oh dear, oh dear.'

He placed an avuncular arm around her and allowed her to weep into his chest. After a minute she drew away and wiped her eyes, smiling at her foolishness.

'I'm being silly,' she said.

He felt like saying she *had been* silly in losing touch with Tom, but there was nothing to be gained from that now. Tom was lost to her.

'I wish I'd written to him. It was really rude of me not to write to him.' Then she argued with herself, something she'd done a lot since that night. 'But if I had, he'd have felt encouraged and I didn't want to give him false hope.'

'You did what you thought was best,' Monty said, lifting up her chin with his forefinger. 'Anyway, as your manager I want to see a smile on this face. Lucrative gig tonight, remember. Joe reckons there'll be a lot of bookers there tonight.' He was referring to Dove's new agent, Joe Weller. 'They're looking for acts for next year's summer seasons. Could be a worthwhile night.'

'I'll be okay,' she forced out a smile. 'I always am.'

'That's the spirit.'

Dove's appearance at the West Yorkshire Trades Club attracted a good audience. During all of Dove's show business activities Monty had kept himself very much in the background, avoiding publicity, especially press photographers. But it couldn't last for ever.

At a recent charity event when he'd been photographed at Dove's table, sitting between her and Frankie Vaughan, who was raising money for Boys' Clubs, someone had told the photographer he was Dove's Uncle Monty, and Elisabeth's cousin saw it in the *Daily Herald*. He tapped Monty on the shoulder just before Dove came on stage.

'Montgomery,' he said. 'Nice ter see yer, lad.'

'Ralph,' exclaimed Monty. 'Where the devil did you spring from?'

'Spring? I haven't sprung from nowhere. I've been looking fer yer nigh on five years now. Where've yer been hidin' yersen?'

Monty became guarded. 'I haven't been hiding anywhere. You mean you've been actively searching for me?'

'Not actively ... keepin' an eye out might be nearer the mark.'

'For what reason?'

Ralph had thinning hair, an irritating voice, and a face that bore a grudge. At fifty-three, he was over twenty years younger then Monty.

'Well, apart from the obvious,' he said, 'I were wonderin' what yer had ter say fer yerself about doin' a runner the day our Betty popped clogs ... as if I didn't know.'

Monty was instantly annoyed at Ralph's callous reference to his wife's death. 'If you can't speak with respect about Elisabeth,' he said, 'I suggest you don't speak at all.'

'Come off it,' sniffed Ralph. 'I reckon yer finished her off when yer heard about the will. That's why I lodged an objection straight away, before yer could ger yer sticky mitts on owt. If t' coppers had any sense they'd have had a few suspicions. It were obvious ter me what yer'd done.'

'Ralph,' said Monty. 'What the devil are you talking about? Elisabeth didn't leave anything in her will. And how dare you suggest I killed my wife!'

'I'm not talkin' about Betty's will, an' you know it. I'm talkin' about what were left to our Betty,' his mouth curled into a sneer. 'Just afore yer did her in.'

Monty suddenly snapped and, completely out of character, pushed Ralph backwards into the crowd, saying, 'Go away, you dreadful little snot! I don't know what the devil you're talking about.'

At that moment Dove walked onto the stage to polite applause. Monty clapped, automatically. When he turned round, Ralph had disappeared.

Tom and Johnnie watched her from the bar. She had become one of the most popular club acts on the circuit; but like all club acts she was only as good as her next performance. Every act died a death now and again and Dove was no exception – she had steeled herself for this particular night. Sitting opposite her cracked dressing-room mirror, she had expelled all extraneous and bad thoughts from her head. The term 'The show must go on' reflected the attitude of all true entertainers. She engaged a higher gear; a gear which set her apart from nonperformers. It wasn't Dove who walked out on the stage, it was Dove's talent.

Johnnie's whistle was unmistakable. Loud and piercing at the end of one her more popular numbers. Dove shaded her eyes and just made out Tom's silhouette. She spoke into the mike.

'Tom? Is that you at the back, Tom Webster?'

Everyone turned and looked. Johnnie reached into the air and pointed a finger down at Tom's head. Dove smiled and beckoned her former boyfriend to come to her.

'Ladies and gentlemen. I'd like to bring on stage my good friend, Tom Webster, who got married this morning. I do hope you've brought your beautiful bride along, Tom.'

The enthusiasm injected into her words came from Dove the entertainer. The real Dove was in a different place, but not far away. Tom found himself being propelled forwards by Johnnie until Dove took his hand and brought him up onto the stage. She covered the mike with her hand and whispered:

'Where is she?'

'Where's who?'

'Your wife.'

'I haven't got a wife.'

Dove had inadvertently uncovered the microphone and the audience were fascinated.

'Tom,' she said. 'I thought you were getting married this morning.'

'Damn!' replied Tom. 'I knew there was something I was supposed to do today.'

'So, you're not married?'

He gave the audience a shrug and an embarrassed grin. 'Not that I know of ... any offers?'

A man shouted, 'Yer can have my wife for the price of a pint.'

The woman sitting next to him slapped the man across the face. The audience clapped and cheered and Dove gave them a broad smile.

'Sorry, there seems to have been a breakdown in communication, folks.'

Dove let Tom retreat back into the audience as she began her next number. The weight bearing down on her had suddenly lifted and it showed in her performance. Monty smiled and was happy for her, then he stroked his beard and wondered what on earth

Ralph had been talking about. His comment about the police not being suspicious came as something of a relief – he'd never been sure of that.

Dove was feeling as good as she had in almost two years when she spotted his face in the audience. It was the leer she noticed. Everyone was smiling, but he was leering. Then he drew a hand across his throat as she stepped sideways into the blinding spotlight. When she stepped back again he had gone, but she knew it couldn't be her imagination, or was it? Surely it couldn't really have been Pikey Scullion?

'Come in. Hello, Tom.'

Dove smiled at Tom's reflection in her dressing-room mirror as he came through the door and stood awkwardly behind her. His hair was longer and he'd filled out physically. It was a face she'd always liked – maybe loved, who knows? She was desperately curious to find out about the wedding that apparently hadn't taken place, but she didn't want to appear too eager to delve into his private life. So she settled for, 'I was surprised to hear you hadn't stayed on in the RAF.'

He gave a shrug. 'I was Shanghaied into Civvy Street.'

'Oh, who by?'

'By my, er, fiancée.'

Dove's heart sank and the black cloud descended, once again, upon her horizon. She'd obviously got hold of the wrong end of the stick. He *was* getting married; she'd just got the date wrong.

'Fiancée . . . so, you're engaged, then?'

He pulled a face and gave a dry laugh. 'I, er, I doubt that very much.'

Her heart lightened again as the black cloud evaporated. She spun round in her seat. 'Tom, I'd heard you were getting married this morning. What happened?'

'I couldn't go through with it, that's what happened.'

'What? You mean you left her standing at the altar?'

'Something like that.'

'Oh dear, poor girl.' Dove felt not a morsel of sorrow for his intended.

'I know,' Tom said. 'I feel bad.'

'So you should.'

176

He sat down on the stool beside her and they looked at each other's faces in the mirror.

'You're looking good, Dove.'

'Thank you.'

'How are you ... really?'

'I'm fine,' she said.

'I'm glad you're fine. I worried about you a lot while I was overseas.'

'I'm sorry about your wedding. I hope you didn't get into too much trouble.'

He winced. 'I haven't been back to face the music yet.'

'Oh dear.'

'It wasn't entirely my fault,' he said. 'You're to blame as well.'

'Me ... why me?' Deep down she had a good idea why, and it pleased her.

'Because when I got to the church,' he said. 'I thought about you and I knew she couldn't hold a candle to you.'

Dove stared at his reflection for a long time; then she took his hand. 'I'm glad you didn't get married, Tom. I have to admit, it bothered me when I heard, but I had no right to interfere with your life.'

'Dove, you interfere with my thoughts every day.'

'Sorry.'

'Hope you're not sorry,' he said. 'I hope you're glad to have been in my thoughts every day, making me miserable.' He looked at her reflection. 'Was I in your thoughts, Dove?'

She lowered her eyes and went silent. 'Yes,' she admitted, at length. 'But Tom, I don't know how I truly feel about you. Scullion damaged me in ways I can't explain. I haven't been out with anyone since that night.'

'I'm not going to force myself on you, Dove. I just want to get back into your life. I'd sooner have you as a pal than Monica as a wife.'

'Ah ... and what are you going to do about Monica?' she asked.

'I'm taking the coward's way out. I'm going to stay with Johnnie for a few days until the heat dies down.'

'Sounds sensible.'

'By the time I surface, Monica should have got over the worst,' he said. 'My mam and dad are over from New Zealand. I feel bad about them.'

177

Dove got to her feet, took his hand in both of hers and kissed it. 'Tell me where they're staying, I'll pop in and explain your side of things,' she said. 'Call in and see me when you get back. We're pitched up on McGill's farm out on the Otley Road.' Then she kissed him again, this time on his lips. Softly and briefly. He was the first man she'd kissed since *that* night.

'Tom,' she said, at length. 'You, er ... you didn't see Pikey Scullion in the audience, did you?'

'What, in here?' he shrugged and shook his head in one movement. 'No,' he said. 'I didn't.'

'Probably just me being silly. I've been a bit paranoid since –'

'You're entitled to be paranoid,' Tom said. 'But I didn't see him. I didn't realise he was out.'

Chapter 15

Dove and Henry were waiting for Monty in Collinson's Café. He burst through the door, then elbowed it shut behind him, momentarily allowing in the noise of the wind and rain, which caused customers to glance in his direction. He looked round to locate his two young friends and his eyes lit up when he saw them waving. As he made his way towards them he continually doffed his saturated trilby to excuse himself as his flapping overcoat brushed against annoyed diners.

'What happened?' asked Dove.

'Did something happen?' said Monty, mischievously. They never knew when he was being serious.

'What happened about the will? You've been ages at that solicitor's.'

'Ah, yes ... the will.'

Two pairs of eyes were fixed on him as he took off his damp coat and hung it over the back of his chair. Then he swept his white hair back over his collar with his hands. Droplets of rain still clung to his bald pate, having leaked through his hat.

'I suppose I really ought to get a new one,' he said, examining it. 'Elisabeth bought it for me, you know. It's a very good hat.'

He took out a handkerchief, rubbed his head dry, then blew his nose, loudly, once again attracting the attention of other customers. Then he sat down.

'Evidently,' he said. 'I'm a property owner. Or at least I would be had there not been an objection lodged against Elisabeth's will. Apparently the whole thing's been in some sort of legal limbo, pending my appearance ... or preferably my demise.'

'I thought Mrs Catchpole hadn't anything to leave you,' said Henry.

179

'And if she had, she'd have let you know, somehow,' added Dove, with a challenge in her voice. 'That's what you said.'

'Ah!' beamed Monty. 'I did indeed, and I'm sure she would have, but you see,' he explained, 'she didn't know herself.'

'You mean she left you a property that she didn't know she had?'

'Exactly. Her will was quite simple. She left everything she had to me. She didn't name things specifically because they didn't amount to much ... rings, a watch, stuff like that. My will to her was exactly the same –'

'Will you be ordering, sir?'

A white-aproned waitress hovered by his shoulder with pencil and order pad poised.

'Oh, yes please.' He beamed at her and squinted at the menu through half-closed eyes.

'You need glasses,' said Dove.

'Nonsense! The Catchpoles are reknowned for their ocular excellence. I'll have a pot of tea and a selection of cakes fit for a celebration.'

'Celebration?' said Dove, after the waitress had gone. 'So, there's cause to celebrate, is there?'

'To be truthful, I'm in a bit of a dilemma about the whole business,' Monty replied. 'You see, what Elisabeth didn't know – what neither of us knew in fact – was that she was a beneficiary of her aunt's will. The old girl died a few days before Elisabeth, and left her a house.'

'Blimey!' said Henry.

'So the house goes to you?' Dove said.

'Apparently ... rum do, eh? Met the old girl a couple of times. Odd old stick. Elisabeth was the apple of her eye. Mind you, she had no time for Ralph. What was it she called him?' He ran his fingers through his beard. 'Rubberneck, that was it. Rubberneck Ralph. Always had his eye on other people's business.'

'Seems he's got his eye on her house,' said Dove.

'Your house,' corrected Henry.

'Yes, and that's my dilemma. I feel a bit guilty about it. I mean, I wasn't really related to the old dear, not by blood, anyway. You see, Elisabeth was her only niece and Ralph her only nephew — so he does have a valid claim. He's arguing that the aunt wouldn't have left it to me had she known Elisabeth wouldn't be around to inherit the place. I suppose he has a point.'

180

'It's no excuse for him to call you a murderer,' Dove said.

'I suppose if I hand it over to him, it'll stop him thinking ill of me. I have no moral right to the place.'

'Would Mrs Catchpole have left it to Ralph if she'd known about it?' asked Henry.

Monty laughed out loud and ruffled Henry's hair. 'Dear Henry,' he said. 'You've hit the nail on the head. This is the question the lawyers would be arguing about ... and I don't know if I'm up to an argument at my age.'

'What sort of a house is it?' asked Dove.

'Oh, it's a very handsome dwelling. Detached bungalow at the end of a quiet road. It has a huge garden – well, more of a field really. Elisabeth used to play there as a child.'

'Sounds very nice,' she said.

Monty screwed up his nose. 'Best forget about it, eh? A legal battle would drain my meagre funds dry within weeks.'

'I see,' said Dove, trying not to appear disappointed. It sounded just the sort of house she'd always dreamed about.

'My home is with you,' said Monty, smiling broadly. 'As long as you'll have me, that is.'

'Pity,' Dove said.

'Yeah,' agreed Henry, who could read his sister's mind on this one. 'It is a pity.'

Chapter 16

The following day, Dove was silently brooding over the loss of a potential home when Monty came in with a broad smile on his face.

'Joe Weller's got you an audition for *The Good Old Days* at the Verts.'

'You mean the telly thing?'

'Yes. Barney Colehan rang him up and asked for a couple of support acts for Jimmy Wheeler and Ronnie Hilton. They're recording it next week. Goes out on New Year's Eve. The auditions are tomorrow afternoon.'

'Crikey!' said Dove. 'There's nothing like plenty of notice. I need a music hall act and somewhere to rehearse for a couple of hours at least.'

'You'll only need one song,' said Monty taking a piece of sheet music out of his coat pocket. 'Grab your coat, I've booked a pianist for a couple of hours down at the Harehills Lane Working Men's Club. We'll call in at Homburg's on the way down and see if they can fit you up with something.'

'What?' said Dove. 'Rent an outfit before I've passed the audition. Isn't that tempting providence?'

'Do you want to impress Barney Colehan or don't you?'

Dove sat in the Leeds City Varieties' Green Room. Over the speaker from the stage came the voice of one of the four women who were all vying for the only available female vocalist spot. The male singers had all been and gone and various speciality acts clattered up and down the narrow stairs to the tiny dressing rooms, or to the single, cramped toilet on the first floor.

'She's good,' commented a female impersonator, cocking an ear to the loudspeaker. He was dressed as Vesta Tilley. 'Mind you, she should be. She's been at it since Adam was a lad.'

'Don't be catty, Wilfred,' said a woman in a Burlington Bertie outfit. 'Ethel's a very nice lady.'

Wilfred winked at Dove, who was wearing a top hat and tails. 'You men,' he lisped. 'You're all the same. You only have one thing on your minds.'

Dove smiled nervously as she heard the stage manager call out her number.

'Break a leg, dear,' smiled Vesta Tilley.

Burlington Bertie said nothing. If Dove's voice matched her looks, none of the other women stood a chance. She comforted herself with the thought that no one could sing as good as that.

Dove's heart fluttered as she climbed the short flight of stairs that led to the wings. She walked to the front of the steeply-raking stage and handed her music to the band leader. From the stage, the small, empty theatre looked friendly – cosy even. She suddenly became aware of the many famous people who had trodden those very boards: Bud Flanagan, Lily Langtry, Houdini and Marie Lloyd. In 1896, a youngster called Charlie Chaplin had played there as one of a troupe known as Eight Lancashire Lads, and had returned a year later to do a solo clog-dancing act. But the variety theatres were now fighting a losing battle against television, and strip shows were what the "Verts" was now famous for. That and *The Good Old Days.*

In 1953 Barney Colehan produced a television programme set in the City Varieties called *The Story Of Music Hall* which depicted the development of the theatre from its Victorian days onwards. The programme was to prove so popular that a short series was devised and the Edwardian ingredient was developed with remarkable success. An audience of invited guests got dressed up in period costumes and by 1959 the waiting list for tickets exceeded 20,000. Thus *The Good Old Days* was born.

Sitting on the second row were three men and a woman. One of the men was easily distinguished by his grey hair and flowing moustache. He smiled up at her to put her at her ease.

'Dove McKenna, isn't it?' called out Barney Colehan.

Dove smiled back. 'Yes, Mr Colehan.'

'In your own time, Dove,' he said.

183

As the band struck up with "Champagne Charlie", Dove's nerves turned into energy and she launched into the song which she'd rehearsed for two solid hours the previous afternoon. The impresario instantly knew that all the other women were wasting their time. This girl sounded good and would look spectacular on television.

Henry was waiting for her in the Circle Bar. 'How did you go on?' he asked.

Dove couldn't keep the smile off her face. 'I'm in,' she said. 'I'm going to be on the telly.'

'Well done, our lass. You can pay for my orange juice now.'

'Where's Monty?' enquired Dove, looking round.

'He's not feeling so good. As soon as he'd heard you, he went home. Told me you were a forgone conclusion.'

'I hope he's okay.'

'He looked a bit off colour,' Henry said. 'He reckons it was something he ate.'

'I'm going back to see how he is,' she decided. 'Are you coming?' She detected a faint blush, unusual in Henry.

'I'm meeting someone at the Mecca,' he said. 'They have a lunchtime bopping session for a shilling.'

'Who are you meeting?'

'Just a friend.'

'Is it the girl from the recording studio?' she insisted, in the way that sisters do when trying to elicit information about brothers' love lives.

'Who, Mavis Feather?'

'If that's her name,' said Dove.

'No.'

He said it as though he wished it was Mavis Feather he was meeting.

Dove left the City Varieties by the narrow Headrow entrance and turned left to walk towards Cookridge Street where she'd parked the car. Her feelings were mixed. Elation at the success of her audition was diffused by a tinge of worry about Monty. Of course at his age he was entitled to be ill now and again, but it didn't stop her worrying. Apart from Henry, he was the closest person to her. Tom was in there somewhere, but Dove's emotions were far too confused for her to know exactly where.

As she crossed Albion Street a large man bumped into her from behind, almost knocking her down. The man had a peculiar limp and offered no apology. He turned round and moved towards her until she could smell his foul breath. Then Pikey Scullion spat in her face. Dove was frozen with horror and disgust as he limped off, sniggering, and turned into the Guildford pub. She turned and ran the other way lest he was lurking in the doorway, waiting to spring out on her as she passed. All she wanted was to be with someone she could trust.

She was still crying when Henry spotted her from the dance floor. Within seconds he was at her side, his arm around her as he led her out of the Mecca into County Arcade and over to the window of Barker's music shop, from where Dove bought most of her sheet music. For a full five minutes Henry hugged her and watched her weeping reflection in the window as she leaned her head on his shoulder. Henry's date came to the Mecca doorway, got the wrong idea, and went back inside in a huff.

'What is it, Dove?' he asked, as her sobbing subsided.

It took her a while to get the words out. 'Pikey Scullion. He just spat at me. Oh, Henry, I was so scared.'

'I'm telling the police,' said Henry. 'We'll call down at Millgarth copshop, then I'll get you home.'

Chapter 17

Tom's lip was swollen when he tapped on the waggon door the following afternoon. Monty had one hand inside a sock he was darning when he went to open it.

'Hello, Tom. Oh dear, what happened to your lip?'

'I faced the music with Monica this morning. Just wanted to get it over with so I could get on with my life ... Hiya, Henry.'

Henry, who was absorbed in a drawing he was copying from a magazine, looked up and said, 'Hiya, Tom.'

'And Monica took it badly?' guessed Monty.

'Actually, she took it okay. Well, she told me she'd had a lucky escape and she was glad I did it.'

'Pride,' said Monty. 'You dented her pride.'

Tom nodded. 'Her mother took it badly though ... she caught me off guard. Gave me a right clout.' He fingered his lip tenderly. 'Then Monica got a bit tearful but at least she wasn't violent. She insisted on keeping the engagement ring and I'm being made to pay for the cancelled reception.'

'Quite right too, you should have to pay for your mistakes,' Monty said. 'Still, it's taught you a lesson. You won't be in so much of a hurry to get engaged next time.'

'You're not wrong,' agreed Tom. 'There's a lot of truth in that ... Monty,' he said. 'What are you doing with a sock on your hand?'

'I'm darning it.' Monty removed the wooden darning mushroom, as if to prove his story. 'A skill I acquired whilst I was on the road.'

'Oh. Is Dove around?'

'You mean our TV star.'

'What?'

'She's doing *The Good Old Days* on Monday.'

'Wow! Do you think she'll still talk to me?'

'This is Dove we're talking about,' said Monty. 'She'll never be a prima donna won't our Dove.'

Both Tom and Henry noticed the proprietorial way he referred to *our* Dove, whom he now regarded as his own daughter – or *granddaughter* if he cared to admit it to himself.

'Where is she now?' Tom asked.

'She's gone into Leeds, shopping for clothes. Henry and I insisted she go out and spoil herself. She'll probably come back with a pair of jeans for herself and something for us two. I hope I get socks. Why don't you come in? Henry and I are plotting strategy against a former in-law of mine.'

'I've thought long and hard about this,' said Monty. 'And I've come to the conclusion that the man is mentally unstable. I told him I might consider handing the house over if he would apologise for certain slanderous outburts about me murdering my dear wife.'

'And what did he say?' asked Tom.

'He said he didn't need my charity. The Lord gave and the Lord taketh away – or words to that effect. The way I see it, is that if I hand over the house, in his twisted eyes it's tantamount to an admission of guilt. My trying to buy the Lord's forgiveness, as it were.'

The three of them were sitting inside the waggon, drinking beer out of bottles.

'If Dove comes back,' Monty had warned Henry. 'Stick that bottle out of sight. I don't want her accusing me of leading you into bad habits.'

'How on earth can Ralph accuse you of killing your own wife?' said Tom.

Monty felt a sudden twinge of guilt, which he quickly dismissed from his conscience. 'Because he's a strange cove, that's why, and he's recently found God. I bet God's none too pleased.'

'What does he do for a living?' asked Tom, who hadn't got a satisfactory answer to his original question, but decided not to pursue it.

'Ah,' said Monty. 'Ralph is one of life's failures. He's failed at many things: solicitor's clerk; insurance salesman; bus driver; bus conductor. Right now he drives one of those things that empty street gulleys ... you know, there's a big tank thing on the back and they stick a pipe thing down the gulley and it sucks all the horrible stuff out.'

'We used to call them sludge gulpers,' said Tom. 'You don't get a lot of bible-thumpers driving sludge gulpers.'

'I shouldn't have thought so,' agreed Monty. 'According to my sources of information, namely one of Elisabeth's more distant and agreeable cousins, Ralph has become a victim of one of those travelling evangelists. American chap with a bow tie and very white teeth. He sold God to Ralph for five shillings a week.'

'Me and Dove used to give a tanner,' said Henry. 'Threepence each in the collection.'

'Me and Alice as well,' said Tom. 'Cut-price religion. If you got to be an altar boy you could get your money back by drinking three penn'orth of communion wine.' He grinned at the memory. 'Then our Alice found out and told me I was drinking the blood of Christ – which was enough to put me off.'

'I heard about your sister,' said Monty. 'She was apparently Dove's only true friend.'

'She was that all right,' agreed Tom. 'I used to think Dove could count on me as a true friend until Scullion proved me wrong.'

Monty and Henry looked at each other, and mutually decided not to offer any useless words of comfort.

'Ironically,' said Monty. 'I understand that Ralph's wife, who is several years his junior, has acquired a gentleman friend.'

'Really?' said Tom.

'Yes, I believe abstinence is part of Ralph's new religion.'

'And does Ralph know about the boyfriend?' asked Tom, who had an idea forming in his mind.

'Apparently not. Too wrapped up in his pious little world to notice.'

'What would he do if he found out?' asked Tom.

'Bearing in mind what a dreadful little shit he is – I do beg your pardon, Henry – I imagine he'll pray for her salvation and kick her out on her ear.'

'Which would give him something to think about,' said Tom.

188

'So, why don't we hurry things along and tell him what she's up to?'

'Why don't we, indeed?' mused Monty. 'But wouldn't she simply deny it? Women like her can run rings around simpletons like Ralph.'

'Where does she go, to ... you know?' Tom asked.

'Apparently she entertains her gentleman friend at home whilst Ralph's at work.'

'So, all we have to do is find out when this bloke does his visiting and somehow get Ralph to go home.'

'Well, Tom, when you put it like that, it doesn't *sound* too difficult,' agreed Monty.

Dove arrived home loaded down with carrier bags. Tom greeted her at the door. Her smile of greeting froze when she noticed his swollen mouth.

'Monica?' she guessed.

'Her mother.'

'Ouch! I understand she's a big woman.'

'She's a big, violent woman when crossed.'

'At least it's all over and done with,' Dove said. 'Better than looking over your shoulder for a wronged fiancée. Here, take this bag, it weighs a ton.'

'Thought you'd have your own personal slave now you're about to be famous,' he grinned.

'You heard then.'

'I think it's brilliant. No one deserves it more than you.'

'Thanks.'

'I thought we might go for a walk,' said Tom, taking the bag from her. 'It's a nice afternoon.'

'Okay,' she said, brightly, walking past Tom into the waggon. 'The big bag's for me,' she told Henry. 'The other two are for you and Monty. If you don't like what I've bought, it's because neither of you have any taste in clothes.' She turned and looked at Tom, who posed and did a half turn, awaiting appraisal of his attire. 'You don't want to know,' she said.

The trees were shivering and shedding withered leaves as they picked their way down the path leading to Adel Woods. All the sensible birds had flown south, leaving behind a few emaciated

189

sparrows and the odd miserable-looking wood pigeon. Dove and Tom walked beside a busy stream. They stopped at a clearing scattered with large rocks, worn smooth by the years, and sat on one such rock, side by side. Tom turned up the collar of his coat.

'It's a bit nippy,' he said. 'Come on, let's have a cuddle.' He placed an arm around her and without hesitation she moved in close to him. He was the only young man she'd ever really known and the only person in the world with whom she could enjoy an easy silence – just listening to the sound of rushing water and the wind soughing through the empty trees, content with each other's company and nothing else. After a while she asked a question that had been at the back of her mind since the minute she'd got back to the waggon.

'Tom, what were you lot talking about before I came home?'

He gave a slow grin and threw a pebble into the stream. 'Ah,' he said, as though reluctant to reveal a secret. 'They're, er … they're planning revenge on the evil Ralph.'

'They? You mean you've got no part in it?'

'Well, I'll be helping out a bit. With it being my idea more or less.'

'Oh heck,' Dove said. 'What's the plan?'

'The plan is,' explained Tom, enthusiastic now. 'To give Ralph something else to think about, so he'll stop worrying about Monty and that flipping house.'

'It's a lovely house,' Dove said. 'I went to see it this morning.'

'It's like a millstone around Monty's neck,' said Tom. 'He'd give it to Ralph if the idiot would just apologise for calling him a murderer.'

Dove considered such an accusation a small price to pay for a lovely home. 'Yes I heard about that,' she said. 'So, what's the plan?'

'In a nutshell, Ralph's wife's got a feller on the side and we're going to fix it so he catches them in the act.'

'I see … and this is the something else he'll have to think about?'

'Precisely,' grinned Tom. 'He'll be too busy with his divorce to worry about Monty. We're calling it Operation Monty's Revenge.'

'And this was your idea, was it?' She didn't sound suitably impressed.

'What's wrong with it?'

'I think it's a typical man's plan. No subtlety, no finesse ... just blunder in and hope for the best. Won't you be punishing Ralph's wife as well? She's done nothing to harm Monty.'

'I think we'll be doing her a favour,' argued Tom. 'Anyway, we've planned it for next Wednesday. That's when the boyfriend calls round for his weekly session. Come and watch the fun if you like.'

'If I come, it'll be to make sure you lot don't get into trouble.'

A robin flew onto a rock in the middle of the stream, extracting an 'ah' from Dove. The bird hopped around for a while, then looked at them with its head on one side, as though asking for food.

'Oh, I wish we'd brought some bread,' Dove said. 'I love robins.'

Tom hadn't heard her. 'Tell me what you think, Dove?' he said, suddenly.

'About what?'

'About that night ... about how I behaved. About how I was too useless to stop you being raped.'

'I'd rather not talk about it.'

'Dove, I really do need to know what you think of me.'

She didn't answer at first. 'I'm sure it was Scullion in the club the other week,' she said. 'And I've seen him since.'

'Oh, where?'

'I saw him in town yesterday. I was walking up the Headrow and this man bumped into me from behind, nearly knocked me over. It was *him*.' Her voice went quiet as she went over the incident in her mind. She shuddered and added, 'He spat at me.'

'He what?'

Dove's brow furrowed as she tried to hold back the tears. 'I ran away from him,' she said. 'I wanted Henry to make things right.'

Tom felt an unreasonable pang of resentment. Why Henry? Why not Tom?

'Where was Henry?' he asked.

'In the Mecca. I don't think his girlfriend was too chuffed when he left her for me.'

'You should tell the police.'

'We did. They said they'd have a very stern word with him.'

'I think that should do it.' Tom didn't believe it for a minute. He was just trying to make her feel better.

'I'm glad you think so.' There was more than a touch of irony in her voice, which he picked up on.

'Okay,' he conceded. 'He's a nutter. Best watch your back.'

'I think we'll all have to watch our backs – you included, Tom. You're the reason he got locked up, remember.'

'Glad I could be of some use. I wasn't much use at the time.'

'It wasn't your fault, Tom.'

'I know all that. People keep telling me ... But that wasn't my question. Look Dove ...' He took her by her shoulders and turned her to face him. 'I need to know what you think of me.'

She understood enough not insult him with platitudes. 'In an ideal world,' she said, 'it would have been wonderful if you could have stopped him, given him a good hiding, shown him up for the scum he is. But to do that you would need to be a thug yourself ... and I don't like thugs. You don't have to be a hard man to be a hero, Tom. You're no more of a bruiser than Henry ... and I love Henry more than anything in the world.' She tweaked his knee. 'Don't tell him I said that.'

'So, it hasn't put you off me, then?'

She laid her head on his shoulder. 'It put me off men in general. Not you in particular.'

'And ... are you okay now?'

'What, with men?'

After some hesitation he nodded.

'I'm not sure,' she said. 'I've never put it to the test.'

'I can't help wondering how things would have turned out if Scullion hadn't burst in on us,' Tom said.

Dove smiled and kissed him on the cheek. 'Hey! I don't know whether I'm ready for *that* yet.'

'Oh.'

'On the other hand, who knows?' she added, cheekily.

He pulled her to him and kissed her fiercely on her lips. Dove recoiled, instantly. He turned away and cursed himself.

'Sorry, Tom,' she said. 'You took me by surprise.'

'No, it's my fault. I'm so bloody ham-fisted. Look, why don't we go out on a proper date and see how we go from there?'

'Okay ... but I'm struggling to see beyond this *Good Old Days* thing. I'd get you a ticket but I'm only allowed two.'

Tom nodded. He knew his place in the pecking order. Henry, Monty, then him with a bit of luck.

192

'How about dancing?' he suggested.

'I'd love that.'

'Majestic, week on Saturday?'

'Sorry, I've got a gig in Harrogate.'

'There's a private dance on Friday at the Broadway,' he said. 'I can get tickets.'

Then Dove remembered the forthcoming dealings with Ralph. 'I think I'll let you know after next Wednesday,' she said.

'Why Wednesday ... oh, right.' Tom frowned, now wishing he hadn't become involved with Monty's revenge.

Chapter 18

Dove shared a second-floor dressing room with four dancers. The television programme lasted an hour and it took little more than that to record the whole show on film. There would be no retakes or room for error. Dove was on first, straight after the dancers. It was the most exciting time of her life. The lively audience were singing "Down At The Old Bull And Bush", and the dancers had been called on stage to open the show. Over the dressing-room speaker she could hear the voice of Leonard Sachs, the Chairman.

'My Lords, Ladies and Gentlemen. Tonight we have, for your delight and delectation, a pulchritudinous bevy of terpsichorean titillation.'

His words were interspersed with loud 'Oohs' from the costumed audience; then he banged his gavel on the edge of his box and shouted, 'Bring on the dancing girls!'

There was a loud knock on Dove's door and a voice called, 'On stage in three minutes, Miss McKenna.'

'Thank you,' she called back, hoping her nerves weren't showing. She took a last look at herself in a mirror and adjusted her top hat for the third time. One of the dancers had helped her with her make-up, adding much more colour to her cheeks than Dove would have.

'Them telly lights make yer look like death warmed up,' she explained. 'Me boyfriend thought I'd got bleedin' jaundice first time he saw me.'

She made her way down the narrow stairs and paused outside the toilet, but decided she hadn't enough time. 'Never miss an opportunity,' Monty had once advised her.

194

Ronnie Hilton was standing in the 'star's' dressing-room doorway, chatting to people in the dilapidated Green Room. Two years previously his cover of "Around The World" had been a bigger hit than the Bing Crosby original. He winked at Dove as she popped her head around the door.

'Hello, love. I've been hearing great things about you.'

Dove returned his smile and said, 'Thank you.' Then she felt guilty at never having bought any of his records. Maybe if Elvis and Lonnie hadn't been around she might have been tempted.

'Nervous?' he guessed.

'A bit,' she admitted.

'Nerves are good, love – being frightened's bad.'

Jimmy Wheeler, who was sharing with Ronnie Hilton, looked over the star's shoulder at Dove. 'Tell yer what, Ronnie lad, there'll be nobody interested in us when this shows goes out!' He gave Dove a huge wink, then pursed his lips. 'If yer play yer cards right,' he said, 'I might let yer kiss me.'

'Ugh! It'd be like kissing a dead cod,' said Julius Jones, an eccentric dancer, who was on after Dove.

Dove laughed at this harmless banter, designed to relax her obvious nerves. The dancers came clattering off and Dove made her way past them into the dark wings, where the stage manager motioned her into position behind the gold curtains. Leonard Sachs was already bringing the audience to order with his gavel as she drew in several deep breaths to calm her nerves.

'Ladies and gentlemen. We now have a veritable Venus of vivacity.'

'Ooooh!' went the audience.

'A callipygian cantatrice.'

'Ooooh!'

'A charming chantreuse.'

'Ooooh.'

'To you lot, a singer.'

As the audience laughed he banged his gavel and shouted at the top of his voice. 'Ladies and gentlemen, the delightful, the delicious ... Miss Dove McKenna.'

The curtains swished open to reveal a colourful sea of bonnets and boaters, military uniforms, sideburns and moustaches, and fancy frocks. The band was already playing the intro as she stepped down on to the specially constructed 'run-out' – a walkway that took her around the back of the orchestra pit and right into the audience.

Monty and Henry were sitting in the upper circle, obscured from her vision by the spotlights; but they were the two complimentary seats she'd been allocated and she wasn't in a position to argue.

From where they sat she looked an old hand. Smiling, confident and vivacious in her shimmering blue top hat and tails, a champagne bottle in one hand and a glass in the other. Dove waited until her intro had finished, gave a loud hiccup and apologised to the band.

'Go round again, boys,' she said. 'And I'll do my best to hop on board.'

The people laughed and one of the three cameras zoomed in for a close-up as Dove began to sing. All her nerves had melted under the warmth of the delighted audience. Barney Colehan was already kicking himself for putting her at the bottom of the bill and was wondering if a bit of clever editing might move her up to a more suitable position.

'Could I speak to Ralph, please?'

'He's on his dinner hour. Who wants him?' mumbled the yard foreman through a mouthful of cheese and pickle sandwich.

'Tell him it's Charlie,' said Tom. 'He'll know who I am.'

Tom was in a phone box in sight of Ralph's house. The bedroom curtains were drawn and a gleaming red open-topped Austin Healey 3000 was parked outside, looking very much out of place in this street of drab, terraced houses.

Monty was waiting with Henry and Dove in her car, from where they should get a good view of the proceedings. Ralph came to the phone.

'Hello?'

'Hello, Ralph,' said Tom, cheerfully. 'You don't know me, but I thought you'd like to know about that fancy sports car parked outside your house.'

'What fancy car? Who the hell is this?'

'You should be asking *whose* car it is ... and what the owner's doing to your wife right now. She's just drawn the bedroom curtains. Ralph ... need I say more?'

The phone went dead. Ralph glared, disbelievingly, at the

mouthpiece for a few seconds, then into space to assimilate what he'd heard; then he slammed the receiver down.

'Careful!' snapped the foreman. 'That's council property.'

Ralph hadn't heard him. 'I'm takin' a machine out,' he said, dully.

'Please yerself. Not like you ter work through yer dinner hour.'

Ralph was out of the office before his boss had finished speaking.

'I reckon he's on his way,' said Tom, climbing into the back seat.

'Did you tell him about the boyfriend's sports car?' asked Henry.

'I believe I mentioned it.'

'Good man,' said Monty. 'I wonder if dear Ralph will roll up in his sludge gulper?'

'I'm not entirely happy with this,' grumbled Dove. 'It seems so ... so spiteful. Trying to break up a marriage like this. What's a sludge gulper?'

'It's a machine for cleaning out drains,' said Monty.

'Calling Monty a murderer, that's spiteful,' said Tom. 'Anyway, all we'll be doing is moving things along a bit. If the marriage was okay she wouldn't be jumping into bed with another man.'

'He's got a nice car, whoever he is,' said Henry. 'It's brand new ... must be worth a good few bob.'

Ten minutes later they heard the rumble of a heavy engine approaching.

'I think this is him,' said Tom. 'Here we go.'

The sludge gulper pulled up just down the street from the house and Ralph jumped out. He walked quickly along the footpath and paused momentarily to look at the sports car before going through the gate into his house.

He entered quietly and stood in the hallway, listening for sounds. There was a rhythmic creak coming from the bedroom – a creak he hadn't had much to do with since he had found both God and chastity at the same time. Much to his wife's chagrin.

Ralph climbed, noiselessly, up the carpeted stairs and put an ear to the bedroom door. A wave of shock and anger engulfed him as he heard the sound of his wife's mounting ecstasy coming from within. He clenched his fists and raised them in preparation for storming into the room, confronting them, and giving them both a good thrashing. Then he had a better idea.

The four watchers in the car saw him emerge from the house. He strode, purposefully, to the sludge gulper and drove it alongside the open-topped car. Then he jumped out of the cab, swung the massive hose round and positioned it over the driver's seat.

'Oh heck!' said Dove.

Ralph threw a switch that sent the contents of the tank slurping into the car until it overflowed with vile-smelling slurry. Then he opened the bonnet and repeated the exercise into the engine. Henry and Tom watched the proceedings with grudging admiration.

'Whatever happened to "Vengeance Is Mine, Saith The Lord"?' wondered Monty. He turned to Dove. 'Do you think we've done the right thing?'

'We?' said Dove. 'How do you mean, *we*? This has got nothing to do with me. That poor man, whoever he is, has had his car ruined because of you lot.'

'That poor man, as you call him, is having it off with another man's wife,' pointed out Tom. 'He knows the risk he's taking.'

Monty nodded his agreement.

'My God!' said Dove. 'You men have got very convenient morals. It's Rubberneck Ralph's wife you're talking about. If Ralph's as bad as you say he is, the man's probably just fulfilling her needs. Maybe they're in love ... did you think of that?'

'Dove, we didn't anticipate this would happen,' said Monty, lamely. 'Did we, Tom?'

'Oh no, not for a minute,' confirmed Tom.

'What? You ring a man who drives a sludge gulper and tell him there's a posh sports car parked outside his house and the owner's in bed with his wife ... and you didn't anticipate this would happen?'

Monty and Tom lowered their eyes and said nothing.

His vengeance complete, Ralph calmly got back into the cab and drove away.

'I, er, I think maybe we should go as well,' said Tom.

'Aw ... I want to see the boyfriend's face when he comes out,' grumbled Henry.

'Has to be worth seeing,' agreed Monty, glancing sideways at Dove.

Dove made no comment and started the car. She was more than a little curious herself, but there was no way she would admit it to these three lunatics.

Tom, sitting in the back seat, spoke to her reflection in the rear-view mirror. 'Hey, Miss Prissy Boots. What about the time we scared off them kids who tried to set fire to your waggon?'

Dove tried to hide a smile as she looked back at Tom's reflection. 'That was different,' she said.

'Different? You were galloping around on Boris, shooting fireworks at them like a mad woman. Don't get all sanctimonious now.'

'Watch out!' said Henry. 'He's coming out.'

The four of them stared in mute anticipation as the front door slowly opened. A youngish-looking man wearing work trousers and a donkey jacket emerged. Without sparing the sports car a glance, he mounted a nearby bicycle and rode away.

For a full minute the stunned quartet stared at the sludge-swamped car. The silence was broken only by the quiet rumble of their car engine. A foul stench was beginning to come in through the window. Dove wound it shut then turned to glare, one by one, at the three guilty faces surrounding her.

'I've no doubt there's a moral in all this,' she said. 'I just wish I knew what it was.'

She slipped the stick into first gear and drove off, vowing never again to go along with a plan devised by a man.

Chapter 19

Tom pulled up outside the waggon in a gleaming blue Ford Consul. He thought it had been touch and go whether she'd come out with him after the sludge-gulper episode, but Dove only demurred to demonstrate her disapproval. She came to the door and raised her eyebrows.

'Very flashy, have you just come up on the Pools or something?'

'It's Uncle Frank's car. Husband of the wicked Auntie Margaret. She thinks I'm going out on the town with Johnnie.'

'Oh! And does the wicked Auntie Margaret still not approve of me?'

'Well, she was as mad as hell when she found out Scullion got away with what he did to you. She reckons they should have strung him by his whatsits and lowered him into a butcher's bacon slicer.'

'At least I've got something in common with her.'

'Apparently,' said Tom, 'she was the only one to see the funny side when I didn't turn up at my wedding. Mrs Utterthwaite gave her a bit of a mouthful and it all got a bit heated. My auntie said something about Monica being a plain little thing compared to you.'

'But your auntie doesn't know me.'

'She knows *of* you.'

'Does she now ... do I look okay?'

Tom wondered if it was just him or whether Dove really was the most beautiful woman in the world. Her make-up was subtle, minimal and spectacular. She wore black high heels, a black velvet, knee-length skirt, a white silk blouse and a gold chain around her neck – a simple enough outfit, but on her it looked breathtaking; almost beyond any praise Tom could heap upon her. So he settled for 'You look really nice.'

'Thank you, so do you.'

He looked at his watch. 'I thought we might call for a drink somewhere; then go in to the dance about nine.'

Dove looked unsure, as if a doubt had suddenly crept into her mind. 'I know I've got ready and all that – but to be honest I'm a bit worried about Henry.'

'Oh, why?'

'Well, it's Monty.'

'Monty?' Tom was puzzled now. 'What's Monty got to do with Henry?'

'He's gone off to the theatre with his bookseller friend and apparently he won't be back tonight. And I don't like leaving Henry on his own.'

'Ah, this is to do with Scullion,' Tom guessed.

Dove nodded.

Henry's voice came from behind her. 'Don't be so daft, Dove. What difference would Monty make? Pikey could blow him over.'

Tom climbed the steps into the waggon and looked at Dove's brother, then at her. 'Dove,' he said. 'We can't let Scullion rule our lives. He's only got to say a wrong word to any of us and he'll be back inside.'

'I know,' she said. 'It's just that I don't feel right about you and me going out and enjoying ourselves while Henry's on his own and Scullion's on the prowl.'

'Oh, thanks very much,' said Henry. 'I was okay up until now. You've made me feel so much better.'

'But, Henry –'

'Dove, please. Just get off. I'll be okay.'

'Henry's right,' said Tom. 'Scullion's not on the prowl. He's probably in some men's hostel, eating his gruel and feeling sorry for himself.' He had an obvious ulterior motive for not wanting Dove to stay home with Henry. He liked Dove's brother and wouldn't wish any harm to come to him; but Henry's safety wasn't uppermost in his mind that night.

'Are you sure he'll be okay?' Dove asked.

'Yes,' Tom assured her. 'I don't think Scullion's got any interest in Henry. It's me and you he's got a grudge against.' He wanted to add 'And you'll be safe with me', but he had no right.

'I don't like leaving Henry,' Dove said.

'Trust me, Dove,' Tom promised. He crooked a finger under her chin and looked at her. 'He'll be all right.'

Dove stared into his eyes as Henry grumbled, 'She treats me as though I'm still a baby.'

'Well, if you're sure,' she said.

'Absolutely sure,' said Tom.

'Dove,' insisted Henry. 'Just go, before I throw something at you.'

'Right,' she opened the door. 'But I'm going under protest. I'm not happy about this.'

'G'night, Henry,' said Tom, walking past her and down the steps.

'I'll be back about half eleven,' Dove called out, as she closed the door.

'No rush,' said Henry.

Dove had worked at dance halls before and had been whisked around the floor by many an aspiring, and ultimately disappointed suitor. But this was the first time she'd been to a dance as a patron – and with a date. There was something normal about this and she'd scarcely had a normal day in her life. Normality, that was her dream. It would help if Tom was a bit more normal. The sludge-gulper affair might serve to secure the house she craved but it said little for Tom's normality.

At one end of the ballroom was an upraised stage where the band played – piano, drums, saxophone and clarinet. According to the sign on the bass drum they were the Billy James Quintet, but the double bass player had gone down with flu so the band played on, ever hopeful that they'd be dividing their money between four instead of five that night. The ballroom manager had other ideas.

Henry and Scullion were forgotten as Tom led Dove around the floor in a series of 'modern dances': the foxtrot, the quickstep and the waltz. Then, for the more romantic slow waltz, the lights dimmed and a spotlight picked out the mirror ball, suspended from the ceiling, slowly spinning and casting its scattered reflection on the shuffling dancers. Hands dropped down to clutch at tense buttocks, testing the water for prospects of more amorous

202

fumblings on the way home. Some young men sang tunelessly into girls' ears, lips nibbled at necks, faces were slapped when hands got too adventurous, feet were trodden on and two girls dancing together achieved their goal of being split up by a pair of likely lads.

A shimmering of cymbals announced the end of the slow dances and the lights came on, which was a signal for Billy James to put down his clarinet and, with the skill of a conjuror, replace his false teeth in order to introduce the next set. He wiped a bead of sweat from his brow, tapped at the microphone and tried to inject enthusiasm into his voice.

'And now, ladies and gentlemen, something for the younger end. Take your partners for the rock 'n' roll.'

He hated rock and roll and wished this bloody fad would die a quick death instead of lingering on. He blamed television for encouraging it – shows like *6.5 Special*.

Many of the less able dancers left the floor; some girls abandoned male partners with two left feet and sought out other girls with whom to dance; the piano player switched to an electric guitar, the band launched into a spirited "Rock Around The Clock", and the floor vibrated with bopping youngsters – none more enthusiastic than Tom and Dove. Half an hour later they collapsed, exhausted, on a sofa.

Tom signalled a passing waitress, then asked Dove if she was glad she came.

'Oh, I've had worse evenings,' she smiled. 'And seeing as how you're buying I'll have a lager and lime.'

Tom ordered the drinks, the waitress repeated his order as if to confirm it and went on her way. Tom smiled to himself. Dove jabbed him with her elbow.

'What's so funny?'

'Oh, I was just thinking,' he said. 'The last time I bought you a drink was a Kia-Ora in the pictures.'

'A Kia-Ora and two straws, if I remember rightly.'

'Ah, I was on a tight budget ... but they were good times.'

'We've moved on since then, Tom.'

'Have we, Dove ... and where have we moved to?'

'I wasn't talking about us moving on as a couple,' she said. 'I was talking about us moving as individuals. Things have happened.'

'Is that how you see us, as two individuals?'

She leaned her head against his chest. 'I like you, Tom Webster,' she said. 'I like you very much indeed.'

'And I like you, Dove McKenna. In fact I'd go as far as to say ...' he paused.

'As far as to say what?' She was fishing; perhaps wanting him to tell her he loved her, but not knowing how she'd respond.

'As far as to say ... I like you very much indeed as well.'

He kissed her and this time he felt an immediate response. They were still locked in an embrace when they heard a discreet cough above the general noise.

'Lager and lime and a bitter, was it?'

'Oh, yes please.'

'That's four and a penny, please, love.'

Tom handed the waitress two half crowns and said, grandly, 'Keep the change, Miss.'

The woman looked appreciatively at her elevenpence tip which was at least sixpence more than the rest of the tight sods in the room were tipping her.

'Last of the big spenders,' commented Dove, sipping her drink.

'Guarantees good service,' he explained.

'Ooh,' she laughed. 'Mr Sophistication, eh?'

They placed their drinks on a table and fell into an embrace once more. Tom's hand was perilously close to her breast when he felt a tap on his shoulder. An acid-faced man wearing a cheap wig and dinner suit hovered over him.

'No heavy petting if you don't mind, sir.' The man avoided eye contact as he spoke, as if looking for other sexual miscreants.

'Heavy what?' said Tom.

'Petting, sir. What you were doing with the young lady.'

'Oh, is that what it was?'

'It's just a rule, sir. I don't make the rules. You never know where it'll end. We had a couple fornicating behind them curtains last week.' He indicated the curtains in question with a nod of his head. 'Give some people an inch and they'll take a mile, sir.'

'Right.'

The unconscious innuendo in his last sentence had Tom suppressing a grin. Dove blushed and hid her face. The man oozed away, as if on castors, into the throng.

'That waitress will have told him,' Dove said. 'Money can't buy everything, you know.'

'Not even a bit of heavy petting,' said Tom.

Dove was annoyed. It was the second time she and Tom had had their passion for each other interrupted. One interruption had been more violent than the other, but this second was an interruption, nevertheless. In fact more of an intrusion than an interruption. Then there was that time in York with Norman. The fates were conspiring to deprive her of a love life. Who the hell did these people think they were, trying to run her life like this? The rebel within Dove was working to Tom's advantage.

'Never mind, Tom,' she said. 'The night is young.'

'I thought you told Henry we'd be back at half past eleven.'

'I think we can stay out a bit later,' she said. 'I'm sure you're right about Scullion, I'm just a bit paranoid as far as he's concerned.'

Tom pulled into the car park in front of Roundhay Park Open Air Baths, closed now for the winter. If there was a moon that night it was obscured by heavy clouds. One other car was already there. He drove to the furthest corner and parked under some trees.

'Mr Webster, I hope your intentions are honourable,' said Dove, slightly the worse for drink. She got out of the passenger door and sat in the back.

'I think my intentions are about as honourable as yours,' said Tom, upon joining her.

A sharp, November wind hissed through the empty branches and, by the sound of it, the high waterfall at the back of the swimming pool was in full flow. Dove put her arms around him and kissed him.

'I think I want to do it, Tom.'

'So do I.'

'It's my first time since ... '

'I know.' Tom kissed her forehead and ran his fingers through her hair. 'Just being with you's enough for me, Dove. We don't have to do anything that scares you.'

'In fact it's really my first time ever,' she said, pausing to give him time to say it was his first time. 'I hope I'm better than Monica.'

'How would I know?' he asked.

'You mean you and her never ...?'

'She was saving herself till she got married, apparently. No doubt she'll feel justified right now.'

'Do you think a girl should save herself?'

'No more than a man should.'

'Hmm ... what about you, Tom Webster? Have you saved yourself?'

The gloom concealed his embarrassed smile. He began to unbutton her blouse. 'Dove McKenna, you ask too many questions.'

'Ah,' she said. 'That means you haven't saved yourself.' When he reached the third button, she placed a steadying hand on his and asked, 'As an expert in these matters, do you think we should get completely undressed?'

'It'll be cold.'

'I can stand it if you can.'

They undressed each other, slowly, until they were naked, but could see little of each other in the dark confines of the car. Then they kissed and caressed each other's mouths and faces and bodies, taking up where they had left off on that awful night. Tom was determined to re-enact that moment and this time to end it as it should have ended; to put right a terrible wrong that had scarred his mind almost as much as it had Dove's. Their bodies burned with growing passion until Dove moved beneath him and pulled him down to her. Then she stiffened as an image of Scullion flashed across her mind. She could feel him forcing her legs apart and smell his foul breath.

'What is it?' asked Tom, concerned, sensing the sudden tension in her.

'It's nothing,' she said.

'Dove,' he said, moving away from her. 'I'm not going to do anything you don't want me to.'

Tears veiled her eyes and anger mounted within her. 'And I don't want the bastards to stop us again!' With a great effort of will she blocked out the dreadful images, took Tom in her hand and eased him inside her. There was no memory of Scullion doing this; she'd been unconscious at the time. Mercifully unconscious.

She clung to Tom in desperation as they moved slowly and rhythmically together. Then she took up the pace and forced it along, frantically, as though in defiance of those who had tried to stop her. They came together in a frenzied and noisy climax which provoked amusement and a honking horn from the occupants of the other car.

Then, like all contented lovers, they lay in each other's arms for several minutes. Dove shivered as the heat of their passion was quickly cooled by the night air. She pulled a coat over them and Tom fell asleep. He was a dead weight on top of her when a torch shone through the window.

'Clear off, you pervert!' she shouted. 'You're too late. You've missed the show.'

'I'm not a pervert! I'm the park keeper. You're not supposed to park here at night.'

Tom woke up and Dove clung to him, not wanting him to move and reveal her nakedness. If the park keeper wanted to see Tom's bare bottom, partially revealed beneath the coat, then that was okay by her.

'What's happening?' Tom said. 'Hey! Who's shining that torch?'

'It's the parky,' Dove told him. 'I think he likes your bum.'

Suitably embarrassed, the man switched his torch off, banged his fist on the car roof and sloshed away through a swamp of sodden leaves.

Chapter 20

Pikey Scullion sat in a corner of the Weaver's Arms, drinking alone and exuding an air of menace that had the other customers avoiding his gaze. The bar staff were hoping he wouldn't cause trouble because they didn't fancy the job of asking him to leave; but they had little cause to worry. Pikey's mind was concentrated on one person: a person who would be getting more trouble than she could cope with when she got home at half past eleven. He looked at his watch – ten o'clock; time to make a move, in case she'd got back early.

Earlier in the evening he'd been hiding in the bushes outside Dove's waggon, waiting for her to come out. When Tom arrived to pick her up, Pikey had cursed under his breath, then grinned when he heard her say she'd be back at half eleven. He couldn't quite see who she was with, and hoped she'd be returning on her own. If not, he'd come back another night. Other people posed risks. He'd thought of breaking into the waggon at the dead of night, putting Henry and Monty out of action and having his way with Dove; but there was a risk that one of the three might escape. He couldn't take that risk; all he needed was patience. One night he'd catch her on her own. He'd waited nearly two years for this; another few nights wouldn't make much difference.

His plan tonight was to knock her out before she got back to the waggon; carry her into the bushes, have his way with her, then kill her. This singular thought had occupied his mind for all the time he'd been in jail and only the plan's execution would satisfy him.

He arrived on a bicycle which he had stolen earlier in the evening, hid it in the bushes and sat down against a tree to await

208

Dove's return. As time dragged on the drink began to have a soporific effect on him, his head began to loll, his body slumped and he began snoring. The sound cut through the night air like a buzz-saw and woke Henry up.

At first he thought it was Boris and paid no attention. He looked at the luminous dial of his watch – twelve forty-five. The door to Dove's room was wide open which meant she hadn't crept in while he was asleep. Henry grinned to himself. His sister and Tom would be up to no good by now. He'd like to get up to no good with that girl from the recording studio, Mavis Feather. She definitely fancied him, did Mavis, and she was a far better prospect than the bird he'd met at the Mecca, the one who had given him the brush-off after she saw him with his arm around Dove. Next time he went down there he'd ask Mavis Feather out. He'd have asked her out this morning only the occasion didn't seem to present itself. Very tricky business asking girls out. The girl at the Mecca had actually asked him. What would he do if Mavis said 'No'? How would he get out of that without looking stupid? Maybe he should drop a hint without actually asking her outright. Something on the lines of: 'Do you like going to the pictures?' Then if she said 'Yes', which of course she would – because everyone likes the pictures – he could say, 'So do I.' After which, he could say something like: 'There's a good picture on at the Odeon, I'm going to see it on Friday ... would you like to see it?' If she said 'No' then that would be it – end of story, no embarrassment. But if she said 'Yes,' then he knew he was in with a good chance. He could dive in with his killer line: 'Why don't we go together?'

Satisfied with this classic approach to the age-old problem he turned over to resume his sleep, but the sound from outside penetrated his senses once again. It was much too regular for Boris – maybe there was something wrong with him. He got out of bed, slipped into his shoes and put an overcoat over his shoulders before opening the top half of the door and calling out, 'Boris?'

The horse was lying down, fast sleep. His great head twitched into life at the sound of Henry's voice. Prince stirred from her slumber beneath the waggon and Pikey Scullion snored on. Boris got to his feet as Henry stepped out of the waggon, while Prince began to to fuss around the boy's ankles, hoping for food.

'Clear off, Prince!' shouted Henry, good-naturedly.

Pikey woke up with a start, but not before Henry had identified the source of the noise.

'Who's there?' he called out.

Pikey's fingers curled around the piece of rock he'd brought to stun Dove with. He was wearing gloves so there'd be no incriminating bruised knuckles – just a quick tap to knock her out, strip her naked and whack her about with his gloved fists before doing what he'd come for. Then a couple of blows with the rock when it was time for her to go for good. Pikey was willing the boy to leave well alone – and Henry would have been wise to have heeded Pikey's unspoken wishes. He walked towards the bushes and stood a few feet to Pikey's left, peering into the dark leaves. He never knew what hit him.

The didicoi struck the boy over the back of his head, causing a wound that spurted blood all over Pikey's shirt, enraging him. Enraged because being saturated with blood was the last thing he wanted, not having a change of clothes. As Henry dropped to the ground, Pikey lashed at him with his boots, smashing his ribs, his face and his back and was about to finish him off when Prince hurled herself at her master's attacker. She had developed into a medium-sized, ungainly dog, not particularly intelligent or obedient, but with an enormous affection for Henry. This affection transformed itself into savage aggression as the dog sprang to Henry's defence and clamped its jaws around Pikey's ankle. All of the time Boris had been whinnying and rearing up and pulling against his tether, but he couldn't reach to help. He was near enough to catch the sight and smell of the didycoy, but not near enough to help.

The pikey cursed in pain and rage and hammered the rock down on to the dog's head. He danced around in rage and frustration trying to unlock the dog's vice-like grip; but Prince's skull was pulped and broken like an eggshell before her jaw relaxed and she fell to the ground. Wittingly or otherwise, the dog had given her life to save Henry. A car's headlights approached down the grassy track, causing Pikey to take cover.

He hid behind the waggon and when he heard both a man and a woman's voice, he decided to call it a night. He now needed an alibi and a change of clothes; and there was only one person who could provide those.

Dove didn't immediately spot Henry lying there. What drew her attention was Boris straining against his tether, trying to reach a dark bundle on the ground.

'What is it, Boris?' she called out.

Tom walked quickly past her, sensing something amiss. 'Oh my God!' he said. 'It's Henry.'

The boy was lying on his back, his face a grotesque mass of blood, some bubbling from his mouth as he tried to breathe. Dove screamed in shock and flung herself beside him. Tom was probing inside Henry's mouth.

'He's swallowed his tongue,' he said. 'There, I've got it.'

The boy began to breathe faster – a choking, rattling sound accompanied each breath. Tom gently rolled him onto his side. Henry's coat was lying on the ground a few feet away so Tom laid it over him then took his own coat off to give the boy an extra layer of warmth. Dove was crying, holding her brother's hand.

'I'll ring for an ambulance,' Tom said to her. 'And you're coming with me.'

'But we can't leave him here,' she sobbed. 'He'll freeze to death.'

'Then get some more coats from the van. This is Scullion's work. He could still be around somewhere and I'm not leaving you on your own.'

'Pity you didn't think about that when you left Henry on his own,' she wept. 'I'm not leaving my brother.'

Tom tried to think. 'Look, get in your car and lock yourself in. Turn the headlights on. You'll still be able to see Henry.'

'I'm not leaving him! Just get a bloody ambulance and stop messing about!'

Tom jumped into his car and sped away. He needn't have worried about Pikey, who was far away, unsteadily riding his stolen bicycle towards his mother's caravan. When he got to within half a mile he hurled the machine into a deep ditch and proceeded on foot, congratulating himself on his ingenuity. No one would tie the bike to him and even if they did he'd been wearing gloves so there'd be no fingerprints.

Beulah cursed as loud banging woke her up. 'Who the bleedin' hell's that at this time o' night?'

'It's me, Ma,' shouted Pikey. 'Let me in. I'm in bother.'

211

'Well yer can get yersen outa bother … an' don't come bother-in' me.'

Pikey kicked at the door with his heavy boots.

'You put a dent in my door and I'll put a bloody dent in yer thick head!' she roared.

'Well bloody open t' door, then!'

'Awright, awright … I'm coming.'

She turned on a light, wrapped herself in a gaudy dressing gown and unlocked the caravan door.

'Aw, Jesus bloody Christ!' she exclaimed as the light illumi-nated her blood-soaked son. 'What the hell happened ter you? If yer've been in a fight yer might just as well turn yersen in, yer barmy bugger. What yer thinkin' of? Two minutes outa t' nick an' yer at it again.'

'None o' this is my blood, Ma. I need ter get rid o' this clobber an' put summat different on, afore t' scuffers come.'

'Why would the coppers come here?'

'Because I'm not in t' bloody hostel, that's why. This is t' first place they'll look. When they come, tell 'em I've been here all night.'

'Oh, this gets better an' bleedin' better this does. Yer gonna have me locked up fer aidin' an' abettin'.'

'Nobody saw nowt, Ma. Nobody knows it were me.'

'Why would they come lookin' fer yer then?'

'Look, can I come in or do I have ter stand out here all night?'

Beulah stood back and allowed him in.

'Is Siddy in?' he asked.

'He's through there. Surprised yer didn't wake him with all that carryin' on.'

Pikey grinned. 'It'd tek a bleedin' atom bomb ter wake our Siddy afore he were ready.'

'So,' said Beulah. 'What's happened and why will t' coppers come lookin' fer yer?'

'I knocked Malachy's lad about a bit.'

Her hand swept round in a vicious arc and hit him with a resounding thwack on his ear, sending him staggering backwards. 'Yer brainless little shitehawk! I'll not ask yer why yer did it because I doubt if yer know yersen. Is he dead?'

'He might be, Ma.'

'They'll top yer fer this. Yer know that don't yer?'

'They've no proof it were me, Ma. Once I get rid o' these clothes an' you tell 'em I were here all night.'

Beulah stood there with rage burning in her eyes. Then she walked the length of the caravan and banged on a door at the end. 'Sid!' she shouted.

No answer.

She opened the door and shook her youngest son by his shoulders. 'Wake up, yer dopey pillock!'

Pikey heard loud grumbling. Sid came to his door and stared at his elder brother through sleep-filled eyes. 'Hey up, Pikey.' His vision cleared. 'Bloody hellfire! What happened ter you?'

'He beat up Malachy McKenna's lad, that's what happened,' said Beulah. 'An' he's come here thinkin' we're gonna clean up his mess.'

There was a silence as the three of them stared at each other; then Beulah gave in.

'Right,' she snarled. 'Take everythin' off, includin' yer boots. Sid, get summat fer him ter wear. Yer both of a size.' She went to the door. 'I'll get t' truck started. There's some dossers on Woodhouse Moor. I'll dump yer gear in their brazier.'

'Stay there till it burns, Ma,' sniggered Pikey. 'Yer never know wi' them dossers. They might tek a fancy ter me strides.'

'I need no advice from the likes o' you!' she snapped. 'Just throw yer stuff outside an' get a good wash all over, feet an' all. Yer stink like an owd pig.'

The police and ambulance arrived together, ten minutes after Tom got back. Dove hadn't spoken a word to anyone, clinging to Henry's hand as silent tears dripped down her face. Then, without a word to Tom, she climbed into the ambulance and went off to St James's Hospital with her brother, leaving Tom to deal with the police. Detective Inspector Sykes arrived just after the ambulance had left. A constable briefed him on the situation before he came over to Tom.

'You think it was Scullion, do you, Mr Webster?'

'I know it was Scullion, Inspector.'

A beacon of hope lit the inspector's eyes. 'Ah, you saw him then?'

Tom paused, then shook his head. 'No, Inspector. I didn't see him. It happened before we got back. It just had to be Scullion.'

He cupped his face in his hands to hide his tears. 'God, I'm so bloody useless.'

Inspector Sykes put a hand on Tom's shoulder. 'It was hardly your fault, son,' he said.

'I told Dove it would be okay. I told her Scullion wouldn't come looking for her.'

'I understand she made a complaint about him harrassing her,' the inspector said. 'Sadly there wasn't much we could do about it.'

'She was worried about leaving Henry on his own,' Tom told him. 'I said we can't let Scullion rule our lives. Even Monty said we should watch our backs.'

'Where is he, by the way?'

'He's staying overnight with a friend.'

'If you see him before me, tell him to call down to the station.'

'Surely you don't suspect Monty ...'

'At this stage we suspect everyone. I just want to eliminate him, that's all.'

'Right ... Inspector, I wouldn't mind going to the hospital. Henry looked in a bad way ... and I'm worried about Dove.'

'Yes, well, you get yourself off.'

'What about Scullion?' Tom asked.

'Hopefully, we're picking him up as we speak, that's if he went back to the hostel, which I very much doubt. I'll just poke around here for a bit, to make sure big boots don't tramp all over my scene of crime.'

Dove was sitting next to a police constable in the intensive care waiting room. Apart from a pale-faced old man they were the only ones in the room. Dove scarcely looked up when Tom arrived. He addressed himself to the policeman.

'How is he?'

The constable shook his head. 'Too early to say yet. Are you a relative?'

'No, I was out with Dove – Henry's a friend.' He looked at Dove. 'Are you okay, love?'

Dove stared straight ahead and shook her head, afraid to speak lest she break down in tears.

'I think she's a bit shocked,' said the policeman.

A doctor came to the door and looked around. All eyes fixed on him, expectantly. He walked straight past them and knelt beside

214

the old man, talking to him in a soft voice. The old man buried his head in his hands. Then the doctor stood up and said, 'Can I get you anything?' and the old man said, 'No thank you, doctor. Can I see her?'

Dove, Tom and the policeman watched as the doctor took the old man to see his wife for the last time. As their sad footsteps faded along the corridor, Tom said,

'Shall I see if I can get us a cup of tea or something?'

'I wouldn't mind a cuppa,' said the policeman.

'Dove?'

She gave an almost imperceptible shake of her head. Tom looked at the policeman. 'Milk and sugar?'

'Please.'

As Tom left he heard Dove and the policeman talking to each other in low voices and he felt more isolated than he had in his life. She'd talk to a stranger but not to him. Was his crime so terrible, or was he just a handy receptacle for her grief? She and the policeman had stopped talking when he got back with the tea. Dove was purposely avoiding his eyes.

Two wordless hours ticked by before a surgeon in a green operating gown came in to the room.

'Miss McKenna?'

'Ye –' Her nerves caused her to choke on the word.

'We've managed to stabilise your brother. There were no life-threatening injuries, but he has a lot of tissue damage and broken bones, including his spine, I'm afraid.'

'So he's not going to die?' Tom said.

'No,' said the surgeon, his gaze switching from Dove to Tom and back again. 'He's not going to die.'

Dove was looking at the man, noticing there was no smile on his face, as one would expect from someone handing out good news. She swallowed, composed herself and said, 'There's a problem, isn't there?'

The surgeon shook his head. 'It's too early to say, but I'm a bit worried about his spinal injuries.'

'What? You mean he could be paralysed?' she asked, hoping this man would tell her not to be so pessimistic and that Henry would be okay apart from a bit of stiffness now and again.

To her horror the surgeon said, 'There will certainly be some paralysis. But we won't know the extent for some time.'

'And will this paralysis be permanent?' asked Tom.

The surgeon shook his head, 'It's not looking good,' he said, 'but it's too early to give an accurate prognosis.'

Dove's face crumpled into tears. 'He's only fifteen. He's never even had a proper girlfriend yet.'

Tom put his arm around her but she shrank from him and he knew he'd lost her. This time for good. In her eyes it was his fault they'd gone out and left Henry on his own. Dove hadn't wanted to leave him but, along with Henry, Tom had persuaded her to change her mind. And she was hardly going to blame her brother.

It was four in the morning when the expected knock came on Beulah's caravan door. She was the only one awake, which annoyed her. How could Pikey sleep with a possible murder charge hanging over him? The knock came again; louder this time.

'Who is it?' she called out.

'Police, open up.'

'Why? We haven't done nowt.'

Meekly opening the door without a protest would have been suspicious.

'Just open the door!' The voice was impatient now.

'Awright, keep yer bleedin' hair on.'

Pikey was awake now, but Sid slept on. Beulah went to the door. Outside stood Inspector Sykes, three constables and a sergeant. They were taking no chances.

'Worrisit?' she asked, through a half-open door.

'Good evening, Beulah,' said the inspector, 'I think you know who I am. Is Pikey with you?'

'Good God!' she exclaimed. 'Have yer come mob-handed? Is it just 'cos he's not at that crappy hostel?'

Pikey appeared behind her and looked at the inspector from over her shoulder. 'Oh,' he said. 'It's you.'

'May we come in?' said Inspector Sykes. 'We'd like a bit of a look round.'

'Have yer got a warrant?'

'No, but I can get one if you like … and while we're getting one, we'll lock you all up so you can't hide anything.'

'Yer can't do that.'

'I bet you we can,' said the inspector.

216

Beulah stood back from the door. 'Aw, come in if yer must,' she said, in a defeated voice. All was going to plan; she just hoped one of her idiot sons didn't do or say anything stupid.

The policemen trooped in and began a methodical search of the caravan. The inspector looked at Pikey, standing there in his vest and underpants, neither garment exactly pristine. 'Could you show me the clothes you've been wearing this evening?' he asked.

Pikey pointed to a pile of clothes on top of a cupboard. The inspector picked at them, distastefully, looking for evidence of mud or blood. There was none.

'And your footwear?'

'Under me bed,' said Pikey.

'Could you get them, please?'

Pikey bent down and brought out the pair of boots Sid had given him. He handed them to the inspector, who gave them a cursory look and turned to the sergeant. 'I want you to examine every item of clothing in this caravan and in their truck. Have a look round outside; see if there's evidence of anything having been recently burnt. I mean anything, including women's clothing. You know what to look for and where to look.'

He returned his attention to Pikey. 'I want you to put your clothes on, including your boots, and come with me to the station.'

'Are yer gonna put me back inside, just 'cos I spent a night with me ma?'

'This has got nothing to do with you breaking your conditions of bail,' said Inspector Sykes, his eyes fixed on Pikey. 'Where were you between say, eleven o'clock last night and one o'clock this morning?'

'Yer what?'

'It's a simple enough question!'

'I were here. I'd been out for a couple o' pints an' I couldn't stand the thought o' goin' back ter that bloody hostel. So I came here ter see me ma.'

'That's right,' confirmed Beulah. 'He turned up like a bad penny. I'd have thrown the bugger out if I knew he were goin' ter cause trouble.'

'And what time was this, exactly?'

Beulah shrugged. 'Ten o'clock ... half past ten at the latest. I were about ter turn in. I don't stop up much after ten o'clock

217

nowadays. I haven't got the stamina what I used to have. I'm a bit past it . . . I expect you're the same, Inspector.'

The detective scowled at her. 'Would you be willing to swear to that in court, Mrs Scullion?' he asked.

'I'd swear it on their fathers' lives, if I knew who the buggers were,' said Beulah.

Chapter 21

Dove and Tom were still at the hospital when Inspector Sykes got there. A nurse had already brought him up to date on the situation with Henry before she brought him in to see Dove, who looked up at him and said, without any apparent emotion, 'He's going to be paralysed, Inspector.'

The detective took her limp hand in his. 'I understand it's early days yet, love.'

Tom looked on, enviously. He'd tried to comfort her, but she'd pulled her hand away. Despite her wretched grief she was still stunning. Her dark, shiny hair was scattered over her shoulders, contrasting against the shimmering white of her silk blouse; and her black velvet skirt was hitched carelessly above her perfect knees. In his mind he was seeing her as he'd seen her only a few hours ago: naked beneath him as they made frantic love. He felt himself becoming aroused and was ashamed at having such thoughts at a time like this. What sort of a man was he? He shook his head to clear it of all this unseemly lust.

'What about Scullion?' he asked. 'Have you arrested him?'

The inspector shrugged. 'He's down at the station, but unless we can break his alibi there's not much we can do. I've spoken to one of the doctors. He reckons the attack must have taken place just before you got to him, otherwise he'd have choked to death after swallowing his tongue. By the sound of it you probably saved his life by pulling it out of his throat. Where d'you learn first aid?'

'In the RAF.'

'Ah, Royal Navy man myself. Anyway, Scullion's mother says he was with her at the time Henry was attacked.'

'And you're going to take her word for that?'

'We've no option, lad. Unless we can turn up any other evidence that links him to the crime. But there's not much sign of that, either. I'd like to speak to Henry when he's able to talk. Maybe he can enlighten us.'

'That won't be until tomorrow,' said the nurse. 'We'll be patching him up for some time yet. He's still under anaesthetic.'

'So,' said Tom, 'unless Henry can point the finger at Scullion, the bastard's gonna get away with it, just like he did with Dove? What sort of justice is that?'

Dove sprang to her feet. 'Will you just shut up about Scullion and justice and alibis and forensic bloody evidence!' she screamed. 'I don't want to hear about it. I just want to know that Henry's going to be okay!' She burst into tears and sat down again.

Tom placed a comforting arm around her. 'We all want Henry to be okay, Dove ...'

She pushed him away with all her might, sending him staggering backwards. 'Pity you didn't think about that earlier. If it hadn't been for you, Henry would have been okay!'

'Come on, Dove,' Tom protested. 'That's not fair.'

'Just go away. I don't want to see you ever again. Every time you turn up bad things happen to us.'

Tom flushed and defended himself, angrily. 'That's just stupid!'

'Stupid? My brother's lying paralysed and you call me stupid. I suppose Henry's stupid as well, is he?'

Tom's eyes blazed for a second and the inspector waved a flattened palm to tell him to calm down. The young man nodded his understanding.

'I'm sorry, Dove,' he said, softly. 'I didn't mean to call you stupid.' He looked helplessly at Dove as she collapsed into her chair and he ran his fingers through his hair. 'Look, maybe ... maybe I should go,' he said. 'I seem to be doing more harm than good.' He turned to the nurse for support. 'What do you think?' he asked.

The nurse agreed it might be for the best, so Tom knelt beside Dove, who was weeping, with her face in her hands.

'I'll, er ... I'll go, shall I ... Dove?' he said.

Without looking up she said in a low, sobbing voice that only Tom could hear, 'Tom, there was only one thing on your mind when you asked me out tonight, and it wasn't Henry.'

220

There was too much truth in this for Tom to argue.

'Please go,' she said.

Totally defeated, he stood up and walked out of the room, glancing back to see if she might be watching him. But she wasn't.

As he walked, he fought back the tears. This was the biggest loss he'd suffered in his life, in many ways worse than when Alice died, because his sister was never meant to be his life partner; she would have eventually gone her own way. But he wanted Dove to be with him for ever, and now he'd made a mess of everything. If only he'd stayed with her and Henry. What was he talking about? If he hadn't taken her out last night, she might well have been the victim. Scullion had no cause to attack Henry. Ah, but supposing he was wrong? Supposing it wasn't Scullion? Well, if that was the case, then he'd been right about Scullion not being a danger – and therefore Dove could hardly blame him. Don't be stupid, Webster, of course it was Scullion, the man who raped her – with you, useless Tom Webster, in the same room.

When he reached the stairs he sat on the top step and pressed the heels of his hands against his temples as his mind raced with an unbearable confusion of sadness and self- recrimination.

A passing nurse paused and asked, 'Are you feeling all right?'

'Bit of a headache, that's all, thank you, nurse.'

'I could get you something for it of you like.'

'No thanks. It's not that kind of headache.'

As Tom was descending the stairs, Monty was going up in the lift. Dove lifted her head just long enough to give the old man a wan smile of greeting. Monty mouthed, 'How is he?' to the policeman, who shrugged and got to his feet.

'I'll be going, Dove,' he said.

She looked up and said, 'Thank you, Inspector,' although she didn't know what she was thanking him for.

Monty sat down in his place and remained quiet for a while, before taking Dove's hand.

'Have you heard anything yet?' he asked.

It was almost a minute before she replied, 'He's going to be paralysed.'

'Oh, dear!'

A wave of melancholy engulfed him as he realised how much he loved these two young people. It seemed just too indelicate to ask *how* paralysed Henry was. Being paralysed at all at his age was too much to bear. Dove turned to look at him, with unbearable grief in her eyes.

'He's the only person who ever told me he loved me,' she said.

There was a stark and lonely sadness in this statement that cut deeply into him. He placed his arm around her shoulders.

'It may be of little comfort to you right at this moment,' he said, 'but I love you, Dove. You and Henry both.'

'Any improvement?' enquired Monty.

A week had gone by and Dove had spent most of it by Henry's bedside.

'None,' she said. 'And none expected.'

Henry hadn't been given the prognosis yet. As far as he knew it was a temporary situation which would improve with time and physiotherapy. All he knew was that his brain was issuing instructions to parts of his body, but they were taking no notice. Everything below his neck was dead.

'He asked me about Prince,' Dove shook her head. 'I lied to him. I told him Prince was fine.'

'It was the right thing to do,' Monty assured her. 'We don't want to add to his troubles until we have to.'

'Tom hasn't been to see him once,' she said. 'Henry can't understand it.'

She had just arrived back at the waggon after another long visit to the hospital.

'I think I can understand it,' said Monty. 'And I think you can as well. Why don't you tell Henry?'

'Tell him what?'

'Tell him Tom isn't coming to visit him because he doesn't want to bump into you and cause you further grief.'

'How do you know that?'

'Because Tom told me, that's how. He called in to see me this morning. If you don't tell Henry, I will. It's not fair on either of them.' He looked keenly at Dove. 'Why do you continue to blame Tom? I could maybe understand it at first, but not after all this time. It's hard to imagine how bad he feels.'

'How bad *he* feels?' said Dove. 'Monty, how do you think Henry feels? He's going to be paralysed from the neck down for the rest of his life.'

222

'Now, Dove, we don't know that for sure.'

'Oh, Monty, I hope you're right. But the doctors haven't said one encouraging thing to me all week.'

'All the same, I think you should tell Tom you don't hold him responsible.'

'If it hadn't been for him we wouldn't have gone out.'

'Then what do you think would have happened?' asked Monty.

'Scullion wouldn't have tried anything with three of us there,' she said. 'Too many witnesses.'

'We don't even know it was Scullion,' argued Monty. 'Henry didn't see anything, and even if it was Scullion, what was to stop him biding his time until Tom had gone home, then trying to catch you outside on your own? If he had, I don't think I'd be talking to you now.'

Dove went quiet and poured some water into the kettle which she put on the calor gas stove. Deep inside her, she knew Monty was right, but she just couldn't forgive Tom.

'I don't know, Monty. It just seems that every time something bad's happened to me, Tom's had a hand in it.'

'Oh, Dove, that's an awful thing to say. Tom's a good man.'

'I know he is, but I can't help how I feel.'

She made them cups of tea and sat opposite Monty at the table.

'I think you'd better explain yourself, young lady,' he said. 'I'd like to know how a lovely man like Tom has had such an awful effect on your life.'

Dove sipped at her tea and stared out of the window at the leafless trees beyond. The sky was iron grey and spiky rain began to fall. The weather matched her mood.

'Oh, maybe it's me,' she said. 'Maybe I'm wrong in tracing everything back to Tom.'

'Of course you're wrong ... for example,' he challenged, 'what about what your father did to you? How on earth was that Tom's fault?'

Dove took up his challenge with a marked lack of enthusiasm. 'If you must know, dad was punishing me for getting expelled from school,' she said. 'The reason I was expelled was because I lied about going to Mass. It was Tom's idea that I should lie.'

'Well ... that's a very tenuous connection if you don't mind me saying so.'

'Then there was Alice's death,' she said.

'Alice? You mean Tom's sister, Alice? Surely you can't blame him for that?'

'If she hadn't been late that morning, she wouldn't have got knocked down by that car. It was Tom's fault she was late.' She gave Monty a warning look. 'And you must promise never to breathe a word of that to anyone, especially to Tom.'

'Ah! So, you think enough about him not to want to hurt him,' he said. 'What else is he responsible for?'

'Monty, I'm not saying he was *responsible* for anything,' said Dove. 'He was just ... I don't know, just part of the cause. Take Tom out of the equation and these things wouldn't have happened.' She turned her eyes away from him and added, 'Had he not turned up the night Scullion attacked me, I'd have slept in the pub.'

'But none of this is his fault. Surely you see that?'

'All right. Whose fault was it that Ralph emptied his sludge gulper into that man's car?'

'Well, I suppose it was Tom's initial idea, but none of us could foresee the consequences.'

'I'm sorry, Monty. But it's hard to see beyond all the trouble he's caused me. This awful thing with Henry just brought it to a head.'

The old man shook his head sadly. 'I can't begin to understand the damage that's been done to you over these last few years. No one should have to endure that; but as far as Tom's concerned the fault lies with you, Dove. You're looking at Tom with the wrong eyes.'

'Wrong eyes? I've only got one pair of eyes.'

Monty picked up his cup and stared into it. 'I was in Leeds the other day,' he said. 'And I saw an old man looking in Schofield's window. He was stooped and withered and I assumed he was infinitely older than me. Then he turned round and smiled at me and I realised I knew him. And do you know, the instant I realised who he was, the years dropped off him. He wasn't an old man any more, he was an old artist friend of mine, Larry Pegson, whom I hadn't seen for twenty years or more. You see, at first glance I'd been looking at him with the wrong eyes, and I'd seen a different person.'

He put the cup of tea to his mouth and took a drink; then he regarded Dove gravely.

'It seems to me,' he said, 'that there are two Toms. There's the real Tom, and there's the one who only you can see. Because I certainly don't recognise the Tom you're talking about ... and I very much doubt if Henry does.'

Dove placed her hand on his. 'You're a good man, Monty, and I know you're right. But I can't drive out this stuff that's inside me just like that. I'll tell Henry it's my stupid fault that Tom isn't coming to visit him.'

'There's something I didn't tell you about Tom,' Monty said.

'What?'

'He's been accepted for officer training in the RAF.'

She frowned, 'I didn't know he'd applied.'

'He didn't want to tell anyone until he knew for sure.'

'Do they know he's a walking disaster?'

'Dove!'

'Sorry.'

Chapter 22

Strong painkillers have a dual role. They kill the pain and dull the senses sufficiently to stop the patient worrying unduly. It was the day after they took Henry off drugs that he began to cry; it was one of the few functions he could perform without help. He had been in hospital for seventeen days and he was alone; and he remained alone for over an hour until a nurse noticed him. She summoned a doctor and asked if she should give Henry a sedative, but the doctor said 'no' and Henry cried continuously for another eight days.

Dove spent hours holding his hand and wiping away his tears. She didn't know what to do or what words of encouragement to give to him. She just tried her best. It didn't help that Scullion kept showing his face. Once in the hospital car park, once outside her local grocers and once at the end of the lane leading up to the waggon – places where he knew she'd be.

Monty had rung Inspector Sykes but had been told that unless Scullion committed a crime he was powerless to do anything, as much as he would love to.

Whenever he felt up to it, Monty went with her to the hospital. The damp weather penetrated his old bones, so he said, or he'd have gone every day. He wasn't with her the day her brother stopped crying; it was as though he'd run out of tears. Henry was lying on top of the sheets in his pyjamas. Dove had been reading *The Catcher In The Rye* to him when she noticed her words were no longer being punctuated by her brother's sobs. She stopped reading and Henry turned his head to her.

'Dove,' he whispered. 'My big toe just moved.' He said it as though he didn't want his big toe to hear.

Dove stared at him rather than at his toe. She knew it was

226

wishful thinking as the doctor had told her to expect the worst. Twenty-five days was a long time for there to have been no improvement. Henry met her gaze with some impatience.

'I'm telling you, Dove. I moved my big toe.'

Perhaps only to humour him she looked at the wrong big toe and saw no movement.

'There,' he said. 'It moved again.'

But Dove had seen nothing and she was at a loss what to say.

'Get the nurse,' he said.

Dove stood up dumbly and went to find a nurse. 'He thinks his big toe's moving,' she said. 'But I can't see it.'

'I'll have a look,' said the nurse.

Together they went back to Henry's bed where he lay with his eyes transfixed on his left foot. The nurse leaned over until she was just a few inches away from his toe.

'I think he's right,' she said. Then to Henry. 'Every time I tap your foot, try and move your toe.'

After a series of taps Dove saw the movement herself – almost imperceptible to her, but to Henry, the owner of an erstwhile lifeless toe it seemed hyperactive. The nurse looked up and smiled at him.

'I'll get the doctor,' she said. 'It's about time you made a bit of an effort.'

The doctor arrived and repeated the same tapping, nodding his head each time. The other big toe was subjected to the same test and the effort Henry put in raised beads of sweat on his brow.

'It's taking a lot out of him, Doctor,' Dove warned.

'He might as well get used to it,' said the doctor, who straightened up and looked down at his patient. 'Well done, Henry. That's two toes showing signs of life.' Henry's eyes were asking the all-important question and the doctor nodded understandingly. 'This is where it starts, Henry. You've got all the tears out of your system. This is where the hard work begins.'

'Thank you, Doctor,' said Henry.

This time Dove was crying. When she got home later that day she'd have something else to cry about.

The message had been picked up by her eyes before she entered the waggon, but her brain was too preoccupied with Scullion for it to be translated immediately into her thoughts. It took several

227

seconds for the image to register. Dove stared blankly into space wondering if she'd just imagined it, then she went back outside, very slowly. It was written in white paint right across the side of the waggon:

YOU WILL DIE YOU BICH

She felt her knees giving way and her breath became uneven. She ran back to her car in tears and sat there for over an hour until Monty returned from a visit to the doctor. Scullion's threat had cancelled out Henry's good news. She wanted to be there and watch her brother get better. How would it affect him if Scullion killed her? She was asleep with mental and nervous exhaustion when Monty tapped on the window. Dove wound it down.

'I've cleaned it off,' he said. 'It was only whitewash.'

'Thanks, Monty.'

'It crossed my mind to ring the police again,' he said, 'but they weren't much help last time.'

'I'm frightened, Monty.'

'Oh dear. Well in that case I'll definitely ring them.'

She shook her head as she got out of the car. 'What good would it do? No one believed me when I said he'd raped me. It's as if I don't matter.'

'We could move away from here,' he suggested.

'Not with Henry in hospital.'

'No,' he agreed.

'He's going to kill me, Monty.'

Dove buried her head on his shoulder and he felt the weight of her total dejection bearing down on him. Then he felt sad and useless, because at his age he was too old to be of much help to her. Her placed an arm around her and led her back to their home.

'You mustn't think like that. I'll protect you in any way I can, Dove.'

'I know you will, Monty. It's just that …'

She stopped herself from saying what possible use could Monty be against a thug like Scullion. Her thoughts went to Tom, who once hadn't been much help. Perhaps she'd been too hard on him. Suddenly she wished he was with her, more than anyone else in the world. But he was at Cranwell, training to be an officer and a gentleman. Then Henry displaced him in her thoughts. As Monty brewed a pot of tea, she blinked away the tears and smiled at him.

'Henry can move his toes,' she remembered, annoyed wth herself at not giving Monty such good news straight away.

'Oh, Dove. That's marvellous news.'

'It is, isn't it?'

It was the next day when Pikey Scullion looked down on the boy who had spoiled his plan to rape and kill Dove. Henry sensed the evil presence looming over him and, with some reluctance, opened his eyes. Pikey grinned at him. A grin brimming with evil and without a morsel of humour.

'Missin' yer dog, are yer, lad?'

Henry's eyes widened with fear.

'Excuse me, sir.'

A nurse brushed past Scullion and leaned over the boy to thrust a thermometer in his mouth. When the nurse stood up the didicoy had disappeared. She took the dumbstruck boy's pulse and checked his heartbeats on her watch. Then she removed the thermometer and without bothering to check it, she said, 'I'm just going to get a doctor, Henry.'

'Don't leave me,' he begged.

She smiled. 'I'll be back in a minute.' Then she went.

The image of Dove's naked body was still seared into Scullion's memory. He kept it there and embellished it until he believed the act had lasted much longer than it actually had, and that she'd even been a willing partner to his debauchery. He desperately needed to violate her once again, this time as a prelude to killing her. His body ached with frustration every time he thought about her – frustration mixed with a need for vengeance for all the trouble she'd caused him over the last few years. He wanted her to experience some of the misery he'd had to endure during his last spell in prison. He was glad his last attempt at killing her had been thwarted; it wouldn't have been bad enough. She must know real fear before he satisfied his lust. Then he would subject her to sexual humiliation and death. For her to know the vile and evil thoughts inside his twisted mind would take care of the first part of his plan.

Following her had become an obsession and over the three and a half weeks since his assault on Henry he'd learned the pattern of her movements. Once he knew she'd caught a glimpse of him and he'd seen the fear in her eyes he'd walk away. That was all he wanted – for the time being.

He had timed his visit to Henry so that he would bump into her just outside the hospital. As he blocked her path, Dove's words almost choked in her throat.

'What are you doing here?'

He held out his hands, innocently. 'I've been to visit your baby brother.'

Dove went cold.

'He's not quite as active as I remember him,' smirked Pikey. 'Still, I think he were pleased ter see me.'

The thought of Scullion being anywhere near her helpless brother made her sick to her stomach.

'I'll get the police on to you.'

'Since when were visitin' sick people a crime?'

She tried to walk round him to get to Henry, but he blocked her path again.

'You told 'em nasty lies about me spitting at yer? That weren't very nice.'

'That wasn't a lie.' Her voice trembled with fright. 'Leave me alone, I want to see Henry.'

'I told 'em what a spiteful little liar yer were. I thought it weren't very nice you tryin' ter get me done fer rape that time. Not very nice at all. Good job t' scuffers believed me an' not a little tart like you.'

She found enough courage to say, 'They'll put you back inside where you belong, if you keep bothering me.'

He feigned hurt feelings. 'Now, why would they do that? They've already eliminated me from their enquiries about what happened ter your kid.'

Dove shuddered with hatred and fear, wanting to hurt him but too terrified to try. 'Just let me past, please.' She tried to get by him again but he anticipated her move.

'Did yer enjoy yer night out wi' yer boyfriend?' he sniggered. 'Did he get his leg over this time? Pity yer didn't come back at half past eleven like yer said yer would. Your kid wouldn't be lyin' in hospital right now.'

Her hatred now took the upper hand. 'It *was* you,' she screamed, hurling herself at him.

230

He grabbed Dove's wrists and thrust his face into hers. 'That's right, bitch. It were me – an' you're next.'

There was a cold, quiet menace in his voice that made her skin crawl. 'Only yer won't be alive ter tell the tale.' Then he gave a ghastly smirk. 'Oh, an' yer can tell the cripple that I'll be back ter see him again ... when there aren't any nurses around to watch me top him.'

He pushed her away, sending her spinning to the ground. A group of passing nurses had watched the whole incident with concern. Pikey went over to them.

'Yer saw what happened, girls,' he said, innocently. 'She went for me an' all I did were ter push her away. An' me a poor cripple an' all.'

They all nodded, not wishing to aggravate this evil-looking man with his scarred, leering face. Dove got to her feet and set off running towards the door as Pikey limped off in the opposite direction, satisfied with his day's work.

The doctor and the nurse were standing over Henry when she got there. The nurse gave her a smile of greeting and in answer to the look of concern on Dove's face said, 'His pulse was up, so I called the doctor, but he seems to be all right now.'

'I gather my brother's had a visitor.'

'Yes,' said the nurse. 'A rather rough-looking man.'

'If you don't want Henry's pulse to go through the roof,' Dove said, 'I suggest you don't allow that rough-looking man anywhere near him.'

The doctor and nurse left her to it, suggesting she keep her visit short as Henry might feel better after a little sleep. Her brother looked at her, accusingly.

'How's Prince?' he asked.

Up until now there had been no good time to tell him about his dog. His question took Dove by surprise. By the look on Henry's face, he seemed to know something was amiss.

'Why?' she asked.

'Something Pikey said. He asked me if I was missing her.'

She couldn't think of an easy way to tell him. 'Prince is dead, Henry. Pikey killed her.'

Tears appeared in Henry eyes. Dove allowed him this moment of grief and sat by his bed, waiting for him to speak first.

'Was it definitely Pikey?' he asked after a while.

'Definitely,' she confirmed. 'I ran into him outside. He told me. The police can't prove it, though.'

Chapter 23

The Scullion caravan was parked in a desolate area of Leeds, earmarked for demolition. Whole streets had been compulsorily purchased in readiness for new developments, but it would be months before the demolition balls began their work. In the meantime the Scullions took advantage of whatever facilities had been left behind.

An illegal standpipe fixed to a fire hydrant supplied their water. The didicoys were gradually stripping houses of lead, slates and cast iron; timber joists provided warmth for the fire they lit every night in a brazier, around which they would sit and drink and stare sullenly at the flames. There was no conversation, only the damp breath of wind whistling through broken roofs and empty windows. The only warmth in the Scullion family came from the flickering flames which exaggerated the malevolence in their faces, like the witches in *Macbeth*.

Every Tuesday Beulah and Sid would sell their illegal goods from a legal stall in Leeds open-air market. Pikey had made it plain that he couldn't afford to get lifted by the police for selling dodgy watches, with him being out on parole, so he divided his time between drinking, sleeping, thieving and following Dove, although he didn't confide in his mother or brother concerning the latter part of his daily arrangement.

The combined mechanical knowledge of Dove and Monty, or lack of it, meant that the simplest of jobs on the car had to be handed over to a mechanic.

'I suspect it's a thing called the carburettor,' guessed Monty sagely, as he stood listening to the dimishing power of the battery as it struggled, unsuccessfully, to fire the engine into life. 'Or spark plugs ... or petrol. Have you put any petrol in recently?'

Dove became exasperated. 'Monty, I do know about petrol.' The starter motor gave a dying whine then gave up the ghost. 'I put four gallons in yesterday.'

'It'll be the spark plugs then.'

'Oh, yes, and what's a spark plug?'

'Well, it's a plug thing, in the engine,' said Monty, hesitantly.

'And what's a carburettor?' There was an edge to her voice.

'That's in the engine as well.'

'I'll go on the bus,' she snapped. 'Do you think you could get a mechanic to look at it?'

'It's getting rather late in the day but I'll try.'

An apology hung on Monty's lips but he bit it back because he didn't know what he was apologising for. Dove had been acting completely out of character lately, and he knew why. Pikey Scullion.

In a recent tearful outburst she'd told Monty how she'd like to take a big gun and put Pikey down like the vermin he was. How her life would never be at peace while he was alive. The trouble was that Monty secretly agreed with her, but he didn't know how to help. Her vehemence when she spoke about Scullion frightened him at times. It was as if she was turning into someone he didn't know; an unpleasant, morose stranger.

Dove wiped the mist off the bus window to take a look at the passing world, which was mostly grey, damp and cheerless. As Otley Road became Woodhouse Lane a few urban acres of dusty green parkland, Woodhouse Moor, passed on either side. Leeds had more than its fair share of urban parks, but to call one of them a moor was going a bit too far. Dove checked her watch by the clock on the white stone tower of Leeds University's Parkinson Building. Three thirty. She'd need to swap buses and catch a Number 42 from the Leeds City bus station which would easily have her at St James's by four. In fact she'd have time to call in the market and buy some plums, Henry's favourite fruit.

Beyond the university was a maze of streets, deserted and due for demolition; destined to be the site of more hospital and university buildings, the Leeds Inner Ring Road, and Leeds's first shopping mall – The Merrion Centre. Squatting somewhere among this ghost town of dismal tenements was the Scullions' caravan.

Dove got off the bus at the West Yorkshire Bus Station on Vicar Lane and made her way across the Headrow towards the market. The sullen rain matched her mood as she pushed open a door in the entrance to the covered market halls. It was crowded, mainly with people sheltering from the rain. Occasionally, shoppers spared her an extra glance, some wondering where they'd seen her before, others, mainly men, just to admire an uncommonly pretty face. Anything to light up a dull Tuesday.

'Two pounds of plums,' Dove said to the cheery man at the fruit and veg stall. 'And could I have them from the front, please?'

'Would you like ter pick 'em yerself, love?' he said. 'Front, back, makes no difference ter me.'

It was something she'd heard other women ask for when buying fruit. Certainly, less than scrupulous greengrocers showed off their best wares at the front whilst serving over-ripe fruit from the back. Up until now Dove hadn't had the nerve to say it.

The cheery man turned to an equally cheery woman, working beside him. 'This young lady's casting nasturtiums upon my plums.'

'I don't blame her,' laughed the woman, probably his wife. 'I'm not too struck on yer plums meself.'

'See what I have ter put up with?' called out the man to anyone who was listening. 'Women, that's what I've got ter put up with. Bane o' my life.'

Laughter and coarse remarks came from passing shoppers. The man handed Dove a brown paper bag. 'Here, love. Pick 'em yerself. As many as yer can get in this bag for a bob, now I can't say fairer than that.'

Suitably embarrassed at her unwarranted mistrust of the man, Dove three-quarter filled the bag with randomly selected fruit and handed him a shilling. As she turned to go he saw his chance and shouted to an approaching group of middle-aged women.

'See what my plums can do for yer ladies? Two weeks ago this young lady had a face like a cow's arse. Then she started eatin' my plums an' just look at her now, ladies. You could look like her after two weeks eatin' my plums.'

As the laughing women walked past without stopping, he called after them. 'On closer inspection I reckon you lot'd need the full year's supply!'

Dove hurried off, clutching her bag of fruit, vowing to keep her mouth shut in future. Had she known how near she was to Pikey Scullion she would have hurried a lot quicker.

Pikey was being escorted from the General Elliot by the landlord, who was an ex-wrestler and therefore well qualified to be running such a public house. Had Pikey been sober he could have given the landlord a problem, but as things stood he was deposited on the pavement with his head in the gutter, vomiting the meat and potato pie he'd eaten at lunchtime.

Early evening shoppers gave him a wide berth and none dared meet his gaze as he staggered to his feet, shouting obscenities to anyone within earshot. He swayed like a tree in a gale which couldn't make up its mind whether to topple over or to weather the storm. Pikey just managed to weather the storm. He searched through his pockets for money, cursed loudly at the imaginary thief who must have robbed him, then limped off to secure new funds, to the person who would pay him good money just to get rid of him – his mother, who was running a stall in the open-air market. Rain was howling down, but Pikey took as much notice of it as all drunks do, which was no notice at all.

Rather than get soaked in the heavy rain, shoppers seemed to come in at the top end of the covered market but not emerge at the bottom despite the bargains on offer on the open-air stalls.

Dove spent some time wandering along the row of pet shops at the bottom end, glancing through the windows at the rain and wondering whether to throw caution to the winds and make a dash through the open market which lay between her and the bus station. Then the rain stopped and the crush of shoppers spilled out and rushed to grab the bargains which would most certainly be on offer before the market closed in an hour. The stallholders would sell at almost any price just to offload their wares.

Most of Beulah's wares originated from the pockets and wrists of people a hundred or more miles away. Ever since the incident with Monty's rings she'd taken care never to sell stuff too close to home. Beulah cheaply acquired the ill-gotten gains of local thieves, then every month she travelled down to the Midlands and swapped contraband with her fellow traders, many of whom had travelled up from London.

Her stall was within spitting distance of the Victorian portals of Millgarth Police Station, whose officers often examined her wares and compared them to their lists of goods stolen locally.

She'd give her scary grin and assure them that, 'Everythin's kosher, boys. Bought fair 'n' square off needy folk who'd starve to death if it weren't for the likes of good-hearted souls like me.'

Dove hadn't seen Beulah since that day in court when Pikey had been found guilty of assaulting Tom. It was the only day Beulah had been to court and if Dove hadn't known better she looked as if she'd only come to see her son found guilty. She had given a cruel smile when the judge sentenced him, and was still smiling as he was taken down. It was a smile that had sent a shiver down Dove's spine.

That same shiver returned when Dove suddenly found herself face to face with Beulah, who didn't seem to recognise her, so Dove hurriedly turned and melted into the crowd. The fact that this woman had spawned the man who had made her life a misery aroused hatred in Dove as she stared at her from a nearby tableware stall. Beulah's patter was as good as any and better than most.

'Here, sir! ... a minute of yer time, sir, which yer won't regret wastin'. Here's a brooch and a matching pair of earrings what I'm sellin' on behalf of a dear owd lady what's fallen on hard times. These is real diamonds, sir. Not the biggest I'll grant yer, but who wants big diamonds, sir? Only very vulgar, ostentatious people, an' I can see yer not one o' them, sir.'

The entertainer in Dove felt herself reluctantly admiring Beulah's skill, then a crowd blocked Mrs Scullion from her view as the crockery salesman began his patter. People laughed as the man, piece by precarious piece, balanced a 24-piece dinner service on his hands and arms with the dexterity of a juggler. Then he carried on an incessant patter about how he was a fool to himself to be virtually giving away such expensive bone china. He finally dismantled his array by throwing a piece at a time to his assistant, who seemed to be an even more skilful juggler than his boss, judging by the way he managed to miscatch every item to oohs from the crowd, then aahs as he retrieved it just before another came flying his way.

'If he drops a piece, you can have the lot for nowt,' called out the salesman to a young woman at the front. 'And no tickling him under his arms, missis ... or anywhere else for that matter. I've heard all about you Leeds ladies.'

Everyone laughed but Dove as normal life went on all around: the sounds and the sights and the smells of the market. Shoppers bustled and laughed and apologised for bumping, and cursed when they themselves were bumped, and swore even louder when they realised their bag had been stolen. The appetising aroma emanating from Ishmael Ziegler's Pie Stall was countered by an aroma of an entirely different kind emanating from Old Lizzie Button, who was slumped, comatose, against a nearby wall, clothed in an avalanche of rags and clutching a dark-brown bottle, the former contents of which were running down her legs and forming a pool beneath her.

A shoe salesman demonstrated the suppleness of his wares by bending shoes in two. 'Today is Saint Crispin's Day,' he shouted, 'the patron saint of shoemakers ... and in honour of this, ladies, everything on this stall is two for the price of one. Buy one shoe, get one free. I can't say fairer than that.'

'Yer said it were Saint Crispin's Day last week,' shouted a woman from the back.

'It's been Saint bloody Crispin's Day every Tuesday for t' last six months,' called out another woman.

'What d'yer want me ter do?' retorted the shoe salesman. 'Give yer three for the price of one? ... Tell yer what I'll do. Anyone what's got three feet gets three shoes fer the price of one. I can't say fairer than that.'

A tingerlary man wound the handle of his barrel-organ, on top of which sat a small monkey wearing a bored grin and a bowler hat. Dove threw a threepenny bit into the man's tin, the monkey doffed its hat and the tingerlary began to play "Put Another Nickel In" – the only tune Alice could play on her mouth organ. It made Dove cry.

Pikey had just left his mother when he spotted Dove. He pushed his way through the crowd with a teetering stagger, sending shoppers flying with his flailing arms and hands. Dove's heart froze when she heard his voice behind her; she braced herself for a blow in the back. It came in the form of a push from his shoulder, from which she easily recovered. There was a certain safety in the crowd, despite them very deliberately turning their faces away from the troublesome man. Dove, despite her racing pulse, squared her shoulders and stood up to him.

'Well,' she said. 'Did you want something?'

'Me?' Pikey pointed, innocently, to himself as he tried to make sense of her words. 'What do I want?'

'Why do you keep following me?' she asked. 'Got nothing better to do?'

'Followin' yer? I'm jus' goin' home, ter me home sweet bleedin' home.'

Her courage was mounting when she saw how pathetic he looked. Swaying, barely able to keep his balance. The slightest push would have sent him to the floor.

'Keep away from me or I'll have the police on you.'

Pikey leered at her. Then he reached out a hand to touch her face, and said with drunken deliberation. 'I'll have you ... yer bitch.'

She slapped his hand away and ran round the corner to the Leeds City bus station. Judging from the obscene shouts, he was obviously following her, so she darted into the ladies' toilets and waited behind the door until she heard him go past.

After waiting for several minutes she emerged and walked tentatively to the number 42 bus queue. Pikey was sitting on a bench directly opposite and the heavens opened again. Dove cursed her luck. The nearest taxi rank was on Briggate, almost half a mile away. She went back into the market and bought an umbrella and was about to set off to Briggate when she saw Pikey staggering up the road.

Why she followed him instead of going back into the bus station she didn't know. But follow him she did, through the fading daylight of that dismal evening. The rain ebbed and flowed from drizzle to downpour but Dove, beneath the shelter of her umbrella, noticed it as little as Pikey did. He had suddenly become the object of her intense fascination – fascination of the horrible. This man who had caused, and still was causing her so much pain, was somehow in her power because he didn't know he was being followed. She had turned the tables on him, only she wouldn't be revealing her presence to him, as she saw no purpose in that. He knew where she lived – it was about time Dove found out where he lived. There was no logic to her reasoning; plenty of danger, but no logic.

Pikey limped and stumbled on, heading for Beulah's caravan by means of some homing instinct, without a forward, sideways or backward glance; his unfocused eyes glared at the pavement beneath his feet; he avoided no one because they always avoided him; he walked past Lewis's and turned right up Woodhouse Lane, with Dove following at a safe distance. The street lamps were now on, plus a few pathetic coloured bulbs which purported to be Leeds Christmas lights.

After passing the Civic Hall and the College of Technology buildings on his left, Pikey turned right into the grid of condemned streets which concealed his home. There were no street lamps here, no lights shining from the empty eye sockets that had once been windows but now contained either boards, broken glass or nothing. The rain had stopped now and there was the smell of dereliction about the place. The streets were eerie and littered with broken bricks, glass, dumped rubbish, graffiti and puddles reflecting the light of the moon as it ventured out from behind a raincloud.

A small, bony dog came to plead with Pikey for food and received a hefty kick for its trouble, sending the howling creature ten feet through the air. It got to its feet, licked itself, then whined and sniffed the air, realising another human was in the vicinity. As it approached Dove she darted into a doorway lest Pikey turned round.

'Go away,' she whispered, stroking its head. 'I haven't got anything for you.'

It sniffed at her pocket from where she took out a plum, which the dog licked once then looked up at her as if to say, 'Have you got anything proper to eat?'

Dove couldn't oblige but her kindness was enough. Such a dog would never turn its back on kindness. Kindness always led to food – eventually. Dove didn't mind the dog's company in this desolate place. Besides, she didn't intend going much further. She'd find out where Pikey lived, then go and visit Henry.

The cobbled streets were dotted with oily puddles, which Pikey added to by relieving himself as he walked. Then as he struggled to fasten his trousers he fell, with comical inelegance, headlong into the deepest puddle in the street. He pushed himself to his knees and swore loudly, then moaned at the pain he'd inflicted on his elbow. Dove and the dog watched in silence, each having good reason to hate the man.

He disappeared round a corner and Dove peered round a minute later, half expecting him to jump out on her. But he'd reached the far end of the street and was sitting on the caravan step searching through his saturated pockets for the key. It took him a full unco-ordinated minute to unlock the door and disappear inside. Dove approached, cautiously, drawn closer to his lair by some strange, unexplainable curiosity.

Opposite the caravan was a doorless house from where she could watch him without being seen. Why she wanted to watch him and for how long were questions she didn't ask herself, as she wouldn't have been able to supply an answer which made sense. It was just something she needed to do. As the dog followed her up creaking stairs, her stiletto heel jammed in one of the rotting treads and she had to take her foot from the shoe and sit on the dark and filthy staircase in order to work it free. She then proceeded up to a small landing and pushed open a door leading into what must have once been someone's bedroom. Cobwebs brushed at her face, water dripped from everywhere and pale moonlight leaked in through a hole in the roof, which she could see beyond the skeleton of bare joists above her. The light reflected in the dog's eyes.

'What the hell am I doing here, dog?' she asked.

The animal wagged its tail, excitedly, and ran to a window, leaning by its paws on the ledge as if it knew what Dove wanted to see. She followed and looked down through the glassless frame onto the Scullion's metal home glowing dully in the moonlight – what her dad would have called a tin can.

Then the dog pricked up its ears at a scraping sound coming from above. The noise stopped just as the didicoy appeared at the caravan door, stripped to the waist of his soaked clothing but with a heavy coat around his shoulders. Pikey bent down and began to pull wood from beneath the caravan, which he threw into the brazier. He then emptied half a sack of coal on top, poured in a liberal amount of something from a small fuel can then threw in a lighted match.

It all flared up in a startling sheet of flame which had Pikey retreating into the caravan, to return after the fire had settled down to a steady blaze. He sat on the step, huddled inside the coat, lit a cigarette and tried to warm himself.

Dove drew back from the window lest she be picked out by the light of the fire. Then, as though suddenly alert to the danger she'd

240

put herself in, she decided she'd seen enough of Scullion and wanted to get away from there to visit her brother, as quickly as possible. Maybe there was a back door she could leave through. A cursory search through the gloomy back–to-back house told her she was out of luck. Her only exit would be in full view of Pikey. Damn! She must wait there until he went inside.

It was the man on the roof above her who first drew Pikey's attention to the house she was in. He was stealing lead flashings from the chimney stacks – lead flashings which were the Scullions' to steal and no one else's. Through the grimy, caravan window Pikey had spotted at least one man on the roof, then he'd seen two faces at the window. Shit! There was probably a whole gang of them. Too many for even him to deal with – especially in his state. Pikey had been drunk too often to have any illusions about his capability after a dozen or more pints.

Lighting a fire might do the trick. Light a fire like a night watchman and scare the buggers off, was all his intoxicated brain could think of. No point shoutin' at the buggers, they might come for him.

As he sat by the fire he glared from under hooded eyelids at the roof and noted with some satisfaction that the thieves seemed to have gone. The beer and the heat soon had him nodding off and Dove waited in the darkness for her chance to leave. She had decided she wasn't going to try until he'd gone back inside. But after an hour she began to rethink her plan. Pikey's snoring carried across the street and it was reasonable to assume that it would take a lot to disturb him; besides, it wouldn't be long before the other Scullions came home – which would make things worse. As quietly as she could she made her way back down the stairs, followed by the dog. It was panting with anticipation, aware that something was about to happen and it wanted to be part of it. When she got to the bottom the dog kept running to the door and back to her as if wondering what she was waiting for.

Dove put a finger to her lips and shushed the dog, hoping it understood. It placed its head on one side and looked intelligent, which Dove found to be a relief. This was no time to have an idiot dog with her. As she stepped out of the door the 'intelligent dog' let out a loud bark and raced up to Pikey as if to tell him he'd found a proper friend and he didn't need Pikey and his big boots after all. Dove set off running but had gone no more than five

241

yards when she tripped over a brick and went sprawling to the ground. As she tried to stand up she felt a heavy boot on her bottom pushing her back to the ground.

'Thought yer'd pay me a visit, did yer?'

His voice made her flesh creep. The dog was trying to lick her face and was rewarded with another kick from Pikey which sent it yelping down the street.

'Leave the dog alone!' said Dove in a low voice. 'It's done nothing to you.'

Why she felt any sympathy for the animal which had got her into this trouble, she didn't know. There were many things about her actions that Dove didn't understand. She rolled over and looked up at him.

'Just wanted him outa the way, darlin',' sniggered Pikey. 'Don't want ter be disturbed, do we?' He reached down, grabbed the collar of her coat and yanked her, effortlessly, to her feet.

Dove tried to speak but couldn't. Fear had taken her voice and the cold ice of submission flooded her body as she allowed herself to be dragged over to the caravan. Pikey shrugged the overcoat from his shoulders and towered over her, half naked. She instinctively turned her face away from the animal stench of his body, only to have her hair grabbed and her face pulled within an inch of his.

'I've been lookin' forward ter this, bitch! Only I must say I never thought it'd be handed ter me on a plate.'

As he dragged her towards the caravan door, he kicked over the can of petrol and some of it splashed on his trousers. The momentary distraction caused him to relax his grip on Dove who broke free of him and tried to run away, but managed only a few strides before he caught up with her. As he ran past the brazier a spark flew out and landed on his petrol-soaked trousers, igniting them immediately. He punched Dove full in the face, knocking her to the ground, then danced around in a panic as he ripped off the blazing garment.

His blow had knocked her out and she came to with him standing over her, stark naked, whirling his burning trousers around his head and howling like a mad dog. This was his moment. The moment he'd been dreaming of for years. With a final great roar he let go of his blazing pants and sent them flying over his head to land in the pool of petrol near the caravan door.

242

So preoccupied was he with the delights in store that he was completely unaware of his family's home now being on fire.

'This is it, lass,' he said. 'This is where yer die.' His evil features were stone hard and his voice as cold as the grave. Then his face broke into a fiendish grin; he held out his arms in triumph and roared, 'So yer might as well enjoy yer last shag. I know I will.'

Dove's heart almost stopped as she cowered beneath the foul, naked colossus, silhouetted against the blaze, with its stiffening penis threatening her, like an ugly cannon. Then the dog appeared from nowhere and clamped its jaws around Scullion's ankle. The tenacity of this small animal jolted Dove out of her abject terror. With all the strength she could summon she jabbed her high-heeled foot upwards into Scullion's groin, and such was the power behind the kick that her stiletto heel deeply penetrated that most tender part of his body.

There was a strange silence for a moment as the pain took its time to register with Pikey's drink-sodden brain. His eyes bulged, his knees buckled and he gave a low, shuddering moan. Dove held her arms over her face to protect herself from the expected shower of blows. Then Scullion's howl of agony rent the night air, bounced off the brick walls and echoed down the street, causing feral cats to arch their backs, sleeping house sparrows to flutter away in panic and the dog to release its grip on Pikey's ankle.

Dove shuffled backwards on her bottom, amazed at the distress she'd caused him. He collapsed to his knees with blood gushing down his naked thighs. His tortured screams drowned the sound of Boris's hooves as they hammered along the street, with the waggon in tow. Behind the horse sat Monty, with a manic expression on his face, sawing at the reins like the mad coach driver in a Hammer horror film. His wild eyes reflected the flames as they approached the blazing caravan and Boris's hooves threw up sparks as he skidded to a halt against the cobbles.

It was almost as if the horse recognised Pikey. He gave a loud whinny and reared up over the crouching didicoy. One of his great hooves caught Pikey a skull-splitting blow on the head, delivered with the full force of the angry half-ton animal. Dove got to her feet and jumped up beside her old friend; Monty turned the waggon to go back the way they'd come and Boris's hooves trampled over the prostrate thug. As they raced off down the street the

243

dog jumped on board and they were just turning the corner when a propane cylinder, which was next to the seat of the fire, exploded. A few seconds later a second gas cylinder, which had been unwisely stored inside the caravan, blew the Scullions' home to smithereens. Bits of the caravan flew high in the air and a large, blazing piece landed on Pikey.

The old man slowed the galloping horse to a more dignified walk as they arrived at the main road. He was out of breath. The sweat of excitement glistened on his face. The dog had inserted itself between Dove and Monty and sat there, happily, as Boris turned up Woodhouse Lane and trotted noisily along the tarmac highway.

Despite the horror she'd just been subjected to, somehow Dove felt free of the cloak of malice which had been enshrouding her ever since her first encounter with Pikey Scullion. She knew he would never hurt her again. Why she knew this so definitely, she couldn't say.

'How did you know where I was?' she asked, eventually. Her voice was cracked and hoarse.

'I didn't,' Monty replied, wiping the sweat off his brow with a handkerchief. 'I rang the hospital to try and speak to you about the car and they said you hadn't been. You'd been acting so strangely lately that I panicked and put the harness on Boris to come and look for you. By the way, where did this dog come from?'

Dove rubbed the dog's head, remembering its bravery. 'I don't know, he just latched on to me. So, how did you know where I was?'

'I knew where the Scullions' caravan was. The police told me, only I didn't tell you because I thought you might do something silly. Don't ask me why I went there because I don't honestly know.' He sniffed the air. 'Are you keeping him? Because if you are I think he needs a bath?'

'He's not mine to keep. Do you think it was some sort of sixth sense?'

'I honestly don't know. How did you end up there ... Did Scullion –?'

'No he didn't. He was about to when you turned up.'

'Oh dear.' He looked at her. 'Oh *dear*! Are you all right ... your face ...?'

Dove tenderly fingered the swelling on her right cheek, and

worked her jaw to ascertain that nothing was broken. 'I think so. It was my own fault in a way. I saw him in town and followed him home.'

'Unwise,' said Monty.

They trotted along in silence for a while, then Dove asked, 'Monty, do you think he's dead?'

He shook his head and heaved a great sigh. 'I don't know, Dove. But it would be better all round if he is.'

'He won't trouble us again,' she said.

'I hope you're right.'

Dove smiled and placed her hand over his. With her other hand she tapped her heart. 'I feel free of him,' she said. 'In here.'

Heavy rain began to fall. Dove brought a rainsheet from the waggon and told Monty to stop so she could throw it over Boris.

'He's getting old,' she said. 'By the way, I'm keeping the dog. He doesn't look as if he belongs to anyone, and I think Henry will like him.'

Monty gave the unsavoury but friendly animal a bleak stare. 'I suppose he might,' he said. Then he looked up at the sky. 'It'll do no harm, this rain, no harm at all. Wash away any tyre tracks and incriminating evidence etcetera. If the police don't trouble us over this, I don't think we should trouble them. They've got enough to worry about.'

'So, you think Scullion's dead?'

He looked at her. 'Boris gave him a really vicious knock. If he's not dead, he'll be in a bad way.'

'Worse than you think,' she said, glancing down at her shoe to see if there was any blood on it. There was only mud. Monty looked at her, but she didn't elaborate.

No one called the police or the fire brigade or an ambulance. Some people in the distance remarked, with little interest, on a glow in the sky which lasted until the rain came, and Jez Mulkin, who had been stripping lead flashings off the roof, made himself scarce. There was an outstanding warrant which he didn't want to bring to police attention.

Beulah and Sid returned an hour later to find their home in smoking bits. The latest shower of rain had eased as she seethed and kicked at the wreckage, calling Pikey all the foul names under the sun for doing this to her. Then Sid drew his raging mother's attention to a sound he could hear, a low moan. He pointed to a smoking section of the caravan lying twenty or so feet away from the main wreckage.

'It's coming from over there, Ma,' he said.

Tentatively they walked over to the source of the moans. Sid flicked the metal sheet over with his foot to reveal his brother amidst pieces of charcoaled wood. Most of Pikey's naked torso was blackened by burns and the bottom half was covered in congealed blood. Beulah knelt beside him.

'Are you all right, lad?'

Her son had just enough life left in him to hear her. 'Never bleedin' better, Ma,' he said, injecting as much sarcasm as he could into his last words.

His mother bent over him and listened for signs of breathing, then she looked up at Sid. 'Yer brother's gone, lad,' she said. 'It's just me an' you now. An' we've got no bleedin' home.'

Chapter 24

On New Year's Eve, Dove and Monty sat round Joe Weller's seventeen-inch television and watched *The Good Old Days*. Although the colour of the occasion was lost on the black and white screen the atmosphere within the theatre beamed out of the set like a big smile. By the time the series ended in 1980 it had become the longest running television series anywhere in the world. And it had acts such as Miss Dove McKenna to thank for that. If only she'd been born fifty years earlier.

'Star of the show,' said Joe as he got up to switch off the set. 'No doubt about that. I'll be asking double your money from now on.'

'And the rest,' said Monty, with his manager's hat on. 'She's a big star in the making, if ever there was one.'

'What, you mean she's another Marie Lloyd or Vesta Tilley?'

'Better,' said Monty.

Joe looked at Dove, who knew exactly what he was thinking. 'I can put you out as a top club act, love,' he said. 'You might even get the odd bit of telly. But don't set your sights too high. Tomorrow it's 1960. There's going to be all sorts of different music in the sixties, you mark my words. Stuff I don't even understand.'

'She can adapt,' suggested Monty.

'Maybe,' replied Joe doubtfully. 'But adapt to what? That's the question. All the big theatres are struggling, and there's new clubs opening up. It's all rock 'n' roll now – and Dove's not a rock 'n' roll singer. Let's face it, she's not even a ballad singer. The clubs love her because she looks good, she's got a really pleasant voice and she makes the punters laugh.'

'I'm happy doing what I do, Joe,' said Dove.

'Good girl,' said Joe Weller.

Monty wasn't too pleased at having his authority and opinion usurped so dismissively. Dove kissed him on his cheek.

'Don't be such an old grump,' she said. 'Who wants to be a millionaire anyway?'

Two male voices chorused 'I do' prompting Dove to continue with the *High Society* song, which they all joined in with Joe's wife at the piano. Later that night they'd all be going to visit Henry and see in the New Year with him. Henry had promised the staff that Dove would be bringing her guitar and would do a little show for everyone – only he could have got away with such a promise behind his sister's back. It was the first New Year for a long time that Dove had looked forward to with any great sense of optimism. Her rehabilitation, her casting off the spectre of her father and Pikey Scullion had begun.

Part Four

Chapter 25

June 1960

Dove sat outside the physio department at St James's Hospital, just as she had three times a week for six months. Her head was buried in the *Daily Mirror*, which told of a young US senator called John Kennedy who had just been selected as Democratic candidate for President; such news meant nothing to her. Andy Capp didn't amuse her and she was only vaguely interested in the fact that "Cathy's Clown" by the Everly Brothers was at number one. She looked up as a pair of rubber double doors opened and the back view of a nurse appeared, pulling Henry's wheelchair through before spinning him round to face his sister. It had become almost a ritual. The pain on his face would bring tears behind Dove's eyes, but she knew she must not let them through. She smiled instead and said, 'Been putting you through it again, have they?'

'He's doing very well,' the nurse told her. 'And don't let him tell you otherwise. He's got eighty per cent movement back to the whole of his upper torso, including his arms and hands.'

She hadn't mentioned Henry's legs. Some time ago a doctor had warned her against 'inappropriate optimism' regarding his legs. Henry forced out a smile.

'I'm getting pretty nifty with this wheelchair,' he said. 'Watch this.'

He wheeled himself along the shiny floor of the corridor, spun the chair round in its own length and propelled himself back with a couple of hefty pushes at the wheels, before pulling on one of the brakes and spinning the chair through 180 degrees to a halt. The two women were were genuinely impressed.

'Hmm . . . I must say, I've never actually seen that done before,' said the nurse. 'Mind you, I've never come across anyone like your brother before.'

'When they made me they broke the mould,' grinned Henry.

'That's because they didn't want to risk making another one,' Dove retorted. She took the handles of the wheelchair. 'I'll take over from here.'

'No you won't,' protested her brother. 'That's the worst part about this wheelchair business ... women drivers. From now on I'll do my own driving, thanks very much.' He set off towards the lifts, leaving Dove standing.

She asked the nurse, 'How's he doing ... really?'

'He's really done exceptionally well. When he first started treatment, he was very down – as you'd expect. But now he cheers us all up. I look forward to him coming. We're reducing his treatment to once a week. He's happy about that.'

'I suppose there's no change in his legs?' Dove asked.

The nurse shook her head. 'Sorry.'

'And ... no chance?'

'I don't think so. It's a miracle he's got so much movement back in the rest of his body.'

'So he needs another miracle then,' said Dove.

The nurse took her arm. 'Dove,' she warned. 'Don't give him any false hope. He's learning to accept things as they are.'

'I won't,' Dove promised. 'But there's no need for *me* to accept things as they are.'

Monty was watching through the window of his bungalow, awaiting their return. The battle of Elisabeth's will had gone in his favour when Ralph became too preoccupied with his divorce (just as Tom had predicted) and finding a new job. His act of revenge had been witnessed by many amused eyes and had cost him dearly in damages, a heavy fine and loss of job. The story had already become firmly established in the annals of urban legend and would be told and retold over the years in many different forms – none of which would match up to the original.

In an adjacent field, Boris was chomping at the grass, looking up occasionally at the waggon, now parked in the spacious back garden. There was comfort and familiarity in that waggon. The span of the beast's memory didn't extend far enough back in time to remember Malachy's rough treatment of him. He only remembered Henry, Dove and Monty. And of course, the late Pikey Scullion.

For Monty, things had turned out well, almost idyllically; but he would swap all this for Henry to have the use of his legs back. He'd reached an age where trying to forget things becomes no great chore. His part in the death of Pikey Scullion was not a memory he chose to retain and it therefore occupied a very obscure and rarely visited recess of his mind.

The police hadn't even approached them for questioning, prompting Monty to comment that, as it turned out, it was perhaps a good thing that Dove hadn't complained too much about Pikey's harrassment or it might have aroused suspicion. The news of his actual death came as a bit of a shock to both of them, until they unanimously agreed that it was Boris who should bear the burden of guilt; no human hand had delivered the fatal blows – although it crossed Dove's mind that a human foot had brought a few tears to Pikey's eyes.

'As soon as Boris caught sight of the flames, he ran away with me,' Monty remembered. 'I was panicking a bit, I must admit. I thought he was taking us into the fire but then he made a bee-line for Scullion. He knew it was he who attacked Henry and killed Prince. No doubt about that.'

'And they say an elephant never forgets,' said Dove.

'Maybe he *is* an elephant disguised as a horse,' replied Monty.

'Well, he's big enough.'

She was almost back to normal now, doing gigs at classier clubs at Joe Weller's new, inflated fee, and smothering Henry with care and attention, much to her brother's irritation. They had decided not to tell Henry the story of Pikey's death. That way it would never be talked about and hopefully soon forgotten. If it's possible to forget something like that.

Monty saw Dove's dormobile turn into the driveway, with Henry sitting in the back. It was a recent purchase, specially converted for a wheelchair. By the time she'd pulled to a halt Monty was standing behind the vehicle, opening the back doors, with the dog, which Henry had named Deefer, scampering around his heels.

'How was it today, Henry?'

'Painful. Hiya, Deefer.'

The dog had jumped into the back of the vehicle into Henry's lap and proceeded to lick the young man's face.

253

'No pain, no gain,' Monty said.

'Is that something you just made up?' asked Henry, pushing the fussy animal away.

Monty had to think about that. 'I don't rightly know,' he said. 'Sounds like a little aphorism I might have heard somewhere – and there again I might have just made it up.' He shrugged. 'At my age, it's hard to tell.'

He put the ramp in place and stood back as Henry pushed himself out, almost running over Monty's feet.

'Careful!' exclaimed the old man, 'That's dangerous driving, that is.'

Henry grinned. 'When I get my car, I'll show you what dangerous driving's all about.'

'Hey! I thought you wouldn't be seen dead in an invalid car,' called out Dove, getting out of the van.

'I wouldn't – but you can convert ordinary cars so you don't need your feet. That's what I want.'

'Let's be sure you can't use your feet before we go to that expense,' Dove said.

Henry looked at her. 'Dove, if I've accepted it, why ca –'

'I'm sorry.' Dove interrupted him with her apology. Then she turned away and walked into the house, kicking herself for mentioning it. How could she explain her feelings to him? He was like that because of her. She'd been Scullion's intended victim, not Henry. Her brother being crippled for life was something she could never accept.

Dove went into the kitchen and plugged in the electric kettle, which was a luxury she'd always dreamed of. There was an electric cooker and a washing machine and along the hall was a bathroom and a bedroom of her own. But somehow the solid walls that surrounded her didn't bring her the comfort and normality she'd always longed for. Maybe it was because they weren't *her* walls. Maybe that was it. Whatever it was, she didn't feel right. There was still something missing from her life.

Monty placed a hand on Henry's shoulder. 'It's nearly as hard for her as it is for you,' he said. 'She's crippled with guilt. If she could swap places with you, she'd do it like a shot.'

'I know, Monty,' Henry said. 'But I need to get on with my life, and Dove's going to be getting in the way if she keeps on like this. She's making me feel like a quitter ... and I'm not.'

254

'Good Lord! Henry, of course you're not a quitter. But Dove's Dove – and if there's a chance in a million you'll get the use of your legs back, she'll find it.'

'I don't think there is a chance in a million, Monty. Neither does anyone else.'

Monty gave a resigned smile and shook his head. Then he brightened and held up a single digit to signal the timely return of a recently forgotten thought. 'I've got some news which might interest you,' he said.

'Oh? What news?'

'I bumped into an old friend some time ago, an old artist friend called Larry Pegson – hadn't seen him for years. Anyway we've kept in touch and he rang me today.'

'Good,' Henry said. 'You should keep in touch with your old friends before ...' He stopped, not wanting to finish.

'Before they die, you mean?'

'I didn't say that.'

'No, but you meant it,' Monty said. 'And of course you're quite right. Anyway, that's not the point. Larry's semi-retired now, but he still feels he's got a lot to give. I told him about you and your painting and he suggested you go and work with him in his studio.'

'Sounds like a pity job to me.'

'You'll find out in a few days whether it's a pity job, as you call it. Painting has been Larry's life. If he doesn't think it's your life, you'll be out on your ear.'

'What's the money like?'

'I haven't discussed it with him, but it won't be much, if anything. Larry's a brilliant teacher; people normally pay to be taught by him, not the other way round.'

'I suppose I could give it a go,' Henry said.

'Right, I'll tell him you're overjoyed at the prospect,' said Monty. 'Because you should be.'

Chapter 26

Entertaining was the only job Dove knew. It was enjoyable and well paid at times – and she obviously had a talent for it. But it hadn't been her choice.

The four walls which now surrounded her should have settled that uncertainty which had plagued her for so long – that longing to be safe and the same as everyone else. But she still wasn't the same as everyone else. She had an unusual job, which was okay; she didn't mind having an unusual job. It was the person who had chosen this job for her whom she minded; and she minded him very much. It sometimes seemed that whenever she was on stage entertaining people she was doing Malachy's bidding. What would she have been had she not been Malachy McKenna's child? Was there an important job that she should *really* be doing instead of messing around on stage – *doing his bidding*?

Her father had messed up her life so much. In a convoluted way, had it not been for him Tom would still be around. Dove, in her confusion, had developed a method of linking chains of events until she could settle on a culprit. Tom had been her culprit for most things but she now knew that Tom wasn't the culprit, her father was. Anyone with half a brain cell should have known that. "You Always Hurt the One You Love" – who sang that? she wondered.

Her television appearance had made a few bookers sit up and advertise her as 'The Star of Television's *The Good Old Days*'. As Joe had forecast, it bumped up her money: but as he also forecast there were no offers of record deals or TV appearances.

'I'm sure Barney'll ask you back to do more *Good Old Days*,' he assured her.

*

'Five of these a week and I'll be able to retire before I'm thirty,' she joked with Monty as she got her things together in preparation for a gig in Bradford. 'I'm getting twenty-five quid.'

'Am I coming with you?' he asked. 'According to Joe Weller it's a pick-up, do you need me to do the honours?'

He was referring to the fact that she would be paid in cash on the night, which Monty usually dealt with. Dove preferred not to deal with the money side of things, but his asking this question puzzled her – he usually accompanied her to all gigs as a matter of course.

'Why, don't you want to come?'

'Only if you want me to.' He didn't sound too enthusiastic. 'But to be honest, I don't feel up to it.'

'Are you feeling poorly? Because if you are you should ...'

He cut her off before she could advise him to go to the doctor's. 'Nothing to worry about. I'm like a creaking gate. Anno Domini and all that.'

She saw no reason to force him to come with her. 'No, you stay here and watch that new programme you like, what's it called?'

'*Coronation Street.*'

'That's it. You and Henry can watch it together.'

Monty laughed. 'I don't think these kitchen sink dramas are Henry's style.'

'I wouldn't have thought they were your style, Monty.'

'Well, there's a certain lady in it who has taken my fancy – Elsie Tanner. Now there's a woman to be reckoned with.'

'Montgomery Catchpole! I hope you're not turning into a dirty old man. What would Elisabeth say?'

'I was rather hoping you wouldn't tell her,' said Monty. 'Did I mention that Tom rang me the other day?' He threw the remark in casually, hoping to catch her off guard.

'Why should I be interested?'

'I just thought you might like to know how he's going on, that's all.'

She shrugged and said nothing. Monty returned his attention to the paper, smiling to himself, as he could sense her looking at him. He knew she'd break.

'And how is he then?' she asked at length.

'Oh, Pilot Officer Webster's doing fine.'

'Pilot Officer eh? Did he ask after me?'

257

'He seemed mainly concerned with Henry's welfare.'

'So he should be,' she said.

Monty detected disappointment in her voice that Tom hadn't asked about her. Which he had. 'I didn't mention anything to Tom,' he said, 'about you still blaming him for what Scullion did to the boy.'

'I never said I blamed him,' protested Dove.

'No? You could have fooled me.'

When he looked up she had left the room and he wondered if he was being cruel to her. Then he decided it was for her own good in the long run, to keep reminding her of Tom. One day it might be too late. It was his duty to see her happy. While he still had the time. Henry as well.

It had taken Larry Pegson just a few days to detect within Henry a rare gift with pencil and brush, a gift which far exceeded his own and which wouldn't be hampered by Henry being wheelchair bound. He'd been working in Larry's studio for just a year: mixing paint, cleaning brushes, and learning the various techniques required in applying oil paint to canvas. Larry's own career was over – apart from a couple of paintings in the Royal Academy Summer Exhibition, it hadn't been an illustrious career. He considered himself to be a journeyman artist, a painter of gloomy but quirky northern urban scenes – somewhat bemused as to why his friend and contemporary, Lowry, had, in later life, become a Royal Academician, by painting similar scenes. He would tell Henry of the times when he and his old Lancashire friend had swapped ideas; and that at one time it was generally held that Larry was the superior of the two.

'Mind you, Lowry doesn't get a fortune for his paintings,' Larry said. 'Even with RA after his name. Such is the caprice of so-called art experts, that sometimes you have to be dead to be famous.'

He allowed Henry to vent his anger and frustration on a series of canvases, most of which Larry painted over – on the grounds that the canvas was worth more than the picture. But Henry never became offended at this. Accepting that he would never walk again wasn't easy and his turmoil was soothed by the act of painting. He loved the texture and smell and sometimes even the taste of the paint when he stuck the wrong end of a brush in his mouth by mistake. He loved the vibrancy of the colours as he learned to lay them side by side, in stark contrast to Larry's grey and brown and black. But the old artist didn't want Henry to fall into the same rut as he had. Larry Pegson had often longed to splash on the cadmiums and crimsons and viridians, but he had a living to earn and a reputation for dull, atmospheric scenes painted in Prussian blue and umbers and ochres – and most of all black. But he never preached what he practised, which is why Henry's paintings had the potential to be so much more exciting than his.

His pupil transferred his emotions onto the canvas and once they had been transferred there they stayed – and Larry could do what the hell he liked with them. After several months of teaching and watching and guiding, the old artist stopped painting over Henry's work.

Chapter 27

'Right, that's it, then,' said Henry, propelling his wheelchair down the ramp that led from the door of Oscar Harrington, sports physiotherapist. He'd been Dove's last hope.

She said nothing and her brother looked up at her. 'Do you know what my biggest regret is, Dove?'

She shook her head.

'Throwing good money after bad,' he said. 'We knew a year ago that I'd never be able to walk again. I'm only doing this for you.'

'I was only doing it for you,' she countered. 'And there's always –'

He chopped her off. 'Dove, I'm sorry, I'm not going to Lourdes ... definitely.'

'It'd do no harm,' she muttered, almost under her breath, but not quite.

'Dove!' Henry was becoming exasperated. 'I *do* know. If God wanted me to walk, He wouldn't have me traipsing off to some bloody wishing-well in France. He'd do it here and now.'

'There's no need to swear.'

'You make me swear sometimes.'

Dove chose to say nothing. She wheeled him down Queen Anne Street and turned right into the more medically renowned Harley Street. She couldn't resist suggesting, 'There's probably a man down here who –'

'Dove! Unless he's got a halo and holes in his hands, I don't want to know. Stop it, will you?'

She relented. 'I suppose you want to see some galleries before we go back?'

'I'd better. Larry Pegson said if I didn't spend some of my time seeing how the real artists do it, he'd send back me to London under my own steam.'

'I'll see if I can get a taxi.'

'I'd prefer not to,' Henry said. 'It can't be all that far and I'm fed up of people carting me round all the time. If I'm going to spend the rest of my life sitting down, I want to make the best of it.'

Dove smiled for the first time that day. 'You're the boss,' she said.

'I wish I was,' he grumbled.

It was a fine, warm day and Dove took full advantage of the courtesy people were extending to this dramatically beautiful young woman and her wheelchair-bound companion. Henry was enjoying the energy of the increasingly cosmopolitan London streets. They stopped to listen to a guitar-playing busker in Piccadilly Circus and marvelled at the cascade of coins dropping into his hat, thrown by passers-by who rarely stopped to listen. If they had, they'd have soon realised he only ever played one song, the seasonally appropriate "Here Comes Summer".

They were sitting beneath Eros, watching with fascination the swirl of the traffic and the bustle of the crowds. The busker took heed of a warning look from a passing policeman and moved on to a new venue down in the tube. As soon as the constable was out of sight a saxophone player took up station around the other side of the statue. He sounded better than most of the musicians in the bands Dove had played with.

'I know what you're thinking,' said Henry.

'All right, what am I thinking?' she challenged.

'Going back to busking?'

'Well, I used to enjoy it,' she admitted. 'And have you seen the money they make down here?'

'Ah,' said Henry. 'To make that sort of money you'd have to come and live down here – and that'd be daft.'

'Oh,' she said. 'Why?'

'Now that we've got a proper home in Yorkshire.'

'It's not *my* home.'

'It's *my* home, Dove,' said Henry. 'Monty says I can stay there as long as I want. He's made a will out and named us in it. Did you know that?'

'I'm not sure I want to talk about wills. His wife's will caused enough problems. It broke up a marriage – not to mention what happened to that poor man's car.'

There was a lull in their conversation as he pondered whether to get something off his chest. He looked at his sister and saw beyond the beauty of her face as only a brother could. She could be a bit of a pain but she was all he had. He could never talk about girls to Monty, and his male friends had always been a bit thin on the ground, especially now he was in a wheelchair.

'You know all this boyfriend, girlfriend stuff,' he said. 'Do you think there's the right person waiting for everybody?'

'I think there is,' she said, after some consideration.

'And do you think Tom's the right one for you?'

'Tom? I haven't seen him in ages.'

'You've tried to ring him a few times, I've heard you on the phone.'

Dove's face clouded. 'I've left a few messages with his auntie. I said some things to him that I shouldn't. I just wanted to clear the air with him, that's all.'

'You should try harder. You know what his auntie's like. She thinks the likes of us are rubbish. Tom won't have got any message. You should try the RAF.'

'And you should mind your own business and stop earwigging on people's private telephone calls,' said Dove, sharply.

'I was only sa –'

'Well don't!' she snapped.

They watched the passing traffic in silence for a while, then a mischievous smile crept across Henry's face. 'When you think of him,' he asked. 'Does it make your heart beat strangely?'

'What?'

'I just wondered,' he said, innocently.

Dove shook her head and looked away. Then she turned back to him. 'Beat strangely? Where the devil did you get that from?'

'I read it in *Tales of Romance* earlier on,' he admitted. 'They never have proper stuff to read in waiting rooms ... Well, does it?'

'Henry, just mind your own business.'

He thought for a long time before saying, 'What about me?'

'What about you?'

'Should they, I mean girls ... should they like you, no matter what?'

262

'Are we talking about liking or loving?'

Henry gave a thin laugh and said, 'What do I know? I'm a seventeen-year-old cripple.'

She said nothing. Mavis Feather had been to see him in hospital, but had shown no romantic inclination towards him. Dove had been there when it happened and was sensitive enough to see the disappointment on her brother's face when the girl walked away with a cheery goodbye and no kiss. She hadn't been back since.

The saxophonist was playing "I'm Walking Behind You" and Dove felt like telling the man not to be so damned insensitive; but her brother wasn't listening.

'It's just that I've heard,' Henry went on, 'that when someone comes along, you always know it straight away and if you don't do something about it, you'll regret it for the rest of your life. Is that right?'

'I suppose so.'

He looked at her, 'How am I supposed to do something about it, Dove?'

Dove felt helpless. 'Why ... have you met someone?' she asked.

'Not really,' he said. 'I've only ever met one girl I ... you know, fancied, but I don't know if she's the one. Probably not actually. Not now I'm a cripple.

'Mavis Feather?'

'Could be.'

'I'll have a word with her on your behalf, if you like,' she offered. 'I'll be calling in the studio next week.'

'What would you say?'

She rubbed her chin, thoughtfully. 'I don't know. I'll just tell her that you like her and wouldn't mind a date.'

'A date? No, she won't want to say no, because she'll feel rotten.'

'What do you want me to say then?' Dove asked.

'Tell her I wouldn't mind ... seeing her again.'

'Seeing her? Yes, there's no commitment in that, either way.'

'I don't want her to feel she's lumbered with a cripple.'

'Pity Alice isn't around,' Dove said, without thinking.

'What? You think us cripples should stick together, do you?'

'I didn't mean it like that.'

'How did you mean it, then?'

'I don't know,' she said. 'It was a stupid thing to say.'

'It was stupid all right.'

She didn't respond. Coping with Henry through this crisis in his life was a day-to-day learning experience. Sometimes it was best to say nothing.

'At least we don't live in the waggon anymore,' said Henry. 'So I'm not a crippo gippo ... I'd have no chance getting a bird then.'

'You'll find someone, don't worry,' said Dove, abruptly enough to end a conversation which was getting awkward.

She took out a street map and perused it, studiously, then said, 'Right, there's a gallery on Jermyn Street that Larry said I should take you to. Albert de Vere's – apparently he's expecting you.' She got to her feet and took the handles of the wheelchair. 'According to this map it's ... sort of over there.' She jabbed a finger in a general southerly direction and set off.

They'd gone just a few yards when Henry said, 'Don't do this to me, Dove! I'm not a baby in a pram. I might not want to go.'

She stopped, annoyed at first, then she realised what she was doing to him – allowing his disability to deny him the right to run his own life.

'Okay, I'm sorry,' she said, impatiently. 'That was stupid of me.'

'I just want treating like a normal person,' he complained, 'I'm not *mentally* crippled, you know.'

Suitably chastened, she said, 'Okay, I said I'm sorry. Where do you want to go, O Master?'

Henry grinned, 'That's better.' Then he pointed, 'To that gallery on Jermyn Street. The one Larry mentioned. I think it's over there.'

'Henry,' she said icily, 'don't push your luck or I'll tip you out of this flipping chair.'

As they set off, she leaned over to caution him. 'And listen, Bossy Boots,' she said. 'When we go in to this gallery, you mustn't pronounce his name, Albert. He's French and you have to say "Al Bear".'

'Has he got a brother called Rupert?'

'And you have to treat him seriously.'

'Why wouldn't I?'

'According to Larry he's got a silly beard and you've not to laugh at it.'

264

'Oh heck,' said Henry. 'How silly?'

'Very silly.'

Albert de Vere was in his first-floor office when he saw them approaching. He went downstairs and was at the door when they arrived. In his fifties, he was completely bald and had a narrow beard, like a cartoon Chinaman, which began under his bottom lip and extended halfway down his scrawny chest. For reasons best known to himself, he had dyed it blue. Henry's eyes were instantly drawn to it.

The art dealer held out a hand. 'Albert de Vere at your service. I assume I 'ave the 'onour of meeting 'enry McKenna?'

Henry shook it and said, 'Hello Mister de Beard ... er, de Vere.' He winced as his eyes travelled up the blue beard into de Vere's serious face.

'Do you wish to take the pees out of my beard?'

'What?' said Henry. 'Oh, er ... no, sorry.'

'We wouldn't dream of it,' Dove assured him.

'Ah, so you are the delightful Dove.' De Vere smiled, took her hand and kissed it. 'Larry tried to describe to me 'ow beautiful you are, but I 'ave to say, he failed miserably.'

'Thank you.'

'Please enter my establishment. I 'ave something to show to you.'

He helped Dove push the wheelchair up the single step.

'I must arrange for ... how you say ... a slurp made to allow the wheeler chair up the step.'

'Slurp?' said Henry.

'Slope,' guessed Dove. 'We call it a ramp ... and yes, it would be handy ... Not many people think of it.'

'Well, Albert de Vere 'as thought of it – and it will be done. Please follow me this way.'

He led the way through the shop to a large showroom at the back. Set up on a series of display easels were six oil paintings. Dove gave Albert a questioning look.

'You 'ave never seen them before?' enquired de Vere of Dove.

'Well, no,' she said.

'Do you like what you see?'

'I do, actually,' she said. 'I like them very much.'

'As an artiste of a different genre, you tell me what you see,' challenged de Vere.

265

'Well,' said Dove. 'I see a lot of bright colours that look to have been bashed onto the canvas, hoping they might hit the right spot.'

De Vere laughed. 'And 'ave they hit the right spot?'

'I think so,' she pointed to the one on the right. 'There's a man and a woman in that one – and he's not very pleased with her. In fact he's not very pleased with anything.'

'That's 'cos he's drunk,' said Henry. 'That's dad.'

Seeing these paintings all together on display seemed to dredge up an ugly morass of emotions. He was crying. De Vere looked at him.

'I think your brother appreciates their power and beauty more than anyone.'

Dove turned to Henry. 'What? Are you okay, Henry?'

Henry couldn't speak. Dove looked at de Vere for an explanation. The man smiled and gave a Gallic shrug.

'Your brother is the artist who painted these pictures. Larry Pegson 'as sent them to me one at a time over the last three months.'

'Henry? . . . You never told me,' Dove said.

'I didn't know,' replied Henry, quietly. 'I thought he'd painted over them.'

De Vere smiled. 'This is what we 'oped you were thinking. It is the purest kind of painting. Untainted by any desire for monetary gain. You were painting from the 'eart, with nothing else in mind other than the act of applying pain to canvas.'

'Pain?' Dove said. 'Do you mean paint?'

De Vere laughed. 'Ah yes, paint . . . It is my accent. Then again, maybe pain is the more better word. I make, how you say, a Freudian slip. These paintings are the reflections of your brother's soul at a time of great anguish in his life.'

'Blimey,' said Henry, drying his eyes. 'Is that what they are?'

'What are you going to do with them?' enquired Dove.

De Vere shrugged once more. 'I will try and sell them, of course. I am shortly to 'ave an exhibition of several up-and-coming painters; 'enry will be one of them. In my opinion 'is work is a tour de force and will stand out very much. I 'ave great 'opes for your brother.'

'Wow,' said Dove. 'I didn't expect this.'

'How much will you sell them for?' asked Henry.

De Vere gave a loud, reedy laugh. 'Ah! You are from Yorkshire. Where there is the murk and there is the brass.'

'Where there's muck, there's brass,' said Henry. 'And I was just asking.'

'Ask away my young friend, and I will tell you. It is unwise to demand a fortune for the work of an unknown artist ... but it is equally unwise to ask a little. Wealthy people do not wish to own things of little value. I 'ave priced them all at one 'undred pounds each.'

'A hundred quid?' said Henry, '...each?'

'That's six hundred for all six,' Dove worked out.

'Of which you receive one 'alf,' said de Vere.

Dove and Henry looked at each other, not quite sure why de Vere would want so much.

'Is that normal?' Dove asked. 'You taking half?'

The twinkle momentarily left Albert's eyes. 'It is people like me who create a market for artists like your brother,' he told her. 'My clients rely very much on my taste and expertise. If I think a painting is good, then so do they.'

'I didn't mean to sound rude,' said Dove.

'*Pardonnez-moi*, of course, you were not rude. But I must tell you that although it is 'enry who paints the paintings, it is I who makes them valuable. If I 'ad offered you, say, fifty pounds for all the paintings, you would 'ave, 'ow you say ... grabbed off my 'and?'

'Grabbed your hand off,' said Henry. 'Yes, I think we would.'

'*Exactement* ... That is why an artist needs an 'onest dealer who recognises 'is talent as much as 'e needs 'is own skill and inspiration.'

'I see what you mean,' Dove said. 'Sorry for asking.'

'Not at all. I would 'ave been suspicious if you 'ad not asked.'

'Why's that?' asked Dove.

'I might 'ave thought you were imposters – not from Yorkshire at all.'

'You're a cheeky bugger for a Frenchman,' said Henry.

Chapter 28

Beulah Scullion was taking down her stall of untraceable contraband in Malton market when Sid, who had been missing all afternoon, turned up.

The death of her eldest son had been something of a blow, but in many ways he'd been more trouble than he was worth. His death was as much a mystery to her as it had been to the police. How he came to be lying there naked, with his head kicked in, a gaping wound in his testicles and covered in bits of burning caravan was beyond her. Still, it was a fitting end for a pillock, even if he was her son. The loss of the caravan had hit her harder than the loss of Pikey – the replacement was a cheap lump of tin with no comfort, status or inside toilet.

'Where've yer been, yer idle pillock?' she bellowed to Sid. 'I've been on me own all afternoon. Yer'll get no bleedin' wages fer today an' don't think yer will.'

Sid was obviously drunk, which meant Beulah would be driving. This didn't improve her temper and she fetched him a heavy blow around his ears.

'An' I've told yer about boozin' when there's work ter be done! Bloody frame yersen an' get this lot loaded up while I have a cuppa tea – I haven't had time ter scratch me arse today!'

Sid's face fell into a sulk as he loaded the dodgy merchandise into boxes. He muttered to himself, 'I found out summat this afternoon what I wouldn't o' found out if I hadn't been in t' pub.' Then he flinched as she raised her arm to him again.

'Hey! If yer crack me again I'll not tell yer,' he warned.

She stayed her arm, vaguely curious. 'Tell me what?' she asked.

'What I found out this afternoon.'

'Oh, aye ... an' what would you know that might interest me? Yer've never known nowt worth knowin' in yer life, yer big useless pillock.'

'All right, then. I won't tell yer.'

Her hand came down again. This time sending him reeling to the ground.

'Yer'll do as yer bleedin' told, lad!'

He held his arm over his face to ward off any further blows. Other market traders paused to watch in amusement, laughing and ridiculing the large man cowering beneath the threatening fist of his mother.

'Stop his pocket money, Beulah,' called out a wag.

'I'll thump you if yer don't shut yer gob!' she threatened.

The wag shut his gob as Beulah hauled Sid to his feet by his collar. 'Tell me what yer've got ter tell me; then gerron wi' yer bleedin' work!'

'All right, all right,' he said. 'It were just summat Jez Mulkin said in t' pub.'

'Oh, I might o' known it,' she sneered. 'Jez bleedin' Mulkin. An' when did he ever say owt worth listenin' to?'

'It were about our Pikey,' muttered Sid.

'What about him?'

'Jez reckoned he were there when Pikey got done. Only he daren't tell t' scuffers 'cos they had a warrant out on him.'

'So, he were there, so what?' said Beulah. 'It dunt bring our Pikey back.'

'It weren't no accident,' said Sid. 'There were a fight and t' van caught on fire... an' somebody turned up on an 'oss an' cart, then t' van got blowed up.'

Beulah frowned deeply as she digested this garbled information. 'What else did he tell yer?' she growled.

'Nowt. That were it.'

'Well I think I'd better have a word with Mr Jez bleedin' Mulkin,' Beulah decided. 'An' find out why he never told me nowt about this.'

'Aw, Mam ... I told him I wouldn't tell yer.'

She hit him again. 'Well yer have told me, haven't yer? So where's Jez Mulkin?'

'He's in t' Fellmongers.'

'By the time I'm back I want this lot loaded up, or yer'll feel more o' the back of me hand!' roared Beulah, before she set off towards the Fellmongers Arms.

Jez knew he was in trouble the second his eyes met hers as she walked in the door. He froze with his pint in his hand, then he half turned to go.

'Jez Mulkin, you stay where you are,' she bellowed. The threat in her voice carried over the top of the rowdy conversations of the other drinkers. They parted as she made her way towards the hapless Mulkin, took him by his shirt collar and led him outside.

'Tell me what yer know about that night our Pikey snuffed it. An' tell me now,' she demanded harshly.

Jez was a thin, wretched-looking thief, who was terrified of violence. 'I meant ter tell,' he blubbered. 'But I haven't seen yer since –'

'Tell me now.' She pushed him against the wall and twisted the handful of collar she had in her fist, half-choking him.

'Awright, awright,' he gasped. She eased her grip to allow his words out.

'I were on a roof nickin' lead.'

'That's not your lead ter nick!' she berated. 'That's my bleedin' lead. Nick yer own bleedin' lead in future, yer thievin' bastard! Now tell me what happened afore I throttle yer.'

'I couldn't see much at first,' he began. 'I just heard your Pikey's voice, as though he were talkin' ter somebody. He didn't sound too pleased.'

'Our Pikey never sounded pleased. What happened then?'

'Well, I worked me way round a chimley pot ter get a better look.'

'An' what did yer see?'

He sniggered. 'I saw Pikey wi' his strides afire. He were dancin' abaht like somebody not right in their head. Then he had his strides off an' threw 'em away, like a bit o' burnin' rag. Next thing I saw were him standin' there wi' nowt on an' your van afire. There were somebody else there an' all but I couldn't mek out who it were. They were lyin' on t' ground near Pikey. I reckon he must 'ave given 'em a right good hiding.'

'What about this 'oss an' cart?' asked Beulah, bemused at this stange story.

'This big bloody 'oss came gallopin' up t' street pullin' a big cart. It were like summat outa *Wagon Train*,' said Jez, warming to his telling of the story. 'Ran straight at Pikey like it had summat agen 'im. It reared up and knocked him down. I reckon that's what did fer him. Then whoever were on t' ground jumped on t' cart an' they buggered off back down t' road. Not afore t' oss gave Pikey another good kickin'.'

'Did yer see who were drivin' this cart?' Beulah glowered.

'Oh aye. I saw 'is face when he turned t' cart round ter come back. Saw it plain as day – because of t' fire.'

'An' what did he look like?' she thundered.

'He were an owd bugger wi' a white beard.'

'Oh aye?' Beulah recognised the description. 'Like Father Christmas?'

'Aye,' agreed Jez. 'Onny it weren't no reindeer pullin' his cart. It were a big bloody 'oss.'

'The owd bastard!' she cursed. Her anger transferred itself to her grip and it wasn't until she heard Jez choking that she released him. He slumped to the ground as she strode away with vengeance in her heart. No one set fire to Beulah Scullion's beautiful caravan and got away with it; not only that, but he'd killed her Pikey as well.

The Thames Trader was parked within sight of the end of the lane leading to Monty's bungalow. Beulah glared through the windscreen and lit another Park Drive. Sid wasn't with her; she didn't want him involved in this. She didn't want Sid involved in anything which required quick thinking. He was cleaning out the caravan, after which the day was his to do with as he saw fit. Sid would exhaust his imagination thinking about the many and varied ways he could spend his leisure time, then he'd go to some pub and get blind drunk.

The landlord of Monty's local had informed her of his address after she'd assured him that Monty was 'a dear old mate what she hadn't seen for ages'. He had also mentioned Dove and her converted dormobile in which she drove her crippled brother around. Beulah had driven the lorry up the lane and seen no vehicle outside, and was about to go away and come back another day when she saw Monty moving about inside. It looked like he was on his own, which was good.

By eleven o'clock the cab of the truck was becoming littered with empty beer bottles and cigarette ends. The weather didn't

271

know what to do. Desultory rain soon obscured the windscreen so she started the engine and switched the wipers on to make sure she had a clear view.

A man came out of the lane, accompanied by a small dog tugging at a lead, the man's face hidden by an umbrella. When he tilted it to check where he was going a startling grin contorted Beulah's face. It was Monty. She drove the truck directly at him.

He neither saw nor heard the oncoming danger, mainly due to his umbrella and his ears being bunged up with wax – he had meant to make an appointment at the doctor's to have them syringed. His walk to the pub had become a daily routine. A telegraph pole came into view under the rim of his umbrella; here was where he always turned to cross the street. He peered to his left and saw a clear road, then glanced to his right. By this time the advancing truck was obscured by the telegraph pole as it came at him with one wheel on the wide grass verge and another on the footpath. Monty was yanked off the kerb by the excited dog and Beulah tried to swerve into him, but only succeeded in snapping the pole off at its base, sending it sprawling into a garden in an entanglement of wires. Monty strode on, battling against the enthusiasm of Deefer, who was keen to get to the pub – or to anywhere for that matter.

Beulah drove away, cursing, and vowing to catch him when he came out of the pub at 12.30, as he apparently always did.

'Where are we now?' enquired Henry.

'Warwickshire. Just coming up to the end of the motorway.'

'Fancy another rest?'

'We'll stop at that service station place where we stopped on the way down.'

'I've read they're extending the M1 right up to Leeds,' said Henry. 'That should be all right.'

She looked at her watch. 'When I rang Monty last night I told him we'd be back about two. If there's not much traffic in Leicester we should be okay.'

'How did he sound?' asked Henry.

'Okay ... why?'

'I don't know. He hasn't been as chirpy lately. Every time I mention it to him, he just says he's getting old.'

'Anno Domini, that's what he keeps telling me,' Dove said. 'He did say one thing that made me wonder.'

'What?'

'He suggested Joe Weller takes over as my manager ... I don't think Monty feels up to it anymore.'

'And what did you say to that?'

'I said I really need someone to come to gigs with me. To take care of stuff ... including me.'

'Like a road manager?'

'Yes. Joe's too busy for that.'

'I suppose that'd have been my job,' said Henry.

Dove shrugged. 'You never know. I suppose if you hadn't been in a wheelchair Monty might not have sent you to Larry Pegson. So some good's come of it.'

'I hope Monty's going to be all right.'

'I'm sure he will be,' she said. 'He is seventy-seven so he's entitled to feel a bit off now and again.'

'I suppose so,' conceded Henry. He watched the passing world for a while, then remarked, 'I could have sworn you'd do a morning's busking and set off at dinner time.'

'I thought we'd set off early and try and miss the London traffic ... and I'm definitely done with busking. Did I tell you Joe Weller's got me a residency at that new hotel and nightclub place they're opening in Harrogate?'

'When did you find out about that?'

'Last night when I rang Monty. The money's pretty good as well. Ten pounds a night, two nights a week.'

'You never told me.'

'You were too excited talking about your paintings. I didn't want to steal your thunder.'

'Sorry.'

'Don't be. I'm as excited about your paintings as you are. You'll be able to keep me in the manner to which I hope to become accustomed.'

'You always split fifty-fifty with me,' Henry said. 'I'll do the same ... fancy a mint?'

He held a packet of mint imperials over her shoulder. She rummaged and took a handful.

'I said one.'

'No, you didn't. You said you'd split everything fifty-fifty.'

'That doesn't mean sweets,' grumbled Henry. 'You buy your own sweets.'

Dove smiled. They were getting back to a brother/sister banter as opposed to the carer/invalid relationship which Dove had found hard to shake off. She still felt guilty for what had happened to him. And she was feeling increasingly guilty at the way she'd treated Tom.

To her dismay she was actually finding living in a house to be monotonous. The freedom to up sticks and move off was in her blood, put there by Malachy. She had been determined to fight it, to become normal, but the prospect of normality grew less inviting by the day.

The fine London weather had given way to gloomy banks of clouds; spots of rain hit the windscreen and Dove switched on the wipers.

'So, what do you think about me and girls?' Henry said, taking up yesterday's conversation which had been left in mid-air. His teeth rattled against the two mints he had in his mouth.

'I'll tell you what I think,' said Dove. 'If you play your cards right you could turn this disability thing to your advantage, especially if it turns out you're a successful artist.'

'Do you think so?'

'I know so. You see, a lot of girls like men who are no threat to them. A man they can mother.'

'Oh, I don't want mothering,' said Henry. 'In fact that's *exactly* what I don't want – if you get my meaning.'

'Sorry, I didn't mean mother, I meant . . . look after you.'

'They can look after me as much as they want.'

'You'll just have to make the most of what you've got.'

'And what's that?'

'Are you fishing for compliments?'

'What – compliments from my sister? I'm not that stupid.'

She drove for a while, then said, 'Well, I don't suppose you're bad looking.'

'Go on.'

'Don't push it,' she warned. 'And you can make people laugh . . . even if you have got a strange sense of humour.'

'It's you who's got the strange sense of humour. I'm the normal one. You get paid for making people laugh, that's always baffled me.'

'To be honest,' she admitted. 'It's always baffled me.'

'What else?' he asked.

'Money,' she said. 'If you become wealthy through your painting you'll be beating girls off with a shovel. You'll have to be careful though, because they probably won't be the right type of girl.'

'I'll just have to take my time finding out.'

She turned and grinned at him; then looked back at the road. 'I've never asked,' she said, 'but is everything all right down there?'

'Down where?'

'I think you know where.'

'Of course it is.'

'How do you know?' she teased.

She looked in the rear-view mirror to see if he was blushing. He decided to shock her.

'Well it was all right the last time I tried it out,' he said.

'Tried it out? Henry McKenna, you mucky monkey!'

'It's part of my medical self-assessment programme,' he said, as though surprised she didn't know such an obvious thing. 'If I don't try it out, I get told off.'

'You just made that up, didn't you?'

'You should mind your own business.

Father Mulvaney shook the rain off his umbrella and joined Monty at the bar. 'Did you see the telegraph pole that's been knocked down at the end of your lane, Monty?' he said. 'They say a lorry hit it.'

Monty had been there well over an hour; another twenty minutes and his time was up. He had to discipline his drinking time to suit his wallet and his liver. He looked up from his newspaper and smiled at the retired priest. 'Hello, Michael. What was that?'

Father Mulvaney repeated his question and Monty shook his head. 'No, it must have happened after I passed.' He returned his attention to his newspaper. 'Yorkshire look like winning,' he observed. 'About time.'

'I hope it hasn't knocked my phone out,' the landlord said, picking up his telephone. He cursed. 'Hell and damnation! Sorry, Michael. I were supposed ter be ringin' t' brewery this afternoon. I'll have ter find a phone box what works.'

'How are you today, Monty?' enquired the priest, as the landlord pulled him a pint of bitter.

'Oh, dying nicely. Ears bunged up and the old ticker's on the blink. Must go see the quack again. Trouble is, the only exercise I get nowadays is coming here.'

'Hello, Deefer dog,' the priest bent down to pat the eager dog's head. He always called Deefer by his full name, as if reminding himself of its pun origin. Henry's idea. 'Kids okay?' he asked Monty.

Dove and Henry were, to all Monty's friends, his kids. The very reference to them brought a smile to his face. 'They're marvellous,' he said. 'Young Henry's turning out to be a child prodigy with the old paintbrush. Who'd have guessed it, eh? A young scamp like him.'

'By all accounts, you guessed it,' said the landlord, handing Father Mulvaney his beer.

'Oh, it would have come out sooner or later,' Monty said modestly. 'I suppose this rain will have stopped play at Headingley.'

'Later might have been too late,' observed the priest. 'Time is on no one's side, even the young.' He took his drink to a table, where he opened up his *Daily Mirror.* Monty wanted to talk about cricket and he hated cricket.

For the next few minutes, the priest's words had Monty ruminatively sipping his pint and watching the clock behind the bar tick his life away – and knew that for him, each passing minute represented a disturbingly high percentage of the rest of his time here on Earth. He thought of Elisabeth and wondered how near he was to a reunion. That would nice. Was there a heaven and hell? Because if there was, then surely Elisabeth would be in heaven. But where would he go, with Scullion's blood on his hands? He assumed God would understand why he killed Elisabeth but would He condone what he'd done to Scullion? Pity he wasn't a Catholic, he could confess his sins and be assured of a place in heaven. He drained his drink and waved a dismissive hand as the landlord went to pull him another. Monty's eyes scanned the top shelf and settled on a malt whisky.

'Large Glenfiddich,' he said. 'And a small one for Michael.'

The priest looked up, suspiciously, at the sound of his name. 'It'll take more than a whisky to get me talking about cricket,' he warned.

Monty picked up the drinks and took them over to where the

priest was sitting. Deefer beat him to it and was already curled under the table when Monty set the drinks down.

'I don't want to talk about cricket,' he said. 'I want to discuss religion with you.'

'I thought they were one and the same with you.'

Monty ignored him as he gathered his thoughts. 'You're a Catholic, aren't you, Michael?' he began.

'Not much gets past you, Monty.'

'And I'm not a Catholic.'

'Go on.'

'Well,' said Monty. 'If I were a Catholic and I'd committed a mortal sin, I could confess it and God would forgive me.'

'So far so good,' said the priest.

'So what do we non-Catholics do? How do we escape eternal damnation?'

'Well, the short answer is, you become a Catholic,' said Father Mulvaney.

'What about the long answer?' asked Monty. 'The answer that makes sense.'

'There isn't much sense in religion,' admitted the priest. 'Why are you asking me all this?'

'Can I put a hypothetical situation to you?' said Monty.

'I think I'd rather talk about cricket.'

'Supposing a man's wife was dying in agony and he put her out of her misery, what would God think about that?'

The priest put down his drink and looked hard at him. 'God would want the man to be truly sorry for what he'd done – then He'd forgive him.' He didn't take his eyes off Monty as he said it.

Monty held Father Mulvaney's gaze as he responded, 'But how could this man be truly sorry for allowing his wife to end her life in peace instead of pain?'

'Such a decision is God's.'

'Then God shouldn't have given man compassion.'

'True,' conceded the priest. 'But He also gave man a set of values.'

'He gave different men different sets of values.'

'Tell me,' said Father Mulvaney. 'Does this man's conscience ever trouble him? Enough, for example for him to seek absolution for committing this act of mercy?'

Monty thought about this as he sipped at his drink. 'Well,

277

Michael,' he said. 'Sometimes this man feels as guilty as hell. He doesn't know whether he was doing it for his wife or for him.'

'This man sounds genuine,' said the priest. 'And if God in His infinite wisdom chose not to make us perfect, then maybe that's all God can expect.'

'I've got another one for Him to sort out,' said Monty.

'I hear Ray Illingworth's having a good season for Yorkshire,' sighed the priest.

Monty wasn't even tempted. 'Supposing,' he said. 'That a good man comes upon a bad man who was about to kill this good man's friend and he had the means to prevent the killing but not without doing mortal harm to the bad man.'

'Tricky one,' admitted the priest. 'What were the means at this good man's disposal?'

'A big horse,' Monty said. 'Which didn't much like the bad man. In fact it was the horse who killed the bad man.'

'But the good man was riding the horse?'

'Driving would be more accurate.'

The priest looked at Monty with new eyes. 'Are you a good man, Monty?'

'I try to be.'

'This is a very detailed scenario for a hypothetical question,' said Father Mulvaney. 'Very detailed indeed.'

'And,' said Monty. 'This good man is a non-Catholic.'

'Just like you?'

'Precisely. How does he get absolution for this?'

'I think he takes his chances on Judgement Day.'

'And what would you say his chances are?'

'I'd forgive him,' said the priest. 'But I'm not God.'

'You're good enough for me,' smiled Monty. 'Whisky?'

Beulah was dozing behind the wheel, parked just a few yards from the pub. The rain had stopped and the heavy sky was beginning to break up. A loud hoot from a passing car jerked her into consciousness just as Monty was emerging from the pub. She shook her head to clear it and started the engine. This time she wouldn't miss. The hoot had been a warning to Monty not to step off the kerb. He waved his now furled umbrella at the driver in acknowledgement of his warning, and tugged Deefer to heel; then he looked up the street towards Beulah's truck to confirm it was stationary before he allowed the dog to pull him across the road.

Running down someone who is crossing a road takes a certain amount of timing – arrive too early or too late and you've missed them. In Monty's case it was too late – but only by a split second. He saw the lorry coming and managed to jump out of its way, only to fall heavily on the footpath and bang his head on the ground. But the worst damage was to his heart, which began racing with the shock of such a near miss. Passers-by were on the scene immediately and an ambulance summoned.

Dove and Henry had made good time. The traffic coming up from the Midlands hadn't been too bad and they turned the corner just as the crowds were gathering around Monty. Dove slowed down automatically.

'Oh heck,' she said. 'I think there's been an accident.'

Henry, from his higher vantage point, first recognised Deefer, running around the perimeter of the crowd with his lead dragging loose. Then between the people he recognised a white-bearded man on the ground.

'I think it's Monty.'

His sister pulled on the handbrake and was out of the vehicle in a flash, leaving her brother banging on the window to be let out. She knelt beside the old man and cradled his head in her arms. He opened his eyes and they crinkled into a smile.

'Oh Dove, I'm so glad you're here.'

'You're going to be okay, Monty,' she said, then asked, 'what happened to you?'

'I'm not sure,' he said. 'But it seems to have got the wax out of my ears.'

'It were a lorry, love,' said one woman. 'I saw it go tearin' past. Next thing I knew he were lyin' here. Me husband's gone ter ring fer an ambulance, if he can find a phone box what works.'

Dove looked down at Monty. The blood had drained from his face but he was forcing his eyes to stay open, as if he knew when he closed them it would be for the last time.

'Where's ... Henry?' he asked.

'He's ... Can someone let my brother out of the van, please?' She returned her attention to Monty. 'There's help on the way,' she assured him.

279

'Oh dear, Dove, I think I'm way beyond help.'

'Don't talk like that, Monty.'

'I'm not afraid, Dove.'

'That's because there's nothing to be afraid of. You've just had a nasty bump, that's all.'

'Ah, Henry.' He looked past her and reached a hand up to grasp that of his young friend, who had been wheeled to his side. 'I hear you're going to be famous.'

Henry couldn't speak at first. He took the old man's hand in both of his and wouldn't let it go. The life seemed to be draining from it. 'Don't you go doing anything silly, Monty,' he blurted. 'Me and Dove need someone to look after us.'

'Me look after you?' said Monty. His voice was weak now. 'I want to thank you for looking after me these last few years. I couldn't have hoped for a better and more exciting way to end my life.' His gaze went beyond them into the sky. 'I think Elisabeth had a hand in this, you know. She brought me to you.'

He narrowed his eyes as the sun suddenly came out and shone on his face. Dove moved her head so it cast a shadow over him.

'See,' he said. 'That's her now. Turning the light on. She always turned the porch light on for me when I came home in the dark.'

He transferred his fading gaze to the two tearful faces looking down at him. 'Now, now, what are you looking so sad about? This is my time, don't you see? I've just been to the pub; my two favourite people are here; and my darling Elisabeth is patiently waiting for me.'

Dove took his other hand and squeezed it, as though trying to inject some of her own life into him. 'Surely there's something we can do,' she said, helplessly.

'There is something,' Monty said. 'But it's a bit naughty of me.'

'What?' asked Dove.

'I don't suppose you could kiss me goodbye, could you? Just on the forehead, nothing that would make Elisabeth jealous.'

Dove kissed him, softly, on his forehead, then laid her cheek beside his and hugged him to her, her tears soaking into his beard. Monty looked beyond her at Henry and said, 'What a way to go, eh, Henry? In the arms of a beautiful woman.'

Through misty eyes Henry tried to smile as Monty whispered into Dove's ear, 'Give my love to Tom. He's one of the good men in your life.'

'I know that, Monty.'

'You know? Then stop being afraid of ...' His voice faded away. Dove placed a hand at either side of his face and willed him back to life.

'Afraid of what, Monty?'

He opened his eyes and smiled at her. 'Afraid of loving Tom. I just hope it's not ...'

'Not what, Monty?'

'Not too late,' he said.

Then the light in his eyes went out and the watching crowd held its breath as Dove lifted her head from his and took his hand. Henry still clung to the other one. Neither of them wanted to break the bond they had forged with this dear old man. The silence was broken by the sound of an approaching ambulance which would take Montgomery Catchpole away from them for ever. Despite them being orphans they had never felt such desolate bereavement. Suddenly they felt very alone.

Chapter 29

Dove replaced the telephone receiver and was shaking her head as she came into the living room from the hall.

'I've just rung Tom's Auntie Margaret to ask where I can get hold of him because it was really important.'

'And did she tell you?' Henry asked.

'Nothing, she asked if I was family and when I told her who I was she put the phone down on me. She's getting worse.'

'Auntie Margaret doesn't like you, does she?'

'Doesn't like me? Auntie Margaret's never even met me.'

Tom had been the first person she felt she needed to tell about Monty. This hadn't been lost on Henry, who figured she was coming to her senses at last. If Dove needed anyone in her life it was Tom Webster, but it wasn't up to Henry to tell her, she had to work that one out for herself.

'Ring her again tomorrow,' advised Henry. 'You know what women are like ... blow hot and cold over nothing at all. She's most prob'ly had a perm that's gone wrong, something like that.'

It was a bit of an insult to her sex but he was right. Dove sat down in the chair opposite her brother and continued to exchange words of comfort and memories of their time with Monty. He'd played such a huge part in their lives and now he was gone.

'Tom'll be absolutely gutted,' she said. 'He liked Monty.'

'Monty liked Tom,' said Henry. 'We all did.' He didn't look at her but he knew his words met with her approval.

'Better he went out like that than withered away until all the life drained out of him,' she said. 'He wouldn't have wanted to die like Elisabeth.'

'I think he'd had a bit to drink,' said Henry. 'That must have helped.' There was a long silence before he added, 'He was my best pal.'

Dove smiled. 'I know. It was like living with a couple of kids at times.'

'He liked Tom.' Henry thought it was worth repeating.

'I know he did.'

'He said something about him before he died, didn't he?'

She nodded and thought about that last moment, frowning away a tear. 'He said to give his love to Tom.'

'Then he said something else,' said Henry gently.

The tear made its way out and down her cheek. 'He told me not to be afraid of loving Tom.'

Henry gave this some thought. 'How can you be afraid of loving someone?'

Dove gave a rueful smile. 'If men have given you cause to be frightened it puts you on your guard a bit.'

'I suppose it must,' conceded Henry.

She suddenly shivered. 'He said, Tom's one of the good men in my life.'

'Tom's definitely a good bloke.'

'I know,' said Dove. 'It just reminded me of something old Betsy Lee told me. Now what was it she said?'

She tried to cast her mind back to that eventful day at Netherton Fair. The gipsy's words had been overshadowed by the subsequent events of that day; but they were still lodged at the back of Dove's mind.

'She said something about ... she seemed to know about dad.'

'Oh heck!' said Henry.

'I've forgotten how ... but I just got that impression. Then she said something about there being three good men in my life, and I said something about it adding up to five.'

'And did she tell you you weren't making sense?' commented Henry.

'No ... that's right, she mentioned two bad men and three good men.'

'Well, the two bad men aren't difficult to fathom,' Henry said. 'Dad and Pikey ... and the three good men are me, Monty and Tom.'

'You don't qualify. You're not a man yet,' she said, rather unkindly.

'Man enough to save your skin,' he reminded her.

She capitulated immediately. 'Sorry,' she said. 'I didn't mean that.'

The knock on the door had the rhythm of an official knock, but not the firmness. It was the respectful knock of someone who knew of the grief he was disturbing. As Dove opened the door, Inspector Sykes removed his hat.

'Hello, Dove,' he said. 'I thought I'd come myself instead of sending some young constable who doesn't know you.'

'Oh,' she said, not understanding why he'd come at all.

'I know this is a bad time, but I need to have a little chat about what happened.'

'Right, er ... would you like to come in?'

'Thank you.'

He followed her through to the living room and nodded at Henry.

'Hello, Henry,' he said. 'How are you?'

'I'm okay, thank you, Inspector.'

The policeman hovered over the settee, 'Mind if I ...?'

'Oh, yes,' Dove said.

He sat down, twiddled his hat in his hands, then placed it on the cushion beside him and looked round.

'It's a very nice place,' he commented. 'Bit of an improvement on the caravan. I hope Mr Catchpole made proper provision for you in his will.'

'I understand he left the house to us, Inspector,' said Dove.

'Quite right too.'

'Is that why you came, to ask about the house?'

'Oh, no ... I was just making polite conversation, that's all.'

'Why did you come?' asked Henry.

'Well,' said the inspector. 'Because of the nature of Mr Catchpole's death, there's to be a post-mortem.'

'I thought there might be,' Dove said. 'Have you caught the lorry driver yet?'

'Not yet ... although according to the hospital, in all probability, Mr Catchpole died of a heart attack.'

'Oh,' said Dove. 'So, it was a natural death?'

'Well, it was exacerbated by him being nearly knocked down, so we might be still looking at a death-by-dangerous-driving charge, as and when we apprehend the driver.'

284

'He hadn't been feeling well recently,' Dove told him.

'Well, apparently it could have happened at any time,' said the policeman.

'Did anyone get a good look at the driver?' asked Henry.

Inspector Sykes shook his head. 'Not yet. We don't even know what sort of lorry it was. The only snippet of information we do have is that a lorry was seen parked in the same street just before the accident, with a Guinness label where the tax disc should be.'

'Scullions!' said Dove and Henry, in unison.

'It's hardly likely to be Pikey Scullion,' said the inspector.

'There's more than one Scullion, Inspector,' Dove pointed out.

The policeman got to his feet. 'Right, I'll, er . . . I'll chase it up . . . and thank you.'

Beulah was arrested within the hour and locked up, while the police took a really close look at her contraband. This time they checked further afield when Sid told them they couldn't take his mother because she had business to do in Coventry with some blokes who were coming all the way up from London to see her. His mother made a desperate attempt to throttle her surviving son into silence but was held back by two grinning constables. Then she screamed that Monty deserved all he got because he was the one who had burned her caravan . . . and killed her son.

'Really? Do you know, I think we might be looking at a murder charge here, Mrs Scullion,' said the inspector. 'So, say goodbye to Sid. You might not be seeing him for a while.'

'Suits me if I never see the brainless bugger again,' spat Beulah. 'They've caused me nowt but bleedin' grief, the both of 'em.'

Chapter 30

The next day, Dove was scanning the deaths column to get some idea of the type of notice to place in the newspaper, when Joe Weller knocked and came in the house uninvited. It was his way. He removed his trilby and stood respectfully beside Dove's chair. Henry was sitting in another chair listening to *Family Favourites*.

'I've just heard,' Joe said. 'I've been away overnight and the wife's just told me. I'm ever so sorry. He was a lovely man, was Monty. I'd like to offer my condolences.'

'Thanks,' said Henry, turning off the radio.

'Yes,' said Dove. 'Thanks, Joe.'

'Is there anything I can do?' he asked. He looked around him. 'I mean, what happens to this place?'

'He left it to us in his will,' Dove said. 'We found a copy. And the undertaker's organising everything else.'

'If there's any legal stuff to sort out,' Joe said, 'leave it to me. I don't want you troubled unnecessarily. You're going to have enough to think about.'

Dove frowned. 'How do you mean?'

Joe gave a half smile. 'To be honest I hoped it'd come as better news. All this sort of knocks the shine off it. He'd have been so proud of you, would Monty.'

'What is it?' Henry asked. 'This news.'

Joe sat down on the settee, twiddling his hat between his fingers. He had a circuitous way of arriving at the facts, something which had always irritated Monty. 'Well, you know I said I wasn't here overnight,' he said.

'Yes,' said Dove, slightly impatient now.

'Well, I was down in London. You see, Barney Colehan rang

me a couple of days ago and asked if I could send one of your records down to a booker he knew. Barney'd put a good word in for you – and Barney's word carries a lot of weight in this business. When I heard what it was for I thought, sod just sending the record, I'll go myself and take you as well. Then I realised you were down there yourself with Henry.'

'We came back yesterday,' Dove said. 'We were with Monty when he died.'

'Aye,' said Joe. 'So I heard. I reckon that'll have put a smile on his face at the end.'

'It did,' Henry told him. 'Our Dove was holding him in her arms and Monty said, "What a way to go".'

Joe looked at Dove and imagined the scene. 'There's a lot worse ways,' he said. 'It's always been a fantasy of mine, dying in the arms of a beautiful woman. Don't tell my wife that or she'll think I don't want her there. She's a good old lass, but I wouldn't go so far as to call her beautiful.'

'You were telling us about London,' Henry reminded him.

'Ah, so I was. Well, I went down yesterday morning and went to see this bloke. To be honest I could have saved me fare, Barney had built you up so much. Anyway, to cut a long story short, you've got the job.'

'What sort of a gig is it?' Dove asked.

Joe laughed out loud. 'I've never heard *Sunday Night at the London Palladium* called a gig before.'

'You're kidding!' Dove gasped.

'I never kid,' said Joe. 'Not about business.'

'You mean the proper telly thing?'

Joe beamed. This was the biggest thing in his career as well. 'Bruce Forsyth, Beat the Clock, the lot,' he said. 'It's only a three-minute spot, but that's all anyone gets, except the top of the bill. Which is Tommy Steele, incidentally.'

Dove gave a squeal of delight – Tommy Steele was one of her favourites.

'Tell you what,' grinned Joe 'I'll make us a brew while you get your breath back. Something like this can make or break you.'

As Joe went into the kitchen, the newspaper was still spread out on Dove's knee but her mind wasn't on it anymore. It was on the London Palladium. Unbelievable. It was the biggest show on television. She'd only get one number to do, so she'd have to choose carefully, compress all her talents into three minutes.

A familiar name in thickened black letters penetrated her thoughts of great fame as she brought the letters into focus:

Thomas Michael Webster

The notice was edged in a black scroll and was very businesslike. It gave his name, his age and his address (Auntie Margaret's), and where the funeral and the interment were to take place. But no sentiments, not even the maudlin poem she'd expect from the likes of Auntie Margaret. Just RIP.

Dove began to hyperventilate, still clutching the newspaper between rigid fingers.

'Dove?' said Henry. 'Are you okay?'

Dove's breathing became rapid and out of control.

'Joe!' he shouted. 'There's something up with Dove!'

Joe dashed in and put a hand on each of her shoulders, holding her at arm's length. 'Dove,' he said. 'Look at me ... now start counting to ten, very slowly, and take one breath between each number.'

Dove nodded and gradually regained control of her breathing as he had instructed – but she couldn't shake off the shock of reading about Tom's death. Her face was the colour of putty, her body was now trembling all over and she couldn't get any words out at first.

'I know it's a shock, Dove,' she heard Joe saying, 'but it's only a television show. You mustn't let it get to you. You can do it standing on your head.'

Dove didn't understand him. She looked at Henry, with awful misery in her eyes and said, 'Oh Henry ... Tom's dead.'

As she handed her brother the paper, her face crumpled up and she wept, with deep, searing despair in each sob.

With a sombre face Henry read the notice, then looked up to meet his sister's desolate eyes and wondered if this was going to be the last straw for her. He knew no words of comfort.

Chapter 31

Dove's eyes were fixed but not focused on a weathered old grave-stone that tilted at an eccentric angle and marked the last where-abouts of some long-forgotten man. She wore black velvet, apart from her silk shirt and sandals, both the same deep red as the rose decorating her floppy-brimmed hat, which shaded a face of extra-ordinary beauty from the sunlight filtering through the hazy sky.

The eyes of some of the men in the funeral party strayed towards her as she glanced in their direction. But apart from Johnnie, there was no one in the party whom she knew and Dove had good reason to believe she might well be persona non grata if she joined them uninvited. So she returned her gaze to the grave of the forgotten man who had died in 1861, exactly one hundred years earlier. The late summer breeze carried the priest's sing-song drone across to her: 'O God, the Creator and Redeemer of all the faithful, grant to the soul of this, Thy departed servant, the remission of all his sins. May he not undergo the pains of hell but may he possess everlasting joys.'

No one seemed to realise he had finished. An exasperated glance from the clergyman prompted the Catholics in the group to chant a staggered response of 'Amen.'

Having lost all faith in these amateurs to hold up their end of the service the priest switched to Latin as the undertaker's men began to pay out the ropes that lowered the coffin into the grave, while Dove dug deep into her memory for a prayer of her own. After a respectful period of silent mourning, the people began to drift away, in awkward ones and twos, as if no one quite knew what the protocol was. Onc man bowed and backed away, as though he was leaving an audience with the Queen, taking his wife with him. As she stepped backwards her foot came out of her high-heeled shoe when it sank into the soft earth of a recent grave, causing her to hop around on one shoeless foot and vigorously curse her husband under her breath.

Eventually just two people remained at the graveside, a man and a woman. The unmistakable resemblance between the man and Tom's father told Dove who he was – Uncle Frank – and the woman must be Auntie Margaret – the reason Dove was keeping her distance. But why weren't Tom's parents there? She answered her own question – they were in New Zealand and probably couldn't afford the air fare to get back in time.

Auntie Margaret left first. Her face was sombre but devoid of tears; she didn't look the type of woman given to public displays of grief. Uncle Frank remained for a few more minutes, his head bowed in silent prayer, before crossing himself and following his wife.

Two workmen with shovels approached, one of them whistling "The Deadwood Stage". They hesitated when they saw the young woman walking slowly towards the open grave, her face as grey as dust. The whistling workman was elbowed into silence by his colleague and the men stopped a respectful distance away.

Dove walked with an empty heart and she knew that great, gaping emptiness could never be filled by anyone but Tom. She'd never even told him she loved him.

Why had it taken her so long to realise how she felt about him? Why had she been so blinded by self-pity? Why had she picked on him as the scapegoat for everything that had gone wrong in her life? She should have gone to him earlier, heeded Monty's advice – and Henry's for that matter. Maybe she could have saved his life? God! She didn't even know how he had died.

Thomas Michael Webster, Age 22

The name etched into the brass plaque on the coffin also etched its way into her heart, before fading behind a mist of tears. She took the rose from her hat, dropped it on top of the other flowers, then she clasped her hands together and spoke to him.

'I seem to have left things a bit too late, Tom … I'm sorry.'

The workmen moved out of earshot and disappeared behind a marble monument for a smoke. Dove picked up a handful of earth and sprinkled it, bit by bit, on top of the coffin as she continued, 'I honestly don't know what I'm going to do without you. Monty's dead as well, you know. Sorry, I suppose you know that. He knew we were meant for each other. So did Henry. So did you probably. I was too full of my own troubles to see the truth. So I'm very sorry for blaming you. It was too stupid for words. So stupid. Blaming someone because you love them and you're too stupid to know it.'

She picked up another handful of earth and let it run through her hands onto the coffin, forming a link between her and him.

'Goodbye, Tom Webster. I love you and I always did.'

'And I always loved you.'

Dove's heart went cold with shock and her legs gave way beneath her. Another second and she'd have been lying on top of the coffin. Two arms caught her as she fell into a faint. One of the workmen saw what had happened and called out.

'You okay, mate?'

'Fine thanks. She just had a bit of a shock, that's all.'

Dove came to, sitting on the ground with her head buried in his chest. He tilted her chin so he could see her face.

'Okay now?' he said.

Her eyes streamed with tears. She just didn't understand anything. What the hell was going on? Had she just woken up from a bad dream ... or was she dreaming this? She couldn't stand it if this was only a dream. She didn't want to wake up from this dream. Ever.

'I'm really sorry about this,' he said. 'I should have realised.'

Dove reached up a hand and touched his face. 'Tom?' she said.

'I suppose you must have seen it in the paper. It never occurred to me –'

'You're alive.'

'Yes,' he confirmed. 'I'm ever so sorry.'

Epilogue

They were in her car but she was in no condition to drive. Tom had taken the wheel and was heading in the general direction of anywhere away from the cemetery – as far away as possible. He placed his hand over hers.

'When Johnnie told me he'd seen you in the cemetery,' he said, 'I dashed straight there from the pub.'

'Pub? What were you doing in the pub?' Dove's voice was still subdued.

'I felt a fraud,' he explained. 'Michael and I never got on. To be honest I thought he was a bit of a prat. He took after his mother in many respects. I went to the service but skipped the burial. Johnnie volunteered to go in my place. I had some sorrows to drown. Good job or you might still be there.'

'Good job,' Dove repeated. Her head was devoid of all original thought. Then a question arrived.

'Tom ... why was your name on the coffin?'

'That's just it,' he said. 'It's not my name.'

'Yes it is. Thomas Michael Webster. Age twenty-two.'

'Michael Thomas,' he pointed out. 'My name's Michael Thomas. Me and my cousin were born around the same time and when Dad told Auntie Margaret they were going to call me Thomas Michael she said that's what she was going to call her baby.'

'Don't tell me any more,' Dove said. 'I think I can work it out.'

Tom insisted on explaining. 'Dad gave in and switched the names around for the sake of peace and quiet, but mam insisted on calling me Tom.'

'Good for her,' said Dove. 'Your Auntie Margaret's a pain.'

'She always called him Michael,' he went on. 'Never had any intention of calling him Thomas. She just did it for badness.'

'What happened to him?'

'Nobody really knows. He was running for a bus and he dropped down dead. They did a post-mortem and stuck a fancy Latin name on the death certificate, but I don't think they really knew. Doctors eh?'

Dove allowed a respectful silence to elapse. She was glad it was his cousin and not Tom who was dead, but it didn't seem appropriate to say it. Although no doubt Tom would have agreed.

'At the cemetery,' he said. 'I heard you talking. To me ... in a manner of speaking.'

'Did you?' She tried to remember what she'd been saying. He reminded her.

'You told me you loved me.'

Dove left it a while before she said, 'I know.'

'Then I told you I loved you.'

'I heard you. It's a bit of a shock when a dead body tells you he loves you.'

Tom laughed. 'I should have hidden behind a tree and kept it going. I could have had some real fun.'

'There'd have been *two* dead bodies in that grave if you had.'

'Now I'm alive, does it still count?' he asked.

'Does what count?'

'You saying you love me.'

'Tom, stop the car. If I don't kiss you I'm going to go mad.'

Tom obliged by pulling into a pub car park and driving to a quiet corner. 'I don't want you taking advantage of my body,' he said. 'Not in broad daylight. I know you show-business types.'

'Tom Webster, I love you. Now just shut up and kiss me. I need to know this is real.'

They melted into one another and embraced with a mutual greed fired by the desire to make up for lost time, and each knew that kissing wasn't going to be enough. Over Dove's shoulder Tom spotted a sign saying the pub was residential. She followed his gaze and within minutes they were booking themselves in as Mr and Mrs Webster to a sceptical landlady who hesitated before being persuaded by Tom's money.

'No funny business,' she grunted. 'Not durin' openin' hours anyroad.'

293

'We're just tired,' Tom assured her.

'We've come a long way,' added Dove. 'We got lost.'

The room was very basic, the bed was hard and they made love with passion and energy all afternoon. Dove was so overcome by the turn of events she hadn't even noticed his slight limp. As he got out of bed and walked over to the wash basin she opened a sleepy eye and complimented him on his body.

'All this RAF training seems to have done you good. When do you go back?'

She didn't mind him going back. Flying had always been his dream; and you don't interfere with anyone's dreams, not if you love them. Just as long as he was alive, the rest could take care of itself.

'I'm not going back,' he said. 'They wouldn't let me fly a Tiger Moth, never mind a Vampire.'

'Oh, why's that?'

He turned and partially lifted his left leg. 'That's as far as I can lift it,' he said. 'Broke it six months ago.'

'Oh, no! What happened? Was it a flying accident or something?'

'In a manner of speaking. I was on the wing when I broke it. The right wing, playing for the squadron.' He smiled at her. 'I was flying all right – flew straight into this left back. He was built like a brick sh ...shed.'

'Will you be able to play football again?'

He shook his head. 'I can't even march properly. I got word this morning to say I'm going to be invalided out. God knows what I'll do in Civvy Street.'

'Is that what you meant when you said you had sorrows to drown?' she asked.

'Yes,' he said. 'I'd only just got started when Johnnie came in and told me about you.'

'I didn't realise he'd seen me. He didn't even acknowledge me in the cemetery.'

'He knew all about Auntie Margaret's funny ways,' Tom explained. 'He suspected you were keeping your distance for a reason.'

'Before I saw the notice about you ... your cousin, in the paper, I rang to tell you about Monty,' Dove told him. 'But she put the phone down on me. Not for the first time either.'

'She was gutted about Michael,' Tom said. 'I suppose she had an excuse to be rude, for once.'

'Yes, I suppose she did. I'm really sorry about your leg.'

He once again demonstrated his leg's limited flexibility. 'I keep telling myself that worse things have happened,' he said. 'I mean, all it's done is ruin my whole life ... and what's that in the great scheme of things?'

'Oh Tom, are you feeling really sorry for yourself?' The words were cynical but she said them with compassion.

'I was trying to, until you came along.'

'And I spoiled your bout of self-pity.'

'You most certainly did. I was looking forward to it as well.' He looked at his watch as he stood on one leg. 'I'd planned on being *completely* legless by now.'

Dove inwardly chastised herself for feeling so selfishly elated at Tom's bad news. It was as though fate was at last conspiring to put things right for her. About time too.

'I'll be needing a manager now that Monty's died,' she suggested hopefully. 'Could be good. Things are picking up for me. I've got a very big telly booking.' She hadn't mentioned the Palladium to him. The fact that he was alive overshadowed any good news she might have.

'Dove, I'm pleased for you and I'm really sorry about Monty, but –'

'We could go on the road,' she said. 'In the waggon. Just you and me. It'd be wonderful.'

'I thought you didn't like living in the waggon.'

In between their lovemaking she'd told him about Monty dying and the house and Henry being a promising artist. Then she'd felt safe to confide in him about how Pikey Scullion died. Neither she nor Monty had mentioned it to anyone, not even to Henry, who had enough to worry about. Tom winced when Dove told of how and where she'd kicked Pikey.

'But it was Boris who saw him off, was it?'

'It was,' said Dove. 'I'm not sure I could have lived with someone's death on my conscience, not even Scullion's.'

'It wouldn't have troubled *my* conscience,' Tom said. 'Boris has done the world a great favour. I just wish I could have been as much help to you.'

'Tom, you're helping me just by being alive. When I thought

you were dead it was as if my world had come to an end. It really brought me to my senses. Nothing meant anything anymore. The house, my career – nothing.'

'Really?'

'Really ... Tom, what do you think about you becoming my manager and us taking to the road in the waggon?'

He gave her a quizzical smile. 'You once told me that all you wanted was to be normal. To live a normal life in a normal house like normal people.'

Dove looked at him, then her gaze became distant and she seemed lost in thought. 'That's all I ever wanted when I was younger,' she said. 'A normal house with a normal mam and dad to love me and take care of me.' Her eyes suddenly brightened as she added, 'Like yours. There was never any security in my life. Henry was all I ever had. But now I'm big enough to take care of myself.'

'So,' summed up Tom, 'You don't need anyone?'

She wrinkled her nose. 'Now, Tom, I didn't say that. I think I've realised that I only ever wanted what I couldn't have. The grass is greener and all that. I've probably been very selfish.'

'You're many things, Dove, but selfish isn't one of them. On the other hand ...' His eyes narrowed and he sat on the edge of the bed. 'Is that why you didn't want me – because you knew I was yours for the asking?'

'Listen, you great gormless lump! I'm trying to tell you I've been stupid. My life got all messed up by horrible men and I was too stupid to separate you from them. Don't make me explain all the stupid things I've done, it'd take all night. She placed her arms around his neck. 'Please say you'll be my manager.'

He kissed her, gently, on her lips. 'I'll do whatever it takes to make you happy,' he said. His eyes were brimming with love for her and Dove realised she wasn't being fair to him. Yet again.

'I'm sorry, Tom. Just forget I suggested it. Being my manager's a poor job compared to what you've lost. It was your dream to fl ...'

'Hey, hey!' Tom cut her off by pressing a finger against her lips, then kissing her again. 'Dovina Mary McKenna,' he said. 'Pugilist, juggler, musician, comedienne, singer ...'

'Excuse me – less of the pugilist, if you don't mind. It was just the once and Jubby had it coming.'

He ignored her interruption. 'When I saw you standing by Michael's grave I thought you were so beautiful I could hardly breathe. And then . . . when I realised that all those things you were saying were meant for me, well, it was just . . . I don't know, just the best moment.'

'Didn't you feel just little bit guilty, listening to me going on like that – thinking I was talking to a dead man?'

'Hmm . . . no, can't say as I did.'

'Tom Webster, I think you've got a wicked streak in you.'

He smiled. 'Dove, I've only ever wanted two things in my life. One was to fly jets and the other was to marry you.'

'Wow,' said Dove, softly.

There was a long moment of silence as she considered the implication of those last two words and Tom was inwardly kicking himself, wondering if he'd pushed things on a bit too fast. Clumsy as ever. Then she placed her arms around his shoulders, kissed his neck and murmured into his ear.

'Well, you know what they say.'

'Do I?' said Tom, uncertainly.

'They say half a loaf's better than none.'

'You're not exactly half a loaf, Dove.'

'No – what am I then?'

He pulled her back on to the bed. 'You're the whole bloody bakery.'